Killer Kowalski
Takes the Mat

Don Eron

Contingency Street Press LLC

Never regret thy fall,

O Icarus of the fearless flight,

For the greatest tragedy of them all

Is never to feel the burning light.

Contents

PART ONE: MARY WELLINGTON

Nocturnal Running, December 12, 1970

Here's Dan Bluestone (aka Biggie) easing into his stride:

On Lincoln Avenue South, dressed in a rubber suit with two pairs of gloves and a wool cap, at 11:30 p.m. A thin sheaf of ice glazes the walkway. He'd been in bed waiting to fall asleep, but his stomach was killing him. The next moment he was pulling the rubber suit out of his closet, then a moment later he was out the door. There'd been no *decision* involved. Suddenly here he was, trudging like a demented halfwit. A *determined* demented halfwit, to give Biggie his due.

In the freezing air his neck ached the entire two miles back home, but two miles were nothing. He could run two miles with a broken neck, or with no neck at all.

The pain in Bluestone's stomach, too, grinded as he ran. Indeed, if he wasn't the picture of health, he'd think that he was having a sudden appendicitis attack. But there was, according to the laws of general principle Biggie relied upon as a personal constitution, no possibility that he was having an appendicitis attack. No *plausible* possibility. He was the toughest seventeen-year old not only on the planet, but in the planet's history. He was Power Incarnate. Not two hours before, he'd won the Highland Park Quadrangular, the third year running. That said, even more worrisome than the grinding were the acids surging through his stomach, splashing his esophagus, searing his lungs. Laws of general principle? When Biggie hadn't taken the time to properly digest before trying to sleep, he knew that this raging flood of acids was imminent.

The *reason* Biggie hadn't given himself the time to digest is that he ate feverishly from the moment he got home from the Quadrangular. Before he sat down, he'd gotten Mom to toss a chuck steak into the oven. He drank a large glass of chocolate milk as he waited, reading the *Daily News* sports he'd already skimmed in the late afternoon, after he read the *Sun-Times* sports and the *Chicago Today* sports. The *Tribune* they didn't subscribe to. Three daily subscriptions were enough, according to Dad. Plus the *Trib* was reactionary, Mom chimed in whenever the issue was raised, as if it were a contagious disease.

On the *Sun-Times* Friday Prep Page was a half-page feature on the immortal Rick Berkenmeier from up in Mundelein, the wrestler's would-be rival. Included was a large picture of Berkenmeier looking like the combination of a blond-haired All-American kid and a grizzled Marine veteran, edgy outside the war zone. For a moment, Biggie looked into Berkenmeier's eyes in the picture and fought the temptation to evade his steely gaze. The story itself was disappointing, focusing strictly on how great Berkenmeier was, not merely on the mat with his work ethic—rated #1 in America after winning Jr. Nationals in Evanston last summer (spectacularly pinning his way through State Champs from Pennsylvania, Ohio, Oklahoma), with a scholarship to Wisconsin signed and sealed, where his brother wrestled first string—where his coach won NCAAs four years ago—Berky was *connected*—but also great as an All-State fullback and greater yet as a human being. The roll call of admirable attributes never ended. At Mundelein High, the article noted, Berkenmeier was in line for class Salutatorian.

The kid did everything but volunteer weekends as a candy striper. Biggie practically found *himself* pulling for Berkenmeier to take State. He could barely stand to finish the article and thought of tossing the newspaper against the wall for dramatic impact, and may well have if anybody had been watching.

Waiting for the chuck steak at the kitchen table, Bluestone managed to answer Mom's questions patiently. He also had a bowl of ice milk and broke into the cabinet for a fistful of Oreos. He scarfed the salad buried in Thousand Island dressing she'd left in the refrigerator for him and was contemplating another raid on the cabinet when Mom returned to check the oven and told Biggie that the steak was cooked.

She kissed him on the forehead. Biggie winced. He remembered now that Giselle, his sister, had promised that morning to make a German chocolate cake after she got back from the Quadrangular.

"Did Giselle make a German chocolate cake?"

"Giselle's over at Mary's."

"Oh."

"Remember to clear your dishes when you're finished."

Biggie said he'd remember.

Mom looked Biggie over skeptically. She was a school social worker, at Evanston High School, one of Highland Park's rivals, but sometimes she looked at him as if she'd never seen his like. "When you're done, take out the garbage."

After the steak and another bowl of ice milk, Biggie walked into the living room, where he collapsed to all fours for a set of 200 pushups. This set was challenging when he applied scrupulous attention to form, as he often did, each pushup methodical to the point of tedium, chest touching the floor, arms quivering back to full position seconds later, but now he breezed through, concentrating not on form but on numeral—"137, 138, 139"—and was breathing calmly enough when he finished that he added another hundred to the set. When he was this lackadaisical (though he assumed that any Marine drill sergeant would find the form satisfactory) he could rip off 400 pushups. Still, cheating was cheating, whether or not a conscientious observer called the infraction. Biggie was disappointed in himself for taking the easy route and wondered idly if the shortcut would cost him down the line. If Berkenmeier ever ripped off cheesy sets of 300, the article didn't mention it.

Theoretically, the long set of pushups triggered the thyroid gland, firing up his metabolism so that the prodigious consumption provided mainly fuel. When he'd step on the scale Monday, he knew he'd find out otherwise, but was convinced the results would be twice as disastrous without triggering the thyroid. Back in the kitchen he had his third bowl of ice milk and slammed a half glass of chocolate milk. Suddenly his thirst was so deep, he filled up the glass again and drained the chocolate milk down his throat, imagining as he did that he'd *invented* chocolate milk, then a glass of water. Reminding himself that this was *it*, once he left the kitchen the process would begin again, tapering off to practically nothing—bouillion cubes and lettuce by next Wednesday—he briefly considered firing up a hamburger or waiting in the kitchen until Giselle came home to make the German chocolate cake. Still, Bluestone cleared the dishes, securing a last fistful of Oreos and an onion bagel smeared with margarine before reluctantly peeling himself off the refrigerator door.

By the time he'd reached his room downstairs, a large bedroom off the rec room, his stomach was already killing him. He walked into the rec room, turned on the TV—nothing of interest, though he nonetheless doubled over, knees and elbows on the floor, and listened disconsolately. Fifteen minutes later he made his way to the bathroom, then his bedroom, where he collapsed fully dressed, eventually closed his eyes and awaited sleep.

An hour later, Biggie was in his rubber suit and wool cap on his double-gloved run up Sheridan Road. The furious acids, the undigested clumps of the huge chuck steak, the salad buried in Thousand Island, four bowls of ice milk, four glasses of chocolate milk, the onion bagel, the dozen and a half Oreos, waged their war. The Battle of the Bulge?

Sheesh. The wrestler knew that by Tuesday—anticipating the prospect of sixty hours of bouillion, lettuce, water—he'd look back *longingly* to the relative misery he felt now. It amazed him that he'd spent less than an hour in the kitchen, which was apparently all the time necessary for a belly to transform from an empty sack into a huge sputtering keg of acid.

At the driveway Biggie slowed, then walked, shrugging his shoulders, dangling his legs, as if—were it not for his breathing in the freezing air in huge gulps—he were loosening up before trotting onto the mat.

Sometimes it felt like he stopped his run just at the point when he could bolt forever.

Biggie, trembling from the freezing cold, got to the door and fumbled with his house key. Despite his immense strength, his hands were too numb to turn the key in the lock, and he wondered why he'd felt it necessary to lock the door, as if someone was going to break in and kill everybody at two in the morning. Though that's pretty much when they *did* break in to kill everybody, he considered idly. Look at Senator Percy's daughter.

Now Biggie buried his double-gloved hands in his rubber-suit pants pockets and for several seconds clenched his fists, willing them to warm up, grabbing a thatch of synthetic rubber for extra measure.

Seconds before he became convinced that they'd discover him frozen to death tomorrow morning, numbed hands clutching rubber-pants in the middle of the porch, his life accurately summarized by the woeful image (and his hideous fate a lucky turn for Rick Berkenmeier), Biggie's circulation fired. Quietly he turned the key and walked inside, feeling his way downstairs without turning on the light until he got to his room, where he found the *Sun-Times* sports on the floor. Though his fingers still throbbed from the cold, he took his scissors from the top of his dresser and cut out the photo of Berkenmeier, then walked back in the dark, upstairs to the kitchen. He felt a roll of scotch tape in the first drawer beneath the counter, then turned and walked the three steps to the refrigerator.

Miraculously, Biggie refrained from *opening* the refrigerator.

Taped Berkenmeier's photo to the freezer door.

The List, December 13

It wasn't that no girl would *look* at Biggie Bluestone.

The next afternoon, as they stood in the kitchen, his sister Giselle told him, "Mary thinks you're cute." She meant Mary Wellington, her best friend.

"I'm sorry. I didn't catch that."

"Okay, if you're not interested in hearing." Giselle turned back toward the oven, where she was finally making the German chocolate cake she'd promised, though it was already too late for the wrestler to devour more than a single heaping slice. Giselle was a short, stocky girl with long black hair and huge brown eyes. She was a tough kid, too, stubborn and unbending when she wasn't giggling or crying her eyes out, and Biggie often thought that if she were a guy she'd be a wrestler and possibly give Biggie himself a run for his money.

"Who's he?" Giselle pointed at the imposing headshot of Rick Berkenmeier he'd taped to the freezer door last night.

Biggie told her.

"I wonder if he has a girlfriend."

"He's the competition, Giselle. That's why I put him on the freezer."

You tape a picture of your nemesis to the freezer so you'll remain ever vigilant, and Giselle wants to date the guy.

"Mary?" Biggie said, steering his sister back to topic.

"She thinks you're mus-cu-lar," Giselle said, articulating each syllable precisely, until it seemed she took a full minute to get the adjective out.

"I've barely said a word to Mary Wellington."

"Biggie, I'm not accusing you. A lot of girls think you're cute and mus-cu-lar. I'm your sister and they tell me, that's all."

"Who, exactly?" he asked absently.

Obligingly, Giselle revealed the list of girls who'd told her they found her brother cute and muscular: Gina Biano, Gloria Wasserstein, Diane Heard, Suzy Applebaum. Of course, Mary Wellington, too. Not really a list of Highland Park's finest, no incipient Sara Shermans—by acclamation the most beautiful girl at Highland Park High School—not even any seniors as far as he could tell, though the wrestler certainly didn't mind hearing about it. Bluestone had this conversation with Giselle periodically. The list had remained stable since the end of last season when he'd lost disastrously in Districts. Mary was the new entry. Gina Biano and Gloria Wasserstein he'd had conversations with—if you count passing them in the Bluestone kitchen and exchanging hellos; theirs enthusiastic, Biggie's muffled. Diane Heard and Suzy Applebaum he couldn't picture specifically—there was an approximate image of two small, nondescript, long-haired girls blending in with a dozen others halfway up the bleachers at the wrestling meets. They were part of the Mat Gals, an organization Giselle had started last year, who would cheer at the meets from the bleachers, wearing their uniforms of blue blouses and blue skirts and white socks. They ran the public address system and the scoreboard, and made posters during the week, which they hung on bulletin boards or held above their heads as they sat in the stands in their Mat Gal section, cheering their heads off on the infrequent occasions they were paying attention. While their disproportionate encouragement was touching, often Biggie couldn't hear what they were saying over the PA, and between periods the coaches usually had to go over and fix the scores they'd put up on the board. Mostly freshmen and sophomores, a few juniors like Giselle (and Mary Wellington before she quit after making JV cheerleaders, who doubled as the cheerleaders for the wrestling meets). Few of the Gals *looked* like high school girls. Mostly they reminded the wrestler of middle school girls—braces, acne, gawkiness—but in limbo, where one day, their names called, they'd mysteriously wake up and shed their braces and discover their complexions cleared up. But Biggie would probably be wrestling in college by the time Diane Heard woke up looking like a high school girl; as pleased as he was that they found him cute and muscular, it was like hearing that somebody's parents liked you, or their pet turtle thought you were great. "Terrific," Biggie said.

The most promising on the list was the latest, Mary Wellington, a small, nervous girl who was pretty. She was a junior like Giselle and might look like a legitimate high school girl if she didn't wear braces. She was very thin, so fragile-looking that when she leaped into the air on her JV cheerleading stunts he was often half-surprised she came down intact.

They had history, too.

Once last summer, Mary came downstairs as Bluestone was stretched out on the couch watching a Cubs game. Mom and Dad were off at a party in Glencoe. Giselle had immediately invited over the Society of Wayward Girls, as Dad called them, who were prepared to convene the instant somebody's parents left. That night the SWG was making a racket upstairs which quickly spread from Giselle's room to the living room to the kitchen.

There were two couches in the basement rec room, ten feet apart, facing the TV sideways so that you could lean back in the cushions and face somebody directly as you talked to them. Biggie looked up between innings to see Mary Wellington standing by the other couch. He hadn't heard her come down and wondered if she'd been standing there a long time. Biggie tried to remember if he'd scratched his nuts or picked his nose or blithely farted in the last five minutes; it was hard to imagine not.

She wore jeans and a purple turtleneck that had the effect of making her neck appear elongated, as if she'd grown two inches exclusively in the neck in the week since he'd last seen her. Still, Mary Wellington looked pretty, as if her stretch in limbo was scheduled to end soon.

"I was wondering what you do on a Saturday night. Now I know. You watch baseball."

Biggie began to say something in response, something like "Wha?" but lost the thread before the first syllable reached fruition.

"Who's playing?"

"The Cubs and the Cards."

"From St. Louis?"

Where else would they be from? "I thought you were a cheerleader."

Mary smiled curiously; she was only JV. The varsity knew sports.

"You can sit down if you like."

There was a chance that when Mary Wellington finally looked like a high school girl she would *really* look like a high school girl, with her long brown hair and startling dark eyes, the kind of girl that came to mind when Biggie read about smart, stylish high school girls like Franny Glass hanging on the arm of a sophisticate. Sitting on the couch across from her as the Cubs battled the Cards with Biggie suddenly providing commentary to supplement the cornball commentary of Jack Brickhouse and Lloyd Pettit on WGN, he envisioned Mary's thin cheekbones as flaring, her startling dark eyes as luminous, her hair, already pretty, as gorgeous, her teeth de-braced, her chest full-breasted. As he found himself pontificating about the Cubs' All-Star double-play combination, Kessinger to Beckert to Banks, Bluestone contemplated positioning himself for that moment, already wondering if, when the time came, her status as Giselle's best friend might prove awkward.

"The way Ernie's hitting now I'm not sure he'll *get* to 500 home runs."

"Have you ever been to a Cubs game?"

"Wha? Sure. Some guys I know, like Wing Terrill, have been to dozens."

"Wing's been to dozens?"

"Ask him if you don't believe me."

When the inning ended Mary went back upstairs to the Society of Wayward Girls.

Bluestone's one other moment with Mary Wellington also occurred last year, and to Biggie it pretty much encapsulated his entire junior year. He'd been sitting in the stands before Oak Park with the rest of the varsity, watching the JV action, talking to Rich Becker, the star heavyweight, about football scholarships. Colleges were desperately trying to sign up Rich Becker to play linebacker. According to Rich Becker, the Michigan State head coach, Bill Boscoe, had personally informed him that he was their #2 recruit in the entire Midwest—right behind a quarterback from Minnesota.

"Boscoe said I was the athlete they have to land. The standard shit."

"If they don't land the athlete from Minnesota," Biggie suggested, "maybe they'll play you at quarterback."

Becker dismally shook his head.

Biggie had wondered if Becker's mock incredulity expressed a genuine modesty, as opposed to the false modesty Biggie himself dished out after anybody complimented him on his wrestling. Suddenly, with Becker shaking his head dismally in incredulity ("The standard shit," as if that were the worst kind of all), the wrestler's sphincter blindsided him. Doubled over with cramps, he hurtled down the Oak Park bleachers to the locker room and the stalls.

On the gym floor Mary Wellington walked from the opposite direction, wearing her blue-bloused, blue-skirted, white-socked Mat Gal outfit. He couldn't secure an alternate route to hustle around her. She looked concerned, as if sensing his dire predicament: Instead of clearing the pathway, or smiling at Biggie and saying hello as she always did when she passed him in the kitchen upstairs when the SWG congregated, Mary stopped. Biggie, with no choice but to stop politely in his tracks, desperately squeezed his sphincter as Mary Wellington gazed solicitously into his face. "Are you okay?"

"Cramps," Biggie admitted.

"I'm sorry."

"I'll live."

When Mary lifted her hand toward Biggie's unshaven face, lightly grazing her fingers along his two-day stubble, he couldn't have been more surprised if she'd squeezed his nose, or suddenly stuck her fingers in his ears. "Biggie, does the beard make you feel tough?"

With Mary Wellington touching your face you can't exactly shove her away then make a desperate run for the toilet, hoping you can control your sphincter until you plop down on the seat. "It makes me *look* tough," Biggie told her flatly. "Anyway, it's not really a beard. It's *stubble*." Biggie didn't bother to explain that hair grew on his face—the same face her hand grazed now—like it was going out of style, as opposed to the top of his head, where he already had a bald spot you didn't have to concentrate feverishly on to see—and if he shaved every time he needed a shave he'd spend half the livelong day shaving. "Instead of talking to you, Mary," he didn't add.

And then she wasn't touching his stubble anymore, was hurrying down the aisle toward the bleachers where her pals in the Mat Gals were watching them.

The wrestler reached the john before his bowel exploded. Still, he was sluggish during the match, a maul and push affair where he couldn't focus and ran out of steam early. He gave up an escape on a sit out with a minute to go, couldn't take the guy down after that, barely tried, his strength evaporated, and the guy—who was pretty good, Biggie had to admit in fairness to the idiotic Biggie he was last year—stalled out the last minute. The score ended 4-3.

Junior year Biggie Bluestone lost five matches. That was one.

Later that afternoon, after hearing the latest from Giselle about Mary Wellington and indulging himself with a heaping slice of German chocolate cake, the wrestler sat in the stands at McGaw Hall in Evanston, where the Northwestern University Wildcats were taking on the Southern Illinois Salukis. It was then that Biggie realized that, at heart, *he* was Killer Kowalski, the most intimidating, feared, vicious, homicidal-looking wrestler on the planet.

He'd been going to the Northwestern wrestling meets since middle school; back then his dad would drive him down, at first watching with him, later just dropping him off—afterward Biggie would walk over to his dad's office, stopping off at the dispenser in the basement to buy a salted nut roll for a quarter, daydreaming about wrestling for Northwestern someday. Back then his dad was already probably the most famous guy on campus *next* to the wrestling coach, Roy Gosley. Roy Gosley had coached the Wildcats for at least twenty years. He'd also wrestled in the Olympics, coached in the Olympics, and was the expert commentator when they'd telecast NCAAs or the Olympics. "Wrestling's foremost ambassador," Biggie had read once in the newspaper, a reputation that he considered as good as you could have.

In less than half an hour, Roy Gosley would introduce himself to Biggie and tell Biggie Bluestone that he was on their recruitment list, but at that precise moment Biggie was watching the Northwestern guy in his weight class, Drake Watson, demolish the Southern Illinois guy, and was thinking that 1) with all these college girls in the stands straight out of the pages of *Playboy* it was tough to get too excited that Mary Wellington had a crush on him, and 2) next year, Jesus, Watson would kill him with his hip throws and misdirections. He'd be lucky to last a minute with Watson's blocks and trips and headlocks that would end up with Biggie on his back, set to be pinned—and Watson wasn't even that *good* as far as college wrestling went, an All-American but far from the pinnacle—he'd seen guys destroy Watson as effortlessly as Watson would destroy him unless he was a thousand times tougher than anybody. *That's* when it hit Biggie that *he* was Killer Kowalski.

Back in middle school, he'd been assigned to write a report on a famous American who *wasn't* a president. While everybody else in the class did George Washington Carver, Albert Einstein, or Helen Keller, Biggie reported on Killer Kowalski. The others nodded knowingly as Biggie proudly read his report to the class. The odd thing was that Biggie *hated* professional wrestling; he hated that people confused it with *amateur* wrestling, which was the greatest sport on earth and in which the twelve-year-old Biggie, star of the seventh grade team, had already resolved to win the State Championship once he reached high school. Most days it was all he thought about. Oh *wrestling*, people would say when he mentioned his ambition, nodding but rolling their eyes inwardly, thinking Biggie meant *professional* wrestling, which probably made more sense to his relatives and his parents' friends, now that he thought about it, watching Drake Watson execute his hip throws and misdirections, since Biggie was an oafish, oddball kid. But there was a lot these people didn't know about the boy other than when his bar mitzvah was scheduled. From the moment in the fifth grade when the gym teacher rolled out the mat, lined up the kids and demonstrated the single leg takedown, it was love at first sight.

He wasn't sure he'd *heard* of Killer Kowalski, whose heyday was around the time Biggie was born, and whose signature moment in the ring—when he ripped off Yukon Eric's ear on a mis-aimed "throat stomp"—occurred in 1954 when Biggie was one year old. He'd never seen film of Kowalski that he could recall, though he remembered watching grainy-filmed programs featuring Bruno Sammartino, Bobo Brazil, and Bearcat Wright on the television in his grandmother's den in New Jersey when he was small. (If they had such TV stations in

Illinois, they didn't come in on the Bluestone set.) He still had this image of a fat curly-haired Gorgeous George dressed like a woman, holding some flailing adversary down in the ring, though Biggie wasn't certain if the image germinated in something he'd seen or from the evocations of the name itself. But Killer Kowalski? That's the name that came to the twelve-year-old, and the name Biggie had looked for when he went with his dad to check out books on professional wrestling from the Highland Park Public Library.

Killer Kowalski wasn't a "scientific" wrestler, and it seemed to Biggie now that that's what he must have seized upon as a twelve-year-old, as if sensing he'd never be too scientific himself, with a bevy of subtle, complex, scientific maneuvers. Also, most wrestlers have mechanical facilities, can take apart automobile motors by feel and piece them back together, still blindfolded, before certifiable dunderheads like Biggie, who barely knew how to check the oil, would notice. According to the books there were scientific wrestlers around at the time, like Verne Gagne, NCAA champ and Olympian, but they were no match for the Killer. "Everybody always said Killer Kowalski was the toughest wrestler they ever faced," Biggie remembers reading from the report, gulping as he read, tremors of pride catching in his already changing voice. He was ruthless, he'd do *anything* to win: gouging, kicking, clawing when the referee was distracted, biting if necessary, along with the world famous throat stomp, where he'd leap high in the air landing feet first on the hapless guy's voice box. "Killer was the most intimidating wrestler in the history of the world," Biggie remembers reading to the class. "And he wouldn't let anybody think they were in for an ordinary afternoon," Biggie had added. "He'd play with their minds, toy with their psyches." Had he really said *psyches*? At twelve? Such passion elevates your sensibilities. "They'd step through the ropes wondering if this was the day *their* ear would be stomped off, their voice box crushed by the soles of Killer's glittering gold boots." That was part of the Kowalski con, too. He'd enter the ring shirtless in purple tights with lightning bolts sewn into the sides, and glittering gold boots. The alliteration itself was magical to the kid.

And outside the ring—this is what got the twelve-year-old Bluestone most of all, cemented what five years later he could see was his identification, for he really didn't want to crush anybody's voice box and was a sweet, bashful boy on the inside, practicing his *haftarah* every night—*outside* the ring Killer was a sweetheart, a softie, a deep reader, a painter dabbling in the arts, a quester often sighted at religious retreats, a gentleman.

The guys he wrestled knew that. Some had even conducted long, intellectual discussions with Killer in the locker rooms. But that just made them fear Killer more.

In a real match, Biggie imagined now, Verne Gagne, a great wrestler and a champ but sometimes Killer's fall guy, a "scientific" wrestler too, an Olympian, would have handled the Killer. As Killer leaped into the air for the throat stomp Verne Gagne wouldn't have lain supine but scrambled up, caught the glittering boot easily, wrenched the leg, tossed Killer to the mat like a frightened boy in his first match with the junior varsity. Biggie knew that, perhaps even realized it as the voice-changing, hero-stunned twelve-year-old dreaming of taking State once he got past his bar mitzvah, and as he sat in the stands at McGaw Hall, then later as he took the long drive down Sheridan Road, turning around, the radio blaring to WCFL, dreaming of the con, even if he was only conning himself, knowing that perhaps *he*, as a seventeen-year-old undefeated, unscored upon in fourteen matches, already could handle Killer Kowalski in a real bout, an honest encounter (it was hard to imagine otherwise when he looked at it squarely), that what he was buying—no half-ass equivocations but completely, for now—was the fantasy, just so much myth, because he couldn't very well lope onto the mat shirtless with purple tights and glittering gold boots—stiff high school regulations prescribed uniforms, head gear, wrestling shoes—for the purpose of scaring the shit out of the poor guy from New Trier standing across the circle (for a moment Biggie, like Killer, a good guy off the mat, *empathized* with the soon-to-be vanquished), though myth spoke louder than costume, cut deeper than rules. Biggie thought he could still be Killer Kowalski, even if nobody knew.

Half an hour after he'd realized he was Killer Kowalski at heart, Wrestling's Foremost Ambassador recognized Biggie Bluestone. On his way out of McGaw Hall, Biggie inconspicuously lingered by the mat, soaking up the college atmosphere. The Northwestern Wildcats had clobbered the Southern Illinois Salukis. Biggie noticed the towering, thick-haired personage talking to two elderly men in the bleachers across the floor. The bleachers were too far away to hear anything more than the two old timers laughing their heads off at every syllable the famed coach uttered, as if standup comedy were the living legend's true calling. Except for the three men, the arena had emptied. Lights were dimmed. Biggie had already tied his shoes, adjusted his coat, reached into his coat pocket to examine the contents (a ticket stub), and put the stub back into his pocket. If he hypothesized that they wouldn't let him stand there all night because he liked the feeling of standing near a college mat, he was willing to test the theory. What if it were Killer Kowalski? Imagine. It would take half-a-dozen security guards; that would be just for working up the *nerve* to walk up and ask if there was anything they could do for him. ("Sir, we're closing. You'll have to leave now." "Why?" "Because it's private property.")

A dozen to escort Killer Kowalski away, if they'd even try.

"Dan Bluestone!"

Biggie turned to see Roy Gosley jogging toward him. Momentarily, he thought Gosley must have recognized him from showing up for the Saturday home meets since he was kid. As he slowed up, the famous coach did a brief double take as if he really did recognize the hero-worshipping kid, or the trace of Killer Kowalski, or—*sheesh*, Biggie thought—a remote resemblance to his dad—his parents' friends sometimes remarked upon it—Biggie couldn't see it—whom Gosley must have *seen* walking across campus—then the towering, thick-haired personage grabbed Biggie's hand like he intended to sell it for parts, and squeezed Biggie's bicep with his free hand as if anticipating an arm drag.

Biggie's head measured up to Gosley's chin.

"You looked good at the Quadrangular last night. Don't see many high school boys with your power. You're a real strongboy, I'll say that for you, Dan. How are your grades? Your test scores? Did you take the ACT? The SAT?"

"Both."

"Good." Gosley gave an avuncular wink to the high school wrestler, who was staring glassily at Gosley's huge neck. "Keep up the good work, Bluestone. We'll be in touch. By the way, thanks for driving down to see us. Next time call ahead and we'll show you around."

This Gosley said as if Biggie was negligent in not thinking to call ahead *this* time. ("Hi, I understand you have a meet scheduled." "Hi, who's this?" "I'm Bluestone, the strongboy. I looked good in the Quadrangular last night." "Bluestone, we've been expecting your call.") "Okay," Biggie said.

Beyond that, Biggie didn't take much in, though later, as he drove down Sheridan through Evanston and on through Rogers Park to Lake Shore Drive where he turned around before he got lost, WCFL blasting, he replayed the moment obsessively.

When he got home, he tossed the car keys on the kitchen table, then thought better of it and tossed them into Mom's purse. He could hear his parents in the living room, where Mom was talking as Dad read the paper and periodically agreed with her. His dad was always reading the paper when he wasn't working.

Biggie considered cutting a beeline for his room downstairs, where he'd turn on the hi-fi and do a thousand jumping jacks to quick-start his metabolism before dinner, but went instead into the living room to tell his parents about meeting the icon incarnate.

"Does that mean he'll offer you a scholarship?" Dad asked, going so far as to put down the paper. Even Mom stopped retelling a compelling story her sister Ada back in New Jersey had told her, from what Biggie had heard walking in as he tossed the keys into her purse.

"It means they'll keep an eye on me."

"Northwestern." Dad said wistfully, savoring the sound: *Northwestern*. You wouldn't have thought he'd taught there for twenty years and was probably the most famous guy on campus. "You're certain that you want to wrestle in college? You know that you don't have to wrestle, Biggie."

He shrugged. His dad was under the impression that if Biggie didn't spend so much time wrestling and working out, then working out again when he wasn't reading about wrestling, which he was doing when he wasn't daydreaming, he might spend more time studying. The wrestler suddenly registered the uneasy impression that his dad expected him to develop other interests once he got to college.

"We'll swing it without the scholarship."

"We're proud of you either way," Mom joined in.

Proud either way. It wasn't so much that Mom expected him to develop other interests, but that she *hated* wrestling. She went to all the home matches and enjoyed sitting with the other parents, hearing how great Biggie was, *kvelling* as she watched the ref raise her boy's arm, but she hated that Biggie had to end up losing twenty pounds every week to make weight. Biggie knew this because she lamented the predicament regularly. It ran contrary to every maternal impulse—after being so proud of him, his entire life, for being a growing boy who could eat a horse, it was, technically speaking, impossible to turn around and watch him not eat, even if it was for a good cause. She didn't even approve of Biggie fasting on Yom Kippur.

To give his parents their due, they were fitness-oriented as parents go. Mom did these halfway sit-ups on her bed every morning; Dad swam laps in the gym on the Northwestern campus, or parked his car several blocks away so he could work in a walk. When he was a child, he'd watch them play tennis; they'd let Biggie be the ball boy, a self-satisfied idiot scampering across the court, tossing Dad the ball when it was Mom's serve. Sometimes, even now, they looked at him as if he were about to toss Dad the ball on Mom's serve, and Bluestone imagined that these two sitting in the living room were mystified to have hatched a son, of their own flesh and blood, a billion times more talented at slipping in the half-nelson than at algebra. "I may be getting more offers as the season goes on. After all, last year I didn't get past Districts, you may remember, so nobody's going to knock my door down yet. Lots of times those deals don't come through until after the State Tournament."

"We wish you luck, son." Dad tended to call him *son* at moments when he offered fatherly advice, like "Do your homework, son," or, when he was younger, "Don't hit your sister, son."

"Is Coach Gosley a good man?" Mom asked.

"The best."

"It's hard to imagine another boy being stronger or working harder at building his muscles," Dad said.

"There's a mental part to the sport, too," Biggie snapped.

"Don't go off in a huff, Biggie. Of course there's a mental part to the sport."

Well, Biggie's mood lifted. He wondered if he'd overreacted. One thing about his dad, he could get pretty sarcastic when you took stuff seriously that he didn't think was all that important. He could say something like, "Of course. Physics is nothing compared to the mental game of *wrestling*," which may be true, but was liable to take the edge off the exhilaration you were feeling because Northwestern—a Big Ten wrestling school despite the Ivy League academics, the place you'd dreamed of going since you were hatched—had you on their recruitment list. Dad wouldn't even be aware he was taking the edge off your exhilaration. But now he was holding back, and Biggie resolved to be a little less sarcastic himself when people were all fired up about things he didn't take seriously which, when he thought about it, were just about everything.

Still, standing in front of his parents, Bluestone felt like he was boasting. Other high school kids, as far as he knew, had in-depth conversations with their parents about current affairs; Biggie tended to fire off a few idle boasts, then head downstairs.

"I think Illinois and Iowa could show some interest, too, after the State Tournament." Biggie developed the theme. "They have excellent programs."

"We're happy for you, Biggie," Dad said.

As long as he was standing there, Biggie thought about telling them that they were looking at the next Drake Watson.

He sure as hell wasn't going to tell them he was Killer Kowalski.

Christmas Break, December 21-January 3, 1970-71

Several days after Christmas, Biggie wasn't the least bit surprised when Gloria Serpentino called him for the second time in his life.

"Dan, it's Glory. Gloria Serpentino. How arya?"

Nobody called him Dan. *He* liked the name, but seldom heard it.

"I'm the girl who almost ran you over two weeks ago," Gloria explained after Biggie didn't respond.

"I'm afraid I don't remember."

"Don't try to be funny. I just called to see how you are. What have you been up to? I mean it."

I can't walk two steps without my shoulder killing me, *thanks to you*, he almost told her, then almost added that Coach Wetzel had given the wrestlers five days off after the Lake Forest Christmas tournament—five days in which Biggie ran six miles daily, then knocked himself out with the weights, along with several hundred pushups every time he entered a room, along with fifty chinups and fifty pullups each morning despite his aching shoulder and an eternity of tiny laps in his room as the hi-fi blared—but no *dieting*, not till practice started again next week—and then almost topped it off with his pontifications on all the college girls who'd fall in love with him once he was a big star next year at Northwestern, none of which Gloria Serpentino needed to hear.

"If you really want to know," he informed Gloria, "I won a couple of Christmas tournaments. Last week at Grant, this week—last Saturday, I mean—at Lake Forest. At Lake Forest I took the trophy for Outstanding Wrestler." The information about the trophy wasn't true, and Biggie was taken aback at how readily he'd dished out the lie. He'd always hated guys who became somebody else when girls were around. Yet here he was, talking to a girl on the phone, lying through his teeth.

"It's not 100% true that I took the trophy for Outstanding Wrestler," Biggie amended. "I should have in my opinion, that's what I meant."

"Is that what you meant?"

"I pinned three guys and won 10-0 in the final. But this kid Dale White from Wheaton Central, a defending State Champ, wrestled at 138, so they gave him Outstanding Wrestler because once you win State, you're royalty. He had three pins, too, but didn't get the shutout in the final. Gloria, if you look at the score without the royalty razzmatazz, *I* was more outstanding."

"Are you a wrestler?" Glory asked.

He deserved that. "On the other hand, his competition was better than mine, you're right. A couple of guys at 138 were downstate material. Nobody at 167, save *moi*. The same thing at Grant, too. I racked up the wins, but whom did I vanquish, really? I see your point."

"*Moi*?"

"You better believe it," Biggie said into the receiver.

"Dan?"

"What?"

"Are you above average in height?"

"About 5-10."

"That's not what I asked, Dan. As a policy, would you rather get there sooner rather than later, or later rather than sooner?"

"Get where?"

"Answer my question, please."

"Sooner."

"Would you rather see the movie before the book or after?"

"Excellent question."

"I have to go," Gloria Serpentino told Biggie. "I'm glad you vanquished everybody at Lake Michigan."

"Lake Forest," Biggie shot back, but she'd already hung up.

Had he said something wrong? Biggie didn't like it too much when people were abrupt, and to an extent went out of his way not to be abrupt with others, except for his parents, who really didn't mind and had plenty of their own stuff to do without Biggie always shifting his weight from foot to foot, hemming and hawing, just so he wouldn't come across as being abrupt. It didn't surprise Biggie that people perceived him as odd. Given that he considered himself to be pretty shy, unless he knew people well, he didn't have much to say even if he had plenty to say, so when he stalled out of sheer politeness around people he didn't know pretty well just so they wouldn't think he was the kind of abrupt guy he hated, Biggie had the impression people took him for an idiot.

He spent a few minutes after she hung up trying to decode her questions, before deciding that any way he'd answered them would have been wrong; that's assuming she wasn't just playing a game where the rules were known only to Gloria Serpentino. For a moment he found himself wishing that Wing Terrill were around—Wing was in Michigan City with Gail Abernathy and her family for the week, which struck Biggie as a pretty mixed deal—to fly the bizarre conversation by Wing.

Odder than the questions, which he could only assume he failed with his half-answers, non-answers, and answer-answers that never quite comprehended the questions, was still the outright bubbamagumba he'd dished out. *I should have won the trophy for Outstanding Wrestler.* It was true, but not the sort of thing you wanted to run around saying. Somebody could say it *for* you—which is exactly the sentiment that his teammates, Wing Terrill and Luigi Cravi, heralded after the trophy presentation, as did Coach Wetzel, who was walking by as Wing and Luigi commiserated melodramatically, "Should have been *yours*, Biggie." "Who counted the votes?" "It's just because Dale White took State last year."—and *then* you could reply, "Nah, that's nuts, that's crazy. Dale White deserved it," and everybody would understand not only that you agreed, but also that you appreciated the sentiment. But, according to the laws of general principle, you couldn't go ahead and say it yourself without making everybody ecstatic you didn't win the trophy.

The first time in his life Gloria Serpentino called him was a few days after she'd almost killed him. This was two weeks before the second time she'd called Bluestone. He'd just finished a thousand jumping jacks and a single page reaction paper to *A Separate Peace,* the best novel ever written—along with *The All-American* by John R. Tunis—when the wrestler, bundled in a rubber suit and wool cap, jogged toward the front door.

"Where are you going?" Giselle asked from the hallway, passing into the kitchen.

"To the moon."

"Send me a postcard."

"Biggie, it's *dark* out," Mom yelled from the kitchen, where she was finishing the dishes.

"Mom, I need to speed up my metabolism." In addition to the conditioning edge, Biggie had read that constant vigorous exercise sped up your metabolism.

"It's icy out there, Biggie. Cars are sliding all over."

"Mom, I've gone outside before—I can handle going outside again. I'm seventeen years old!"

"Leave him alone," Dad yelled from the study. "The big shot's seventeen years old!"

"You don't have to be so compulsive, Biggie."

"*Mom.*"

"Don't be so compulsive, Biggie," Giselle said.

Mom walked into the hallway and looked at Biggie. She was wearing her apron and rubber gloves. "Be careful, please. Okay?"

"Sure." Biggie said, deliriously happy that Mom wasn't lapsing into one of her Cautionary Tales, often recounted before he left the house, of a boy she knew in high school who'd gotten killed when a car skidded off an icy road and ran him over on the sidewalk. She had a story about a guy getting killed for almost every occasion.

Still, as he turned onto Forest and eased into his run, the constant entreaties began to irritate the wrestler. Usually, her observations rolled off his back, whereas Giselle was always at her throat: nothing rolled off Giselle's back. But *compulsive*? As if both his dedication and his desire to spare himself the misery later in the week, when a glass of water could prove disastrous, was an affliction like claustrophobia, or penis envy.

A large Buick was at the stop sign at Forest and Lincoln. Before turning, Biggie looked straight through the windshield at the driver. He faintly saw her face in the streetlight, and for a moment thought she looked familiar. The girl nodded and Bluestone made his turn onto Lincoln.

At the same time, she turned the Buick and, seeing the runner, slammed on her brakes and skidded clockwise. Though Biggie pivoted and dove, the front fender brushed his leg, knocking him from the road into a snowbank as the skidding Buick spun a full turn on the ice.

Shit.

For a second Biggie lay in the snow, collecting his wits. Slowly he stood in the snowbank and checked out his legs. Gingerly, he shook his arms. No tingling or numbness in the extremities. The wrestler bent his knees then lunged from the snowbank to the car. He instantly thought of lifting the Buick and dumping it on its side, but instead jerked at the driver's door handle. Inside, the girl sobbed into the steering wheel.

"Watch where you're going!"

The girl didn't respond except to sob harder and squeeze the steering wheel. The engine had stalled out. Her bobbing face banged against the steering wheel. Biggie sensed she was bracing herself as if he would momentarily reach across twelve inches of freezing air and strangle her, an idea with considerable appeal, and for a moment, standing on the corner of Forest and Lincoln shaking and hovering over the trembling girl, the wrestler felt pathetic. "Where'd you get your license, Monkey Wards?" That's what his dad liked to shout whenever somebody cut him off in traffic.

The girl turned from the steering wheel and looked at Bluestone as if beholding an escaped convict. In the misty half-light he could see she had a broad face, wet from sobbing, and her brown hair was glistening wet.

"You could have killed me! You could have broken my leg! You could have put me out of commission for the season. Jesus! Where would I be then? *Shit! Fuck!*"

"Are you okay?" the girl asked so softly that Biggie wondered if she was trying to make him feel like an asshole for overreacting, a familiar strategy in which Giselle was the world's ranking specialist.

"Can you promise me something? Will you drive carefully? Please."

"I don't know what happened."

"Stay off the roads if you're not going to pay attention. It's icy out here. A guy was killed when a car skidded off the road and hit him on the sidewalk."

The girl didn't say anything.

Biggie figured he'd worn out the theme, but added, "Watch where you're going, Miss," before telling her to turn the engine.

She nodded and the stalled Buick fired up.

Before the girl could knock him over again Biggie was running off down Lincoln Avenue South. His left arm and left shoulder and leg throbbed and ached, but within a hundred yards the aching dulled. He was afraid to stop running for fear of what he'd discover, afraid to flex his arm for fear he couldn't or loll his leg in the air to test the range of motion, but he ran, and once he saw he could, he considered it cowardly not to continue. He'd been hit by a car—almost killed—though with each step the description struck Biggie as ever more melodramatic. But then he'd picked himself up, cold-blooded as the breeze, said a few choice words, shrugged like she was asking him for directions to the expressway, then continued his run. Which, when you thought about it, was precisely what Killer Kowalski would do if *he* were hit by a car. Nothing could stop Killer Kowalski. Hitting him with a car was approximately the same as not hitting him with a car. ("The stud was hit but came out sprinting," they'd say. "That's Bluestone. Indestructible. What's his secret?")

The wrestler slowed down when he reached the driveway and walked the steps onto the porch the way he always did, as if he hadn't just been hit by a car, almost killed, and then kept running like Killer Kowalski would. He promised himself he wasn't going to tell his parents that a car skidded on the ice and hit him. The consequence would be unbearable, according to the laws of general principle. His mother would worry every time he left the house, convinced that every Cautionary Tale in her head applied, every story she'd ever read about some guy getting killed, a portent.

Soon she'd be telling him how to breathe.

The moment he walked through the door, Bluestone peeled off the wool cap, hesitated, then walked down the hall to his parents' bedroom. He knocked before entering. Dad was sleeping, but Mom was reading and watching the news playing softly on the TV and glanced appraisingly at her son.

"A car skidded on the ice and ran into me."

She looked at the wrestler uncomprehendingly.

"I mean it, Mom."

"Are you okay?"

"Of course. I just wanted you to know. It was nothing. I finished my run afterward. A close shave, that's all it was. Anything interesting on the news?"

"You *finished* your run?"

"I'd barely started. It was bad enough the car ran into me."

Dad awakened and saw Biggie standing in the doorway in his rubber suit. "Goodnight, son," he smiled and fell back to sleep.

"Doesn't the TV keep Dad awake?"

"Are you sure you're okay?"

"Of course."

His mother smiled at Biggie and said goodnight as she turned back to the news.

That was his mother. She'd worry endlessly over his getting hit by a car, but after he was actually hit—seeing he was still ambulatory—she didn't give it a thought, instead worrying about his getting hit the next time, or shaking her head that her son was nuts to finish the run, then back to the weather report.

That made Biggie feel even more idiotic for telling her in the first place. He was constantly doing things like that, but took some solace in knowing that for things like that, there was nothing you could do about it. When you were hit by a car, almost killed—at least in the Bluestone family—the mother *knew* whether you told her or not. The knowledge was in the genetic coding.

A few minutes later Biggie stood in his basement bedroom and steeled himself, trying not to look away as he undressed. Cuts and scratches riddled his arm and leg; he hadn't felt them, and wondered if he'd bounced on the road before landing in the snow—and a bruise the size of a baseball smeared his shoulder. His leg was bruised from thigh to knee. He knew that if he'd fallen the *other* way after being hit, the Buick would have run him over. He could picture the screaming girl kneeling by his head running her hand through his hair. Then an ambulance would come and haul him away. ("Where do we take the stiff?" they'd ask the girl. "Dump him straight in the cemetery?" "Sure," she'd respond. "That sounds efficient.")

Biggie dropped to the floor. His shoulder throbbed, but after fifty pushups he didn't notice. At 200, home free though his form was shot to hell, he stopped counting. The wrestler thrust himself into the air and slapped his chest for the last dozen, then collapsed to the floor, listening to his racing heart for several minutes.

He went into the bathroom, grabbed a towel, then walked upstairs and turned on the kitchen light. He tossed some ice cubes into the towel and wrapped it around his shoulder so his shoulder wouldn't explode overnight. Then he noticed again the face he'd taped to the freezer door the week before, after the Quadrangular. Perhaps it was his throbbing shoulder, or almost getting killed, but suddenly he knew that everything he wanted was impossible.

Now Biggie clutched the towel to his shoulder and stared at his putative rival—realistically, Berkenmeier wouldn't know him from a hole in the wall—and permitted himself several items of feckless indulgence:

1. The wrestler bet Berkenmeier didn't have a mother who assumed he was pathological. He bet Mrs. Berkenmeier—he pictured a toothless woman wearing a crew cut—didn't have a story lined up about a guy getting killed for every occasion. Also, Biggie bet she didn't go nuts just because Berkenmeier had to lose twenty pounds a week. As he saw it, Berkenmeier's mother ridiculed Berky when he *ate* or *didn't* take a run on the icy roads after two hours of practice.

2. Berkenmeier's brother, Lane Berkenmeier, won State three years ago, and now wrestled first string for the Wisconsin Badgers, as the *Sun-Times* article had noted. An even older brother twice made it to Sectionals. Bluestone pictured Berkenmeier being thrown around like a rag doll by his brothers from the second he was tossed into the crib by Ma and Pa Berkenmeier; not terribly wholesome, perhaps, not the by-the-numbers rearing that Biggie enjoyed, but in the process absorbing all kinds of holds and strategies that Biggie—whose sister hadn't been willing to wrestle him for years, and whose dad walked a couple of miles a day to stay in shape but wasn't about to get down in referee's position and roll around on the rec room floor so Biggie could hone his gut wrench—was just *now* beginning to catch onto. The truth was that Biggie grew up wishing he had a brother, even now. "Mom, if I had a brother I can guarantee he'd take State as a *soph*," he'd be tempted to hint, if it weren't so pointless.

3. Up at Mundelein, Berkenmeier's coach, Zach Reese, who'd won NCAAs at Wisconsin four years ago, was even *now* in training for the

Olympic Trials. "If Berkenmeier can take me down in practice, he can take down anybody," Coach Reese was quoted in the *Sun-Times* article. *Great for Berkenmeier.*

Down at Highland Park, Coach Wetzel's back went out whenever he looked at Biggie. Wetzel—huge, baldheaded, "Running to seed," according to Wing—had wrestled in college, too, for Rutgers, but that was shortly after the time of the last Ice Age, and Biggie had the impression Wetzel had wrestled mostly to stay in shape for football, where he starred at pulling guard. So while Biggie was concentrating during practice on going easy on Wing Terrill, not doing too much so he wouldn't throw out Coach Wetzel's back, keeping Pete Hoffman healthy for Yale—considerations it was difficult to imagine from Killer Kowalski—Berkenmeier was practicing hip tosses full-throttle against a guy who could pin him in a minute. Biggie liked the romance of being mostly self-taught, but the reality had its limits. For example, Coach Wetzel always had *suggestions*, but they amounted to encouragement rather than expert advice. "C'mon, Biggie, ride him tough," Wetzel would yell from the corner. "Turn him over, Biggie. You can do it!" Bluestone wouldn't mind pointers on *how* to ride him tough or turn him over. But those nuances he'd leave to you. Instead Biggie—not complaining—relied on stuff he read in books. Often, too, he wouldn't know if he got the moves right that he was applying from the photos of *Advanced Wrestling for the High School Athlete* he'd squint at before falling off to sleep the night before. The captions tended to be as ambiguous as the instructions for assembling a hi-fi system. What's more, against Terrill and Hoffman and Cravi and Wetzel, the moves worked just as well if he executed them wrong.

4. Not mentioned in the *Sun-Times*, but which the self-taught wrestler found implicit: Berkenmeier wasn't Jewish. At Highland Park, half the school was Jewish. *Biggie* was Jewish—proud of it—but when you scanned lists of recent NCAA champs, or recent State champs, or

even—lowering the bar yet farther—examined the State Tournament brackets from recent years, you didn't find a lot of guys who struck you as Jews. Rich Becker made it downstate last year—pinned in the first round—and he was the only Jew; Biggie would have known, too, because if there'd been any other Jews they'd probably be from Highland Park.

When he was a kid his dad bought him a book featuring profiles of star Jewish athletes. The book, an illustrated encyclopedia, was surprisingly hefty; mostly boxers from the twenties and thirties like Barney Ross and Bennie Leonard and Slapsie Maxie Rosenbloom (whom it was hard to imagine being all that good, Biggie remembered thinking), plus the heavyweight champ Max Baer, whose mother wasn't Jewish and called himself a Jew for promotional purposes, plus a bunch of fencers and yachtsmen, a couple of weightlifters and archers, a few basketball players, and about fifty pages each dedicated to Hank Greenberg and Sandy Koufax.

The only wrestler in there was a guy named Henry Wittenberg, who won the Olympics in 1948. Realistically, the wrestler wondered if he should use *Henry Wittenberg* as his persona, rather than Killer Kowalski. Two Jewish boys, a generation apart, kindred spirits. But *Henry Wittenberg* didn't quite carry the same force for the wrestler. ("Uh oh. Who's that across the mat?" "*Henry Wittenberg.*" "Terrifying.")

That was the litany. He wished he'd written the list down, so he could tear it to shreds. *Sheesh.*

He replenished the ice in the towel and went downstairs. ("Bluestone," they'd say. "Indestructible. What's his secret?")

A few nights after the calamity with the girl in the Buick, she phoned him for the first time in his life.

Mom had called down to say it was for *him*; this didn't happen often unless it was Wing calling for a ride to practice because his Fiat was in the shop.

"Hi, Biggie. It's Glory."

"Wha?"

"Glory. Gloria Serpentino. I met you the other night. I'm the beautiful girl in the Buick. Remember? You were running in your wrestling outfit. About 10:00 Tuesday. In the p.m.? Did you knock your head when you fell?"

"I don't remember any beautiful girl in the Buick," he managed.

"I deserve that."

"That wasn't a wrestling outfit. It was a rubber suit and a jacket with a wool cap and a shawl."

"A shawl?"

"A scarf, I mean."

"Are you okay?"

Biggie had almost told her *sure*, automatically, until he wondered if she had a recording device, so that if he later sued for damages the devious girl would play the device in court and clear her name. Still, it was nice of her to ask. Often, when people asked Biggie how he was, he genuinely appreciated the question, pleased that they were interested, even when they were obviously just being sociable. It ran in the family. He'd heard people ask Giselle that same question; half an hour later he'd walk by and Giselle was still filling them in.

"Biggie. Biggie Bluestone. That's an unusual name, Biggie. Is it on your birth certificate? No, I don't think so. How'd you get it?"

"First, everybody thinks it's an unusual name, and second, what business is it of yours?"

That had cut Gloria Serpentino to the quick, but as he felt the surge of satisfaction, he thought he'd gone too far. Though she'd almost killed him the other night—apparently she'd been under the impression they'd been "meeting"—she was pretty nice about it now. He wondered if she'd mentioned to her mom that she'd almost killed a guy in a wrestling outfit, and her mom insisted, "You better call and see if he's okay if you want to use the car again," with her dad chiming in, "Make sure you get his answer on the tape recorder. Sweet-talk the boy if necessary." Bluestone thought of playing up the injury angle, maybe depicting his bruises as "serious contusions with ligament involvement," tossing in—against the delayed reaction possibility—"likely whiplash and skull fractures." If there were a way to say that without sounding vain and self-indulgent, he'd have let her have it double, and almost did nonetheless.

"Touché," the girl said.

"My real name's Dan. In elementary school I was bigger than most kids, so they called me Biggie. Who wouldn't like that? Then, come middle school, I hated the name, but everyone still called me Biggie anyway so I caved in to the inevitable. My *grandmother* calls me Biggie now. Even Coach Wetzel calls me Biggie, though in the newspapers he's always saying, 'Danny really got after it today. Danny's really having a great season,'" Biggie said, reminding himself of a whiny mosquito. "Otherwise I'm Biggie."

"You're in the newspapers?"

"Just the *Highland Park Life* weekly sports page. Nobody outside the HP boundaries reads it. Or inside either, evidently."

"I'll call you Dan."

"Biggie's okay."

"I'm sorry I hit you the other night, Dan. I didn't see you. I guess I wasn't paying attention."

"Sure. Apology accepted." He'd found himself saying, "It was a snowy night with poor visibility. You should see my dad drive." Before he could apologize to *her* for getting in the way as she'd innocently peeled away from the stop sign, the girl said, "Good night, Dan."

"Wait. You sound like you know me."

"You're the strong boy."

When the strange girl hung up, Biggie had the vague impression that she was crying.

Biggie went down to his room in the basement and turned on the hi-fi and played *Tea for the Tillerman*, the greatest album ever recorded.

Did Killer Kowalski leave 'em crying?

Before Midlands, Dec. 27, 1970

That afternoon Mom and Giselle were off shopping. Dad was at work—Mom would pick Dad up at the train station at 5:07, she'd informed Biggie, which meant the garbage had better be out by 5:06—so he answered the phone when Gloria Serpentino called again. The third time in his life.

She still didn't say hello. "I'm giving you one more chance, Dan."

"That's fair."

"Should people be responsible to others, or responsible to themselves?"

"Others," Biggie guessed.

"Then they should neglect their *own* interests, Dan?"

"I guess responsibility to others should be their interest," Biggie said.

Glory paused, then softly sighed into the receiver. "Do you mean that?"

Did he mean that? He wasn't even sure what he said. "Yes!"

"I see. Are you an emotional person, Dan Bluestone, or are you a logical person?"

Biggie was going to give her query the glib retort it deserved, but instead found himself ruminating. The truth was, people took him for being unemotional, a cool cucumber, unflappable. When you said Biggie Bluestone, that's what people said back. But at heart he knew he wasn't; he was just different. For example, most people—even guys like Wing

Terrill—would take a slap in the face then immediately yelp and slap back twice or three times before deciding the next day they'd overreacted, that there were other points of view they'd failed to consider, that really—now that they'd thought about it in the calm light of recollection—they'd gotten what they deserved. Contrite, they—these guys who were like Wing and everybody else—walked the streets looking for somebody to apologize to, that's what he told Glory. But the great Biggie? "I shrug like I'm all composed, Glory, a cool cucumber, unflappable, *contrite*—"

"Contrite?" Gloria said.

"I take the insult to heart. I immediately see my degree of culpability—"

"Culpability?" Gloria said.

"They slap me and *I'm* looking to apologize, that's me. *Then* I wake up a few days later wanting to slap the guy back three or four and worse! Maybe it's a delayed reaction."

Gloria didn't say anything.

"So I'm both, I guess—emotional and logical—but logical first."

"Do people insult you often?"

"Outside the family, you mean?"

"That's what I mean, Dan."

"I bench 380," Biggie said, inflating his best lift by 20 pounds by way of making the point.

"Hmm." Biggie had the impression she was screening the next question on her list. "Is it fun to be you?"

"Gloria." The wrestler sensed he was finding his rhythm, the way when he set up the deep double there was no way the guy would ever block the move. "It's all the fun I've ever had."

"What are you doing?"

That should have been obvious, though he wondered if she suspected he was beating off or drooling to the sound of her voice. "I'm talking on the phone."

"Tonight. What are you doing tonight, Dan?"

"I'm going to Midlands."

Midlands was a huge wrestling tournament staged every year at Mc-Gaw Hall; hundreds of the best wrestlers in the country would be at Midlands, mostly from college teams, but a lot of guys who *were* big college stars now training for the Olympics also wrestled. "Most schools consider it the toughest meet of the year next to NCAAs," Biggie informed her, like it or not. Tonight was the quarterfinals. He didn't tell Gloria—but almost did, deciding at the last second that it came under the heading of "unnecessary information," that he'd been looking forward to Midlands all week, almost as much as he'd looked forward to the college girls strutting the hallways in their underwear as he stretched in the dorm lounge next year. Biggie had gone the last couple of years—first with his dad, who was nice enough to drive him; last year with Rich Becker. This year he'd drive himself, and, here's what he balked at telling Gloria Serpentino, he looked forward to going next year, too, only next year he'd be there as a *wrestler*, and for years after. He imagined even when he stopped wrestling, when he was an ancient guy of forty-five with dentures and grandkids, he'd still go back as a pilgrimage to his long-lost youth.

After deciding not to tell her, Biggie, though pleased with his restraint, broke down and told her.

"Dan?" Glory said when he finished.

"What?"

"Have a good time at Midway."

"Mid—"

After she hung up, Biggie wondered if he was supposed to ask her along. He wondered again if he'd told her more than she wanted to hear; after getting an earful of the true Biggie Bluestone, was Gloria Serpentino bored to tears?

What got to him was, he'd only seen her through the misty half-light when she had tears streaming down her face, and didn't know what she looked like. Who knew how accurate his observations might be, given he'd just come within an inch of being run over?

One afternoon last week Biggie had stood outside The Sergeant, where he'd learned that Gloria Serpentino worked. The place was on a side street between Central and Vine, with a large display window of pipes and hippie clothes, and a narrow door beneath an awning that stretched across the sidewalk. He'd stood there for half an hour, knowing there was no way he'd go *inside* to scout her out. Biggie, freezing to death, figured she'd come out, or he could spot her in the window and, as happened with movie victims scanning mug shots, her image would instantly correlate with the girl he couldn't quite picture. But nobody he saw through the window resembled the terrified girl in the car. Biggie was half freezing to death, bundled beneath several layers, looking for a girl whose looks he couldn't remember, whom he wasn't all that certain he hoped to confront in the first place. *Confront?* If Glory did come out of The Sergeant there was a good chance she'd be bundled beneath several layers of clothing herself. Curling his hands into tight little balls buried in his pockets, he'd known that she might have already left, bundled in a babushka in front of his eyes as he stood freezing to death trying to steal an inconspicuous glance through the window. *That's* how ridiculous he'd become.

Since Roy Gosley, the legendary coach, had introduced himself two weeks before, Biggie hadn't worked up the nerve to call for the guided Northwestern tour. But last week, *before* Lake Forest, he'd received a letter in the mail from the University of Illinois wrestling coach, Monte

Safredo, something to get excited about, triumphantly waving the letter in the air.

It turned out to be an impersonal note with an attached questionnaire, as if Coach Safredo wondered if he were one of possibly a million guys—probably everyone above the level of Wing Terrill got the questionnaire—who might be interested in Illinois. The wrestler had immediately filled out the questionnaire, laboring over items such as "field of interest" and "career ambitions"—were they looking for identical answers or different?—before mailing the sheet back, feeling good for an hour or two about being recruited now by *two* Big Ten schools. It still felt good, until you considered that all they really cared about was how you did downstate. If they sent you a *hundred* letters, if they called you a dozen times, if they positioned an assistant coach to move into your basement, if you didn't win State or finish second, they'd thank you for the hospitality and leave. That was the general principle. Since last year he'd lost in *Districts*, he ought to be amazed and grateful he was even on the letter list. But Biggie, who'd always been a dreamer, thought: Why not dream for the best?

All stuff Wing Terrill would understand if he weren't in Michigan City, but stuff just scratching the surface of things you could never tell him, so it was just as well Wing was in Michigan City.

Waukegan, December 30, 1970

The wrestler sat on the bus to Waukegan, contemplating the contents of the traveling bag on his lap: three roast beef sandwiches, a thermos of apple juice, an apple and a package of Oreos he'd devour after weighing in.

Beside him Wing Terrill was honing his Sara Sherman Dissertation. "Last night her parents were awake, so I had to crawl through her window. This will surprise you, Biggie, but Mr. Sherman doesn't like me. They argue about it all the time. He says she's too young to be head over heels. She says that she's old enough to make up her own mind. It's her body, her emotions, not his."

"Hasn't Mr. Sherman ever been young and in love?" Professor Pete Hoffman asked from across the aisle.

"According to Sara," Wing related, "if she wasn't too young to be popping some guy every spare moment she wasn't composing sappy poetry about him or writing the guy twenty-page letters vowing her eternal love, *I'd* be the guy he'd want for her."

"It's because you're so great," Biggie Bluestone commented.

Wing nodded thoughtfully. "He's the one paying the bills, what can you do? I've made my peace with it. Most nights I toss pebbles at her window like a schoolboy, that's our secret signal, then I sneak like a fucking bandit through the window into her room, where Sara has already pulled off her jammies at the signal."

"Pure poetry," Hoffman said.

"In the black of midnight her skin's golden against her pillow," Wing added defensively.

"Is that so?" Luigi Cravi yawned across the aisle.

"Fuck you, Cravi," Wing said.

"I don't want to sound like a fucking schoolboy, but I'll concede that Sara Sherman's pretty," Pete Hoffman acknowledged, next to Cravi across the aisle.

Pete Hoffman was the master of understatement. He was also the only guy on the team going to Yale next year, which he had this way of thinking you wanted to hear about every second, so they called him Professor.

"Pretty? You call that hair pretty? Those eyes? You call Sara Sherman's ass *pretty*? That's all? Her *ass*? Cravi's an idiot, but don't *you* get the point of her ass, Hoffman?"

"The point of her ass?" Cravi asked.

"It's an existential question," Professor Hoffman suggested.

Wing Terrill had been in love with Sara Sherman since elementary school, though it was known that they'd never had a conversation beyond, "Sorry I knocked your books over, Sara," or "I didn't mean to kick you in the shin, Sara. It was an accident." Sara Sherman probably still held it against you if you kicked her in the shin in elementary school. Every guy Biggie knew had been in love with Sara Sherman since elementary school, and she'd never spoken to any of them. Wing even had a steady girlfriend, Gail Abernathy, who was nice looking and smart and funny, but not somebody you'd be in love with since elementary school, and probably not somebody—Biggie imagined—who liked to think her boyfriend spent nearly every second he wasn't with *her* winding toward obscure points about Sara Sherman's ass.

Still, what the point was about Sara Sherman's ass Biggie wanted to know, for the archives if nothing else. There was debate both within and without the wrestling team as to exactly who was the most beautiful girl at Highland Park. Some said Lisa King, a curvaceous blonde, though a lot of guys would tell you Jo Anne Feldman or Janey Porter, but Sara Sherman was the consensus among the guys who weren't the type to go along with the consensus; since that described every wrestler, Wing probably saved a lot of time just by saying "Sara Sherman." Nonetheless, it was difficult to see what her ass had to do with any of it. Sara Sherman's ass was fine, as far as Biggie could tell, but indistinguishable from Janey Porter's, and Porter was known for her *legs*, after which—it had been noted in the halls of HPHS—pythons modeled their natural behavior.

"With girls like Jo Anne Feldman, Janey Porter, Lisa King, one day they're gangly, wearing braces, the next some college guys have picked them off the vine," Wing Terrill lamented regularly.

"Do you have a copy of one of those letters with you?" Biggie asked Wing. "One where she swears her eternal love?"

Wing looked at Biggie like *he* was a fucking bandit.

"It sounds farfetched to me," Luigi said across the aisle.

Wing suddenly seemed to doze off, presumably dreaming about Sara Sherman, which he was liable to do even in the midst of a Sara Sherman soliloquy.

Biggie was tired, too; having to wrestle a match in a few short hours could take the starch out of you, though the nerves usually wouldn't kick in until after weigh-in. Before weigh-in you were too busy going out of your mind wishing you could eat, as well as fighting off the drowsiness, to get too worked up about the match itself. Even when the guy you were wrestling—in this case, Lamont Garcia, whose record was 16-3, according to the Waukegan *Sun*—was good. Biggie wondered if, when the time came, he'd even give Berkenmeier a thought before weighing in. Once you weighed in, though, in the hours before you wrestled, the nerves ate you alive. Often Biggie would emerge from the fog he went into before his match and look out on the mat and see two guys stalling and hanging on to each other, as if they'd decided by mutual decree that nobody was going to get humiliated out there in front of everybody. Wing's matches tended to be that way.

Biggie elbowed the dozing Wing in the arm.

"Bluestone, give me a break. Can't a guy take a nap around here? I have a match to wrestle."

"Can I go out with Abernathy? Since you're busy with Sara Sherman."

"Why ask me?" Wing yawned. "I thought you were already going out with Abernathy."

Gail Abernathy and Wing had been going out since sophomore year. They were a matched set, like the salt-and-pepper shakers or blustery wind and the lake. How that squared with Wing's relentless rhapsodizing about Sara Sherman every spare second wasn't the sort of thing you could ask Wing, who'd look at you like you were an idiot. It was the sort of thing you could barely stand to think about yourself. Still, Biggie imagined the riffs were Wing's way of talking about Gail Abernathy without talking about Gail Abernathy. If you told everyone how much you were in love with some girl you were really in love with, the guys—Hoffman, Cravi, Bluestone himself—would know you were pussy whipped. "A terminal case," Professor Pete Hoffman would say so sadly and definitively that you'd want to cry. But this way Wing could say what he had to say and all the guys could get a kick out of it, even if it was a joke you really didn't want to understand.

That might be the point of Sara Sherman's ass, Biggie thought.

"I snuck into Abernathy's room last night," Luigi Cravi said across the aisle. Since Cravi was 260 pounds, the image was funny. "It was interesting," Cravi added.

Wing glowered at Cravi. "Shut your trap, Fat Boy."

For a guy who could dish it out, Wing Terrill didn't take it too well. Biggie thought a lot of people were that way, beginning with his sister.

Cravi snorted jovially.

That was Cravi. If you called Cravi "Fat Boy" he'd assume you were being funny and let out a jovial snort, even though he weighed a good 260 and it wasn't precisely all muscle. The heavyweight's easy disposition—Biggie assumed—was because he'd made All-Suburban League at tackle last fall and would have had a lot of colleges after him except for his low grades, though the low grades didn't seem to bother him either. Luigi wasn't Rich Becker on the gridiron or the mat, but Biggie imagined that something about being All-Conference made you not mind so much when guys called you Fat Boy.

A while later, Cravi and Pete Hoffman debated across the aisle. "You know your problem, Cravi?" Professor Hoffman was saying, nodding his head somberly. "You've compromised too readily. You've cut a deal with yourself at the expense of your sensuality and the wild man within. You're civilized, Cravi."

"That's true," Cravi admitted.

"But at what cost? You don't permit the whole man free reign. You're not proactive. I trust that you've read Norman O. Brown?"

"I *am* Norman O. Brown," Luigi said.

Biggie quietly asked Wing, "Do you know a girl named Gloria Serpentino?"

He didn't want to ask too loudly. In fact, he didn't know why he was asking.

"Glory? Sure I know Glory. Went to Northwood." Northwood was a middle school in Highland Park. Whenever somebody's name came up everybody in Highland Park immediately identified them by where they went to middle school. If Mahatma Gandhi were from HP, everybody would say, "Oh yeah, *Gandhi*. Went to Northwood." It was one small thing Biggie hated about the place.

With a lot of guys, if you mentioned a girl they'd automatically say, "Oh yeah, that whore," whether they knew her or not. Wing wasn't like that. With Wing she'd have to literally be a whore—working out of some bordello in Highwood, probably—if he called her a whore; even then Wing would probably think that was a good thing and be happy for you. Still, it was encouraging that Wing hadn't laughed in his face when he mentioned her name.

"Why do you want to know? Biggie, do you like Glory?"

"She only almost killed me a few weeks ago. I was out running and she practically ran me over."

"Fucking lady drivers," Wing said.

"She's called me up to apologize," he added.

"Decent of her. I haven't seen Glory around much the last couple of years," Wing said. "I think Gail told me she works at The Sergeant."

Biggie nodded. A lot of pretty girls hung out at The Sergeant, trying on dresses and scarves and staring into the mirrors. Biggie had found it encouraging that she worked there, even knowing there was no guarantee that because pretty girls liked to hang out at a place that they only hired pretty girls. It was known that The Sergeant also hired girls who were full of spirit, whom you'd mostly hang around with because, in addition to soaking up their spirit, they might put in a word with their pretty friends.

Biggie almost asked Wing if Gloria Seprentino was one of the Fifty.

Out of 2,600 students at HPHS, half were female. While a substantial portion hadn't developed into what Biggie considered to be high school girls and may as well be eleven or twelve, and while many others—Biggie thought—nobody would think to look twice at, some because they were so quiet when in class or moving through the hallways that it wouldn't occur to you to look twice, though when you did—Biggie had discovered—you could be surprised. Many of these quiet girls that you never noticed bore remarkable resemblances to the pretty girls who were all you thought about, though it was as if there were a dull light inside them that kept you from especially thinking of them as "girls." In the *Little Giant*, though, they'd look good. Last year, looking over the class photos, Biggie resolved to pay more attention, but it turned out that you never noticed these girls in the first place, even when you were looking out for them. Invariably they escaped the Bluestone radar.

That left fifty girls on the radar. The Magical Fifty. The name itself—he'd heard of the Fifty as far back as middle school—summoned the powers of myth. They were the ones who made walking around the halls, or leaning back against the wall in the passageway between the gym and the east classroom building during lunch or optional study hall talking to Wing Terrill or Luigi Cravi—but generally by himself leaning against the wall for fear of keeling over from starvation—pleasant.

Of the Magical Fifty, he knew the names of half. Their lives were opaque, impenetrable. Did they know how pretty they were? In the hallways the question bore consideration. Biggie thought *that* might be the difference, that the fifty who by consensus were what everybody meant when they talked about "girls" knew how pretty they were, while plenty of others, who looked great in the yearbook, for one reason or another—shyness? personality?—didn't possess that degree of self-awareness. Sometimes, as these girls walked down the hall, on the rare instances when he noticed them in the first place, Biggie thought about pulling them aside and telling them flat out. *Those* would be the girls who'd go out with him, though it was always one of the Magical Fifty he pictured driven berserk by euphoria, praying, crying, clenching their fists, desperately hugging each other during his incredible journey to the State title. Naturally, he envisioned one of the Magical Fifty when he envisioned Gloria Serpentino.

"Next time you see her tell her to take driving lessons," he told Wing.

When the two teams weighed in, you had two lines of guys stripped down, waiting to hop on the scale. You never said anything to the other team or acted like you were paying attention, but you kept your inner eye intensely perched on the guy you'd wrestle. It was often misleading because a lot of guys who were tough on the mat didn't look that tough when they stepped on the scale, while sometimes guys who looked like they ought to be behind bars while standing in line to weigh in were the same guys who held and stalled during a match and were just happy to get through without getting pinned or puking all over the mat.

Still, Biggie was sure he'd won some matches just by the way he looked. It wasn't only his stubbled face that looked tough. When you wrestled at 167 and could bench 360 and military press over 250, there was no way you'd be a guy who was just hoping to hang on. Most guys looked at Biggie and figured the match would be over before the first period if they didn't stay away from him and stall it out; even then they'd get pinned right away. "A man among boys," Wetzel described him as the team watched a video of the Quadrangular final a few weeks ago. "Biggie's a man among boys this year." The top guys—Berkenmeier, Dixon Boyd of North Chicago, Bluestone—were often men among boys. When you got downstate half the guys in the weight class were "men among boys." Most of the others were guys who, though they looked like boys among men, could really wrestle.

Against Waukegan you didn't have to wonder whether the guy you were wrestling was tough. Nobody remembered the last time that Highland Park beat Waukegan—"a hundred years ago," Professor Pete Hoffman speculated on the bus—or a year when Waukegan didn't win the Suburban League or weren't top five in Illinois. Making it close in the dual was the best you could hope for; even *that* never happened. Last year Biggie lost in the dual, 6-3 to Perzonelli, who went downstate. Lamont Garcia concentrated very hard on not looking at Biggie as he stepped on the scale.

"Boo!" Biggie felt like shouting.

Then it was Biggie's turn. Killer Kowalski made weight.

He always cut a beeline for the water fountain as soon as he made weight. If there was a line, he'd hunt down another water fountain. This even before he drained his thermos and attacked the sandwiches, if only because the last two days, water fountains were mostly what he dreamed about; not the State Championship celebration at Henrici's, but the moment he made weight and took a long cold drink at the fountain. In his imagination the water always ran cold. When the reality didn't match the dream, when the water emerged lukewarm from the spigot, Biggie would stand for a moment shaking his head, not comprehending the discrepancy. He'd stare at the fountain a moment longer, as if he might tear it off the wall and hurl it through the window across the gym.

The nerves wouldn't hit for an hour and a half—late in the JV meet, they'd explode, until he was uncertain he'd make it all the way to the john before his sphincter collapsed. Still, he never vomited before a match. A lot of guys did, including Wing Terrill. Wing gave no outward indications, didn't get frantic and start pacing—unlike Biggie, who was liable to break into paroxysms of pushups. One second Wing would be talking loudly, so mindlessly free-associating that you *wished* he'd start talking about Sara Sherman's ass; the next second you'd hear him retching in the stalls. Wing wasn't even a guy with much at stake, as far as Biggie could imagine. If Wing harbored illusions about getting through Districts, nobody else expected him to. It's not like—after being pinned by Biggie twenty times a day during practice—Wing Terrill cultivated illusions. Still, even if you had no illusions, there was something about the prospect of getting the stuffing beaten out of you by some guy your age in front of a packed gym that could send you into the stalls to puke your illusionless guts out.

He hadn't given a thought to Lamont Garcia yet. Sometimes when guys made weight, particularly those who killed themselves doing it, they tended to forget that on top of it all they still had to wrestle. To an extent that was Biggie's problem, too.

The Waukegan bleachers were packed by the middle of the JV match. Pete Hoffman, Biggie's backup at 167, lost 15-2 to a kid who showed improbable quickness moving in on the single—twice he took Professor Pete down to his back after kicking out the leg, then showed enough mat sense to immediately move in with the half, something you didn't see too often on JVs—Biggie marveled that as recently as last year, when the other team's second-string guy looked unbeatable, it would drive him nuts trying to imagine how good the kid *he'd* have to wrestle must be. He'd feel like he was about to die of thirst if he didn't first keel over from heart palpitations, but now he thought, "Fuck, that's just Hoffman. Hoffman, for crissake. He may have been undefeated on JVs until now, but it's Hoffman." *Hoffman.* Shit. When Hoffman signed up for wrestling, after eyeing the activities entry on the college application, he hadn't imagined a massive gymnasium full of Waukegan fanatics screaming their heads off. It was bound to throw off Hoffman's JV equilibrium.

During the JV meet, the lower weights wrestled in private. By the time they got to 167 there were about 2,500 idiots going berserk.

The point of no return came when you slipped on your togs.

Highland Park had great uniforms, state-of-the-art, tight and sleek, whereas some teams wrestled in loose-fitting garments with what looked to be a pair of diapers on the outside draped over the pelvis and butt. The uniforms were new last year—the JVs wrestled now in the old varsity loose-fitting garments—black tights and a black singlet that made you look tough even when you weren't. In this spirit, wrestlers posed in the locker room mirror in their sleek togs, knees bent, palms out as if they were about to shoot in at their mirror image for a takedown.

Looking at himself looking tough in the mirror, Biggie wasn't too certain how *he'd* fare against himself.

They pulled on their elegant black sweats, the weight classifications stitched to the backs like badges of honor, and gathered around Coach Wetzel, whose huge bald head glistened, staring sullenly into the faces of his men. "These guys think they're the best team in Illinois. Men, let's see how good they are. Listen up. Be aggressive. Go after it. But be patient out there."

Be aggressive but be patient. That was Wetzel.

Wetzel's big face shook now with sweat as he eyed the squad one by one. "Let's go out there and have the time of our lives. This is our test, men. Let's remember who we are."

"We're Highland Park Little Giants," Jerry Bray said solemnly. Bray, the co-captain along with Biggie, wrestled at 132 and was undefeated so far, though everybody knew he'd lose tonight. The Poster Boy for School Spirit, according to Wing. As Biggie watched Bray smolder with school spirit, it occurred to him that Wing had a name for everybody. The Professor. The Poster Boy for School Spirit. Fat Boy. Looking back, Wing was the one who came up with "Biggie" one day as Danny walked through the halls of middle school bumping into lockers. When Biggie thought about it, "Wing" was the sleekest name in the bunch.

The squad lined up behind Jerry Bray and Biggie. The Poster Boy for School Spirit led the team through the chute onto the gym floor, where the Highland Park Little Giants sprinted to the mat to a burst of deafening murmurs and a few scattered yells, ran two laps around the mat and circled around Jerry Bray and Biggie Bluestone for calisthenics.

After sprinting around the mat again like a squadron of spirited idiots, they stretched and loosened. Biggie rolled around a few minutes with Cravi, then crawled to the far corner of the mat, eventually spinning through a series of bridges. Here he liked the feel of pressing his head and face into the mat—the wrestler loved the way wrestling mats smelled before a meet—and for a while, balanced on toes and forehead, appeared to burrow into the mat as if digging for China.

Back in the locker room, Biggie stared steadfastly at the floor. The crowd outside erupted, cheers generating louder cheers, as the Waukegan Bulldogs took the mat for warm-ups and Biggie remembered the fireworks breaking over Ravinia Park when he was a kid.

Nobody talked to Bluestone. *Other* guys talked. Co-captain Jerry Bray busied himself going from wrestler to wrestler pumping them up, rubbing their backs, slapping their shoulders, "Whadya say, Mandel?" "Whadya say, Teagarden?" "Whadya say, Pelligrini?" A few muttered back to the Poster Boy, in polite response to an honest question. "Good,

Jerry. Fine. Thanks for asking." Biggie often wished *he* could be more of a gladhander, frothing at the mouth with team spirit, and sometimes wondered if his teammates—who'd *elected* him co-captain and presumably harbored at least minimal expectations—sensed a cruel indifference. ("Bluestone wishes us well, but he doesn't care as long as he wins. He'd sell us up the river.") Not even Wing made an effort to talk to Bluestone. Nor did the Fat Boy, Cravi.

Biggie blocked out everything but the crack in the floor he stared at. There was no team, no city of Waukegan, no crowd outside but the soothing, deafening echo from the lake. He listened hard to the rhythmic beauty of distant Lake Michigan against the raw winter beaches.

The Little Giants lined up behind Jerry Bray and Biggie Bluestone, sprinted out again, now circling the Waukegan Bulldogs, then crowded onto half the mat, intensely oblivious to the guys they were soon to wrestle.

Everybody stood for the Pledge of Allegiance.

Biggie never understood why they made you pledge allegiance to your country because you were about to wrestle Waukegan, which the last time he checked was also in America. It wasn't only America, though. Something about sports made otherwise rational people want to leap to their feet and thank their countries and pledge their loyalty. Biggie pictured some guys in Bulgaria right now thanking Bulgaria for the opportunity, in the spirit of Bulgaria. Guys were probably looking at each other, squaring their jaws, tears falling down their cheeks. "Only in Bulgaria," they say in Bulgarian.

The reason, though, that saying the Pledge of Allegiance before a *wrestling* meet against *Waukegan* made him crazy is that the wrestler always wondered if he should stand for the Pledge at all.

Last football season this kid from Niles North refused to remove his helmet for the national anthem—before the game, when everybody snapped to their feet, this guy stood but wouldn't take his helmet off—and while everybody in the newspapers made an international incident over such a colossal display of disrespect, calling the kid a communist, ungrateful for the opportunity America offered, indicative of our youth's moral decay, Biggie admired the hell out of him. If he felt as this kid did—and he wasn't altogether sure he didn't—that he didn't care to honor certain things his country stood for, namely the war in Viet Nam but possibly including material values, and anyway the great thing about America was that you didn't *have* to take your helmet off for the national anthem, not if you didn't want to, as a matter of principle—Biggie, though a natural subversive, suspected he wouldn't have the guts that this kid had—who was the same age, too, so there weren't too many ready defenses he could launch on his own behalf, as if the issue weren't courage but chronology, Biggie biding his time, his light under a bushel for the time being, but give him a year or two, then *hold on to your hats*! ("There goes Big Dan Bluestone," they'd say; nobody would call him Biggie anymore, assuming he wasn't killed in Viet Nam by then.) As it happened, all these old guys who called the kid a communist and would be quite happy to send the kid to Viet Nam *now*, tried to get him expelled and kicked off the football team. Even Wing was all upset about it—"The kid should move to Russia!"—though with Wing you never knew what he really thought, especially when he told you.

Of course, everybody knew the kid had *rights*. Still, just because you had a right didn't mean you'd exercise that right if everybody was not only going to call you a communist but, also, a kid who was just looking for attention—as they called this Niles North guy, who'd spend the rest of his life as a symbol of ingratitude—so Biggie never made that big a deal about it, just sort of stood up for the Pledge but was careful not to put his hand over his heart, as some guys liked to, and also made a point of looking bored and distracted. That way nobody would get the impression he supported the War or was big on material values.

Last year, in fact, Biggie was suspended from the football team for the last half of the season *because* he protested the war, so you could say he'd already taken a stand. For National Moratorium Day, Biggie had skipped school and practice. There was this rally in a big park where he sat down and listened to a bunch of speeches, mostly by students from his school who struck Biggie as both a million times more mature than he and better informed. Half of Highland Park High School was there—it was practically an HPHS-*sanctioned* protest; they'd met at the school and marched over, Biggie marching behind a girl he'd never seen before with long black hair who wiggled her butt as she walked—just as the bombshell sexpots did in the old movies. The thing about being in that park on Moratorium Day was that even though these were mostly kids he didn't know and hadn't seen walking in the hallways, which is the sort of thing that can happen at a big suburban high school, the really pretty girls being ones you never even got to see in the hallways, everybody *smiled* at him. It wasn't as if at the time he was a school legend. But on Moratorium Day, in that park near the school, as he listened to speaker after speaker and began to think that it was possible, they really could stop the war, not the suburb of Highland Park by itself but towns, villages, cities like it all across the country, if people would just refuse to do business as usual, on that day in that park hundreds of girls smiled at Biggie Bluestone as if synaptically connected.

What was amusing in retrospect, from the vantage point of the guy he was *now*, undefeated, unscored upon, the putative sure-shot State Champion, is that Biggie was suspended from the football team for participating in Moratorium Day and missing practice. At the team party after the season, when all the players and their parents got together to reminisce about their trials and tribulations, the coach told Biggie's dad how much he admired Biggie for showing up at practice every day and not complaining, even though he was suspended for the season because he missed practice that day. Even though, when his dad told him, Biggie considered all that a crock—the head coach was the kind of guy who'd call the Niles North kid a communist and want to send him off to Viet Nam *now* if that's how little he appreciated America—also first string guys missed practice but were right there in the lineup Saturday—nobody bothered to *inform* him of the suspension. "If you're suspended, they should tell you about it," Bluestone told his dad, who agreed.

He'd attributed not playing to his being, all in all, a lousy football player. Interested, but no aptitude. It's not like he'd made any tackles all season when he'd been in there on the suicide squads.

Still, when he stood for the Pledge of Allegiance, Biggie liked remembering that he'd made something of a stand himself, technically; suspended for half the season because he participated in the Moratorium to End the War. But it wasn't the same thing as *knowing* there'd be a price to pay, or doing it on your own without a thousand others, including hundreds of smiling girls standing around and doing it with you, or the kind of stuff his dad did all the time; at home Dad mostly read the newspaper and yelled at Giselle and Biggie to shut up when they argued with Mom, but outside the house he was always taking stands. Last year, for example, after his dad joined the Highland Park Dad's Club, Rich Becker's dad, who was not only president of the club but went to every Chicago Bears game home and away (if there was anybody the precise opposite of his dad it was Becker's), proposed that the club purchase these athletic jackets for a price that was not only a steal, but since the jackets were obviously hot—this Dad told him later—really *were* a steal. Still, everybody thought it was the greatest idea since sliced bread. Dad stood up and made this speech about how they were supposed to be role models, and buying jackets that were obviously hot so they could get a good price and being proud of themselves about it was the sort of thing they should be ashamed of. Then—Biggie liked to imagine a hush falling over the place—Dad walked out of the meeting room. That's the sort of thing that Sanford Bluestone would do, telling off a roomful of people, including some who had been nice to him. (Becker's dad in particular loved having the famous professor in the club, and before then was always calling him up.) Naturally, Biggie often found himself wondering if he would fill those shoes himself someday and take a stand, by himself, if necessary, if a stand was called for, even if he *knew* it would cost him. Or if he'd *not* take a stand, talk himself out of it ("It's not that important," he'd say. Or: "I'll get to it later."); that would probably say just as much about the Bluestone people would see when *he*'d walk into a room.

The Niles North kid didn't have to wonder; though—*sheesh*—with the way things worked, probably *his* dad was the kind who would call him a communist and be content to ship him off to Viet Nam *now*.

As the 98-pounders went at it, then the 105s, the 112s, the 119s, Bluestone leaned back in his mat-side folding chair muttering comments with Wing Terrill, neither of them able to hear but both barking, "The half, Artie, the half!" in the direction of the mat. Next, in the spirit of thinking about anything but his match twenty minutes away, Bluestone watched the Waukegan cheerleaders.

They were a thousand times more organized and athletic than the Highland Park cheerleaders. Half of them were Black girls, just as half the Waukegan wrestling team was Black. Though Biggie had beaten Black guys before, he'd often feel at a disadvantage, as if the Black guy had reservoirs to draw upon that he couldn't imagine as a rich suburban Jewish kid. The Highland Park cheerleaders, on the other hand, were the JV cheerleaders most of the year, but were reborn as the *wrestling* cheerleaders during the season, when the varsity cheerleaders were off hooting and hollering and jump-splitting the basketball team to inspiration.

Even if you didn't already know that the wrestling cheerleaders were the JVs, you could tell. They didn't look like the way Biggie pictured cheerleaders, so much as like studious girls, interesting to talk to, who wanted to be cheerleaders. They looked trustworthy. You believed the cheers. From what Biggie could tell, they were to cheerleading what the JV wrestling team was to wrestling. Other than Rona Lefler, Mary Wellington, Cindy Shelton, and Kelly Lipschutz, Biggie never noticed any of these girls before they'd shown up on the JVs, and sometimes wondered if he'd notice any of them now outside their uniforms—which, like the JV wrestlers' uniforms, were loose-fitting, hand-me-down garments. Mary Wellington made JV cheerleaders this year, and Biggie occasionally got a charge out of somebody he knew, whom he'd even briefly contemplated making a play for, somebody he'd often see in his kitchen who was alleged to find him cute and mus-cu-lar, on the JVs, and often listened for her voice, ringing slightly off-key, and would find himself looking at Mary Wellington during other guys' matches.

The cheers they'd manage for Biggie were garden variety ("Give me a B! Give me an I! What's that spell?" "Bluestone, Bluestone, he's our man!"), punctuated by shallow leaps into the air, while the Black Waukegan squad broke into a Radio City Rockette routine. You wanted to watch the Black girls because they were so spectacular, but you also wanted to listen to them because their chants were so clever. Thus, as the wrestler considered the issue, with half his attention directed toward the mat, muttering "Go, Mandel, go!" it seemed *appropriate* that Mary Wellington made JVs. If the Bulldog cheerleaders were like Broadway showgirls on tour, their Little Giant JV counterparts were like your sister's friends. They didn't incite the crowd so much as inspire curiosity. Still, at home meets, when practically nobody showed up, it was always nice hearing feminine shrieks when you took somebody down to their back, then look up to see a group of well-meaning girls attempt to leap into the air in synchronization.

You could say the same for the Little Giant wrestlers, who were similarly in over their heads. Teagarden, the 98, who was *pretty* good, lost

10-2 to Waukegan's Chimarski, who was *very* good and would probably place downstate. The 105, Pelligrini, fell 12-3. That's how it went. Nobody got pinned, everybody fought like hell, you weren't ashamed to be their co-captain, but nor could you overlook, just because you were co-captain, that for Waukegan it had quickly become a solid workout conducted under meet conditions, everybody screaming in the showgirl ambiance.

Biggie knew if he wasn't ten times as good as anybody else, nobody would have voted for him for co-captain, other than Wing, Cravi, and maybe Hoffman. Biggie himself voted for the Poster Boy. Still, when Wetzel announced, "Bray and Bluestone, you're co-captains. Congratulations, men," he'd looked around the locker room and thought, "These men *elected* me," and swore to himself that he'd represent his constituents well.

It turned out that even if you didn't really care if you were elected captain, when you were ten times as good as anybody else, you wanted to be elected anyway, just so everybody wouldn't assume you have leprosy.

That applied even if you didn't practice with the team half the time. Usually, after the flopping up-downs for conditioning, the technique demonstrations, the sit out drills, standup drills, takedown drills—all proscribed and punctuated by Wetzel's tinny whistle—then after the 3/4 speed rolling around drills, which Wetzel tried to make fun—one wrestler would stay in the middle of the circle where another would challenge him until somebody took him down, then, as in a child's game, *that* guy would take the middle—though these contests often became confusing, guys jumping into the circle simultaneously and stopping at Wetzel's whistle, which he was invariably blowing at the action in another circle—also, nobody really knew whether they were going 3/4 or 1/2—after the hour of serious scrimmaging—wrestling full-tilt in furious twenty-second bursts—during the practice matches (informal, though you were expected to try more than 3/4), everybody avoided him. He'd work up a sweat only because he was wearing a rubber suit and the wrestling room temperature was set to 80. He'd need to get a workout in, so finally he'd tell Wetzel that he was going down to the indoor track, which circled around on the basement level under the gym. There he'd run twelve laps to the mile until he got dizzy or lose count. By the time he'd finish, at last working up a real sweat, at last looking forward to weighing himself, emerging back into the wrestling room glistening, set for a final bevy of drills, everybody was showering.

It turned out, Wing told him once as they drove home from practice, with Biggie ruminating thoughtfully, and Wing in the passenger seat, his Fiat in the shop, that Wetzel *preferred* that Biggie descend downstairs for his laps.

"You're kidding."

"No."

Apparently the practice level elevated as the fear level diminished. They could peel themselves off the wall, as exhausted as they'd ever been in their lives, and not feel like they'd been loafing. Hoffman suddenly became tenacious when he grabbed your legs on the double. Cravi, with no Biggie Bluestone around, could jut out his massive belly and really swagger like a 260-pound heavyweight, an immovable object. Even Coach Wetzel, now participating beyond blowing his whistle, was quick to pair off, fearless on behalf of his back. "It's not the same when you're down there," Wing allowed.

"I guess that makes me an asshole."

"Don't take it that way. We can finally get some practice in."

Biggie considered marching up to Wetzel the next day and resigning his co-captaincy. But he'd been elected, a case could be made either way, and nothing really tilted the scales.

Though the men deserved a co-captain who'd overflow with constant advice, pumping them up at all times, Biggie was co-captain enough to watch while his co-captain wrestled. Bray was always good for six minutes of enthusiasm and intensity; he was fun to watch even for the Mat Gals and parents, who didn't really know what was going on. You could count on the Poster Boy throwing a dozen moves a minute. Bray was big enough, too, that he *looked* like a wrestler. Unlike most guys at the lower weights, at 132 Jerry Bray looked formidable, almost as tough as Biggie himself, weight-adjusted, with plenty of well-defined muscle and plenty more sinew where there wasn't muscle. Tonight Bray was wrestling a short Black kid with enormous arms named Crockett, who in all likelihood would take State next month. Whereas a lot of guys backed off and tried to stall it out against a monster like Crockett—as they did against a monster like Biggie—there was Jerry Bray circling to his left, shooting the single in the first ten seconds, getting in on the single, lifting, knocking out Crockett's left leg. Crockett toppled to the mat, looking up on all fours with the most limpid expression Biggie had ever seen on his taut, round face. Bray slipped in the leg and tried to angle into a tight crossbody, as if it weren't *Crockett* he were trying to ride. But it *was* Crockett, so Crockett escaped within five seconds. There were no more takedowns for the rest of the period as Bray shot a dozen times. Crockett fought off Bray's pesky shots. 2-1 Bray.

At the beginning of the second period, Crockett stood up, only to have Bray lift him and throw him down. Biggie Bluestone, co-captain, led his team as they leapt into the air. It was almost too much to take in. The Waukegan crowd, intensity diminished through the series of lopsided, tedious matches, also turned berserk, chanting "Crockett! Crockett!"—as if by their deafening pitch they might ignite their supernova. Five seconds later Crockett stood up again. Crockett peeled Jerry's hands before he could lift, broke free for the escape, 2-2, then clasped Bray's wrist before he could circle, snapped him down with an arm drag. The escape and takedown happened within ten seconds. The lift—when Bray slammed Crockett down after he stood up—already seemed improbable, something they imagined or that Bray deserved because he was such a conscientious team guy. For the next minute and a half, then again through the entire final period, Crockett rode Jerry, hooking a leg, holding Bray's wrist with the two-on-one, relentlessly grinding Jerry Bray into the mat. He'd slip in a gut wrench or pick an ankle, Bray would kick out in panic, otherwise relentlessly grinding with the two-on-one.

Bray—Biggie knew—felt like he was being crushed by several tons of cement, wondering, as Crockett dug his mouth and face and shoulders and torso into the rubber, slowly circling as if to erase the circle with Jerry Bray's hide, if he were going to suffocate. Biggie wondered if Bray would just give up—let Crockett slip in the half and turn him for the pin; he'd seen guys do that against Crockett many times. What else could you do when time stops? Thirty seconds, which seems like nothing when you're crossing the kitchen, may as well be eternity when you're drowning. Twice the ref warned Bray for stalling—the ultimate affront to Mr. Intensity—and appeared set to penalize Jerry at the buzzer. The score 4-2, the closest match Crockett would have all year, was incredibly respectable, though Bray was no closer to beating Crockett than if he'd been pinned in a minute. *Everybody* knew it. Biggie watched his co-captain waddle off the mat. A layer had been peeled off Bray's visible skin; his Poster Boy face, shoulders, arms, scoured raw.

Jerry Bray sobbed like an infant.

The wrestler left for the locker room. On the concrete floor in front of the lockers he broke into a long set of pushups, then burst into the air and landed with a set of 100 jumping jacks. Disregarding his dead shoulder as always, he tried another 100 six-count burpees accented with a pushup when he hit the floor, then later flying pushups punctuated by claps. For a moment he felt he was going nuts, but if he didn't work out now like a lunatic he'd be twice as exhausted when he stepped on the mat, only a few minutes away. He sprinted to the stalls, listening as he strained to the voluminous cheering from the bleachers overhead, thundering to such a crescendo that the stalls vibrated. Blake, who had never been pinned before except by Bluestone every day during practice, must have been pinned at 145.

Crestfallen Bray meeting crestfallen Blake stumbling off the mat.

Biggie ran with conviction through the doors to the warmup mat behind the bench. He vaguely took in that he was nodding at Bray, who had stopped sobbing and was looking at him eagerly: even with his cheek scoured into one monstrous rash, Jerry Bray was going to tell him to watch the *kelly*. Biggie faced the mat, vaguely aware that Hatch was being mauled by Waukegan's Cresper, still another downstate candidate, to an inch beyond his tolerance.

He never took in a thing from the 155. Hatch may as well have been wrestling in a different galaxy, Biggie observing implacably through a billion miles of murk. Out of which he emerged, pulled off his sweatsuit, pulled off the gray t-shirt he liked to wear beneath the sweats, flexed until he could feel his arms again, feel who he was from that moment, feel the blood rushing through his veins, feel the sigh that momentarily stilled the crowd, which soon began to buzz again, then chant.

With a hint of menace, coolly, icily, Killer Kowalski took the mat.

Through the murk came clarity as Lamont Garcia also took the mat and nodded to the referee: You get Garcia off balance, you find an angle to turn in with a hold. You force him to commit, then surge with every-thing you have into the direction of the kid's momentum. That's all you had to do. And even if Biggie knew he wasn't as strong as he looked, Biggie Bluestone never had to wrestle himself. Garcia flexed his own big muscles and half-smiled at Biggie across the circle as if commenting to his pals screaming from the bleachers ("Can you *believe* this guy?"); most guys looked startled when the moment finally came and they saw Biggie

Bluestone across the mat, and he admired Garcia for the full-hearted, if desperate, con job.

"Biggie, he's tough. Let's go," he took in that Wetzel was telling him.

Mary Wellington and the JV girls calling out, "What's that spell?"

It amazed him what he heard and what he didn't.

Garcia moved in and locked him up, banging his forehead, already breathing hard. He pushed Garcia away. Garcia moved in again, harder, as he grabbed Garcia behind the neck with one hand, behind the arm with the other, snapped Garcia down as he still came forward, spun, knocked out his arm (Lamont Garcia hadn't quite taken it in yet) as if he were slicing down a fence post, slipped in the half, turned him in the same motion, shot back his legs and gripped the mat with his toes as he dug in with the half. Garcia tilted toward, then left, then swung back as the ref slapped the mat.

Biggie emerging through the murk, the ref raising his arm.

Garcia gripping his hand, looking up through the same wary smile. The Waukegan announcer droning over the PA, "The winner by fall in 39 seconds. . ."

"Is there anybody Biggie Bluestone can't pin in a minute?" Pete Hoffman yelled from the bleachers, in triumph and despair.

———◦———

Last Semester of High School, January 4-7, 1971

Since kindergarten—it seemed to Biggie Bluestone—he'd heard classmates speculating on how they'd spend their last semester of high school. Everyone knew you lived in a free zone last semester, unaccountable to rules and order. You could skip all the classes you wanted—whether because you'd already proven yourself, or the teachers figured you were a full-blown adult so didn't care, Biggie didn't know—and if you flunked your classes in the process they passed you anyway because they didn't want to keep you out of college. Even if you weren't going to college they didn't want you hanging around the hallways grousing about how the bastards kept you out of college, so they passed you anyway. It was also well known that in the last semester all the girls who never bothered to say hello to you were suddenly willing to at least give you a blow job, because they suddenly felt homesick about leaving the place and already were feeling sentimental because you'd shared the same homeroom or row of lockers.

Biggie figured the rumors about last semester of senior year kept a lot of guys in school who otherwise would have dropped out long ago. That's why they circulated them in the first place, to keep a lot of guys from showing up on the factory strip along Skokie Boulevard with their shipping-receiving applications filled out the morning after Miss Geddenking screamed at them for passing notes during Geography. (One class, she'd even screamed at Biggie, who wasn't passing notes but whispering quietly to Luigi Cravi.) The rumors, along with the fact that if you dropped out or otherwise didn't go to college, the draft board automatically listed you as 1A the second you turned eighteen, kept a lot of guys enrolled. To hear some guys talk about it, they shipped you to Viet Nam the next day, providing the basic training and everything over there, just so you wouldn't harbor illusions that you might get out alive.

Biggie didn't give some of the rumors too much credence. He couldn't see, for example, Sara Sherman, the most beautiful girl at HPHS, giving him a blow job for old time's sake. The college guy she went out with probably wouldn't appreciate the nuances, though it seemed odd to Biggie, now with college around the corner—he'd already applied to Northwestern and Illinois, along with Knox—that if you were a college guy you ought to be able to do better than go out with a high school girl, even an Imperial like Sara Sherman. Probably you had to be a second-string kind of college guy to *want* to go out with a high school girl in the first place (which Biggie suddenly saw as a step below not going out with any girl at all), given all the co-eds you saw every day on the dormitory floors. It made you wonder if Sara Sherman was even aware that her boyfriend didn't rate any higher than all the other guys she wouldn't say hello to. Suddenly Biggie found himself feeling sorry for the guy, who was probably desperate about now to get his blow jobs in, assuming Sara Sherman even knew what a blow job was—a hand job maybe, Bluestone could see that—because he sure wasn't about to get any next fall once Sara Sherman was in college.

Whether or not the rumors were true, the seniors seemed more relaxed. Suddenly everybody was saying hello to Biggie in the hallways. And if he was by himself—say in the passageway between the gym and the cafeteria, watching the passing parade—leaning against the wall, passing the time, and a group of seniors nearby huddled together, several would look over to Biggie, smiling, as if he were free to step in and add his two cents' worth whenever he pleased.

The trouble you'd gone to back in the fall of filling out a college application and mailing it off guaranteed they'd pass you along. Everybody knew it. Cravi even filled out his papers for Harper Community College in Lake County, where the football coaches already had him convinced if he got his grades up Notre Dame would be after him. Professor Pete Hoffman, who wrestled behind Biggie at 167, would be choosing between Stanford and Yale, assuming his tenure on the JV team put him over the top in the application pool. Wing Terrill had applied to Bates in Maine, Utica in New York, and Lewis and Clark way out in Oregon, which was causing all kinds of problems with Gail Abernathy, who was set to go to the U. of Illinois where her sister pledged ZBO. (Wing applied there but didn't think he'd get into the Business School; at least that's what he told Gail. All the other places he applied were liberal arts colleges, but if Wing went to Illinois it had to be the *Business* School.

Biggie figured he'd still end up going where Gail Abernathy went.) He'd heard that Sara Sherman had applied to Smith, Sarah Lawrence, and Northwestern, the latter a possibility that tripled Biggie's resolve to land the scholarship. There were times, doing laps in his basement room as the hi-fi blared the soundtrack to *Hair*, that Biggie envisioned the imperial, magnetic Sara Sherman marching up to him to discuss their college plans since she'd heard he was also considering Northwestern. Or else running into her on the Northwestern campus, once he made All-American, that faint hint of recognition, then the fervent reminiscence about their high school days, then Biggie's starring as the protagonist in Wing Terrill's pipe dream. By then, though, he'd probably have a dozen similarly imperial girls after him. In college so many were imperial that you barely drew the distinction. That was the kind of reverie last semester of senior year gave license to. You even found it realistic.

Gloria Serpentino, who wasn't certain she'd accumulate enough credits without summer school, was thinking about Northern Illinois in Dekalb. She told him so on the Monday after Waukegan, when she called up Biggie to discuss college plans.

"Dan, do you think it's better to be good than lucky?"

"If you're good you don't need luck," Biggie told her.

"I'd better be lucky if I'm going to graduate this spring. I'm still a class short."

They'd let her graduate anyway. "Can't you carry an extra load?"

"Dan, I work twenty hours a week. You're lucky you don't have to work."

"I take out the garbage and mow the lawn." Biggie feared he'd revealed himself as a guy who was all luck, no substance, so he added, "Sometimes I clear the table."

"Well, you are lucky, Mister."

"Glory, I run and lift weights twenty hours a week. And that's on top of practice, which is on top of sitting in my chair thinking about wrestling, which is on top of staying up at night sifting through the pages of *Advanced Wrestling Techniques for the High School Athlete*." It wasn't the same thing—after all, his pursuit was voluntary; Gloria probably didn't *want* to work her way through high school. It was hard to envision somebody working in a store and *liking* it, especially in a place like Highland Park, where everybody else had doting parents and huge allowances. Most guys he knew—those that worked—worked for their dads or at the Bobolink Golf Course. Biggie added, "Though I guess it's not the same thing."

"Why do you do it, Dan?"

"Do what?"

"Lift weights twenty hours a week and put yourself to sleep dreaming about wrestling some guy to the floor."

"The mat."

"The mat," she corrected.

"I guess I like it."

"Does it make girls fall in love with you?"

"That's right, Miss. They don't want to fall in love with me, but it *makes* them."

"Then you like it because you're good at it? Is that all there is to it?"

While Biggie wasn't sure where this was going, that's what he liked about talking to Gloria. Usually when he talked to people, even his parents and Giselle and Wing Terrill, he'd have the impression they'd had the same conversation before, or one enough like it you could substitute freely and not notice the difference as you kept talking away. That fact itself he took as proof he was ready to graduate. "Yeah. Sometimes I think I'm the best there is at it, for the age and weight at least, in Illinois. Most anywhere, too, though. You watch. Come February I'm going to take State."

"Wow, Dan."

"I like the smell of the mats, too, Glory. I like the excitement from making weight. I like the anticipation. I like when I step into the circle and know nothing in the world can stop me. I like when I'm afraid, or when I'm so stricken I know my next step will be my last, but I work through it anyway, that's when I put the throttle down, and my next step isn't my last, after all, but the step leading to the next step, which leads to the one after that and suddenly the pattern's clear. I like the instant my guy realizes he's in over his head and caves in, though I like it when they don't, too, when they suck up what might be their last breath and meet me halfway. You want it to end but you never want it to end, if you catch my drift. I like it when I'm running and people think, 'There's Biggie Bluestone, the star wrestler. They say he's good.' That's what I imagine they think, Glory. They think, 'It must really be something to be Biggie Bluestone, best in Illinois. Power Incarnate. Such steel, that Bluestone. Such iron and fiber!'"

"I get the idea," Glory said.

"Sometimes what I like most is working out. You don't have the pressure—though I like the pressure, as I said. But when you work out you can just close your eyes and dream. Since you asked, Miss Serpentino."

"Oh, what if you couldn't wrestle anymore?"

She was teasing him. Anyway, the question seldom crossed his mind. Certainly, that regrettable day might come, but it would be after college when he'd have his hands full anyway between fighting off the sleek twenty-five-year-old post-college girls and staying out of the war, which would probably still be going strong. And trying to make a living, too. As for a living, he'd applied almost as little thought to what he might do to make one. Maybe a wrestling coach, he thought. Bluestone could see himself as one of those hotshot former wrestlers who gave their teams a monumental advantage, unlike Wetzel, who'd played pulling guard at Rutgers back before the Ice Age—"So they made Wetzel the *wrestling* coach," as Wing once put it, thus filling out the perfect equation.

If it turned out that he wasn't any more of a coach type than he was of the co-captain mold, he could see himself as a social worker, like his mother, or actor. Maybe he'd run for governor, something in the limelight like that. Whatever it was, he knew he didn't want to work in a store. "I guess I'd concentrate a lot more on football if I couldn't wrestle."

"Dan, you're incorrigible."

That was Dan: Incorrigible. Whereas *Biggie* was unscored upon.

Still, he kind of liked the "Dan" shit, coming from Glory. Now he almost asked her, while they were baring their souls and dreams, to describe herself or possibly send him a photo. Could you say that to a girl without her getting the wrong idea? It didn't seem like you could wrench a right idea out of that, from her point of view. Like looks were all you were after. Well, Biggie wouldn't pretend otherwise if Glory put the question to him straight out. Still, if she didn't have the looks it would be nice to have a picture to attach to her voice as long as they were baring their souls. "It's work in a way, Gloria. I don't think of it that way, that's not what gets me out of bed in the middle of the night so I can run five miles and almost get run over for my trouble, but it's work, too. My dad sees it that way. It's going to get me a scholarship."

Gloria didn't say anything. Immediately Biggie entertained second thoughts over the crack about "almost getting run over for my trouble," and figured, if he was going to say it at least he should add something like, "What's more, almost getting run over by a pretty girl." If she hung up on him, at least he'd know that avenue was closed.

Even though Bluestone felt like he could say anything to Gloria, there was plenty of other stuff he'd do really well not to say. He already felt rotten about mentioning college scholarships while she wasn't sure she'd have enough credits to *graduate* after working her way through high school. "I see," Gloria said finally. "Do you have a lot of wrestling scholarship offers?"

Biggie couldn't tell if she was mocking him. "None really, not yet. Northwestern and Illinois have shown interest. I've already applied there. But last year I lost in Districts to a guy from Deerfield, Bob Stuth—it's still a sore point, Gloria—so they don't know me too well. Some guys, like Berkenmeier, this kid from up in Mundelein I'm going to have to wrestle, for certain in Sectionals, again downstate, have scholarships already. That's because they had great junior years. Berkenmeier signed with the Wisconsin Badgers, where his brother already wrestles. That makes a big difference, too. He also has a coach who was a big star. Colleges pay attention to guys like that. He also won Junior Nationals last summer, so he's rated #1 in the country. But a lot of schools—really good ones, too—wait until after the State Tournament to see how you fare. Then they make their final choices."

"From what you say, Dan, your plans aren't any more settled than mine are. Despite your tone."

"My tone?" Biggie said. When he thought about it, though, maybe his plans didn't sound all that *finalized* yet. "As I said, Northwestern and Illinois are at the top of my list." He didn't point out to her that it wasn't quite the same thing, his plans not being finalized, versus Glory having none at all that he could see, and decided he'd do well not to point out the discrepancy. She wasn't even sure she'd *graduate*. "When you get the credits, Gloria, where do you figure you'll go?"

"Northern Illinois University in Dekalb, Dan. I've already applied."

That was surprising. The wrestler had figured she'd wind up at Triton, or College of Lake County, or—for crying out loud—carpooling with Luigi Cravi to Harper Community. "They have a good team, too," Biggie said.

"My cousin Patty goes there. She says I can live with her. So you can see, Dan, I'm all set. I only have to get lucky."

"What do you plan on majoring in, up at Northern Illinois in Dekalb?"

As Gloria paused Bluestone tried to visualize her through the phone line. Her long brown hair swayed. Strands were in her mouth as she said his name. Strands covered the receiver. It struck him now who she looked like: Katharine Ross in *The Graduate*.

Strands fell down her shoulders to her tits.

"Well, Dan, it won't be wrestlers."

Gloria had this way of working their conversations that kept him thinking about what in the world she meant long after the conversation ended. When Biggie thought about what she said at face value, it was obvious Gloria was telling him to steer clear. On the other hand, it was hard to know if he should take anything Gloria Serpentino said at face value.

That was Biggie's stance on the matter when Gloria Serpentino phoned the next night. Mom yelled down from upstairs. Mom hadn't asked too many more questions since Gloria first called a few nights after she'd almost killed him, when—to throw her off the scent—Biggie told her the girl was calling about a homework project. "With a girl?" Mom asked.

"They come that way, too," Biggie said, though Biggie assumed by now she was wondering just what kind of homework project this was that spanned the semesters and required constant phone calls.

This was the *Tuesday* after Waukegan. Biggie, delighted to have found himself only eight pounds over after practice, told Glory as soon as she said hello. She didn't show much interest in the curious development. "Dan, do you like to go for long drives?"

If this were anyone else Biggie would assume he'd be expected now to ask if she'd care to go for a long drive, but this was Gloria, so he didn't know what she meant. Possibly it was the sort of thing she just liked to ask people. "Sure, if I'm in the mood. If something especially good happens, or if I think something especially good *may* happen, I like to turn up the radio and cruise." If something *bad* happened, too, but he didn't care to open that can of worms at the moment. If so, she'd probably ask him about the kinds of bad things which happened, or he feared would happen, and the way they were going he might end up telling her just to sound like he had something to say, thereby giving a form and a name to the darkness and asking it in.

"I know," Gloria said. "What stations do you like listening to?"

"WCFL. WBBM-FM, I guess." He might have added WLS, which he listened to more than the others, but Wing had once asked him the identical question, then pointed out *nobody* listened to WLS anymore unless they'd never heard of WBBM-FM. Wing hadn't said this to ridicule Biggie, but as a point of information. "Who do you like listening to?"

"It depends on my mood, Dan."

"On whether you're feeling good or feeling lucky?" Biggie cracked, wishing he could take back the quip before it left his mouth. Sometimes he thought that the major difference between himself and others is that others were equipped with a mechanism for blocking the inflammatory remark *before* they said it, whereas Biggie invariably said the stuff, the mechanism kicking in an instant too late, putting him in the position of having to apologize every time he said anything. He was guaranteed to insult somebody; there was a one-to-one ratio between remarks and apologies uttered, even when, as in this instance, somebody had been mocking *him* and deserved it. "I'm sorry."

"You say that a lot, did you know that?"

"It's because I'm an idiot," Biggie lamented.

"Well, you don't need to say it to me so often."

"Thanks."

"I'll just assume the apology is in everything you say."

Usually this was when his conversations ended, after the swapping of insults, but Glory continued, "Do you have brothers and sisters, Dan, since you're so lucky? The other day you mentioned you had a sister."

Biggie said, "I know it's hard to imagine."

"There you are, apologizing again."

"I wasn't apologizing."

"You were apologizing for being alive," Glory said. "You do that a lot, too, after you say something. You make a self-deprecating remark."

"I'm trying to be *funny.*"

"Well, you're not."

"Thank you."

"What's her name, this sister you claim to have?"

"Giselle."

Everybody who knew Giselle knew Biggie Bluestone was her brother. When they were kids, after everybody suddenly began calling Bluestone "Biggie"—with news of the nickname spreading through Lincoln School like a common cold—they'd sometimes call Giselle "Little Biggie."

"I know who Giselle Bluestone is. Short. Built like a brick shithouse. Long black hair. She's friends with Suzy Grossman and Mary Wellington and that group."

"I'm impressed," Biggie said. "Do you have a similar dossier on everybody at that school?"

"Try me," she challenged.

"Wing Terrill."

"A jock like you, Dan. A guy's guy. I've heard he's a sweetheart. They say he's all but engaged to Gail Abernathy."

"Okay. Pete Hoffman."

Gloria paused. "I don't think I know Pete Hoffman. I'm stumped, Dan. You win. Who's Pete Hoffman?"

"He wants to go to Yale."

"*Now* I remember," Gloria said. "I met Pete Hoffman at the last gathering of the National Merit Scholars."

"He was there. Even if you weren't."

"These are your best friends?"

Biggie considered. "I don't know if they're my best friends. I wrestle with them every day in practice, if that's what you mean. Along with Luigi Cravi." Along with Wetzel, he didn't bother to add. Wetzel was probably forty years old. You didn't run around calling guys like that friends. You called them Coach. "Do you have brothers and sisters?"

"Dan, did I say you could ask me questions?"

He thought about apologizing but instead said, "No, you didn't."

"I have a brother eight years older. Then there's my little sister, Vicky. Victoria Serpentino. Vicky's a doll. She's my sweetie."

"I'll bet they called your brother Snake Serpentino!"

"I'll thank you to keep your gratuitous remarks to yourself. Especially ones like that one, which is *so* original."

"Okay," Biggie conceded. "Okay, it was unoriginal."

"Do you have a mother and a father?"

"I believe I do, now that you mention it. Hmm. Yes."

"Watch it, Dan," Gloria warned. "Are they divorced?"

"Not to my knowledge. Hmm. I mean, they've never mentioned it."

"And you'd be the first to know, I suppose. Is that what you're saying?"

He wondered if he'd be the first to know. It seemed to Biggie now that he wasn't the first to know anything. For instance, it seemed to him that Glory had a better idea whether he was about to ask her out than Biggie himself had. Still, it was impossible to imagine his parents getting divorced, whether he'd be the first to know or the second or the last. It was impossible to imagine Wing Terrill's parents getting divorced, or Luigi Cravi's, whose parents sat with Biggie's, the four huddling together in the stands at the home meets. He wasn't sure he knew *anybody* whose parents were divorced, other than Rory Pruskin's. Pruskin was the quarterback on the football team. He'd heard that Pruskin's divorced mother went out once with Tom Lloyd, who was this famous meteorologist on

Channel 7. But probably there were others, too; all kinds of kids walking around the halls at HPHS whose parents were divorced, though you didn't hear about it much unless they happened to tell you. Every year or two, back in elementary school, he'd hear about somebody's parents getting divorced; next thing you knew they moved away. It was like hearing that somebody's mom or dad had cancer, when usually word didn't get around until they were dead. It was bizarre when Bluestone thought about it: One day you have both a mother and a father, the standard nuclear unit, then the deck gets shuffled and the next day your mom's going out with Tom Lloyd.

"My parents are getting divorced, Dan, did you know? And I wasn't the first to hear, I assure you of that."

Biggie waited for Gloria to continue, until it occurred to him to tell her he was very sorry to hear it. "That's terrible."

"Thanks. Don't go telling me, though, about being the first to know. Some things you don't know until it's too late. *Then* they tell you, then you spend half your time trying to talk them out of it, as if they'd listen or really let you know what's wrong—my mom pretends to let me know, but my dad's impossible, let me tell you—you spend half your time blaming yourself, and another half of your time trying not to think about it. Then you drive around in your mom's Buick at night trying not to think about anything at all, but of course all you do is think about what's happening, just like when I'm at work I try *not* to think about anything, which only makes it worse, because then I pretend I really don't care. Sometimes it gets so bad I really think that. I love both dearly, but sometimes I think both of them have knifed me in the back. And worse, knifed my sister Vicky, who's eleven years old. Even my mom, who I don't think even *wants* the divorce, though she claims she's going along with it. I think they're both so selfish, thinking of themselves rather than Vicky. Or me. But then I think *I'm* being selfish, putting my needs ahead of theirs. After all, they're entitled to happiness, too. But Dan, how can they be happy if I'm miserable? I wonder about that a lot. And none of that has anything to do with being lucky or good or any combination thereof. Dan, that's what I was thinking when I ran into you."

Jesus, again he felt like apologizing to *her* for getting in her way when she was out driving the Buick to get her damn thoughts in order. Biggie felt terrible for her. Terrible for the world, too, including little Vicky. But now he thought he understood why she'd been calling him these last few weeks. It was getting clear. He was touched, too, that it meant so much to her to explain to him why she'd almost killed him while he'd been innocently running the icy roads at night. Better, too, that she apologized *this* way, roundabout, over several calls, rather than saying she was sorry at the outset and never talking to him again. That's the way people usually apologized for things, saying they're sorry immediately. And you sort of immediately accepted the apology, before you even fully realized what they were apologizing for. But by then you'd let them off the hook. It still scared him to think how close he'd come to disaster that night, at least a broken leg. Maybe a crushed chest or skull. His shoulder not just wrenched but shattered. Biggie didn't imagine that was lost on Glory, either. "*Generous* of her to take such pains to explain herself," that's what he thought now, though, generous as she was, it was clear that she hadn't been calling him all along because he struck her as an extremely interesting person.

"Are you still there, Dan?"

"Yeah, I'm here, Gloria. I get your meaning, too."

"You sound upset."

"Of course not."

"Dan, what I just told you, about my parents and fuck-all, does that come under the heading of 'more than you wanted to know?'"

"I'm glad you told me, Glory."

"Will you not tell anybody? Not Wing, not Pete, not Luigi or Giselle. I don't care who knows, really. Half of me knows nobody cares, but half would prefer it not be grist for public consumption. You know what that can be like."

"Jesus, Gloria, give me some credit for discretion. Plus, if I told somebody you'd probably run me over in your mom's Buick."

Now it was Gloria's turn not to say anything. Biggie figured she was probably deciding if the part about running him over if he tells anybody was a gratuitous crack which, now he that thought about it, she'd probably run him over for making. You couldn't win with Gloria Serpentino. If you were coming, she had you going. If you were going, she had you coming. Still, he felt comfortable holding onto the phone on his end saying nothing, while she was holding onto the phone on her end saying nothing, and to an extent he regretted that, now that she managed to finally explain herself about driving around in a daze and almost killing him, this was liable to be their last conversation. In a way it amazed him that he'd had this entire played-out episode with a girl his age, they'd even gotten to *know* each other a little in the process, and he not only didn't know if she was pretty or not, but by the end of the episode had pretty much stopped wondering.

"Dan, can I ask you something?"

"Shoot."

"Do you like it when I call you?"

"Sure, it's okay. I like it."

"It's okay? You like it? You're sure?"

"That's right."

"I've noticed you never call *me*, Dan. Do you have so many girls after you, Mr. Jock, you can't make an innocent phone call?"

"Who said it would be innocent?"

"Let's try it this way: I know this is the age of women's lib, but if you want to talk to me again, you call me."

"I will," Biggie said automatically.

"And one more thing, Dan. Congratulations on being eight pounds over."

Before Biggie could ask Gloria her phone number, she hung up.

He knew if it came to it he could look her number up in the Directory, but a lot of times when you tried to call somebody up it turned out their number was unlisted, or else there were a dozen people listed with the same last name. There were probably fifty Serpentinos in Highwood. Biggie pictured himself calling each, asking if Gloria was there, until he tried the fiftieth number, when a divorced woman picked up the phone. "You must be Dan Bluestone. Gloria has been waiting for your call."

The wrestler turned the light off and lay back on his bed. On the hi-fi he played *Tea for the Tillerman*, by Cat Stevens, in his opinion the greatest album ever recorded. For some reason that made him think of Giselle, who'd gone through a stage in middle school by responding to every opinion Biggie uttered by saying, "That's asinine." "This prime rib is *good*," Biggie might exclaim to their parents over dinner. "That's asinine," Giselle would comment from across the table.

Did Gloria like Cat Stevens? It was the sort of question he could ask her, once he asked her out and they went on that big date. Afterwards—*if* he played it right—she could be here beside him on the bed, lights out, bodies entangled, clothes off in the darkness. If the mood fit, he'd sing, "Where Do the Children Play?" which he could sing and sound almost like Cat Stevens as long as he sang it while the record played.

This Friday night they were wrestling Niles East. He'd ask her along to watch him pin the guy—which should take about twelve seconds—and take his bows, then afterward they'd go for a long drive, perhaps into Chicago, or north, to Kenosha, Wisconsin (where Wing sometimes drove with Gail Abernathy). Biggie could picture Katharine Ross in the passenger's seat.

For all his savvy where girls were concerned, the wrestler had never gone so far as to ask one out. For one thing, despite the reports of girls who found him cute and mus-cu-lar, it was difficult imagining one *wanting* to go out with him; and for another thing, it was too late to start now, what with Northwestern around the corner where he'd start over with a clean slate; so what was the point of calling up Gloria? What's more, if he began showing up with a girl on his arm it might *occur* to people that they'd never seen him with a girl before. ("Is that Bluestone with a girl?" "Tell me another." "Thought I'd never see the day.") Similarly, he wasn't crazy about being associated with a particular *type*. He could picture himself, forty years old if he's a day, and Giselle calls him up to say, "Met a girl who's your type." You could be pretty sure it wouldn't be Katharine Ross. Also, it's not as if he was going to marry her. He promised himself he'd make that clear from the start so they'd both know where they stood. Even if, face-to-face, she really looked like Katharine Ross; even if it became something that in vulnerable future moments he'd look back on and *wish* lasted forever, though as far as he knew he wasn't a guy to latch onto a girl in high school and close the books, never letting go. (Nonetheless, Biggie could see himself forty years old if he was a day, sentimental to a fault, mourning the one who got away.) You'd have a history where you hate each other, even though you swore you'd be friends, calling each other all the time as if nothing had happened ("At least we gave it a shot." "Better off as friends."), then never talking to each other again because you got jealous when she talked to another guy at a dance or movie or ballgame or *shul*—vice versa, too, Gloria screaming at Bluestone, betrayal staining her tears—the kind of shit that you heard about that was driving guys nuts as far back as middle school.

All of which you never heard about happening at Northwestern, which doubled Biggie's resolve to land the scholarship, lying on his bed in the dark, staring at the ceiling.

There wasn't *too* much he was afraid of. Staring at the ceiling, the wrestler composed a mental list:

1) Dying young.

2) Giselle dying young.

3) His parents before he was ready, if you were ever ready for something like that.

4) Speaking up in class, though there was a legitimate distinction between being *chickenshit* and realizing that you had nothing worthwhile to contribute, especially if you had the tendency to sound like Professor Irwin Corey whenever you opened your mouth.

5) Taking stands, like the Niles North guy who wouldn't remove his helmet for the anthem.

6) Not taking State.

He almost added, as #7, *Gloria Serpentino*, but decided it would only be because he had a list going. Once you began a list, the list never ended. Soon he'd be wondering if there wasn't more he was chickenshit about than that he wasn't, and, as usually happened when he made a list, he wished that he'd written the list down just so that he could tear it up.

The Man of the House, Wednesday, January 13

As was his practice every morning at 5 A.M., Biggie rolled out of bed to hit the floor: 200 pushups. For five minutes he stared at the ceiling, then 200 more pushups, concentrating on keeping his back level. For ten minutes he paced about the room in small circles, then worked up fifty pullups on the bar his dad helped set up years ago in his bedroom door frame. He did thirty before slipping off. He attacked the bar again immediately, his arms set to explode into shards of ligament and bone, squeezing the pullups at the rate of three or four, falling off, attacking the bar again until he hit fifty by his count, then two more for good measure. Ten minutes. Then fifty chinups, which were easier. Throughout the sets his shoulder that jammed into the road when he'd jumped out of the way of Gloria's mom's Buick as she'd pulled out from the stop sign was killing him—it killed him wherever he went, working out or walking through the halls at school or on the mat or talking to Gloria on the phone, but he couldn't give it two seconds of thought. Wrenched, but not shattered, was his self-diagnosis. They weren't going to postpone the State Tournament so his shoulder could heal; nor would Berkenmeier go soft on his shoulder if word got out. While sometimes it was as if somebody had just blindsided him with a hammer blow, more often there was a dull ache that accompanied every breath he took, like an ironic chorus mocking his fate. Sometimes, too—since there wasn't any-thing to be done about it—he even *liked* the idea of his bad shoulder, as if when they wrote up "The Adventures of Biggie Bluestone, State Champ," the shoulder would be front and center, along with how he never complained to anybody.

Biggie gritted his teeth and breathed deeply, settled in for leg lifts and situps, then pulled out his rubber suit and wool cap and trudged five miles up Sheridan Road, as he did every morning when he didn't run the night before, regretting for the thousandth time that *last year* he hadn't taken extra runs during the season, or lifted weights on top of wrestling practice—telling himself his muscle fibers needed the time to rebuild—he'd really believed that—which, as far as Biggie was con-cerned, is why Berkenmeier was the one on the *Sun-Times* Prep Page, and he was the one reading about it on the freezer door.

For breakfast he had a bowl of Wheaties dampened with skim milk, half a grapefruit, which he hated, sprinkled with saccharine, and was guzzling his third glass of water when Mom came into the kitchen, followed by Dad.

Both sat at the table, double-teaming their son, who briefly suspected that they'd overheard his telephone calls with Gloria and were about to tell him the facts of life. ("If you like her *call* her," he could hear his mom saying. "Don't be chickenshit, Biggie." "Plenty of fish in the sea," Mom adds. "If you can't catch this one," Dad adds.)

It wasn't too often that Dad was around by the time Bluestone got to the kitchen. Usually he left for Northwestern at 6:30, though to-day—Biggie remembered now—Dad was going to drive up to Milwau-kee to speak at a luncheon for a pediatrician's group. Over the weekend he'd be in New York speaking at another conference. He was always flying all over the place to lecture about the sociology of early childhood development to pediatricians or parents' groups or other interested or-ganizations. When TV or radio stations needed a sociology professor to lend a tone of enlightened gravity to topical concerns, they called up Sanford Bluestone, the hotshot sociology professor.

"Biggie," Mom said, now that they were seated across the table, as if they were a college admissions committee, or police interrogators. Either way, you didn't have much of a chance once they laid down the law. "I've decided I'm going to New York with Dad this weekend."

"Can I come along?"

Mom looked at Biggie, contemplating the question an instant before brushing it aside. When you raised Bluestone kids you quickly disregard-ed most of what they said.

"Will you be okay? We can ask Mrs. Baker to stay here."

Mrs. Baker, the neighbor's, Mrs. Zeisnintz's, cousin, was this ancient widow who lived in Glencoe. Until a few years ago she always stayed with them when his parents went out of town to conferences or on quick vacations that usually accompanied one of Dad's speaking engagements. Usually, Mrs. Baker stayed in Mom and Dad's room, where she watched TV when she wasn't in the kitchen boiling potatoes for kugels. Biggie said, "I think I can handle the responsibility."

"You'll be the man of the house," Dad cracked. It was the same line he'd been using since Biggie was three years old; back then, whenever Dad left the house, he'd tell Biggie, "You're the man of the house."

"I'll leave a list for you." Ah, Biggie thought. One of Mom's lists. She'd list about 4,000 things she wanted Biggie to do over the weekend while she was gone, like take the garbage out and lock the doors at night, along with voluminous details about what was in the freezer, all stuff Biggie either knew how to do or could find out anyway by opening the freezer door.

Still, it wasn't worth getting worked up over. If you pointed out stuff like that to Mom, it just tended to reinforce that she was right. "Yeah, leave all the information on the list. Where you'll be, that kind of stuff. What there is to eat, where I can find the light switch."

"I want you and Giselle to get along," Dad said.

Because half the time when his parents were around Biggie and Giselle were screaming at each other, Dad assumed that's how they were when they weren't around. Usually, though, they got along as long as nobody made a big production out of it when you didn't clear the table or wash the dishes. It helped a lot that Giselle had a little TV in her room.

"That's up to Giselle."

"Giselle said it's up to you," Dad said.

"That figures."

"You're in charge. Remember that." Dad stood up, clutching his briefcase, and stuck out his free hand. That's one thing his dad always did that annoyed Biggie. He was always shaking his hand, man-to-man, another habit carried over from when Biggie was a tyke that Dad continued to find wildly amusing. "And beat Niles East, Co-captain."

Considering the source, the sentiment was surprising. Usually Dad knew they had a meet, but couldn't tell one school from the other. Biggie never had the impression—until it was clear that a scholarship could be at stake—that his parents cared whether he won or lost, other than that *he* cared.

"Niles East?" Biggie said. "They're fish."

Niles East, Friday, January 15

A fish was a guy who flopped around on the mat like a fish.

As Niles East lost every match except at 105—even Weinberg won at 119, a miracle—Biggie found his pleasure at HP's victories—after all, he was co-captain—diminished by annoyance that Niles East didn't take wrestling any more seriously. Niles East had a bunch of sophomores on the varsity who couldn't *help* but be lousy, but he still took their ineptitude personally. As for his own match, Biggie didn't want to be a conceited bastard, but he knew he could start the match on his back, with his guy—whose name was Leaver—fitting any pinning hold on him that he wanted, if he knew any—also enlisting the aid of any of his teammates—and Bluestone could *still* pin Leaver within thirty seconds. And pin Leaver's teammate with his other hand. Not to be judgmental, but it was hard to get too worked up about being Killer Kowalski when wrestling Niles East, which was like wrestling a middle school, and he briefly feared he might lose his rhythm and find himself out of synch next week—Proviso East was scheduled—against Ward Pinsker, who was tough. In fact, last year he barely beat Pinsker.

Biggie pinned Leaver in twenty-one seconds, his fastest stick of the year. He had the impression—perceptible but indistinct—that Leaver swooned toward the mat before Biggie *began* his throw, as if exposing his jugular, accepting the inevitable.

Here's what redeemed the disgusting Niles East spectacle: Wing Terrill won on a pin.

Wing won about half his matches because the competition at 185 was so soft. He had been pinned several times but had never come close to pinning anyone. Tonight, up 3-1 in the second period (a high score for Wing), and next thing Biggie knew Wing had the guy on his back and the ref's hand was slapping the mat. After the ref raised Wing's arm, Biggie sprinted onto the mat and hoisted Wing Terrill aloft as if Wing had singlehandedly conquered the Barbarians. The others watched, bewildered, until Co-captain Jerry Bray followed Biggie onto the mat and leaped on Biggie's back as Biggie held Wing aloft.

"Wing, Wing, he's our man!" Mary Wellington and the JV cheerleaders chanted.

"What was the move you took him down with?" he later asked Wing in the shower. Sincerely.

"The stumble and fall," Wing said. Sincerely. "It's a classic takedown."

"He learned it from Leaver," Hoffman said. Even though Professor Pete wrestled JV, he had a way of hanging around in the locker room after the varsity match, soaking up atmosphere for his Yale interview. Still, Biggie had to give the Professor some credit. A lot of seniors would quit if they hadn't made varsity by then.

"Fish is fish," Biggie said.

"Practice makes perfect," Luigi Cravi chimed in.

Tonight Luigi won by forfeit. That happened a lot at heavyweight. Some schools that *had* heavyweights didn't like trotting them out against a big guy like Cravi, so he ended up getting a lot of forfeits in addition to a lot of pins. Biggie often thought if you could transpose Jerry Bray's spirit and tenacity into Luigi's body—an arrangement that would satisfy neither—he'd be State Champ. He'd even—in his capacity as co-captain—told this to Luigi once, hoping to inspire the heavyweight. "That's the kind of crap I've heard my whole life," Luigi told Biggie. It turned out that, while it failed to inspire Luigi, it did serve to make Luigi detest Jerry Bray.

"Let's go to Virginia's."

Virginia's was a restaurant in Highwood some guys on the team went to after matches to celebrate their victories. Dick Pasquasi, who was a star on the team back when Biggie was in middle school, had a cousin who ran the place. The team was feted each Friday night with all kinds of extra helpings of lasagna and garlic bread and free Cokes. But as each year went by, the connection became more remote, so when Biggie tagged along once last year with Rich Becker, nobody but the bored-looking waiter came over to the table, then they were charged full price. No extras, either. "You'd think it's a lousy French restaurant," Becker complained.

"I can't tonight," Biggie said to Luigi. "Other plans. Thanks for asking."

Luigi grunted and squinted, toweling off his massive shoulders. The effort appeared self-sustaining: the more Cravi toweled off, the more water remained. Luigi was such a great guy that Biggie felt like going along to Virginia's for the sole purpose of not disappointing him. Luigi *looked* disappointed, turning his squint from Biggie to Wing to the wet towel, though you never knew with Luigi. The Fat Boy often flared this leery, dyspeptic expression, as if he wanted to turn you in to the cops, or was constipated and suspected it was a permanent condition. That's when he wasn't feeling jovial over making All-Conference in football and signing with Harper Community. Once, when Biggie lent him ten dollars, Cravi looked him over disdainfully, disappointed but not surprised that Biggie didn't know any better.

"Good to see you get your pin in front of a full house," Biggie said to Wing. They were combing their hair, staring into the long mirror before heading off into the night.

"That's my flair for the dramatic," Wing said, smoothing his hair back as if he were one of those greasers Biggie used to see in juvenile delinquent movies.

That was like Wing, to try to look tough *after* the match.

"Must have been thirty fans screaming their heads off," Cravi chimed in.

When they wrestled good teams at home—Waukegan, Evanston, North Chicago, Oak Park, Proviso next week—they practically packed the gym, even though everybody knew HP was going to lose. But when they had a sure win on their hands, they were lucky if fifty fans showed up. "That's the operative mentality around here," Wing summed it up, smiling when he said it, Biggie noticed. Since he got pinned a lot, Wing was happy nobody came, except when they wrestled a bunch of fish.

The Mat Gals showed up tonight. The wrestling cheerleaders showed up. The parents, of course. His own parents would have if they weren't in New York, just because they thought that was the kind of *caring* activity parents were supposed to pursue. There'd be times Biggie felt like telling them he understood—and appreciated the gesture—but they really didn't *have* to show up at the meets. But their sense of what parents were supposed to do, even if it was far from their concept of stimulating entertainment, overrode considerations of sheer common sense. When his parents came, they huddled with Cravi's parents, which Biggie always got a kick out of. Luigi's parents, immigrants from Modena, Italy, dropped out in the fifth grade. They'd never *heard* of sociology, which made Biggie wonder if his dad liked the Cravis so much because he could take a night off from being a famous guy. There were times famous guys probably wanted to blend in so that nobody felt obliged to listen respectfully to everything they said, in case they felt like screaming, "*Where'd you get your ref's license, Monkey Wards?*"

None of the Magical Fifty showed up tonight. Gloria Serpentino didn't show up tonight, needless to say, though the wrestler imagined her walking up to him, then introducing herself: Katharine Ross looks gorgeous and Biggie mus-cu-lar in his togs, as un-chickenshit-looking as any seventeen-year-old on the planet.

"See you at Virginia's," Luigi said.

Usually after meets, Biggie would cut a beeline to the kitchen. A chuck steak. Ice milk. Oreos. Salad scarfed with Thousand Island. Chocolate milk. Onion bagel buried beneath margarine. Ice milk. Oreos again. Then long sets of pushups designed to trigger his thyroid, otherwise doubling over to salve the furious acids, his knees and elbows on the floor. But that was usually, when his parents weren't gone for the weekend.

When he walked inside, Giselle was congregated in the kitchen with the Society of Wayward Girls. Bluestone could hear Mary Wellington and Suzy Grossman, a waifish, moon-faced girl half the sophomore guys at Highland Park were crazy about, along with a chunky, pretty blonde, Lauren Gelfin. They were the Society's current core.

Mary and Suzy sat at the table with Lauren Gelfin, attending to a box of Vanilla Wafers. Giselle stood at the counter. With the SWG, you always felt like you were barging into secret proceedings.

"Great match!" Mary Wellington said as Biggie cut straight toward the freezer. She was still wearing her blue and white JV cheerleading outfit.

"Niles East," Biggie shrugged.

"Anybody can win against Niles East. They're fish," Giselle explained from across the counter.

"I don't know about that." Biggie clutched the carton of Butter Brickle and waived it reproachfully at Giselle, as if she'd violated a general principle. "It's a tough sport." *He* could call somebody a fish, and tell everybody they were fish, but if you weren't a wrestler, you didn't have the right.

Giselle made a face.

"What's your record now, Biggie?" Lauren Gelfin asked.

"He's shy," Giselle told Lauren before Biggie could say anything.

"24 and O."

"Ask how many pins," Giselle said.

"How many pins?"

"Twenty."

Lauren creased her brow. The edge of the pretty girl's mouth settled into a contemplative smile.

"Who's that boy on the refrigerator?" Suzy Grossman asked.

It amazed Bluestone that half the sophomore guys at Highland Park were nuts about Suzy Grossman. "Berkenmeier."

"He's cute."

"You can visit him up in Mundelein," Biggie suggested.

"Will you get a wrestling scholarship?"

Biggie addressed Suzy and Lauren. "Depends on how I do downstate. A few places have contacted me—Northwestern, Illinois—but it all depends on the Tournament."

The SWG didn't know what to make of that. Giselle was still making the same face at Biggie, as if they were five years old and she were challenging her brother to wipe her expression off.

Biggie refilled his bowl of Butter Brickle and grabbed a fistful of Vanilla Wafers for downstairs.

"Biggie, can we use the Dart?"

"What if I have to use it?"

Giselle laughed.

He *already* felt like an asshole, which is what always happened around the Society of Wayward Girls.

Giselle didn't officially have her driver's license, but she drove around with Mom and Dad—stuff he never did when he had his permit—and he wouldn't put it past her to grab the keys and drive off on her own. She'd done that before, even on weekends when Mom and Dad were around. She never went too far, usually a few blocks over to Mary Wellington's.

"Why are you asking me?"

"You're in charge. Quote unquote."

Lauren Gelfin laughed, then covered her mouth.

"When you get your license you can drive, Giselle. You know the regulations."

"Don't be so *officious*, Biggie."

"Officious?" Lauren said.

"Never challenge Giselle to Scrabble," Mary said.

He wondered if Mary Wellington really had a crush on him, or if that was just Giselle's way of making life interesting.

"Never challenge *Biggie* to Scrabble," Giselle said. "He knows every word in the dictionary."

"Never challenge Giselle to jacks," Lauren said. Back in sixth grade, Giselle had won the city elementary jacks championship, nipping Lauren in the final.

"Lauren has her license, Mary has her license. Suzy has hers. I have my permit. It's okay to drive if they come along. Those are the *state* regulations."

"We'll get you a cheeseburger at Burger Chef," Mary Wellington promised from the kitchen table. "*Please Biggie?*"

"A triple cheeseburger," Suzy promised.

They'd probably practiced this shit before he got home.

Now it was Lauren's turn. "Biggie, come with us!"

Giselle refrained from rolling her eyes and snickering.

"Be back by 10," Biggie Bluestone ordered.

Surprisingly, there was only one Serpentino in the Highwood listings. Several times Biggie began dialing, abandoning the call before he'd finished to pace his room and reconsider.

He imagined he'd have to work through half-a-dozen mothers, aunts, and grandmothers commiserating over the divorce before getting her on the line, but when he finally completed the call Gloria answered.

"It's me."

"And who might 'me' be?" Gloria inquired.

"Bluestone, Asshole."

A patented Bluestone move, as if he were calling Glory an asshole, rather than referring to himself, Asshole Incarnate.

"Gloria is not in this evening, Mr. Asshole."

"Gloria—"

"You have the wrong number, sir."

"Okay."

"Is it Dan? Is it possible? Is that you?"

"Do you want to come over?" he asked her flat out, because at this rate he'd kill himself before Gloria stopped torturing him and he might arrive at a strategic point in the conversation where he could ask her to come over. The way the conversation was going he wasn't sure he *wanted* her to come over, even with the house empty.

"Are you asking me on a date?"

"Look, Gloria, we're getting off on the wrong foot. I thought you wanted me to call. I didn't intend any disrespect."

"Apology accepted, sir. What would we do if I came over?"

"Watch TV, play some records, maybe make a German chocolate cake. My mom has some chuck steaks in the freezer we can fire up."

"And will Mom have the chuck steaks with us, Dan?"

"My folks are in New York for the weekend," Biggie boasted.

"We'll have the house to ourselves. I see, Dan. Will you answer something honestly? Do you really think if I come over, we're listening to records, our bellies full of chuck steak, Mommy and Daddy gone to New York for the weekend, we'll *fuck*? Dan, I sense sinister notions lurking."

This was a peculiar conversation to be having with somebody whom you didn't even know precisely what she looked like. Although there was no way to know how to interpret a single thing Glory said, it was still encouraging to think that this was what a lot of his telephone conversations would be like next year in the Northwestern dorm where girls he barely knew would call Bluestone up, or vice versa; before you knew it they'd be talking about fucking. "Gloria, I don't even know what you look like. To me you're this disembodied voice poking me like I'm a mound of putty. I hope that satisfies you."

"Well, I deserve that," the disembodied voice said finally.

"Even if I wanted to and you wanted to and *we* wanted to fuck each other—"

"Don't be vulgar," Glory said, but in this husky, sexy way, like one of those bombshell movie stars from the 30s.

"I don't even see how we could. For one thing, Giselle's going to be home soon with the Society of Wayward Girls."

"The Society of Wayward *Girls*?"

"That's my dad's name for Giselle and her friends. It's some sort of joke, I think."

There he went, wrong move #90, reminding her about fathers when her dad's moved out.

"Do you fuck the Society of Wayward Girls? When your parents aren't home?"

"Not all of them."

"I'm sorry, Dan. You don't deserve that. I'm pretty fucked up."

"I understand, Gloria. I just thought I'd call and ask if you wanted to come over. No harm no foul."

"No harm no foul? What does that mean?"

Biggie felt on surer footing. "It's a basketball term. They won't call a foul unless you practically kill the guy. Otherwise it's no big deal."

"Nothing ventured, nothing gained."

"I suppose."

"Thanks for venturing, Dan. I can't come over tonight, I'm sorry. But I think you're one of the good guys, Dan. I hope I didn't rain on your parade."

Biggie had the feckless sensation of not quite knowing how to get out of the conversation; he wished the Wayward Girls would barge through the door upstairs with the triple cheeseburger to provide him with a pretense. "It's not completely that I've felt the disembodied voice was toying with me," Biggie admitted. "I liked hearing it. It's most of what I think about when I'm not thinking about wrestling. I like picturing a face and a body behind the voice. Half the time I don't even care what the face and body look like. I just need a frame of reference, or things can tilt off-balance. You're not even in the yearbook. I spent one whole afternoon hanging outside The Sergeant, trying to get up my nerve to walk in and introduce myself so I could see what you look like. It was snowing all afternoon, a fuck-all blizzard. I froze my nuts off, Gloria. If I never have kids, I'll trace it back to that moment my nuts froze waiting for Gloria Serpentino."

"Gloria Serpentino, femme fatale," Gloria amended.

Bluestone felt awkward letting her know she had the drop on him and wondered how to take it all back.

"Will you run away with me, Dan?"

"Wha?"

"Will you? Can you do that, Dan? Can you act spontaneously? Can you go in the moment?"

"Gloria, one second you won't come to my place, the next second you want me to run away with you." This wasn't chastising her for inconsistency, so much as clarifying the chain of events.

"Where would we go if you ran away with me? Imagine this with me, Dan, please. I need that now."

Proviso East was next Friday, with Ward Pinsker whom he barely beat last year. If Biggie ran away, he wouldn't want to go too far. "We could go down to Champaign-Urbana," Biggie offered. It's where the State Tournament would be next month, at Assembly Hall.

"Are you just saying that?"

"Okay. How about Chicago?"

"What about Amsterdam? Or Rome, Dan? Would you go there with me? What about Alexandria? Have you read *Justine*? Go with me to Alexandria."

Where was Alexandria? "This is pretending, right, Gloria?"

"Yes, we're pretending."

"I'd go to Alexandria with you. As long as we're pretending, I can leave in five minutes."

"You're sweet. I mean that. Not pretending."

"I'd go with you to the moon. I'd go with you to Russia," Biggie said, filling out the theme.

"Enough."

"Agreed."

"I can't take it, Dan. I don't know what I'm going to do."

"Gloria, why are you fucked up? What's going on?"

Now Gloria didn't say anything. Biggie felt alive to the air between them, as if he were a wild animal sensitive to a quivering in the stratosphere. For a moment he was all but overcome by a premonition of doom. He wanted her to be the way he imagined, the long-haired Katharine Ross wrapping her legs around him as they lay on his bed in the dark listening to *Alice's Restaurant*, conversing like civilized people. Dirty-minded civilized people.

"I don't know if I should tell you."

Don't tell me, he thought. Still, she'd gone this far; Biggie sensed if she left what remained unsaid to the obsessive reconfiguring of his imagination, Katharine Ross was gone anyway. "You have to tell me now, I guess."

"I don't *have* to tell you anything."

"I wasn't talking about the *law*, Gloria. About *regulations*. Of course you don't have to tell me. I'm not sure I want to hear. But you've gone this far. It's not like I've been holding back too much myself. I already told you I think about you all the time. So I'm not just a guy on the street. Is this about your mom and dad?"

"Yes, no. I don't know. I guess."

"Now you're making fun of me. You don't have to say anything, of course. But if you want to talk about anything anytime you have my number, I believe. Not just so you can unload. There's plenty of interesting crap I could tell you, too. That's Rochelle 6-9214."

Gloria laughed. "I love the way they used to have words for prefixes, back when we were kids. It was so much more civilized than barking out a number. You'd feel like you were dialing up an idea or a concept, not just operating a machine trying to connect with another machine."

"The machinery of destruction," Biggie observed.

"Of course, it's about my mom and dad, Dan, but that's not all. Well, do you know Victor Post?"

"Victor Post? I don't know Victor Post." This wasn't altogether honest. There was a guy named Victor Post who played ball for Highland Park back when Biggie was in middle school. Biggie remembered him as a tall, gangly safety who had a knack for batting the ball away at the last instant after he was beaten on deep pass patterns, but a guy, too—as Biggie recalled—who'd be easily blocked or run over on end sweeps. Victor Post was the kind of back who could assist on a tackle pretty well if the guy was already half-down but shied away on big solo hits when the guy was coming straight at him full steam. *Chickenshit.* Still, this wasn't a character judgment. A lot of defensive backs fit that description. They weren't really football players half the time because they didn't get the piss beaten out of them every day in practice. You need them back there to break up passes and assist on tackles when the guy was already half-down, but if you were a defensive back and made the starting lineup it didn't mean you were all that tough.

Victor was also a relief pitcher in baseball.

"I used to go out with Victor. I saw him today. It made me really, really angry."

"Just because I say I don't know him, it doesn't mean I don't know who he is."

"Victor works at Bruno's Body Shop on Maple. Do you know the place? During his break, if the sun's out, he just stands in front of the shop, eating his sandwich out of this greasy paper bag, ogling the girls who walk by with this idiotic grin on his face. He's the last person in the world I needed to see, but I drove by, and Victor was there."

"How old is Victor now? Twenty-three? Twenty-four?"

"He's twenty-three, the Asshole," Gloria said.

Biggie was going to say, "What's he going out with high school girls for?" though he refrained in that Gloria was the high school girl in question. Still, it was incomprehensible how big a loser you had to be to be hanging around with high school girls at twenty-three, going on dates with them, sighing over the phone, whatever, probably the same shit Biggie was going through now. When *he* was twenty-three, he'd probably be on City Council, not in Highland Park but Chicago or somewhere, or otherwise famous. What kind of loser—though, when you thought about it, if a guy was twenty-three, still in Highwood, working in a body shop, ogling high school girls, a guy whom running backs didn't have to put a move on to avoid, they could just steamroll the guy (you knew the most he'd venture was an arm tackle), it was pretty much the definition of a loser. It's not like you'd be telling the guy something he didn't already know if you bothered to point it out to him. That girls couldn't see that was even more incomprehensible, though it didn't seem like a productive question to pose at the moment. Sometimes, even when they *knew* the guy was an asshole, a loser, they still fell for him anyway, like they figure all the guy really needs to suddenly right the boat is a blow job or two.

"It drives me nuts, Dan, that he's still there ogling girls, still eating his greasy lunch everyday with the same idiotic grin on his face like nothing happened."

"Maybe you should take an alternative route next time," Biggie suggested. "Guys like that don't change, if that's what you're expecting."

"I don't know what I'm expecting," Gloria said.

He knew it was coming. She couldn't *not* tell him, any more than actors in a play could *not* perform the final scene, and any more than you could *not* watch it.

To begin with, it wasn't an accident that she drove by Bruno's Body on Maple today. She drove by it every day. That was the only way she had to see Victor. Otherwise he wouldn't see her. "He'll have nothing to do with me," Gloria declared.

"Why won't he talk to you?"

"Victor's furious."

"Because you split up with him?"

"He thinks I killed our baby."

"Wha?"

That was the upshot. As Biggie listened to the story he asked a few questions, like, "When did this happen?" and "How did you feel about that?" mostly to show he was listening and interested and didn't hate her—that was becoming a big theme of Gloria's, just as Biggie was beginning to think maybe he did hate her. Several times she'd say, "You're going to hate me for this, Dan," to which he'd say, "Of course I won't, Gloria. I like you," until he figured out his protests weren't really necessary, her statement was mostly a transitional device, Gloria's way of saying, "Dan, here's what happened next." Once she began the story, he saw she wasn't going to stop—she was saying it as much for herself—and he didn't have to say anything. Though he didn't like the story, he was surprised to find how pleased he was that she felt comfortable enough to tell him, and that pleasure sustained Biggie as he listened, whether she saw him as an ear or a heart.

She'd begun going out with Victor over a year ago. By then she was disgusted with Highland Park High School and all the rich girls filing their nails in the hallways, as well as the material values the place stood for. "Where everyone wants to be Sara Sherman. Or Max Factor." The cosmetics tycoon lived in Highland Park and it was thought—even Biggie had heard—that his grandkids attended the middle school. "Victor was different. He didn't care about any of that. He felt the same way about the place."

Although Victor wasn't materialistic and felt the same way about the place, to hear Gloria tell it, he wasn't too shy about tossing his own money around to impress her. He wore expensive clothes and had a state-of-the-art stereo and drove a Maserati. (It was *used*, according to Gloria. Victor picked it up for a song from a guy down at the shop.) Right around the time Gloria was telling Biggie about how sensitive and bright Victor really was, though he'd never been encouraged to study, Biggie considered pointing out the contradiction. Victor took Gloria to dinner and shows. One weekend last summer he took her over to Michigan City, Indiana, the same place Wing had gone over Christmas with Gail Abernathy and her family, where they stayed at a lakefront resort. "It was splendid. We had some good times, Dan."

The bottom fell out when she got pregnant at the end of the summer. "You're going to hate me for saying this, but I don't know how it happened. Victor used protection."

"That's thoughtful," Biggie said.

She told her parents she was pregnant, which was probably the biggest mistake she'd ever made. It was close to the last straw that broke her family apart. Her dad grounded her for the rest of her life, other than school and work. Her mom defended Gloria, not that she was pregnant, at which she was disappointed, but that she wasn't Evil Incarnate *because* she was pregnant. Her dad wanted to kill Victor, and even contacted him at Bruno's Body Shop where they ended up talking it through; her dad came home saying Victor was willing to marry her. "He was *willing*," Gloria said. "How gallant of him."

Other than the report of Victor's willingness, she hadn't heard from her boyfriend since she'd told him she was pregnant two weeks before. This was over dinner at The Nightingale, where they went every Saturday. The first thing he said was, "Everything's going to be all right, Glory. We have each other," though he didn't squeeze her hand but sat back from the table, the blood draining from his face as he looked her over. It was almost as if there was a five-second delay between what Gloria said, and what Victor took in, because the second thing he said, five seconds later, was, "Is it mine?"

There was no third thing, until her father walked through the door after three weeks of humiliation and recrimination and said Victor was "willing" to marry her.

It was out of the question that she would have the child. This was understood between mother and daughter. Although it was a sin in the eyes of Jesus Christ, Gloria wasn't going to have to pay forever for it. On this, Gloria's mother was determined, while for her father it was cut and dry. She wasn't Gloria anymore, with her own hopes and dreams, of his own flesh and blood, she was a *slut*. Becky Tomasetti's mother knew somebody, and three weeks later Gloria's mom drove her to Waukegan, where an hour later, after a heavy local anesthetic, she lay back in stirrups while the doctor impassively operated a suction device that sucked her clean, the man never looking at Gloria's face or saying her name. It was done. The next day, she was back on her feet, and a week later back in school, though nothing was ever back to normal again.

"That was the last straw with mom and dad," Gloria said. "He thought she arranged it all behind his back, and she thought—I thought—he didn't care if I was a human being or his daughter. I lived with him for seventeen years but that didn't matter one way or the other, Dan, not compared to the Pope's arbitrary opinion on abortion. Thanks for being so sensitive, Dad! He was so satisfied when he came up with the solution—he'd get Victor to marry me—he didn't give a thought to whether *I* wanted to marry Victor. Nothing could be more beside the point to Dad, the prick. What counted was the Pope's opinion, and that nobody think *his* daughter was a slut. Whether I had to ruin my life to justify that view really wasn't worth considering."

"I thought you wanted to marry Victor," Biggie said.

"Maybe. But whether I wanted to mattered as much to Dad as whether I didn't want to. And now Victor, who didn't want anything to do with me—'Is it mine?' he asked." Here Gloria paused. Biggie thought she might begin sobbing, but she just caught her breath. "One day he's calling me a slut, then avoids me for two weeks, that same guy who'd held me in Michigan City and whispered his dream was to spend his life with me, that he thinks I'm a star that will disappear if he looks away even for a second, and the next day he's high and mighty about how I killed his baby. That's what he told me today. He gets to take the high road, eating his greasy sandwich, chasing the next teenage girl he can find. *I'm* the whore."

"Oh," Biggie said, "I'm sorry this stuff happened to you, Gloria."

"Dan," Gloria said, "it's so galling. I can't tell you, it's just so *galling*."

"Fuck 'em if they can't take a joke, that's what I say."

He thought she was going to curse him out for insensitivity, but she caught on he was trying to lighten the atmosphere. "Thanks for saying that, Dan. That's what I say, too."

What if he asked her if she had any second thoughts? For a moment he wanted to, though he immediately knew better. He wondered. Probably this was the kind of stuff you couldn't bear too many second thoughts about. If you probed and probed you just hit raw nerve. Maybe he'd ask her someday, but for now he thought by asking he wouldn't be showing her much more respect than her dad had, in her view, or Victor Post. There was time to talk about stuff like that later, maybe once the wounds healed, if she was still talking to him then. Sometimes, to show you cared, you really had to keep your mouth shut.

"I'm not the girl for you, Dan. That much must be evident by now. I like it a lot when we talk, but I'm fucked up. You stay away from me now. I'm damaged goods."

It was encouraging that she was taunting him again, if that's what she was doing. "Let me be the judge of that, please."

"You see, Dan, the way I'm feeling now," Gloria was saying, "if I went over there, I'd never want to leave."

That was plenty to feel sky high about, Biggie thought when they hung up after a few more niceties. "I mean that, Dan," she'd said wistfully, but in a way he knew she meant it. "I'd never want to leave. Will you go with me to Alexandria, Dan?"

"Sure."

That he was feeling sky high now, Biggie figured, told him something about himself that wasn't too pleasant to know. After all, Gloria had just told him a story about how her life was practically ruined, joint traumas running wild, not just the abortion but discovering her father cared more for his self-image than about her, the destruction of her family, to say nothing of her relationship with the guy she thought she wanted to spend her life with, even if it was a loser-guy like Victor Post, and all because she says something nice to him, with a vague promise—"If I went over there I'd never want to leave. I mean it, Dan"—he hops up feeling sky high, not the least bit burdened by her calamity.

Walking upstairs to fire up a chuck steak—where was Giselle? He looked at his watch. He'd talked to Glory for two hours. It was possible Giselle had already come and gone with the Society, not bothering to leave his triple cheeseburger on the counter where he would find it, or had been trying to call about her change of plans—well, he was starving like he'd never been and wouldn't mind the triple cheeseburger to tide him over while the chuck steak thawed—it occurred to him that a month ago he'd never met a girl he knew for absolute certain had had sex with a guy, though he'd heard plenty of rumors and there must be dozens of girls at the high school—he'd wondered about it plenty watching them in class, though it always struck him at the end of the reverie as unlikely—though you had to figure, for example, that Wing had slept with Gail Abernathy, though it was nothing you could really ask, any more than you could ask Gail Abernathy if she were still a virgin, and all Wing Terrill ever talked about was Sara Sherman, whom he'd never even said hello to—now here Biggie was, *sheesh*, half in love with a girl who'd had an abortion.

Half in love?

All because she said *fuck*, Biggie thought as he polished off the fistful of Vanilla Wafers that remained in the box on the kitchen table.

Floodgates, Saturday, January 16

It was so much like Giselle Bluestone not to return with the Dart (much less the triple cheeseburger) anywhere near the time Biggie instructed her, Biggie was disappointed to find himself surprised. If you told Giselle 10:00, she assumed you meant 10:00 Pacific time. And if Biggie called her on it, as he would the instant she stepped through the door, she'd accuse *him* of being selfish. The more he thought about his sister, the more annoying she became.

He could remember a million times when he'd hear Giselle and Mom, who'd make the mistake of thinking *she* was in charge. You could hear them clear across the house, Giselle mocking Mom, scoffing, screaming, ridiculing ("Mom, I'm not a baby. I'm *sixteen years old*! You can't tell me what to do!") because Mom told her she had to finish in the kitchen. It was pretty funny, really. Where Giselle was concerned, she'd already finished in the kitchen. She got grounded a lot, usually for screaming at Mom. That's about the only time Dad got worked up, when they were being rude to their mother. Dad would put up with the screaming for ten minutes, then charge to the scene and announce that Giselle was grounded for a week—this after Mom had grounded her for *two* weeks, which generated a round of clarifications. ("*Mom*, Dad said a week!" "Why did you tell her a week!" Mom would scream at Dad.) A lot of times they'd compromise and Giselle would be grounded—confined to her room, no visitors—for three or four days. Once, while this was being settled, Biggie, exasperated, shouted upstairs, "Three days? Try *ten* days!"

"Shut up, Biggie!" Giselle screamed.

"Mind your own business!" Dad yelled downstairs.

Biggie and Mom had their share of shouting matches, so he could understand getting irritated when Mom told you what to do every second.

Giselle still wasn't home the next morning when the wrestler returned from his five-mile run. After showering, Biggie slowly jogged the several blocks to the HP Public Library. Saturday mornings the library was usually empty except for hordes of kids tracking down homework assignments. "That information is available in the *library*," he remembered every elementary school teacher telling him after he asked a question, as if tracking down the information built character. If the teacher answered the question, all Biggie would get was the information.

He liked to sit in the soft chairs by the periodical section and read a pile of Waukegan *Sun*s; one of the few newspapers the Bluestones didn't subscribe to. Biggie liked reading the *Sun* because the Sports carried coverage of the northern Lake County teams, not just Waukegan but the other wrestling powerhouses, Mundelein and North Chicago. It wouldn't take long to track down that Berkenmeier had pinned some kid from Grayslake or Wauconda in ten seconds. After checking for other results, Biggie would place the stack of *Sun*s back on the shelf, then slowly jog the several blocks home where nobody at the Bluestones' knew he'd left.

Today, he noticed Dixon Boyd of North Chicago, second in the state last year at 155, was still wrestling at 167, where he'd pinned a kid from Zion-Benton in twenty-two seconds. Everyone thought Boyd would eventually drop down to 155 for the Tournament, as he'd done last year. Boyd was a spectacularly muscled Black guy who was also twice as quick as anybody else Biggie ever wrestled—which they'd done two years ago, both sophomores wrestling varsity at 155, Boyd winning 10-4, Biggie knowing he was lucky to keep it that close. Biggie thought he was even better than Berkenmeier. Today the *Sun* noted a distressing development: despite that everyone thought Boyd would eventually drop back down to 155 for the Tournament, according to the article, the football coaches at Purdue, where Boyd had already signed as a running back, wanted Dixon Boyd to keep his weight up and stay at 167.

In the spirit of not ruining his morning more than it already was, thanks to his sister, Biggie *still* figured Dixon Boyd for dropping to 155.

Later, as he stretched in front of the TV, Bluestone planned his afternoon. If the Dart ever got back, he'd 1) drive down to McGaw Hall where

Northwestern was taking on Indiana. Then 2) tonight Deerfield was wrestling Glenbrook North in a dual meet worth driving into Deerfield for.

That required the Dart.

That's what Biggie was considering, along with Gloria Serpentino, and Dixon Boyd possibly not dropping to 155, when he heard the Dart pull into the driveway.

He was upstairs by the door already when Giselle walked in, dark circles beneath her brown eyes, her hair tousled in a million directions, a zombie in a sullen trance walking past her brother.

Biggie told her, "I didn't say you could have the car all night!"

"Fuck you, Biggie." Giselle stalked by him, then turned down the hallway to her room and slammed her bedroom door.

Bluestone walked deliberately into the kitchen. Another chuck steak was thawing. He looked at his watch; he had an hour before driving into Evanston. He poured some chocolate milk cut with skim milk—an indulgence—and sat at the table reading the *Daily News*.

Giselle came into the kitchen. She had changed into a sweatshirt and jeans from the dress she'd been wearing and sat across from her brother. Biggie looked over the paper at her. "I'm sorry, Biggie. I shouldn't have said, 'fuck you.'"

A tear the size of a fingernail descended her cheek. If it were anyone but Giselle, he'd ask her what the deal was, but now he mostly wondered if he'd ever *seen* a tear that large. Because it was Giselle and not anybody else, in fact, he remembered a time when they were kids and he'd broken his favorite glass; the glass fell right out of his hands, as if purposely, and shattered into a dozen pieces against the floor. Later he told Giselle about it, working the angles, going on about how much the glass meant to him, how he always had his ice milk mixed with grape juice in that glass, how—when they were even younger—*that* was the glass Dad always poured the milkshakes he'd make for Biggie and Giselle into, how—Biggie really pulling out the stops here—he'd even liked thinking when he was older and got married and had kids he'd bring the favorite glass with him and give it to his son, how—going too far, with anyone but Giselle—he'd always felt it was as if the glass had feelings of its own. By then Giselle was crying full bore. Huge tears descended her face. Her tears didn't dissolve but accumulated, so it seemed to Biggie, the small lake expanding across the room, the flood of tears wading across fields. Tears ebbing at Giselle's knees.

Since it was Giselle, though, he disregarded the tear. "That's okay. I really didn't need the cheeseburger. A triple cheeseburger, was it? Thanks for leaving some Vanilla Wafers."

Giselle laughed.

The best thing about his sister is that she laughed at everything he said. He could count on Giselle to *understand* when he was trying to be funny, which was always. When his cracks were off the mark, Giselle still thought they hit the mark. Sometimes her giggling was frantic, uncontrollable as she let out these loud honks—"honk, honk, honk"—that only accelerated the laughing frenzy until *Biggie* was on the floor laughing. By then there'd be no pretense that they were laughing at Biggie's crack. Often, when Giselle was hanging out in her room with the Society of Wayward Girls, he could hear laughter from upstairs across the far hallway of their sprawling suburban house as he hoisted weights down in the basement rec room, or lie on his bed in the dark, playing his hi-fi as loud as he could without provoking Dad or Mom to rush downstairs to yell at him, visualizing wrestling moves; periodically, upon hearing a song he liked, he'd rise from his bed and run small frantic laps around his room as the fantasy played out, and when the song finished and Biggie returned to his bed and closed his eyes, he could still hear Giselle laughing upstairs.

As exhausted as she was, with the black circles dampened by the stupendous tears falling from her gigantic eyes, with her world-weary tousled hair, Giselle didn't look much older than a thirteen-year-old playing a twenty-five-year-old in a middle school play. "Look, Giselle, I'm in charge, but I'm not Mom and Dad. It's not like you owe me an explanation. I just need the Dart later. It's only fair, since you had it last night. I know you think I'm not being fair because you want the car. That's how it is. I need to go to McGaw Hall, then to Deerfield later. They're taking on Glenbrook North." The wrestler was disappointed in himself for offering an explanation. *Any* reason was sufficient, even if he wanted the car for driving up and down the driveway.

"Biggie, you can have the car later."

Jesus, now he felt like offering to let Giselle *have* the Dart. Just because she didn't fight him tooth and nail.

This was another aspect of his personality Biggie wasn't crazy about. He simply wasn't confrontational. He couldn't stand showdowns of any stripe, though he didn't mind seeing others go at it. A lot of people thought he was confrontational because he looked twenty-five. He looked like he could dismantle you with one hand behind his back under the flimsiest pretense. But he was always letting things pass just because he didn't want to make a big deal about it—things he *should* want to make a big deal about, and, unknown to everybody else, really did want to raise the roof over. This stuff didn't happen too often because people steered clear of Biggie or preferred to glad-hand the star wrestler. Sometimes, though, he'd get really worked up about telling somebody off because they'd insulted him vaguely—more likely, insulted somebody he knew—but the next time he saw them, if *they* acted like nothing had happened, *he* was more than happy to act like nothing had happened, and would end up feeling relieved and grateful that there was no confrontation. One problem was that the one or two times he didn't oblige their reluctance—"I remember something you said yesterday, Goldfein. Don't act like you don't remember. It still doesn't sit well with me." —Goldfein—or whoever—would act like he didn't know what Biggie was talking about, or else be so apologetic, practically tearful, that Biggie felt like an asshole for bringing it up and getting so worked up about it in the first place. That was the general principle with confrontations. You felt like chickenshit for avoiding them, or like an asshole for calling their bluff.

"Biggie, Mary's in the hospital."

"Wha? Is she okay?"

Even though he was Giselle's big brother, and she thought of him as being a hundred times smarter than anybody else did, Giselle had this way of looking at him, sort of tilting her head and assessing Biggie from the corner of her eye, as if confirming that he was the village idiot. "She's not in the hospital because she's *okay*, Biggie. She has a concussion."

"A concussion?"

Giselle began shaking and throbbing, the tears rushing out in furious spasms. Biggie felt like he should say something to comfort her, but he needed to get the story. "What happened?"

"We were at Burger Chef."

"*Sheesh*. You really went to Burger Chef."

Through her sobbing, Giselle glared at Biggie.

They'd been in the parking lot outside the Burger Chef on Old Skokie Road. Biggie pictured the lot, which merged with the Kentucky Fried Chicken lot, which, in turn, connected with the Arby's, one long series of sandwich joints connected by the lot out past Edens Expressway. He knew a lot of kids from school hung out there weekend nights, though hanging out in your car in a half-empty parking lot with a bunch of kids who were high or drunk always struck Biggie, as did most activities you could mention, as a waste of time. "Mary and Lauren wanted to ride on the back," Giselle said. "Biggie, I let them. They jumped on the trunk and I drove around, very slowly. They were yelling at me to go faster but I didn't want to go faster, so I started turning in circles. They fell off. Lauren scraped her knee. Mary hit her head."

"I hope Lauren's okay."

Giselle glared at him again.

"Was Mary knocked out cold?"

"She stood up right away and yelled at me, '*Very funny, Giselle*,' then threw up and fell down again."

Suzy Grossman ran into the Burger Chef and told somebody to call an ambulance. Somebody called the police, who were down the street anyway and were already writing up a ticket for Giselle as they waited. By the time the ambulance arrived Mary had come to, though she was too groggy to say much. They took her to Highland Park Hospital. Giselle followed with Suzy and Lauren. At the hospital Mary was still groggy. They didn't let Mary say much, so they mostly sat around her bed in the emergency ward talking with Mary's mom and dad and sister Myra, who was Biggie's year at Highland Park. That's where they'd been most of the night, then went to Lauren's after the hospital kicked them out. "I tried calling you but the line was busy." Giselle looked skeptically at Biggie, as if he must have accidentally knocked the phone off the hook. "They're holding Mary over at the hospital for observation. After a concussion, they like to watch you for twenty-four hours."

"They'll let her out this afternoon, right?"

Giselle nodded. For about fifteen seconds, Giselle again sobbed ferociously, then raised her head and looked pleadingly across the table at her big brother.

"You didn't mean for Mary to hit her head. You guys were having fun. She's the one who jumped on. That sounds like Mary," he added. He didn't know if that was true. He could *picture* Mary jumping on the Dart, but he didn't know if that was like her or not. About all he knew about her was she had striking dark eyes and had once touched his face. She also laughed a lot in the Bluestone kitchen. It was still a stupid thing for Giselle to do, that much was true but not worth emphasizing at the moment.

Giselle looked up from her tears. "Mom and Dad will be mad about the ticket."

An hour later Lauren Gelfin drove by in a new silver '71 Volvo, to pick up Giselle. They'd spend the afternoon at the hospital, then go over to the Wellingtons for dinner after Mary was released. It struck Biggie that he'd *noticed* Lauren was driving the new Volvo, and that it was a 264 GL, because that was the sort of observation that he'd never had before. There were plenty of kids in school whose parents bought them new silver Volvos—or Jaguars or Zs—when they turned sixteen. While *he'd* never notice, it was just the sort of thing that turned Gloria Serpentino's stomach, and Biggie wondered if that kind of shit would begin to turn his stomach, too.

A few minutes later, he was driving the Dart, off for McGaw Hall to watch Northwestern take on the Indiana Hoosiers, Activity #1. As soon as Bluestone turned south from the driveway down Sheridan he thought of swinging by the hospital and marching up to the tenth floor to surprise Mary Wellington. Mary would appreciate the hell out of it. She probably thought he was an idiot—by definition, as Giselle's brother, everything he did was tarnished by Giselle's jaundiced view—but he was also the star wrestler and she was a wrestling cheerleader. General principle suggested she'd get a kick out of it. Suddenly he likes picturing the look on Mary Wellington's face as he walks in and she emerges from her grogginess. Still, he suspected that Mary probably wasn't looking her best, what with the concussion and sweating through the night at the hospital. Also, she had the alleged crush on him. She might not be too crazy about Biggie seeing her that way.

The wrestler knew this was an excuse—he'd be late for the Northwestern meet if he stopped in—and lamented that he wasn't the kind of guy for whom such graciousness came naturally. Would Wing Terrill hesitate to drive over to the hospital and stop in, just to show Mary

Wellington that the wrestlers *cared*? It wouldn't surprise him if Wing was there already, half-showing Mary the wrestlers cared, half-wondering why Biggie wasn't over there pulling his weight. Jerry Bray was likely there, too, in his official capacity as co-captain. You could count on Jerry Bray to show up in the hospital room and take the bows, bringing out the bells and whistles, presenting Mary with a bouquet of roses, starring in the Co-captain Jerry Bray Show. The poster boy had probably already arranged for a gift certificate at Rueger's. The thought was enough to make Biggie want to stop at the hospital just to show Mary Wellington it could all be done with tact and dignity, not Bray-style.

As Bluestone drove down Sheridan Road into Glencoe, the issue of whether to stop in to see Mary Wellington resolved itself by the southward momentum of the Dart.

Though Indiana was the worst wrestling team in the Big Ten, the Hoosiers would clobber most major college teams in America. This consideration summoned a conversation he'd had with Wing a few days ago. Driving home from practice, he'd suddenly become forlorn about wrestling scholarships and found himself in a blue mood. Other than the handshake with Gosley and the form letter that Illinois sent everybody who knew a half-nelson from a sit out, Biggie still hadn't heard anything from colleges, and the more he considered it, the more unlikely it seemed that the handshake with Roy Gosley, the Icon Incarnate, meant Northwestern had *their* eye on him.

"I could be 100% wrong about the floodgates suddenly opening after the State Tournament."

"Open them yourself," Wing suggested.

This was the problem with getting advice from people, even Wing. They'd say things like, "Open the floodgates yourself," inspirational advice at first blush, but they didn't tell you *how* to open the floodgates, or even what the floodgates were. They smugly left you to your own devices, trying to solidify an abstraction. And it wasn't as if Wing marched around all day opening the floodgates himself, though Biggie imagined he might, if he were undefeated, which you had to be in order for there to be floodgates to begin with.

"Can't Wetzel help?" Wing said, helpfully. The *football* coach was always calling around to colleges, trying to place guys.

"Wetzel's a football guy at heart."

"Wetzel doesn't have the wrestling connections," Wing agreed.

Watching from the stands at McGaw Hall, Biggie figured if the Hoosiers didn't wrestle a Big Ten schedule, the Hoosiers might have thought *they* were tremendous. Did the general principle hold? It was hard not to consider whether, as a wrestler, he was an Indiana—thought he was great, but only because of the weak schedule—rather than a Northwestern, a team that not only considered itself great but held its own against other teams that considered themselves great.

Open the floodgates?

During the matches through 150, featuring Northwestern guys who'd been taking their licks lately wrestling the top guys in the country, clobbering Indiana guys who'd been winning lately against teams that were good but merely, the wrestler wondered what the odds were against his summoning the nerve to march over to Salt Tepper, the Indiana coach, this ancient guy who looked like Senator Dirksen with his shock of white hair and eyes that twinkled from fifty feet away, right after the meet, then politely introduce himself, letting Tepper know he was available for the scholarship. He was pretty sure he wouldn't, and wondered if the *reason* he wouldn't was because he was a chickenshit weasel, or because the chances were about 999 out of 1,000 that he'd stand there shifting his weight from foot to foot, hemming and hawing, barely managing respirations, while Tepper looked at him like he was a wino.

By the time of the heavyweight match, the crowd had dispersed until barely half remained. It happened a lot in wrestling that people left early when the team match was decided. Often, hardly anybody remained for the heavyweights. Even at the college level, when you watched a couple of heavyweights, they mostly leaned into each other the whole bout—that's how it looked from the stands, though you knew from experience they were working their butts off trying to work angles and find leverage for throws. But because they'd didn't shoot in for a lot of quick double leg takedowns, which you'd try only with extreme trepidation against a guy 260 on a wrestling scholarship, the fans and often the refs (who should know better) thought there wasn't too much going on in there. In a lot of heavyweight matches, there were more stalling warnings than points scored. Even at the State Tournament, a lot of people wandered off to beat the traffic by the time the heavyweights took the mat.

But when the team match was still on the line everything changed. Then everyone went *nuts* during the heavyweights, getting a thousand times more worked up than they'd been during the other matches, even Biggie's this year. You'd think you were watching the Beatles on Ed Sullivan rather than two blobs who were crapping in their leotards trying not to humiliate themselves, all for the bragging rights between Highland Park and Glenbrook North, for example, that in Biggie's experience nobody exercised anyway. But you'd think the free world was at stake.

The Indiana heavyweight was an All-America linebacker named Nick Tucci. When football players wrestled in college, sometimes they were so tough that they were terrific, but usually they'd get kicked around the mat by the other heavyweight who looked like a blob who'd never lifted a weight in his lazy, slothful existence on the planet, which is why football players didn't turn out for wrestling too often in college. In college you could bet the blobs were tough as hell beneath the Jello. Underneath mounds of insulation covering their chests and stomachs were steel walls reinforced by steel cables. Their legs: buttresses. Now the Northwestern heavyweight, a junior blob named Higgins, rode Tucci for almost the full eight minutes. Late in the match Tucci turned the wrong way. Higgins, adjusting the half, pinned the football All-American within seconds to a smattering of cheers, and Biggie found himself lumbering down the stands toward the Indiana bench.

Biggie felt like he was in a daze and crossed toward the exit as if slicing through fog in the Dart. Coach Tepper was hunching over Nick Tucci, speaking softly as the football star, still looking a thousand times as tough as the blob Higgins celebrating across the mat, leaned over sweating and gasping with such deep inhalations they sounded to Biggie like the shrill and coarse whistles from a siren.

If it weren't for Tucci's gasping, Biggie might have kept veering toward the exit, then spent the rest of his days as a chickenshit weasel. He could already see himself someday an old man of fifty, still sheepish, veering away, feeling like everybody was always looking at him as though he were wearing his undershorts on the outside. He stepped onto the warm-up mat behind the bench, and before he could change his mind stuck out his hand. "I'm Dan Bluestone."

From three feet away Salt Tepper didn't look senatorial to Biggie, with eyes twinkling like Everett Dirkson. He looked like a man who wanted to know where Security was.

Coach Tepper, after noticing Biggie's extended hand, shook it tentatively, as if fearing Biggie was set to slip a hand buzzer into his palm. That's how a lot of these top wrestling guys were. They either took your hand off when they shook it, like Gosley, or acted like you were a clown liable to prank them with a hand buzzer. They *assumed* you were a dipshit. Salt Tepper looked over Biggie's shoulder.

"I wrestle for Highland Park at 167. We're a north suburban school, Coach Tepper. I'm undefeated and intend to stay that way."

He was pleased with himself for getting it out, even if Tepper looked at him like he was a wino.

"I'm interested in Indiana. Well, I think we'd be a fit."

Biggie imagined guys came up to Tepper all the time with similar pitches; probably even real winos went around introducing themselves looking for tryouts and scholarships. Biggie had the sense Salt Tepper had heard similar lines so many times before, multiplied by a thousand in his memory, he almost wished he'd veered all the way toward the exit instead of slicing through the fog.

With the immediate predicament so awkward, he looked over Tepper's shoulder. He felt like closing his eyes and drifting away, back into the stands before he'd lumbered down in a daze. But across the mat, fifty feet away, Mr. Wrestling Roy Gosley stared straight into Biggie's eyes.

Tepper straightened up and winked. "Your name again?"

Roy Gosley stared at Biggie another five seconds, then turned back to the guy he'd been talking to, whom Biggie recognized as Canham Janes, the Northwestern athletic director.

Canham Janes then looked at Dan Bluestone, 167 pounds, undefeated, unscored upon, shaking Salt Tepper's hand.

Floodgate *that*.

After taking another run, Biggie wound down with 300 pushups and 1,000 jumping jacks as the radio blasted through the darkness of his room. He showered, tossed back a bowl of salad, sliced a grapefruit sprinkled with saccharine, baked two chicken pot pies, and grabbed three small chocolate chip cookies. Instead of immediately driving to Deerfield for the Glenbrook North meet, Biggie surprised himself again: He called Gloria Serpentino to see if she wanted to go along.

"To a wrestling meet? How charming."

"It's not the activity, it's the company." Not that there was anything wrong with the activity.

Gloria sighed. "I'd better not. I have homework."

On a Saturday night?

Biggie didn't *want* to sound like one of those dumb-panned guys who were always pleading with girls to go somewhere, not getting the hint. "C'mon, Gloria. It'll be a good time. You can do your homework later."

"It's not the homework, Dan. You know that."

"You just said it was the homework."

Gloria sighed again. "We've gone over this. I don't want to get involved with you—or anybody. Not yet. It's too soon."

Biggie sighed. While Glory had implied the sentiment in their last conversation when he'd asked her out, he'd assumed it was open to negotiation. "Okay, Gloria, I'm just trying to keep my head above water."

"Apology accepted."

"Plus I'm sorry for putting you in an awkward position by asking you out."

"I like us the way we are, talking on the phone like this. If we got to know each other, Dan, if we actually became involved, things might get out of hand. We'd ruin what we have now. I've seen that too often."

Biggie couldn't tell if he was being rejected or accepted. "Sure."

"Don't be hurt, Dan. It's not like that. If you really want me to come along I will. I hope you know that. But I don't think I should."

Thus began the strangest conversation of Biggie's life, edging out for first place every other conversation he'd ever had with Gloria Serpentino. Now he debated aloud, mostly to himself, whether he *really* wanted Glory to come along. "I was feeling an incredible high, see? I did something today. So I wanted to talk to you, not just over the phone but face-to-face. I wanted to look you in the eyes and see your smile." As he said this Biggie wasn't sure he wanted to look her in the eyes and see her smile, first and foremost, or whether he said it because that's just the kind of crap you say to girls all the time, even when it's the first time you've said it. Even if you don't want to say it, you've heard it said so often that's what you ended up saying.

"What makes you think I'll be smiling?" Gloria asked.

"I'm not predicting anything, Glory," Biggie pointed out. "I'm just describing my dreams. If I saw you—if you saw me—well, who's to know what would happen, right? Seeing each other could jeopardize our great conversations. That's the kind of thing seeing each other does, I guess. That's when you can't see each other and talk at the same time."

"Dan, you know what I mean. We may not *feel* like talking to each other anymore."

"Whereas if all we do is talk to each other on the phone all the time, we'll naturally feel like talking to each other forever."

"I'm not ready to go out with you."

"Okay. I'm not going to beat a dead horse here."

"Do you still like me?"

"*Gloria*," Biggie said, the way his mom and sister always said *Biggie* when he did something ridiculous. He finally began telling Glory about the Northwestern meet, marching up to Salt Tepper afterward with his hand extended to introduce himself. "It went okay, I guess. He didn't call me a dipshit to my face, anyway."

"Will Indiana recruit you?"

Gloria really sounded proud of him, as if introducing yourself to a Big Ten coach, even of a bottom feeder like Indiana, might be on the order of driving a used Maserati. "He had the student manager take down my name and said he'd keep his eye on me." Biggie secretly suspected Tepper used that piece of paper to blow his nose the exact second Biggie turned around. Still, it wasn't something everybody would have done. It may have *sounded* a lot like blowing his own horn, but Biggie *dared* Indiana to call his bluff. "I know that makes me sound like I'm blowing my own horn." In his heart of hearts, though he was chickenshit about calling up girls and buttonholing coaches, Biggie sensed he was something of a conceited bastard. "Do I strike you as a conceited bastard?"

"I think you're the nicest guy I know."

"Wha? The way I feel now, if Indiana offered me a scholarship I'd take it in two seconds. But the important thing is Roy Gosley—that's the Northwestern coach—Mr. Wrestling—saw me shaking Salt Tepper's hand. Now maybe *he'll* call my bluff."

"You're a real bluffer, Dan."

"He's probably trying to get through right now as we speak. So this is goodbye, Gloria."

"Is that also a bluff?"

"I guess it is." That was true. The last thing he wanted to do was hang up, though if he wasn't out the door in ten minutes, he'd be late for the Deerfield meet. He'd promised Wetzel he'd take scouting notes. Biggie resolved that if he ever had a girlfriend, she'd be the type that, in addition to being beautiful and willing to talk to him in person, wouldn't consider it a federal offense if he cut off a high intensity conversation because he had to leave for the Deerfield-Glenbrook North wrestling meet. "It sort of works that way, though," Biggie conceded, "asinine as it sounds. You can have the same guy and if nobody recruits him nobody wants him. But if a few schools are after him—the same guy, remember—suddenly *everybody* wants him. I'm talking guys who are State Champs, too, whom nobody wants because the other guy doesn't want him. It's asinine," Biggie repeated, though he couldn't help thinking he was referring to himself. "It's like nobody can think for themselves and fuck-all."

"They need outer validation and fuck-all," Gloria said. "You got that from me, didn't you? Fuck-all? I said it first."

"It's a lot like being in middle school, recruiting is. The important thing isn't whether you like somebody, but whether you get jealous because she likes somebody else, or pretends she does, or somebody else likes her. Then suddenly you go nuts and decide you've loved her all along. Your knees get weak and fuck-all."

"I see you know a lot about women," Gloria said.

"The general principle applies to everything," Biggie suggested.

"That's a very mature view of human nature."

"It's got me where I am today!"

"Dan, what are you wearing?"

"Right now?"

"As we speak. What do you have on?"

He wondered if he was supposed to tell Gloria the truth—he was halfway out the door to Deerfield; did she think he was wearing a Mickey Mouse costume?—he was in his *street clothes*—or if she wanted him to talk dirty. "Nothing. And you?"

"Nothing."

"I have to leave now to go to the wrestling meet you don't want to go with me to."

"Your timing is opportune and exquisite."

"That's what they've been telling me," Biggie said, "since middle school."

"Will you wear nothing to Deerfield?"

"In my heart."

"Dan, has Northern Illinois recruited you for wrestling?"

Well, how could he tell her he wouldn't be interested? "You see, I want to shoot for the top. I have that in me. I think I can be the very best. Also, I want to go to a place I can't get into without wrestling. Otherwise all the time I've put into it—you can't begin to guess—means nothing. This may make me sound like a dipshit, but I couldn't take that. Plus, it's bleak in Dekalb; I mean the weather."

"If you went to Northern, we could talk for hours on the phone every night."

"Though there's a lot to be said for Northern Illinois," Biggie said. "I'll let you know."

Usually, Gloria had a way of responding instantly, either topping his remarks as if he were her straight man or opening up an entirely new direction. While it was unlikely that she knew what he was going to say before he said it, she advanced that impression. Bluestone supposed the tendency could be annoying, were she Jerry Bray, but with Gloria, it made him feel like they were tethered. He couldn't remember a time, in their conversations so far, where there was an awkward pause or a ponderous silence. When he talked to other people, that's mostly what he got and gave.

"Another milestone," Gloria said after a while. "Our first time at a loss for words."

"We've run out of things to say."

"We'll start repeating ourselves."

"That would be asinine," Biggie said obscurely.

"Do you like talking to me, Dan?"

That's the kind of question it was known that girls came up with all the time. You just finish talking to them for half an hour or more—the latest in a series of such discussions—and then they ask if you like talking to them, on the chance you've been performing a community service. "Do you want the truth or a funny remark?"

"First the truth."

"More than anything," Biggie said truthfully.

"Dan, when we stop talking, I hate it."

That was the highlight of Biggie's day, along with being proactive, opening the floodgates, shaking Salt Tepper's hand.

The lowlight was Deerfield.

He was able to sit midway up the bleachers with nobody too close—the way he liked—as he took the scouting notes. Biggie took a lot of scouting notes for the team and considered it an expression of his co-captaincy. He imagined people secretly assessing him because of his official-looking clipboard, a twenty-five-year-old dignitary attending the meet in an official capacity, and sincerely wondering what kind of big shot he was—college scout? Famous coach? Journalist? Just the kind of self-important shit he was liable to imagine even without a clipboard in his lap.

It was always instructive to compare Deerfield, the Little Giants' sister school and sworn rival, with Highland Park. You couldn't *not* tell, even at a glance, that there was a lot more going on at Deerfield. The crowds at Deerfield were large and attentive. At Highland Park half the crowd shuffled in and out of the bleachers the entire match looking for friends, while the other half spent a lot more time talking to their friends—or else watching the doors expectantly—than watching the matches. Here at Deerfield, from what Biggie could tell, they watched the matches *studiously*, almost like at McGaw Hall, offering the kind of persistent shouting, astute encouragement, and cogent advice ("Watch for the half, Larry! Turn away!") that you never heard at Highland Park, though the two schools were a mere five miles apart and in the same school district. The Deerfield girls were a lot more down to earth, too—this phenomenon Wing Terrill, who'd talked at length with Deerfield girls, had also observed. You could get to know Deerfield girls as a natural expression of youthful existence; should a steamier opportunity arise, you took it in stride. Whereas at Highland Park, Biggie couldn't look at a girl without sensing the quotation marks around the term. She was a "girl," you were a "guy," and the assumptions smothered you to death with bullshit. If you talked to a girl at Highland Park, even if you just asked her about some damn assignment, half the school would start gabbing that you were in love with her, and, coming from Highland Park, you were so convinced yourself by the boy-girl dynamic that you probably *were* in love with her. At Deerfield you sensed it wasn't the same omnipresent deal. All of which made Biggie regret that Highland Park wasn't 1,000 times more like its sworn rival, or that he hadn't gone to Deerfield himself since day one.

It carried over to a lot of things. For example, while Deerfield didn't have a club of Mat Gals, which should give an edge in the one area to

Highland Park, you couldn't help thinking that *if* Deerfield had a Mat Gal Club, the girls would be a lot prettier in a full-blown high school girl way, plus down to earth, too, *plus* there'd probably be a bunch of seniors in the group. So you ended up giving the edge to Deerfield instead. And while—intellectually—you knew Highland Park had the Magical Fifty who could stack up beauty-wise with any high school on the north shore, if not anywhere in America, you sensed Deerfield didn't have a Magical Fifty, just a lot of nice girls named Suzy and Katy and Laura and Alice. You sensed they didn't have materialistic values but were deep into sports and intellectual activities. It was the kind of place where Gloria Serpentino would fit in, and Biggie found it vaguely depressing that Gloria was stuck at Highland Park, where she didn't fit in at all.

As depressing as he found the general picture, the low point was watching Bob Stuth wrestle.

You needed to brace yourself before watching Bob Stuth.

Bob Stuth was tall and lean—6'1" to Biggie's 5'10"—with a crossbody ride that, while effective and useful for gaining leverage to tilt some guys for back points, against better guys only served to stall out the clock. Still, Stuth was very hard to score on. Last year, they wrestled in the District semi-finals. Stuth was ahead 1-0 going into the third period, with Biggie on the bottom. Biggie bided his time—since mid-season it seemed his strength had eroded, so he saved himself, wrestling in spurts rather than full-tilt whistle-to-whistle. Of course, the *reason* his strength had eroded is that he hadn't lifted weights during the season, trusting to the rigors of practice and competition to sustain his power, which to Biggie now was like driving on the wrong side of the road, trusting in the skills and judgment of the other drivers to avoid hitting you—so he bided his time in the third period, waiting to break loose in the kind of sudden tidal frenzy he was still capable of only in bursts, but Stuth had his legs in; every time Biggie made a move he couldn't quite gain control before Stuth crawled off the mat or swung around to keep him under control.

With about ten seconds to go, he leaned back into the move, as if to break Bob Stuth in two, to snap the goddam leg hold like a pencil, but by then, in addition to not having the strength, Biggie was pretty exhausted. (He didn't run five miles a day during the season either, trusting to the rigors of practice and competition to sustain his endurance.) Stuth tilted him for a two-point predicament. Before Biggie could fuck up even more, the match was over, 3-0, as was his season.

The most humiliating moment of Biggie Bluestone's life. That nobody else made that big a deal about it was—in its way—equally humiliating. Coach Wetzel was obviously disappointed, Biggie being the #3 guy on the squad last year, but his chips were stacked on Rich Becker making a run at the State Tournament, so Wetzel merely whispered, "Next year, Biggie," as a disoriented Biggie stumbled off the mat in the depths of humiliation. His parents didn't grasp the significance of the loss—even if they had, they had this annoying way of cheering Biggie's triumphs while emphasizing the bright side when he lost. They could always locate a bright side, expressed with such enthusiasm they appeared to expect *Biggie* to endorse the whitewash. (Luckily, he didn't lose often enough for the whitewash to become an issue.) The other guys on the team were consoling and sympathetic, but since Biggie was making a pretty big deal out of consoling them for *their* losses, there wasn't much emphasis. Biggie wasn't even favored in the match, seeded third to Stuth's second, with a 20-4 record going in (soon to be 20-5) to Stuth's 22-3. Evenly matched wrestlers, even result, until the bullshit in the last fifteen seconds. Afterward, Stuth went up to Biggie in the locker room; it turned out that Stuth was such a winning guy, Biggie couldn't help feeling happy for him. Better to lose to a great guy, he found himself rationalizing.

Could you have a most humiliating moment in your life if nobody else realizes it's humiliating? Even as Bluestone was rationalizing away, warmly congratulating Stuth, wishing him luck at Sectionals, he knew the reason he'd lost was that he hadn't been ready—hadn't lifted weights or run during the season on top of regular workouts; he'd devised a cockeyed strategy, conning himself into wrestling in mere, if furious, spurts, rather than furious full-tilt whistle-to-whistle—thereby turning his back on what had been his dream from the first time he'd stepped on a mat back at Lincoln Elementary School; he promised himself he'd never let it happen again, that he'd back the promise with every last shred of self-respect remaining.

But—here was the thing—you couldn't *get away* from grabbing a bright side. That's one thing Biggie hated about himself; he was always seizing a bright side when things blew up in his face. In fact, he was will-ing to tell anybody if anybody asked—would probably tell Gloria right now were she beside him—that losing to Stuth turned out to be the best thing ever, without which, Christ, he'd probably mope through another season without extra lifting and road work. ("Best thing that ever hap-pened to me, Gloria. Really.") Still, the "best thing that ever happened to me" was mostly the kind of shit you told yourself so you wouldn't feel so humiliated. *Sheesh*. That's still the way Biggie felt around Bob Stuth, now from midway up the stands, clutching the official clipboard.

The Glenbrook North wrestler, a short, stubby, muscular guy named Wilder, whom Biggie beat 14-0 last month at the Quadrangular, took Stuth down in the first with a nice arm drag. Stuth reversed him with an efficient sit out and switch—completed by the time Biggie looked up from the clipboard—and got the legs in on the crossbody ride. That was all she wrote. Stuth kept Wilder entangled most of the next five minutes, twice tilting him for the same predicament—Wilder leaning back into the move—he'd gotten Biggie with. Stuth was the star of the Deerfield team with plenty of downstate hopes, so the Deerfield folks yelled a lot of down-to-earth encouragement throughout ("You got him this time, Bob! Tilt, *tilt!*"), but mostly it was like watching an octopus devour a muskrat. While the cheers were good-natured, the enterprise was *pro forma* once you caught on. Biggie found it encouraging that Stuth lacked the extra gear to inspire the crowd to a frenzy, rattling the rafters from bleachers to roof, the way he would if *he* wrestled for Deerfield, where they watched the matches rather than the doors.

Stuth wasn't even undefeated. He'd lost to Berkenmeier 12-3 in the semi-finals of the Waukegan Christmas Tournament, that same weekend Biggie pinned his way through a weak Grant field. Biggie wanted to stick around and talk to Stuth after the match about Berkenmeier. After dispensing with Wilder, Stuth spent the rest of the meet staring at Biggie from the Deerfield bench. If it were anybody else, he'd think Stuth was wondering, "What the hell's Bluestone doing spying at the Deerfield meet; doesn't Highland Park have a fucking wrestling schedule?" But since it was Stuth, you knew he was thinking, "Nice of Dan to drop in."

Although humiliating was humiliating, after the heavyweights, Biggie walked up to Stuth, holding out his hand. "Nice work, Bob."

Stuth smiled warmly, looking down at the stockier Bluestone, then glancing at the clipboard. Stuth had blond hair and a sharp hawk face that always veered into a smile, whatever you said.

You couldn't not walk up.

"Thanks, Dan. Still unscored upon?"

"Only because I haven't wrestled you," Biggie said. "I see you're working the legs as always, like an octopus. How was Berkenmeier?"

"You can beat him, Dan," Stuth said, which was awfully nice of him to say, but it was part of why Stuth was such a great guy. He'd praise you to the skies, acting like you'd handle Berkenmeier, whereas he, little ol' Bob Stuth, had already jumped into the fire and fell short, 12-3, while both of you knew all along who'd won last year at Districts.

"Think Boyd will drop to 155?"

"He'd better."

It was more than Biggie could take. "See you at Glenbrook South." That's where Districts would be.

"Thanks for coming," Stuth shook his hand again, firmly but not as if he wanted to grind his fingers to powder, as if the only reason Biggie drove out—breaking off an intense conversation with Gloria Serpentino to do it—was for the pleasure of seeing Bob Stuth wrestle.

Which, come to think of it, was true.

Biggie blasted the radio the entire drive back.

Putting the long day into perspective, laying plans for beating Berkenmeier, deliberately not contemplating Dixon Boyd, reminding yourself that last year's loss to Stuth was a positive, in retrospect, imagining—realistically—that Roy Gosley was calling Wetzel right now for a character reference—only to find the line busy because Salt Tepper's simultaneously calling Wetzel for the first-hand report—replaying the conversation with Gloria Serpentino where she testifies that she'd practically die if she couldn't talk to you all the time, reassuring yourself that you'd now *twice* asked girls out, you could do just as scrupulously in the strict austerity of peace and quiet, in study hall or a phone booth or even, conceivably, driving with the radio *off*. But the same shit came across as a thousand times more compelling when you entertained the notions with the radio blaring to WCFL as you drove up Deerfield Road. Biggie wondered if this suggested there was a hollowness in his life, that the soundtrack was required to make it interesting.

After pulling into the garage, walking inside and looking around, Biggie wondered if he should worry that Giselle wasn't home yet, didn't, then wondered if he should call Gloria to report on both the Deerfield meet and the current state of his insights, didn't, gave a thought to swooping half a bowl of ice milk washed down with a bottle of Fresca, did.

Reckoning, Sunday, January 17

Fifty pull ups, fifty chins. Biggie imagined his arms falling off, then exploding afterward while detached in the waste basket.

He pictured his shoulder as a broken meteor crashing to Earth, disintegrating upon contact.

Ran six miles. When he returned, Giselle *still* wasn't around.

Parents away for the weekend, she was gone. Under ordinary circumstances, he barely noticed whether she was home unless she was engaged in a shouting match with Mom, or the Society was holding proceedings in the kitchen. Still, you didn't like somebody playing you for an idiot when you were in charge, even if it was Giselle and she probably had her hands full with Mary's concussion.

He could tackle somebody in the hallways at school and they'd have more in common than he had with Giselle.

It was unusual for Biggie to catch the rhythm of lifting weights on Sunday morning—during the season he usually lifted *Saturday*s, when there was a Friday meet. After stretching, he did 100 pushups, then cautiously set the bar for a 155-pound set of curls when the phone rang.

It wasn't Gloria, but Giselle.

"Where are you, young lady?" His tone let her know she crossed him at her peril. He wondered if he was authorized to ground the hell out of Giselle. "Did you go to Mary's last night?" he added, then softened. "How's Mary? *Did* she go home?"

"No." Giselle's voice was muffled, giving Biggie the sensation she was speaking to him through a blanket. As kids they'd sat around on Giselle's bed Sunday mornings with blankets over their heads, pretending they were having normal conversations but for the technicality of the blankets, conversations that lasted a good five seconds before they'd break out giggling like miniature morons. "Mary's having an operation this afternoon, Biggie. She has a subdural hematoma, something like that. It's a blood clot."

"Wha? Will she be okay?"

"They'll know better after the operation, Biggie. That's what they said."

Biggie almost asked how Mary's parents were, then caught himself. He knew how *his* parents would be if anything happened to him or to Giselle. It was an asinine question, really.

Giselle said distantly, "She looks peaceful, as if she's about to wake up."

"How are Mary's parents?"

"They want Lauren and me to stay with them during the operation."

Biggie asked if he should run over to the hospital to lend his support and regretted not having done so yesterday.

Giselle didn't say anything.

"When will you be home?"

"I don't know, Biggie."

"Call *immediately*, will you?" Subdural hematoma? "She'll be okay, Giselle." Biggie couldn't think of anything else to say which wouldn't backfire.

"Do you promise?"

"If it was really a problem they'd operate *now*, so it can't be too bad," Biggie told her. Still, how could he promise that Mary Wellington was going to be okay? Other than that it was hard to imagine otherwise? Giselle often retained the view that her big brother was imbued with extraordinary powers, borderline extrasensory, if only because it was assumed between the two of them, from infancy, that Biggie knew a thousand times as much about *everything*; that was the view he'd never hesitated to encourage and, as the years passed, believe. There were *things* Giselle knew more about, like the interests of her friends, jewelry, makeup, stores, other shit girls gravitated toward, whether bellbottoms were in or out, whether you were better off wearing Levi's or Lee jeans. Rumors at school, she was the authority. Just the way Biggie knew more than his dad about lots of things, but a thousand times less about anything that counted. Biggie knew something about blood clots, too, because he was always reading in the sports section about a high school football player in Ohio or Idaho who'd get up after a hard tackle—the stories were always the same—start walking back to the huddle, then collapse. It usually made him feel pretty fragile. But after a while you tended to forget, and feel a lot less fragile, and think it was an Ohio or Idaho sort of thing, a regional issue, or one of those one-in-a-zillion shots, like being struck in the head by a meteor as you walked to school.

Such a pall had spread over the morning, as Bluestone returned to his weights, that by the time he'd finished his third set of curls he still couldn't find a rhythm. He tried psyching himself up, pretending he was going down the stretch against Berkenmeier, but the exercise came off as unconvincing. He wondered if his whole day would be ruined—when nothing caught fire and he staggered about, consigned by fate to go through the motions, and directly blamed Giselle and Mary Wellington for his predicament, as peevish as it made him feel to blame a girl in the hospital because he can't focus with any intensity because *she's* in the hospital. But sitting on a moving vehicle, or driving a car, even really slowly, with people sitting on the trunk? Fuck-all, it always amazed the wrestler what people did in the name of reckless youth or hormonal exuberance or whatever the blanket rationale was that people were always applying to the youth of America. You read about stuff like that all the time in the papers. They always said—these articles—that teenagers—how Biggie hated that term, too—thought they were immortal, then succumbed to an endless succession of losing bouts with stupidity, at the end of which they emerged from their reckless youth as adults, mature, in full command of any situation. *If* they survived believing they were immortal, that is. That's the kind of shit you read all the time, until you find yourself saying it.

Biggie thought there were a lot of myths like that that you found yourself believing, even if they probably weren't any truer than the myth of reckless youth; like if you were diagnosed with terminal cancer a girl would sleep with you automatically. Or if your girlfriend cheated on you and you found yourself the subject of public humiliation, no girl could resist you. Or if you asked somebody if they were a narc, they were legally obligated to tell you. It seemed to Biggie that most of these myths ended up with girls having sex with you. If you were a star athlete at a big high school, for example, being the ultimate aphrodisiac. Being a star athlete at a big high school and seeing that the girls weren't exactly lining up to fulfill *their* end of the bargain made Biggie happy he didn't fall for some of these myths. It would be monumentally disappointing to come down with terminal cancer or have your girl cheat on you only to find out that these were mere myths, the kind of stuff everyone believed but, when push came to shove, didn't turn out to be any truer than any of these other myths. These myths were probably designed in the first place to keep guys from starting a revolution, or to give them the hope that, if they couldn't get laid, they always had one more card to play.

Like the immortal shit. Biggie didn't think he was immortal. You had to figure he was as close to being Superman as any high school guy in Illinois, too. Even if he *were* immortal—here was the thing—that didn't mean he'd do half the "I'm immortal" stuff he heard about—like getting stoned and climbing onto somebody's roof to play frisbee, or driving a thousand miles an hour on the wrong side of the Eden Expressway. He really couldn't see what all that had to do with feeling immortal anyway, but this was everybody's assumption. Like this was all stuff anybody—any adult, like his dad—would naturally do, only they didn't because they realized they weren't immortal. It was a lot like the posturing you always heard on talk shows from religious fanatics, saying if you don't believe in God what's to stop you from killing, cheating, robbing, and raping everyone in sight? People always had tendencies to confuse concepts that you could see really had nothing to do with each other, like God and morality, or feeling immortal and being an idiot, when you gave it five minutes' thought.

The wrestler was so worked up by the time he finished his third set of military presses—with 180 pounds today—he finally found his rhythm. Sunday or no Sunday, completely back in stride. It was during his backward presses—performed behind his neck, head bent forward—that required, if he couldn't clear his head on the final repetition, walking to the couch where he'd sit down and roll the bar down off his back, when he heard the door upstairs open.

You could always distinguish Mom coming into the house from his sister or Dad or Mrs. McKinny, the lady who took the train up from Chicago once a week to clean. Only *Mom* was driven to call out within two seconds, "Biggie! I need help with the bundles!"

"Hi Mom! I'm lifting weights."

"How's everything?" Dad yelled from the top of the stairs.

"I'm busy, Dad. Lifting weights."

"We need your help with the bundles!" Mom yelled again.

Even if his mom was returning from O'Hare after a trip across the continent, exhausted, beat, eager to see her offspring, she couldn't pass Dominick's without stopping off to take advantage of the specials.

When he invoked lifting weights, it was usually sacrosanct and nobody ran down to bother him, if only because—as now—he'd work up such a sweat they really didn't feel too much like walking around down in the rec room, not even Mom. But they also knew Biggie wasn't liable to stop lifting for anything. He didn't *mind* hustling upstairs and hauling in the bundles when he wasn't in the middle of something pressing, though there were plenty of times when she'd returned from the store and he wasn't around, she'd managed to bring in the bundles on her own. Mom considered such action a shameful waste of resources, however, when she had a son who could bench press 360. A child of the Depression, that's what it was. She was determined to get her money's worth. Upstairs he could hear his old dad, another Depression child, bringing in the bundles, then the luggage. "I'll get them in a minute!" Biggie yelled.

With luggage and the bundles and other stuff you had to haul from the garage to the house, though, the stuff could never wait a few minutes. Biggie figured that was another of those Depression lessons. You couldn't count on tomorrow. It had to be done that second, or else his dad would do it, or his sister, or, as a last resort, to be avoided at all costs, Mom herself. It was the sort of trap Biggie was always falling into. If he didn't drop everything and snap to, it was like a Secret Service agent yelling out, "I'm busy, Mr. President! I'll catch that bullet in a few minutes!"

The shuffling in and out the front door stopped, so Biggie went ahead with his squats. When the phone rang again, Bluestone was relieved they were home so he needn't drop everything to answer it.

Ten minutes later *Dad* yelled from the top of the stairwell.

He liked finishing his workout by cleaning and pressing 225 pounds, once, which is all the weight he had, in a symbolic flourish indicating that, even after a full workout, on the verge of muscle collapse, Biggie Bluestone remained a ball of fire. Hercules. Killer Kowalski. The toughest seventeen-year-old in the history of the planet. Since his *dad* was screaming, Bluestone quickly jerked the weight instead of pressing it—which required concentration and resolve—then dropped the weight and walked to the basement stairs.

Dad was ashen faced, looking down from the top of the stairs. His shirt was still halfway off, and it occurred to Biggie that certain phone calls never caught you at the right time. One thing about Dad, though he was a hotshot, always immaculately dressed for work and conferences and spent half his time sitting around the living room dressed up as he waited for Mom, the rest of the time he had this way of looking like a bus driver—Biggie liked that—and that's how he looked now, blank and pale, staring down at his son. Biggie could never remember a time when Dad was at a loss for words, or the very words that were the right words, as if he were pre-programmed to say the perfect thing. He used to think it was a quality all adults had, but his mom wasn't always that way. Wetzel was the opposite. "That was Giselle, Biggie. Why didn't you tell us?"

At the top of the stairwell Dad turned around before his son could answer.

After showering, toweling off, slipping on his street clothes, Biggie went upstairs to explain.

Mom and Dad were in the kitchen talking. Both looked set to collapse but had their coats on anyway. Biggie counted his blessings that he'd caught them before they left.

"How was New York?"

Mom glared at him, which made what she'd say a thousand times worse than the words themselves, because you knew she was refraining from telling you what she meant. She wasn't like that often. Usually, she didn't hesitate to let you know. "We're very disappointed in you, Biggie."

"I was *going* to tell you."

"You should have told us, Biggie, the second we walked in."

"You should have called us in New York, young man," Mom said.

Dad sighed.

Biggie wondered whether this was one of those transgressions that would be lost in the deafening clatter of events, or never forgotten for a second, so Mom and Dad would be regaling his kids someday with tales of the time Biggie wasn't immediately forthcoming. "I used poor judgment," Biggie admitted. "How's Mary?"

"She's still in surgery," Dad sighed again.

The furniture practically rattled.

"Do they know anything more?"

"We're going to go to the hospital in five minutes. We don't know when we'll be back. There are pot pies in the freezer. I just bought some roast beef and turkey at Dominick's. Do you need anything else? You know where the cookies are."

"I'll be okay, Mom."

"I hope you will," said Biggie's dad.

Nobody was spared.

That night his father explained what a cerebral hemorrhage was.

"The brain is composed of a Jello-like substance contained within a netting of thousands of tiny blood vessels. In reaction to a violent jarring the Jello-like substance crashes against the hard shell of the skull. Sometimes—a statistical improbability—in the crashing, the tiny veins may tear; that's why concussions are so dangerous, and why they kept Mary in the hospital for observation. We're lucky they did, Biggie. The bleeding may offer no immediate symptoms other than a terrible headache, natural for a concussion anyway and, as such, undetectable for hours. By the time it's detected, the bleeding may be uncontrollable. The blood fills the space between the hard skull and the soft brain and then runs out of space. With no place to drain, the blood compresses, ultimately squeezing the brain to death if they can't reduce the swelling. That's what I understand the case to be."

"Fuck," Biggie said.

They were sitting in the living room a couple of hours after his parents had returned from the hospital. The surgery controlled the bleeding, but it was always touch and go at this point; the next twenty-four to forty-eight hours would tell the story.

Dad looked him over. *Fuck.* Though it wasn't often that Biggie swore, he doubted this was a time his dad would yell at him about it. He figured his dad would probably be swearing himself right about now, if it wouldn't set such a bad example.

"But she'll probably pull through, right?" Biggie asked. "Percentage-wise?"

"I hope she will," Dad said. "Oh dear. Mary, Mary."

"How's Giselle taking it?" This was a question he'd asked before. In fact, he'd talked to Giselle himself as she called every twenty minutes with updates from the hospital. Still, it bore repeating. Anyway, his dad always answered differently. Sometimes he'd talk about Mary's parents, and sometimes he'd talk about Giselle, but stuff that didn't directly address the way she was taking it. At the moment, she was still at the hospital, calling every twenty minutes with updates presented through a blizzard of sobs. She'd probably spend the night again—along with Lauren Gelfin—at the Wellingtons'.

"You know Giselle cries uncontrollably one moment; she's giddy the next. The Wellingtons, Biggie, are extraordinarily solicitous of her emotions. They're quite remarkable people under the circumstances. I don't know if I'd be as remarkable. Do you know Myra?"

Myra Wellington, Mary's sister, was one of those girls known to never say anything except to her friends, and whom you never had cause to notice. Their sisters were best friends, they were the same year at Highland Park, yet he wouldn't know her from Myra Breckenridge. "No."

"A pretty girl." His dad thought every girl was pretty. Biggie wondered if he'd be like that himself when he was fifty years old and a father, if he made it that far.

It was the sort of conversation he didn't have too often with Dad these days. While part of Biggie wanted to run downstairs and call Gloria Serpentino—which he couldn't do anyway because they had to keep the lines open for Giselle—and he also needed to find half an hour to translate about twenty simple-minded sentences into Spanish for school tomorrow, plus about a thousand other things he had to be doing rather than shooting the breeze with Dad, he knew he'd better stick around upstairs for a while, talking to Dad, just to show he wasn't a selfish, uncaring bastard. That's something his parents worried about sometimes because he spent so much time by himself, didn't run upstairs to carry in the bundles or take out the garbage, and did things like not telling them right away about Mary, finishing his lifting instead. They feared he might be a selfish, uncaring bastard. Biggie was pretty certain he wasn't. But the truth was you didn't get too many opportunities to *show* you were really a caring, unselfish bastard. Because you couldn't just make the announcement to clear up the issue, occasionally Biggie had to do things like hang around the living room showing he cared, talking up a storm, when he really had a thousand other things to do waiting downstairs. Still, talking to Dad could be pretty interesting; he found himself asking questions like whether Mary felt any pain in her coma, figuring his dad would know because Dad spent several weeks in a coma back during World War II and still suffered the effects, according to Giselle.

"Poor Mary. Poor Giselle," Biggie said. He wasn't being insincere about it, he really felt that way, but understood it was necessary to let his dad know he felt that way.

After a while Mom came in from the kitchen and sat beside Dad on the couch. She kissed him above the ear and grabbed his hand, as if they were a couple going steady who had to steal away to see each other. They were always making these affectionate gestures that tended to annoy and embarrass Biggie. It took extra effort not to grimace and look askance, rather than directly at them.

Sometimes he felt like he was about the touchiest guy alive.

He asked his mom now to tell him the story of Dad's coma, back during the war. It was a story he'd heard dozens of times over the years, but his mom was a great storyteller. She liked telling it even more than Biggie liked to hear it, and a lot more than his dad liked to hear it. The short version was that the very day his dad was scheduled to be shipped to North Africa, he hitched a ride in a Jeep with some other soldiers into New York, where he was expected to propose to Mom. The Jeep he was riding in, however, was hit by a train; two people were killed, Dad fractured his skull, broke his clavicle and all his ribs. He was in a coma for two weeks, delirious for a month afterward. That was the short version. Mom never told the short version but fleshed out the story with a lot of details about what she was doing while waiting for Dad to show up at Grandma's, and how she heard, and what it was like going every day to sit by his bed at the Aberdeen Proving Ground Military Hospital as he babbled away. Sometimes she'd squeeze his hand, and he'd squeeze back very faintly. That was the only sign of hope.

It was the kind of story where everybody has a favorite part, even Dad, who usually rolled his eyes and tuned out when Mom began. About fifteen years after the injuries, when Dad became a hotshot famous sociologist, there was an article about a study he'd done in *Time*. Biggie's Grandma read the article and shook her head. "Just think what he could accomplish if he was right in the *noggin*," she said, adding to the stock of family lore. Whenever Mom told that part, he'd look up from the newspaper and smile at her. *Biggie's* favorite part was where the same day he stopped babbling deliriously and they clamped up his skull, still in the hospital bed, they handed him his military discharge papers to sign. The fractured skull was his ticket out of the war. He had this image of his dad, head wrapped in bandages, looking the papers over with a maniacal glint in his eye. He tore them up in the Colonel's presence—this last a flourish Biggie himself added. The next day, skull clamped, not babbling, they flew him to the North African front to fight Rommel and the Germans.

There was a part of the story that Mom never mentioned. When Biggie pressed, neither she nor Dad would furnish details. In fact, he'd only found out about it years ago when he was poking around in a box of letters in Grandma's closet in New Jersey. When he came to from the coma and delirium, Dad *didn't* ask Mom to marry him, not right away. Maybe he planned to later? Maybe he didn't recognize her? They got into this horrible fight, the details of which both parties claimed profound memory occlusion, especially his mom, who could probably tell Biggie what she ate for breakfast every day of her childhood.

They didn't see each other again for seven years.

During this time, a dozen guys proposed to Mom. Mom would get this faraway look in her eyes when she talked about one of them, who died of a brain tumor not long afterward. Sometimes he thought *that*—the proposals—were Mom's favorite part of Dad's war injury story.

It never occurred to Biggie until now, but maybe the reason that was his favorite part of the story—the fight nobody talked about, followed by the seven years in exile—is because he really *is* a selfish, uncaring bastard.

When Mom finished the story, they talked a bit more about Mary, reiterated what they knew about the operation. This led to more stories. Then Biggie announced that he needed to go downstairs to finish his Spanish translations.

His dad's arm was slung on Mom's shoulders. "You're a good guy, Biggie," his dad said as Biggie stood to go downstairs to the homework and the thousand other things.

"You're a real *mensch*," Mom said proudly. She called him a *mensch* sometimes, when he paid attention to her and talked to her and did things like carry in the bundles after she only asked him once, the kind of responsible attention he had the impression she expected from him all the time. *Mensch* was a Yiddish word meaning caring, unselfish bastard.

Biggie hustled downstairs before they reassessed his character.

Infinity, January 18-22

As a real *mensch*, at least for the duration if not long afterward, he thought he'd get through this.

But then the fog rolled in.

By the next morning Mary's condition was unchanged.

He found himself walking through the school halls in a daze, never spoke in his classes, was seldom called upon. He sensed people looking at him oddly, as if he walked toward them along the floor of a giant aquarium like the one at the Field Museum; or they were the fish he saw swimming through the glass. He'd hear people talking about Mary, or about Giselle. They shut up when they saw Biggie groping toward the glass.

He didn't remember practice. He knew he went because the body was a machine, but didn't retain a single image until the next day, Tuesday, when he threw both Luigi Cravi and Wing Terrill against the wall. Then Coach Wetzel screamed at him to go to the track if that's how he was going to be, so he threw Wetzel against the wall; a huge vein throbbed in Wetzel's temple as he picked himself up and stared at Biggie and began to say something. Biggie groped toward the door, descended the stairwell and ran in endless circles around the oval. The next day he left History class early to return to the track. Bundled in his rubber suit he ran in circles. He imagined doing this forever, until he hit infinity. He imagined digging beneath the track, through the layers of the Earth all the way to China. He cut Chemistry altogether to stay on the oval, felt himself again part of the infinite process. He remembered now thinking if he ran in circles forever, where would he end up? Sometimes students in gym classes, or on the indoor track team, passed Biggie on the oval. Sometimes he passed them. When there were too many of them and he felt them piercing through the circle, he sprinted toward the weight cage where he lay on the cold cement floor, closing his eyes so fiercely he feared—hoped?—his skull would swallow them.

That night, Wednesday, he insisted Mom make him a chuck steak for dinner. Afterward he broiled another on his own as Mom stood at his shoulder. By then he'd finished off a box of chocolate chip cookies and a half gallon of Butter Brickle. "Do you know what you're doing?" Mom and Dad both asked.

Since when were they so concerned if he fuck-all made weight, thanks. It was *his* weight.

"That's it," Dad snapped and returned to the study.

Because Wednesdays meant he was on a grapefruit diet, he had a grapefruit then ran seven miles. Before showering he grabbed a jar of nuts from the kitchen, then consumed the dry roasted cashews in one continuous motion of hand into jar into mouth.

Thursday Wing walked up to him in the hallway. "This is too bizarre. What's going on?"

"Fuck-all's going on," Biggie told Wing, then turned to walk toward Spanish class in the west end of the building.

Sometimes he thought, as when walking away from Wing, if he walked straight through the wall the wall wouldn't stop him.

Gloria Serpentino called three straight nights. He wouldn't talk to her.

On Thursday Biggie sat in Spanish class contemplating the fog. At one point a girl named Kerry Lipschutz, one of the JV cheerleaders, looked into Biggie's eyes as she returned to her seat from the blackboard. Though she hadn't been crying a moment before as she stood at the blackboard conjugating verbs, her eyes were moist when they searched Biggie's. Their eyes met for but a second, but it was a moment of such intensity he was uncertain he'd ever return from it. He thought she was going to stop at his desk and say something important to him, or to touch his face, or to let him say something to her. Neither said a word, but for a moment as she passed his desk, the fog lifted.

After that, as he walked through the crowded hallways, pathways magically cleared.

Thursday at practice Wetzel pulled the star aside when Biggie was walking from the locker room to the oval. He hadn't been to the wrestling room in two days. "You're not wrestling against Proviso East on Friday."

"I am. Ward Pinsker's good."

"You're not," Wetzel said. "You may be the toughest kid in the history of the program, but I'm the coach here. As long as I'm the coach here, I have the say."

"Fuck-all."

"You haven't practiced with the team in two days. You're not above the team, Biggie. Look at yourself, you're freaking out. You're fifteen pounds over. You look like you want to kill somebody. You knocked the crap out of Wing and Luigi the other day. You looked like you wanted to kill me. I know the situation, Christ, I know the situation. Your reaction's understandable. If you want to talk my door's open. But I won't let you wrestle against Proviso."

"I'll wrestle 185 if I can't wrestle 167."

"No."

"Fuck-all."

Wetzel looked at him a moment longer. He was well over six feet, wore a crew cut with the little hair he had, had a high pitched voice and a fat scar on his chin from a tackle he'd tried to make against Jim Brown of Syracuse, Coach liked to say, and Biggie had the image of Coach Wetzel closing the hole, where the great Jim Brown met him, helmet exploding into Wetzel's chinstrap. Still, he'd made the tackle, the coach liked to say, though sometimes Biggie wondered if it wasn't some other ball carrier, but that saying it was the great Jim Brown, then believing it, made the scar more congenial, even flattering, when Wetzel met his face in the mirror.

Everybody has a thousand stories.

Coach Wetzel shook his head and walked toward the wrestling room. Biggie walked toward the oval.

Sometimes when he ran the fog lifted.

Sometimes after the fog lifted, he'd run interminably, maniacally, until the fog engulfed him again.

Giselle never came home except to change her clothes. The rest of the week she was at the hospital or the Wellingtons', where she slept in Mary's bed.

One night—Tuesday or Wednesday, perhaps both—Biggie awoke to find a shadow standing over his bed. He thought it was his dad, looking down at him. He felt Dad wanted to speak—wanted Biggie to say something, or hear what he had to say—but Biggie turned over and closed his eyes.

By Thursday night, the fog cleared for good, though for days afterward Biggie wanted the fog back. It would seem to him he saw people too clearly. He wanted the murk because the murk wasn't the murk but the core of his sanity. He wanted the aquarium and the pressurization from the air and the green aquarium water. It was possible people looked at him no more than they did before, but now, when they'd reach for him, they'd touch only glass.

Mary Wellington died Friday morning. As Biggie dressed for school, the phone rang, and a little later his mom came down to tell him.

That afternoon Giselle came into his room. He hadn't seen her for days and didn't realize she was home. Giselle didn't say anything, but lay her head in his lap and cried as Biggie stroked his sister's hair.

PART TWO: FOG

Nothing changed in the Bluestone household in the weeks after Mary Wellington's death, at least on the surface. No household rules were altered or in the least way suspended.

Biggie ran laps, lifted weights, rode his bike with the tires deflated for extra resistance, did his homework then closed the door.

The next day he opened the door and did it all again.

Mom and Dad came and went as before, too. Dad read the newspapers, looked up when necessary, said the right things in the right way, went back to the newspaper. Later he'd retire to the study for another hour or two of work or paying the bills. Mom cleaned up in the kitchen, yelled for Biggie to charge up the stairs to take out the garbage *now*, got into the same old screaming fights with Giselle when they weren't talking like best friends.

Giselle came and went as before. She'd spend a lot of time in her room crying—he'd hear her wailing from downstairs as he lifted weights, then listen for a moment before turning the television louder—then she'd leave her room to go to the kitchen and fight with Mom or to leave for school or go out with her friends. She'd speak for hours on the phone, as before. In the days following Mary's death, some of Giselle's friends came over to spend the night. He'd awaken to chattering in the kitchen, wave at the Society of Wayward Girls sitting around the kitchen table in their nightgowns and socks as he headed out the door for his morning run. That's how it was for a few days afterward. After a few days, her friends stopped coming over.

Then there were the local ordinances, which remained unchanged as well. Then there were the universals, the natural laws like gravity, none of which paused in the least or stopped even momentarily to register the minute disruption in the universe, the murmur or its echo in the stratosphere, before resuming their incorrigible rhythms.

The wrestling cheerleaders made a decision not to replace Mary Wellington. For the rest of the season, as Bluestone sat in his folding chair watching the matches, leaning forward, he'd find himself glancing over at the cheerleaders stationed at the side of the mat going through their yell routine without Mary Wellington, and he'd picture a hole in the floor. On the mat, loosening his arms and hopping around before entering the circle, he'd listen for Mary Wellington's voice. He knew he wouldn't hear it, but it struck the wrestler as a nice thing to do.

He thought about doing nice things more than he remembered thinking about doing nice things before. For one thing, Gloria Serpentino called every few days. Biggie still wouldn't *talk* to her, but he sometimes imagined calling her up and apologizing for not talking to her. That would be nice. He thought, too, of telling Gloria—when he made the nice gesture of finally talking to her again—that he was dedicating the State Championship to Mary Wellington. He'd decided at the funeral, which the wrestling team attended *en masse*, as an official show of support and because the ceremony was scheduled during practice. The wrestlers had entered the chapel in their suit coats and dress pants like a busload of Young Republicans. It was the first funeral Biggie had attended—and the first embalmed body he'd observed, so porcelain-like the name *Mary* didn't apply, or else it did apply but as a term rather than a particular girl, to what had been Mary Wellington, polished like a replica of herself in the open casket. As the official 1,000 strong—according to estimates in the Highland Park *Life*—stood crushing together in the brief service that followed the viewing, Biggie wondered if he'd remember this funeral. Maybe when he was an old man of fifty, because it was *Mary*, whom he'd remember as his sister's friend who'd once thought him mus-cu-lar. Or would he remember just because it was the first funeral he'd ever attended? Bluestone got that idea because everybody made such a big deal out of milestones, as if they reconstructed their lives to conform to a chronology, the kind listed at the beginning of a biography.

After the service, Mr. and Mrs. Wellington—his name was Caspar, hers Gretta—stood at the head of the chapel exchanging greetings and somber regrets. Myra Wellington, Mary's sister, stood beside her parents shaking people's hands, looking them squarely in the eyes, smiling as they passed before her. Myra was a strikingly pretty girl with long black hair; pretty enough in her dark green dress to be in the Magical Fifty if she wasn't so quiet that nobody noticed her. He'd never heard anybody mention Myra Wellington, indeed was seeing her now for the first time he could recall; not even Wing had ever mentioned her, who'd mentioned every girl worth mentioning during the bus rides back from Oak Park or Berwyn, bumper to bumper on the Kennedy, with everybody else pretty much thinking about everything they were going to eat once the bus pulled into the school lot and they found their way home.

There was Myra Wellington on the worst day of her life, burying her sister, trying to sound gracious as the procession of mourners passed by, acting like an *adult*—a battlefield promotion if ever there was one—and all he could do was stand around and assess how she stacked up as a *girl*. Biggie felt diminished for heaping one more indignity on her. Already he was moved by the image of Myra shaking all these hands, thanking people as they spoke their regrets—making the effort to smile as everybody else started sobbing—while all she wanted to do—Biggie bet—was curl up in the fetal position and bawl, anything but stand here beside Caspar and Gretta, wondering how she'll ever go back to school in a few days and sit through her classes and take the fuck-all tests and graduate in the spring. How could they expect her to? Wondering, if she had the energy for such frivolity, how she'd get through a single day beyond that, when all you accomplished was getting through a day while there was still another day ahead and another one after that—Christ, it never ended—and still, as loudly as she bawled from the fetal position, there was no awakening from the nightmare; Biggie could appreciate the difficulty of her position—it occurred to him he'd never done anything as difficult or as transcendent as what Myra Wellington was doing in this moment—he could praise her grace and courage which was nothing beside the grace and courage she'd need tomorrow and onward, possibly replaying every second of her sister's life, their rivalries and affections (which made Biggie wonder about the two of them, if they'd even had rivalries, if they were best pals now, or just assumed they'd *be* best pals when they grew up, like Mom and her sister), yet still the point of reference was that Myra Wellington could be in the Magical Fifty if anybody knew who she was and she wasn't so quiet. That's how pretty she was.

When it came to assessing girls, Biggie was a machine that couldn't be switched off. He didn't even *mean* anything by it, that's what he'd tell Gloria if she hadn't hung up already by this point. Because, if there was one girl in the entire Highland Park High School he knew he'd never go out with, it was Myra Wellington.

Biggie looked around the chapel for his parents and sister and Katharine Ross, who was here for all he knew, couldn't see them, then eventually fished his way in and extended his hand. "I'm Dan Bluestone, Giselle's brother."

Caspar Wellington, a tall, slightly stooped man with thinning black hair, smiled generously then did a double-take, registering approximately a thousand emotions Biggie figured he could identify, including ones in which Mr. Wellington seemed happy to see Biggie, and a thousand other emotions beyond the ken of Biggie's experience—possibly beyond the ken of Mr. Wellington's experience—before coming out of the double-take, smiling again and pumping his hand a third time while thanking him for coming. "I see your team's here," Mr. Wellington motioned to Bray and Mandel and Cravi and a few others standing at the back of the chapel in their suit coats and dress pants staring at Biggie—Wing, decently, had already paid his respects and gone home—and probably wondering if they should return to practice. He had the impression that the Poster Boy for School Spirit, watching Biggie warily, was about to burst into a set of jumping jacks. Still, Biggie was touched that Caspar Wellington knew who he was.

"As a team, we're sorry. I'm sorry, too. As an individual. As Mary's friend."

Biggie was ashamed of himself for calling Mary a friend—certainly an exaggeration—as if he were claiming a piece of notoriety for himself, but Caspar didn't blanche and was already pumping the hand of the man beside him in the semi-circle. Jesus, Caspar probably *wanted* to think they'd been friends. If he ever had a funeral probably everybody would be claiming they were *his* friend and Biggie knew his parents—especially his mom (Dad would know better)—would be glad to hear how thoroughly loved he was, even by negligible bastards like himself.

Biggie wondered if his other apologies—not that Biggie was exactly apologizing to Mr. Wellington, unless it was for not interrupting the service to announce to the thousand strong that he was dedicating the State Championship to Mary—would prove more efficient. In fact, Bray was watching him so intently because he figured Biggie would tackle Caspar Wellington or tell him off from deep in his fog should Mr. Wellington say something he found inconvenient. Well, who could blame him? That's the kind of credibility Biggie had now. While people excused him and understood the situation, which is probably why he hadn't been arrested by now, the idea of going haywire—snapping just like that—wasn't altogether unpleasant. Maybe he really was Killer Kowalski now, an edgy bastard as liable to snap in your face as say hello. Maybe Caspar Wellington took one look at him and was wary that he'd crush his hand to powder when he shook it, though he'd bravely shaken it anyway. The scary thing was that in the fog he really *was* haywire; as much as that made him feel out of control and scared him, now, looking back, he'd enjoyed it too, really enjoyed it, for in the fog he'd felt invincible and that he could do or say anything.

Once the apologies begin, where do they end? For one thing, there were the apologies he owed. Biggie could see himself collaring strangers in the hallway. ("Look, I was in the fog for a while. If I said or did anything that doesn't suit you, sorry does it. I mean, fuck-all sorry." "That's okay," they'd say, terrified he'd toss them against the wall if they hesitated to accept the genuine apology.) Biggie wasn't sure he wouldn't toss them against the wall, which was another thing about apologies. If you were going to go to the bother of individually collaring anybody whose path may have inadvertently crossed yours in the fog, they'd damn well better accept the apology. But you knew nobody was liable to forget that you'd tossed them against the wall.

As long as he was issuing apologies *carte blanche*, it might not be a bad idea to start with his parents, though Biggie considered if he apologized for everything he did to his parents—for not picking up his Tinkertoys as a toddler to snapping at Mom last night when she called from the kitchen—it would take longer than individually collaring every kid in the hallways. He'd be an old man of fifty, teeth falling out, stooped over, and still apologizing genuinely, though with your parents they sort of already *assumed* you'd apologized. And once you got it off your chest, what if they started apologizing to you? The wrestler knew that was their mentality. They were liable to dream up all kinds of stuff, that's how they were, because they wouldn't bear to see him down on hands and knees, exposing the jugular. Well, enough was enough. If he apologized to them, it would be mostly for his own sake, not to open a can of worms but to say he was sorry. He'd make that clear, when they tried to respond by tossing in a thousand apologies of their own.

If it wasn't a sorry world, at least his portion of it—Biggie Acres—measuring one side of his basement bedroom to the other at 1528 Sheridan Road, was pretty sorry.

Street Clothes, Saturday, January 30

Two days later Biggie sat at the end of the row of folding chairs watching Proviso East, one of the best teams in the league, dominate the mighty HP Little Giants.

By now half the team wasn't talking to him. The other half were wrestlers he'd never talked to much to begin with, beyond, "Good match, Pelligrini" or "Watch for the half, Teagarden. The *half*." Wing Terrill and Luigi Cravi sat within five feet of Biggie, observing Proviso tear apart the Little Giants match by match.

Neither did Terrill and Luigi talk to each other, but stared straight ahead.

Earlier, Coach Wetzel had talked in the locker room, where Bluestone buttonholed him on a last second appeal, five minutes before the meet. "Bluestone, why don't you sit with the team tonight. Next week we'll see." He had the feeling Wetzel wanted to apologize for holding him out against Proviso—in view of the situation—because the Coach added, "You shouldn't be here tonight. You should be home with your family. Biggie, they're the ones who'll be there for you when nobody else shows up. Try to forget about wrestling for a few days. There are more important things."

"Sure."

Wetzel looked him over. Biggie couldn't help thinking that Wetzel thought he was apologizing. Biggie sensed the edge of a grin, though the expression receded instantly. The situation was somber. "You're welcome to sit with the team tonight. Next week we'll see."

Biggie sat by the side of the mat in his *street clothes*, which is what he considered any item of clothing not directly part of an athletic uniform.

You went to school in street clothes, hung around the house in street clothes, even walked the street in street clothes, and didn't give it a second's thought. But when you sat beside a wrestling mat in street clothes, you felt like you were wearing a hospital gown with your *tuckus* hanging out the back.

Ten feet in front of him, Pete Hoffman squirmed on his back early in the first period against Ward Pinsker, a kid Biggie was lucky to beat last year. Biggie pictured the Professor firing off a note to Yale that he'd wrestled with the varsity, thus salvaging the experience. Pinsker watched Bluestone warily as he toyed with Hoffman, as if momentarily Biggie might tear off his street clothes and charge.

Pinsker pinned Hoffman in ninety seconds. "Pinsker's looking good this year," Cravi observed.

"He'd pin Bluestone if they wrestled," Wing agreed. Wing stretched with his hands on the back of the folding chair, already sweating though Wing didn't warm up too often before his matches, didn't go into his tunnel, didn't have a tunnel, just jumped up and down in place a few times as if he were preparing to play tennis with Gail Abernathy, then slapped his headgear, waiting for the ref to raise Pinsker's arm.

"Think Bluestone'll ever wrestle again?" Cravi asked.

"I'll bet Oldenhopf pins Wing," Biggie offered.

"Why don't you sit in the stands? Don't think we'd miss you. Fucking Bluestone," Cravi said.

"Fucking Bluestone," Wing echoed.

From here on out everybody would call him *Fucking Bluestone*. ("Fucking Bluestone," Mom would say, "take out the garbage.") He knew he'd blown it already with Luigi and Wing. They'd opened the door with the insipid banter, and he'd closed it automatically, Fucking Bluestone-style, without realizing until—too late—that they'd opened it. *Wing* could say Ward Pinsker would pin Fucking Bluestone because there was no way that Pinsker would pin Fucking Bluestone in a thousand years unless FB made a stupid mistake and got caught in the middle of a move, which wouldn't happen in 2,000 years. Ten Pinskers couldn't pin Fucking Bluestone. But you couldn't say things like "Oldenhopf will pin Terrill," because Oldenhopf *would* pin Terrill.

"Christ, Bluestone!"

"That's who he thinks he is. Jesus Christ," Wing said.

Biggie stood and clapped encouragingly as Professor Pete Hoffman gasped and tottered off the mat.

Wing was finally running in place, as if he had a match in ten seconds. "Don't move in with your arms spread," Biggie offered. "Wing, keep the arms in or else he'll catch you with the fireman's."

"Thanks for the excellent advice."

"Great advice, Bluestone," Cravi nodded his head ostentatiously.

Biggie now looked over at the wrestling cheerleaders and noticed they weren't there. Not just Mary, but the entire squad. It was strange to think the only way to tell if they were there was if you happened to look over. Or else made a point of *not* looking over because you didn't want to see them jumping in the air and shouting out letters without Mary Wellington in formation, then suddenly looked over to find the *reason* you didn't notice them isn't because you were determined not to, as a point of tribute, but because they weren't lined up in formation at all but instead were milling around in the bleachers twenty feet away in the first row. Nobody was paying attention to the match in front of their eyes, as usual, but now it was touching—Biggie thought—that everybody was at a loss because Mary Wellington wasn't around to help lead the cheers. That the fifty or so home-town loyalists in the stands didn't know when to cheer, or the cheerleaders know anymore how to lineup in formation, that outside the Wellington household a piece of the world was at a loss.

In front of him, Wing locked up Oldenhopf, the Proviso guy at 185, at the whistle. The two waltzed around the circle. Oldenhopf reached for a leg—Wing blocked. That was the pattern. Oldenhopf pushed Wing off the circle, the referee whistled them back to the center, Oldenhopf shot a move, Wing pulling him off the mat if he couldn't block it. To Biggie, considering it was *Wing* out there, who barely warmed up, whom he wouldn't think had any illusions about what would happen against Oldenhopf if he hadn't heard Wing groaning in the stalls an hour ago, whom Oldenhopf would pin in twenty seconds if Oldenhopf *knew* Wing was a guy it took only twenty seconds to pin—if you could pin a guy in twenty seconds from any position, the guy really couldn't wrestle well, that's what you tended to think even if you liked hearing Wing expostulate on the nuances of Sara Sherman's ass and gave the guy a ride when his Fiat was in the shop and worried that he wasn't talking to you because you were mean lately—it prejudiced you against the guy's ability—most guys let in so much emotional garbage that they ended up playing it as cautiously as Oldenhopf was now, not opening up, fearing one wrong move would spell doom, sometimes losing to guys whom if they wrestled every day in practice they'd *know* they could beat—Biggie would have a breakdown, or cut a beeline to Dr. Feingold's office for an examination if he couldn't pin Wing in twenty seconds—Biggie thought, considering it was *Wing* out there, this was interesting.

The referee cautioned Wing to wrestle in the center without giving him a stalling warning, so Wing kept tilting toward the edge of the mat where he would drag Oldenhopf, who was reportedly 20-2 on the year, who during football season was an All-Suburban linebacker, off the mat when he felt the earth giving way. It was hard not to lose respect for Oldenhopf. With thirty seconds in the period, Oldenhopf, from the leg position—where he appeared to feel about as comfortable as Wing, which was bizarre—Wing didn't have any moves that Oldenhopf might worry about—grabbed Wing's calf and pulled him toward the circle, Wing landing on his butt, twisting to his stomach before Oldenhopf could pry in the half to turn him. It took Oldenhopf most of the *second* period before he could turn Wing, and then only for a predicament, two points, before Wing managed to frantically turn back to his stomach, where he fought off everything Oldenhopf tried—nothing too imaginative from what Biggie could tell, dismally watching—working the two-on-one to break Wing down, trying to force in the half nelson. In the third period the ref called Wing for stalling; now Wing couldn't just block everything Oldenhopf threw but had to look busy with a few moves of his own if he didn't want to be disqualified. By this time Oldenhopf was up 6-0. Wing, who didn't really have a few moves of his own to look busy with, rushed Oldenhopf, arms ajar. Oldenhopf threw a fireman's, swinging Wing over on his back. The ref slapped the mat with forty seconds to go.

For a second, Biggie felt such anger and resentment toward Giselle—for going out in the Dart that night, for driving with Mary on the trunk—that he looked about hopelessly.

Cravi was already in the third period of his match, a tedious, scoreless affair. Wing was seated beside him—he hadn't noticed this—on the folding chairs sweating like a maniac, his wheezing head buried in a mauve towel. Biggie found himself on his feet walking into the bleachers like a lunatic. He passed the wrestling cheerleaders milling about, into the second row where he stood in front of the Mat Gal who had responsibility for running the PA system. She was a short stocky girl, a sophomore, he guessed, though he didn't know her name or recall seeing her before. Now Biggie loomed above her, waving his arms as she cringed, fully expecting the wrestler to pick her up and toss her onto the mat from her Public Address perch in the second row. "Look," he was talking down to the frightened girl, the words acquiring momentum as they accumulated, "maybe we should say something about Mary Wellington now."

Terrified, she looked up at Bluestone.

"Suggest a moment of silence, that kind of thing. Over the PA." He waved at the machinery to make the point clear.

Biggie felt a hand tugging at his sleeve and turned around to see Rona Lefler, the captain of the wrestling cheerleaders. Last year she was Rich Becker's girlfriend. He'd sat beside her on the ride to Normal when a bunch of them rode down with Wetzel to watch the State Tournament—Becker rode down with his parents—and though they didn't speak the entire ride their thighs had touched copiously as Wetzel's station wagon swerved from lane to lane. She had blonde hair that Bluestone wanted to touch, briefly, the way their legs touched on the way to Normal.

"We had a moment of silence earlier, Biggie. Before the match," Rona said.

He couldn't recall.

Rona looked into Biggie's face. He'd always assumed Rona Lefler—by far the prettiest of the wrestling cheerleaders—would fall head over heels in love with him once he took State. Now he knew that was impossible. He could win the Olympics, and she'd always know he was an idiot. That's what he'd lost within the last minute when he lurched into the stands; the notion that her thigh pressing into his was the result of anything but inertia.

He nodded, then returned to his folding chair between Wing and Pete Hoffman. Luigi was still on the mat, ahead now 3-0. He'd been gone less than two minutes by the scoreboard clock. Nobody on the team noticed that he'd left, or that Biggie Bluestone had returned.

Afterward, the parking lot was mostly empty of the couple of dozen cars that were there minutes ago. He drove the Dart as far as Vine before U-turning back into the parking lot. Bluestone bolted out of the Dart and jogged the twenty yards toward the landing outside the Giants' locker room doors—"Standard prison block issue," according to Wing, who felt like a prisoner every time they suited up. One by one his teammates came through, identified Biggie Bluestone bundled in his down coat and wool cap standing on the landing, shaking like a wet dog, asked if Biggie needed a ride, appeared relieved he didn't. Finally Wing and Luigi came through.

"Speak of the devil. Fucking Bluestone."

"It's Jesus Christ," Cravi said. "The one perfect human being."

"You guys got a minute?"

"What was that shit in the bleachers?"

"During *my* match." The Fat Boy's knit cap stood atop his head like a dunce cap.

"I was trying to deflect attention from the sorry spectacle."

Cravi nodded appreciatively.

"I look up to see Bluestone putting the moves on Rona Lefler," Wing said.

"I slept with her once," Luigi said.

When you mentioned a girl around Cravi, he'd say that he slept with her. It was mostly a verbal tic—Cravi's way of saying, "Rona Lefler wouldn't sleep with a fat boy like me in 10,000 years"—but could still get pretty annoying, even when you knew it was mostly a verbal tic.

"Last night in your dreams," Wing said.

"You guys need a ride?"

Terrill and Cravi shrugged.

"Because if you do, I can call your moms."

Biggie turned down the steps to walk toward the Dart. He walked around to the passenger side and unlocked the door. This was the sort of gesture you'd make for a girl, pretending that you had all kinds of manners and weren't otherwise some sort of lowlife. What lowlifes did around girls, they'd get in on the driver's side then reach across and unlock the passenger door, letting the girl open the door on her own. Once, though, last year, Rich Becker, a lowlife at heart, had given Biggie a ride to Lake Forest, where they rolled around with the Lake Forest College wrestling team, which turned out to be a joke, the college squad no better than half the teams in the Suburban League. When they walked back to the car afterward, Becker cut straight to the passenger side and unlocked Biggie's door—Becker possibly confusing him with Rona Lefler—before circling the car to get in on the driver's side. "Shit, I'm not Rona Lefler," Biggie mumbled. But he thought it was such a nice gesture, particularly for a lowlife like Becker, that Biggie resolved to do it himself whenever he drove somebody somewhere, except when he carted Giselle and her friends to school. They could open their own door.

Looking back, he wondered if he were magnifying the graciousness of Becker's gesture 1,000 times out of proportion. Whenever he unlocked the door for anybody, usually Wing or once in a while his mom, they never made a big deal out of it. Nobody acted as if he'd taken off his coat and spread it across a puddle. They thanked him, but they would have thanked him if he'd reached over to unlock the door from the inside. Still, it was a nice habit he'd cultivated—though one nobody noticed—and felt good about himself for doing, even if, when you got down to it, girls probably preferred guys who were lowlifes.

"The *Deathmobile*," Luigi Cravi announced, climbing into the back seat after Bluestone bothered to unlock the back door for him.

"Is that supposed to be funny?"

"Look who's sensitive," Wing said.

Biggie considered strangling Cravi with his bare hands as he cut over to Sheridan, which he took past Highwood and the Ft. Sheridan enclave into Lake Bluff, "the most exclusive suburb on the north shore," according to an article he'd read in the *Sun-Times.* Half the suburbs on the north shore competed for the title of most exclusive, as if exclusivity was some sort of admirable quality, like sensitivity. It was a warm night for late January. Puddles glistened from the shoulder, but driving through an exclusive suburb you didn't get a lot of street lights glaring into your eyes. He turned up the radio—tuned to WCFL—as a favorite song by Badfinger came on that always reminded Biggie of Gloria.

"*I remember finding out about you,*" Biggie sang along with the radio.

"*Every night my mind is all around you,*" Wing and Luigi sang, drowning out Biggie, which was pretty annoying since Biggie could really sing when he sang along with the radio. According to Giselle, without the radio accompaniment he sounded like a wounded raccoon.

The only two people on the planet who sang worse were Wing Terrill and Luigi Cravi. Artificially elongating syllables, breaking into phony falsetto, transposing lyrics, mocking the piss out of him.

Biggie turned down the radio. "Don't call it the Deathmobile," Biggie said.

Soon Biggie felt the air seeping out of him and a presence in his chest, as if the throbbing that was always in his shoulder surged to his heart. Suddenly he struck the dashboard with his fist, wondering at what point you were supposed to drive to the hospital. If you counted to a hundred and the piercing presence in your chest was still there? He pounded the dashboard again, and would have again if it weren't for the presence tearing through his chest, and would have yelled if he didn't fear the yell would finish him off altogether; instead Bluestone sighed, "I can't win with you two."

"Do you have any idea at all the way you are?" Wing sighed back, then tapped the dashboard, but in such a way you knew he wanted to pound it to pieces.

"Asshole," Luigi Cravi muttered from the back.

Asshole.

He thought of threatening to drive them all the way into Lake Forest if that was their attitude, but Biggie slowed the Dart to turn around and head back to Highwood. The presence in his chest diminished as he turned, and within a hundred yards he wondered if he had imagined it, if at any moment he was capable of feeling a crushing presence in his chest, if this disposition was even more depressing than would be suffering a massive heart attack for his troubles.

"Biggie," Wing said softly, "*Oldenhopf will pin Terrill.* That's a direct quote."

"*That's* what this is all about?"

"*Tonight* that's what this is all about," Luigi clarified.

"Last week you told me to fuck off," Wing said, tapping the dashboard again, then leaning back in the seat and turning toward Biggie.

There were no other cars on the road, not even headlights in the distance. He knew that would change once they approached Ft. Sheridan and then Highwood, which may as well be a chunk of Las Vegas in the middle of suburbia, but for now it was nice to think they were driving through the middle of nowhere, and that just beyond could be a place you've never been. He wondered if that was one of the reasons he liked driving sometimes; you could be suspended in the realm of not knowing, all while under the illusion you were going somewhere new, with the radio blaring, leaving behind who you were *en route* to the future.

"Last week you threw me against the wall."

"Worse than that, you threw *me* against the wall," Luigi said.

"You threw Wetzel against the wall," Wing chuckled.

Nice to think Wing didn't think he was *all* rotten.

"Every day it's something new with you, Bluestone." Luigi again.

"Great seeing you guys today. What's the weather forecast?" Biggie.

"*Keep your arms in. Watch the fireman's.*" Wing.

"*You're* the one who said Pinsker would pin *me*." Biggie.

"That's not the point." Wing.

"Whatsoever it's not the point, Bluestone." Luigi.

"I'm sorry." Biggie thought of pointing out that, from an accuracy perspective, even if Wing *had* kept his arms in, Oldenhopf would have found some other way to pin Wing, but that wasn't the point.

"Okay," Wing said softly. "Okay."

"I don't know what's going on," Biggie admitted.

"Anymore, you think you're so superior," Luigi said. "You weren't like that before."

"We know things are tough with Giselle," Wing conceded.

"Yeah," Luigi said.

"Shut up," Biggie said.

"I'm trying," Biggie said awhile later, suspecting that the admission was indistinguishable from a sigh. "I see that throwing you guys against the wall and throwing Wetzel against the wall and telling Terrill to fuck off when he was trying to help—I'm sorry about that, Wing. I appreciate that you made the effort—everybody else was terrified I might throw them against the wall if they tried to help—and I'll shine your shoes if it will make any difference, Luigi's too, and Wetzel's—well, *sheesh*, not Wetzel's shoes; I draw the line—but I don't see what you guys are talking about. About the superior shit and fuck-all."

"Even Hoffman thinks you're really smug and self-righteous."

"*Professor* Pete Hoffman, who's going to Yale?" Biggie said.

"You act like your shit don't stink, and Pete's and everybody else's does," Luigi said from the back.

"Pete's worked to get into Yale," Wing added.

"He's worked to build his *resume*," Biggie said.

"We appreciate your trying, but that's a case in point," Wing said.

"You have no appreciation of the effort it's taken Hoffman. You act as if he was *born* to Yale. To you it's all a joke because it's Hoffman, not you."

Luigi. Full of appreciation for Hoffman's effort.

Biggie thought, these guys aren't even friends, but mirrors for each other. *Distorted* mirrors. "*Did* Hoffman get into Yale?"

"He's still waiting to hear," Wing said.

"But that's not the point," Luigi said. "Whatsoever."

"Pete's not the point," Wing said.

"I get the point," Biggie said.

"We shouldn't have told you. *I'm* sorry I told you that, Biggie, because now you're going to walk around thinking that Hoffman's green with envy, or that Hoffman's a conceited jerkwad with a huge bug up his ass, while *you're* the one who's really so smug and above it all and couldn't give a flying shit about others. Hoffman's only—"

"An example," Luigi said from the back.

"Thank you for pointing that out." In fact, Hoffman wouldn't be un-defeated on JVs except for Waukegan, without Biggie showing him every damn move Professor Pete could absorb, Biggie thought of adding if it wouldn't come across as self-serving. "Sure, there are always exceptions," Wing would say.

"You're always acting like you're too good to associate with us," Luigi added from the back.

Wing glanced at Luigi in the back seat. Biggie had the impression Wing was warning Luigi off, that whatever they were getting into—whatever manner of personality counseling they were under-going, dissecting Biggie's flaws before he contaminated the Western World—Wing wanted out of. Biggie imagined the two of them getting together after practice, last week after he threw them against the wall in his fog, though it was possible it was weeks—months—before that, when Biggie didn't come along to celebrate at Virginia's, and one of them says, "You know the problem with Bluestone? He's a jackass," and the other, not out of conviction but to explore the concept, in the spirit of camaraderie, says, "You know, I've thought that too," because who didn't you think that about once you got to know them? And now the two had a theme to develop, in increments, day by day, neither really believing it. All of which convinced Biggie that he should have thrown them *harder* against the wall. "Is that how you feel, Wing?"

"It's not like you condescend to wrestle with us during practice half the time. You're always going down to the track to run laps. How do you think we feel?"

"Relieved."

"You look at Wetzel like he's a piece of shit," Wing chuckled.

"You won't go out with us after the meets," Luigi registered from the back.

"Let's test that point-of-view. Did we have a wrestling meet tonight? Are we going out?"

"You never call anyone up. You're always by yourself. You don't *give* anything. You don't notice."

"You just *take*." Luigi.

"Ah."

"At school you stand against the wall with a silly grin on your face. That's what everyone says about you. You're in your own little world, Biggie, which you find a lot more amusing than the one the rest of us slobs are stuck in; or else you look down from your world and find us pretty amusing. It's scary, Biggie. Here's another example: Do you have any idea the contempt you show for Jerry Bray?" Wing.

"And you think Bray's terrific." In fact, *Wing* was the one who gave him the idea Bray was a jerkwad. That was a direct quote: "Bray's a jerkwad."

Wing sighed, "Forget it, Biggie. I'm in a bad mood from Oldenhopf. That's all."

"Forget it," Luigi sighed.

"You think there's nobody worth talking to unless they're undefeated—"

"Enough."

"I know you don't *mean* it, but that can give people the impression you think you're better than them, that you don't have to practice with them, that you can joke about their getting pinned the second before their match, that they don't care if they get pinned by Oldenhopf because they're not fucking unscored upon, in line for some fat ass wrestling fucking scholarship shit."

"That says it all." Luigi said.

"It's not that *you* don't have any feelings, Bluestone. But you assume we don't."

I'm the one who runs the miles and lifts the weights, Bluestone thinks, and pulls the double sessions and does the 100 pullups and 200 chinups daily and dreams of the captions in *Advanced Wrestling Techniques for the High School Athlete*. And *they* could, of course. They could run the miles and lift the weights and knock themselves out at the chinup bar and pull the double sessions and dream of the captions. In fact, they could be fucking unscored upon, in line for some fat ass fucking wrestling scholarship, except they weren't selfish bastards.

"I never looked at it that way," Biggie admitted. "I thought I was knocking myself out. Sorry."

"I know," Wing said, though with such resignation that it suggested he now realized Biggie *was* a different animal altogether, different natural laws to subscribe to, altogether different expectations for what constituted human engagement, all beyond Wing's understanding. Guys like Wing on one side of the wall, undefeated guys like Biggie on the other.

That was an interesting dimension of being undefeated. People cursed you, called you out, twisted every aspect of your behavior so it looked a certain way in an unflattering light, all because you acted like you were better than everybody else, but on a certain level you *were* better than everybody else, or at least a different animal altogether. That's why you were undefeated.

Yet if *everyone* called you a selfish bastard? Even Biggie had to wonder. It's not as if he'd ever given a thought to how Wing *felt* when he lost. Christ, it was surprising Wing or Luigi felt anything when they lost. Also, his sister and Mom had pretty much been calling him a selfish bastard for years, always wanting him to do things he didn't want to, like bolting upstairs at the snap of a finger to take the garbage out when he was in the middle of something, though the truth was—here Biggie feared again he was being self-serving—it was hard to imagine Luigi snapping to and charging upstairs under similar circumstances, or even Wing, who was pretty much the nicest guy he'd ever met (unless your back was turned). Still, you had to consider there might be something to it beyond defense mechanisms operating in overdrive or—as was the case with Giselle—their own tendencies mirrored back in their faces.

"Sorry. I'm a selfish bastard."

"Say that again."

"I'm a *conceited* bastard," Biggie said, wondering if it was the same thing.

Biggie was surprised to find the heartfelt apology was all it took to land back in Wing's and Luigi's good graces. He didn't have to promise to be *less* of a selfish, conceited bastard in the future. When people called you to account, they *wanted* to let you off the hook. The important thing was that they'd pointed it out.

When they got back to Highwood, Biggie pulled the Dart into the lot at Scornavacco's. Though this was a Friday night, the winter air took on the glittering mist of an incipient blizzard, and the parking lot was empty.

"There must be a wrestling meet inside," Wing said.

Wing and Luigi followed Bluestone into the restaurant, the two sitting across from Biggie in a booth. Though the subject of his imperfections was closed, Biggie couldn't help wondering if they'd bring it up again someday, after he took State. ("Good for Biggie." "Now he'll never speak to *anyone*, the selfish bastard.") He wondered too—this is what got to him, for he valued their company and didn't want it hovering over them every time he saw these guys, though the subject was closed—he wondered if he'd ever forgive them for opening fire like that, ever forget that once he came out of the fog and made the move to sincerely apologize, his two friends chose that moment to let him have it both barrels blazing. It wasn't the kind of thing you went around forgetting, any more than you could forget your German Shepherd turning on you.

Biggie's spirit sank again into gloom.

Wing and Luigi chose that moment to ask him what had happened.

"They were driving around in the parking lot at Burger Chef. Mary and Lauren Gelfin hopped on the trunk. Giselle turned—she was driving very slowly—and they jumped off. That was all. Lauren hurt her knee, Mary hit her head. She got up right away and walked toward the car but then threw up and collapsed." Biggie felt it was wrong to mention the part about Mary's throwing up—it hurt to consider that it was her last conscious action—and wondered what he would say differently next time, or not say at all in case he ever talked about it again.

"That's what we heard," Wing said. "It's all so nutty."

"We heard they were drunk and on LSD."

As he looked at Luigi's water glass, Biggie wondered if he reached across the table, placed Luigi's bulbous asymmetrical head between his hands then drowned the Fat Boy in his water glass, if the two would consider him to be a bigger bastard than they already thought.

"You believe everything you hear?"

"I didn't say I believed it."

"Mary was a *wrestling* cheerleader. Did she look to you like she was on LSD?"

Wing turned toward Biggie. "Luigi thinks everybody's on LSD."

"Luigi's on LSD."

"Fuck you."

It was true, though. It came out once you talked to Luigi for a while, on the bus back from North Chicago or Oak Park. A lot of guys on the football team were like that. Biggie could figure it was because they didn't want to think they were missing out on anything: They spent hundreds of hours pushing blocking sleds as the coaches screamed at them and questioned their ancestry, hurtling themselves into the blocking dummies, lining up for the nutcracker drill, but it's not as if they were missing out on anything productive. Everybody else was tripping on LSD, not getting blow jobs or anything significant, but looking at sunsets and going apeshit over the beauty. In fact, you were actually *safer* getting the piss beaten out of you every afternoon, because then you weren't frothing at the mouth over the sunset on LSD, your brains getting permanently addled. That was the view of Luigi and a lot of other football guys. Biggie wasn't completely certain he didn't buy into that view a bit himself.

"Cravi thinks *Wetzel's* on LSD," Wing said.

"Do you know what I heard?" Luigi asked Wing.

"Fuck you," Biggie said.

"Giselle was driving fifty miles an hour."

"That's why the police didn't arrest her or anything, because she was on LSD and going fifty miles an hour in a parking lot," Wing said.

Biggie looked at Wing gratefully until he noticed *Cravi* was also looking at Wing gratefully. Wing was just sarcastic enough in general that you could take half of what he said to support any position you wanted.

"I didn't *say* I believed it, Wing. It's just what people say. Bluestone should *know*."

"Biggie, how's Giselle?" Wing asked.

Now the waitress came with her platter. Because Biggie didn't try to make weight this week, hadn't stepped on a scale in days—he must be 200 by now—he promised himself he wouldn't go overboard gorging. An eagle could as well promise not to soar. Still, he grabbed a fistful of the onion rings before Luigi got started. With Cravi, you could turn around, then turn back to find the rings consumed save for a single shard of crumbling crust.

"Giselle comes and goes. She sits in her room a lot then gets up and roams into the kitchen where she screams at Mom like a raving lunatic, then goes back to her room and turns the record player louder. I haven't talked to her much," Biggie admitted, touched by the question.

"You sound like you're on LSD," Luigi said.

"I knew you were going to say that."

Luigi smiled at Biggie. Cravi could practically accuse your sister of murder, but put a cheeseburger in his hands, a double order of rings within reach, and he was eternally pacified. Biggie picked up his cheeseburger, grabbed a handful of rings, and smiled back.

"What I'd give to have Sara Sherman beside me."

"I'm sure you'll see her later tonight," Biggie said to Wing.

"I slept with her last night," Luigi said.

"How are *you*?" Wing asked.

"I'm doing as well as Giselle," he said honestly. Not the Giselle who was his sister, but the Giselle he'd just described. In fact, Biggie wondered if he hadn't been describing himself. It seemed odd to him now that he really didn't know how Giselle was, or hadn't made any effort to find out, other than occasionally asking her how she was. Although Giselle was liable to erupt if you asked her, like you were accusing her of stealing the brownies, that he didn't know precisely struck him as another serious deficiency in his personality. "Thanks for asking."

"Are you screwing Gloria Serpentino?"

Biggie looked again at Luigi's water glass, then at the basket of onion rings, where two remained.

You spend night after night talking to a girl for hours, thinking about her most of the hours you're not talking to her—full time now, practically, since he wasn't talking to Gloria—priding yourself on keeping the arrangement to yourself, that nobody knew besides your mom and dad and Giselle, they only because they answered the phone—still under the impression Gloria and Biggie were working the homework project—saying nothing to Wing and Luigi, as if half the power of what you felt for Gloria was derived from keeping it a secret, maybe that's the sole fucking attraction, then it turns out an imbecile and fat face like Luigi Fucking Cravi has read your mind all along. While Biggie wanted to cram Luigi's fat face into the water glass—and lucky for Cravi that the onion rings weren't bicycle chains—another part of Biggie wanted to embrace Cravi for providing him with this moment, which so accurately summed up his life.

"Screwing her? I don't even know what she looks like," Biggie said to his friends across the table.

By the time he drove Wing and Luigi home, the snow had stopped, but the roads were still icy. Biggie drove ten miles an hour, telling the two about meeting Gosley and Salt Tepper. In the telling he managed to suggest that Tepper introduced *himself*. "The guy's a double for Robert Frost," he said. He'd already said this stuff to Wing and liked it that Wing didn't accuse him of being obsessive. "But I guess it depends on the Tournament. For places like that, you pretty much have to take State."

"When Wing takes State," Luigi said from the back, "I'll go out with Sara Sherman."

The conversation wasn't going anywhere, but it beat discussing his *personality*. When he talked about scholarships, he only felt like strangling the guys he wrestled, not the guys who cheered him on.

Face-to-Face, January 31-February 4

Biggie decided he'd lift *after* his run, bundled up in sweats after stretching, then barreled upstairs and out the front door.

The morning was so bright for almost February he could barely see the cars going north. After a few blocks, running with his face pointed toward the sun, Biggie began to warm up. That was the odd thing about running in Chicago in the winter: You could run in the middle of the night and freeze your ass off—as would have occurred had Biggie run last night after returning from Scornavacco's, as he was tempted to do before collapsing on his bed—or you could run in the bright morning with your face pointed toward the sun and freeze your ass off with a sore neck tossed into the deal, until you covered several blocks and warmed up. No real benefit, either way. It was the kind of observation he liked telling Gloria Serpentino, all of which made him regret for the thousandth time that morning, the millionth overall, that he was no longer speaking to her.

As Biggie ran, swerving from the street to the sidewalk as the traffic picked up, he imagined what he'd say to Gloria when he finally *did* call her again. Something profound and heroic, the kind of stuff his dad came up with all the time, rather than letting her know he'd found himself shrouded in a fog—due to tragic events about which she may have heard—and was afraid of what he'd say to her from the confusion of the heavy mist.

What he liked about Gloria was that he could be paradoxical, and whereas a lot of people—Pete Hoffman, for example, with his Yalie sense of precision—might say, "Christ, Bluestone, that's paradoxical. Why don't you make up your mind?"—Gloria could see exactly what he meant. Or say she did, which wasn't the same thing but better than telling him to make up his mind in such a way—a Hoffman, Yalie kind of way—that made him regret opening up and telling her in the first place. Most people, when you told them stuff that mixed them up, you ended up regretting telling them to begin with.

The truth was, whether he apologized first or not, here's the kind of thing he knew he'd end up telling her: "Gloria, I had a choice to make this morning. I could run before I lifted, or lift before I ran. If I lifted before I ran, I knew I'd run in a state of muscle collapse, whereas if I ran before I lifted, I knew I'd lift in a state of exhaustion. Well, here's why I ran first. I knew I wouldn't lift less weight—curls with 145, for example, instead of 160—if I ran first, but if I *lifted* first, Glory, you can bet I'd stagger through the run half-throttle!" Nothing profound and heroic, nothing to make Glory think, "Gee, this reminds me of why I've been so upset that Biggie hasn't called," but the kind of thing she'd understand was *important*, so at first you didn't mind telling her, and after a while found you liked telling her. She probably wouldn't even notice there was nothing profound and heroic about it, or she would find some angle invisible to anybody else in which it could be viewed as profound and heroic.

Well, a running, lifting bastard, that's what he was, and Biggie figured he always would be.

Did his parents think of him that way? ("What does your son do, Mrs. Bluestone?" "He's a running, lifting bastard.") The wrestler was *glad* that's how he was. As often as it drove him nuts, Biggie figured it would drive him even nuttier *not* to run and lift all the time. It reminded him a little of when he was nine years old and discovered a pile of old

Playboys in Ricky Nash's garage. For weeks afterward, Biggie—still Dan then, it would be a good three years until middle school—pitied every nine-year-old in the entire goddamn universe who wasn't him or Ricky Nash. Ricky Nash moved away two years later, but Biggie figured the guy was still hiding out in the garage at the place he moved to, thumbing through the pile of *Playboys*.

Crossing Prospect, he eyed a surly black Lab three blocks ahead. Bluestone had the impulse to strangle the creature, or kick him in the muzzle if he snapped at Biggie as he ran by. That's the kind of bastard he was. He had to steel himself against such impulses if he saw an innocent dog ahead as being not a natural dog, pre-programmed through 10,000 generations of crisscrossing genetic signals, in the act of apprehending a hooded, sweat-clothed creature invading his turf, but a dog lobbing personal insults. Luckily for the Lab, the Lab retreated as Biggie ran past, freeing him to wonder if his parents or Giselle—or Wing, too, or Sara Sherman—had something, like lifting and running, that they'd be hard pressed to get by without. You probably didn't want to know, with half the people you knew. You really look up to somebody, and it turns out that the thing they'd be hard pressed to do without is watching *The Ed Sullivan Show*, or skim milk. Take away anything else and they'd get by. It reminded Biggie of a big deal movie he saw in History class, junior year, *Citizen Kane*, where this big deal powerful guy, based on William Randolph Hearst, says "Rosebud" as his last words, which turned out not to be the secret of the universe, the sum of all human knowledge and desire, but the name of the snow sled he played with as a little kid. As if it's the memory of the damn sled that made him tick all those years. That would be kind of disappointing to find out. Even if you saw "Rosebud" as a symbol. That's what one of the girls in class, Robin Wasserman, said during the discussion after the movie. Robin Wasserman was one of those girls, a Highland Park High specialty, who reminded you every time they opened their mouths in class that as smart as you sometimes—secretly—thought yourself to be, there were people out there, though the exact same age, who were ten million times smarter. That was the function of girls like Robin. You couldn't imagine them getting together like the Society of Wayward Girls to bake German chocolate cake and brownies and have macaroni and cheese eating contests. These HP specialty girls didn't sit in the stands with the Mat Gals mangling your names as they chirped into the loudspeaker. You certainly wouldn't ask one of them out. What would be the point? Even if she looked like Sara Sherman, if you got her in the front seat in the moonlight under the dazzling stars and she'd look into your eyes and say, "What are you thinking, Biggie?" all you could think to say back would be, "I'm thinking about what a dumb fuck I am, Robin." And they didn't look like Sara Sherman, Biggie thought as he headed up Lincoln Avenue West, deep in his rhythm now. Even if you *could* get past the way they made you feel like a dumb fuck—same age, 10,000 times the insight and wisdom—they still didn't look like Sara Sherman, though it was doubtful anybody in history could ever get past the reminder of their dumb-fuckery to tell. That's why it could really knock you out sometimes to see some of these specialty girls' pictures in the yearbook. "She's as pretty as a petunia" you think, startled, because face-to-face in the flesh with the living incarnation, all you'd think is that you'd spelled petunia wrong, or that petunia wasn't the kind of flower you meant in the first place. In fact, you're too much of a dumb fuck to think of the kind of flower you meant.

What Robin actually said wasn't as brilliant as it sounded when she first said it. When Mr. Dacker turned the projector off—the movie had taken two full sessions—everybody was guffawing—now that he thought about it in the context of Robin Wasserman, Biggie wasn't certain he knew what *guffaw* meant—"Rosebud, hah, hah. Rosebud. Gee," when Robin quickly raised her hand—of course, Mr. Dacker called on her like a starving man sighting a root beer float—"Mr. Dacker, maybe

Rosebud's a symbol for a vision of youth and innocence and purity he carried with him through his journey into moral decay." It made a lot of sense when Robin said that—she didn't say it in an "I told you so, I'm better than you" kind of way, either; more like she was pointing out that nobody had turned the lights back on, as if, if she didn't come up with the casual observation, the next person to raise their hand was bound to—that the big deal guy supposedly based on W.H. Hearst was a pretty corrupt bastard who'd squeeze you out as soon as look at you—kind of like an industrial version Killer Kowalski without the sensitive side off the mat—but when Biggie thought about it, it was a lot more mysterious and interesting to think Old Hearst went to his grave thinking about a sled. A puny fuck-all sled. Of course, Biggie didn't think to say that at the time. No, he sat there at the time mouth ajar at Robin Wasserman's sheer genius. Even if he *had* said it to show that he wasn't such a dumb fuck after all, you knew Robin Wasserman would come back with some nuance—a dimension as clear as the view of the lake from the top of the John Hancock building—which showed Biggie was a thousand times more of a dumb fuck than even he'd suspected.

What was lifting and running a symbol for? Biggie figured it had to mean hard work, going that extra mile, that he was going to leave no stone unturned, that he would do anything within his power (and he'd make that power as powerful as he could, double powerful, you better believe it, so the symbol suggested), that nothing was going to stop him from taking State if he had two cents to say about it. That he was Killer Kowalski at the core. All true. But it saved you a lot of time just to say he was a running, lifting bastard. That's all anybody really needed to know.

Here's why he wanted Gloria. Wanted the sound of her voice through the receiver cradled against his ear. Wanted the vague image of a pretty girl to shut his lids to at night. Wanted the phone to ring and Mom, flabbergasted, incredulous, calling down that *it's for Biggie*, like it was the Democratic party calling to ask him to run for governor, whereupon

Biggie's down-in-the-dumps spirit snaps to—that's what Glory's voice could do for him, not change the events of the day, maybe not, but smear a brighter sheen over them. Wanted back, too, the world as it was before Giselle took the Dart—with Biggie's *permission* that he's wanted to revoke since Burger Chef, before the fog. Wanted to accept it all—to be a better version of Biggie, tempered by grief, mellowed by dint of his own gig in the human circus. Wanted, too, to ask Gloria Serpentino what *she'd* be hard pressed to do without. You could ask her, too. Stuff you could never ask anybody, you could ask her as easily as asking where she was born, or if she liked to wear hats, and she'd ask you back twice as easily.

That's how Biggie felt turning the corner, picking up speed as he hadn't since before Giselle drove a car full of girls to Burger Chef, with the sensation that he was running toward Gloria Serpentino.

If it was one thing to run toward somebody in your reveries as you race down Sheridan with the only second wind you've had in two weeks, suddenly in the stretch, Killer Kowalski again after a tour through the fog, it was another to sustain the reverie *after* you call and no Gloria Serpentino waiting on the other end. With Biggie Bluestone, things could get ridiculous fast. First her mom answered. Half an hour later it was her sister Vicky. Her mom again an hour later. By now Biggie was exhausted from the weights, punching at the presses like 200 pounds of barbells were stuffed with marshmallows, wondering one second if it was Gloria Serpentino he couldn't do without—proven by his stint in the fog—wondering the next that if it *was* Gloria Serpentino he couldn't live without, was it worth the candle?

The *sixth* time he called, two hours later, Gloria came to the phone.

Gloria thought he was calling to sell her magazine subscriptions. "What do you want?"

"I want to talk to you."

"You haven't returned my calls."

"I've called you six times."

"That's in the last hour. I'm talking about the last two weeks, Dan."

Bluestone found the *Dan* encouraging. Unless she'd said *damn*. The way he was feeling, it wouldn't surprise Biggie if his *parents* meant damn when they signed the birth certificate. ("Here's our boy, Damn Bluestone." "Sure you don't mean Dan?" "I guess so.")

Gloria sighed. "I'm not going to make this easy for you."

"Nothing's been easy for me."

"Do you want to meet?" Gloria asked. "Monday, third lunch period."

If at that moment, she'd asked him if he had a class Monday, third lunch period, he couldn't have said.

All that night and Sunday, Biggie wondered if *meeting* Gloria amounted to a step backward in their peculiar friendship. Was it two weeks ago that it meant so much to her that they *not* meet because if they did she'd never want to leave?

This might be the sort of thing to talk over with Wing to demonstrate he didn't think he was superior. ("Gloria wants to meet. I'm afraid that constitutes a step *backward*.") Realistically, it wasn't the sort of observation guaranteed to reassure Wing about Biggie's personality.

Should he talk it over with his little sister? In the event that women spoke a coded language beyond his understanding, she would translate because he was her brother. The single time he'd talked to her at length since the funeral—this the day after, during a respite when Lauren Gelfin was home getting a change of clothes—Giselle went on and on about mistakes that happened all the time at the hospital where Mary Wellington died. "Alice Milkwood's mother was there with a head injury from a fall at home. She died, too."

"You're kidding. They should investigate or something."

Bluestone was sorry he said what he did about "They should investigate," as if Biggie were more interested in finding a solution than hearing Giselle out. She'd looked at him, that blank look that pretty much proclaimed how useless Biggie was, a look after which she suddenly turned about and walked back to her room; the exact look, in fact, Giselle had given him 10,000 times before to no effect whatsoever, though this time Biggie was *trying* to be useful.

Sunday night Biggie walked down the upstairs hallway and lingered by Giselle's door. He could hear "Teach Your Children" by Crosby, Stills, Nash and Young on Giselle's record player. He didn't know whether she was in there by herself, though the last few days he'd noticed that she was alone more often. After a big tragedy everybody toes up to tell you how sorry they are, but one by one they peel away until at the end you're there by yourself, crying in your room. For a second, he wondered what it was like for Myra Wellington, Mary's sister. He'd bet it was the same way. It would be hard to imagine that Myra was all that interested in talking to Giselle right now—or that Giselle would begin to know what to say or do, other than to burst into tears—but Biggie bet the two had more in common with each other right now than anybody else they knew.

He knocked on Giselle's door. He couldn't hear her crying inside the room. Sometimes when you knocked on Giselle's door, when you wanted to ask her something, like she'd better give you the car key, you could *hear* her inside the room not answering, the vibrations from Giselle freezing in place, if not deafening, then eerie. But now Biggie couldn't sense his sister freezing in place. It wasn't unusual for Giselle to leave the record player on as she went off with friends. The only way to tell if she was *really* there was to sit there with her face-to-face. He turned to walk down the hall, for a moment overcome by the thought that Giselle was there, after all, not answering, freezing in place, and for the first time since he'd noticed years ago that he *always* knew if she was home—how old was he then? Two? Three?—he couldn't sense her presence. That was something you never thought too much about when you had a sister, and certainly didn't think you wanted. If anything it annoyed you, as if you were wearing a dog collar.

Maybe if he really got to know Gloria—if face-to-face it turned out that all the ways he'd envisioned her were mere wishful thinking—and vice versa, he supposed, though certainly she knew well who he was, she had the drop on him there—maybe then Gloria could help him decode Giselle.

When you had a girlfriend, though, you probably didn't spend too much time worrying about things like decoding your sister.

You didn't want to know all that much what made her tick.

Monday afternoon, sitting at a table during third period lunch hour, Biggie promised himself he wasn't going to do the kind of shit that always drove him nuts. Nonetheless, here he was, looking at every girl walking by who hadn't yet transmogrified into a full-blown high school girl, thinking *that's* Gloria Serpentino, just his luck.

Once, even a strikingly pretty girl, already transmogrified, walked by. Jane Bennett, by acclamation one of the Magical Fifty, no Sara Sherman (which was the sort of thing implicit with any girl, though you still thought you had to point it out) but well-dressed, as if she *thought* she was Sara Sherman, a tall blonde with a slightly pointed face that didn't translate well in the yearbook but such a startling smile it was hard to take the view you were anything but the luckiest guy alive when Jane Bennett directed it your way—in fact, you'd have to be a moron not to go out with Jane Bennett if you had the shot, though as with many girls in the Fifty, she was strictly material for college guys, so the situation—going out with her or not—was impossibly hypothetical, no such question could ever exist in the actual world—Biggie found himself thinking as Jane Bennett walked by, whose identity he very well knew and who may well have known his, for they'd been in about two classes per term together since freshman year, who'd once even laughed out loud at a report Biggie gave (a laugh he couldn't imagine ever forgetting), looking at her with an expression of expectation, pure wellbeing (might *that* be Gloria?) until Jane Bennett passed his table and Biggie, as if seeing her for the first time, thought, Bluestone-style, "That's not her, damn. Just my luck."

And then she was there. On a cold overcast day in early February 1971, during third lunch hour when Biggie Bluestone was driving himself nuts from the odor of French fries and hamburgers he couldn't have, Gloria Serpentino sat down across the table.

He hadn't seen her coming. He'd been so caught up in Jane Bennett and his damn luck, Gloria slipped through the fog undetected. Suddenly she was in front of him, as if a day of the week didn't go by when she didn't sit across the lunch table from him. "Dan."

"Hi, Glory." As this didn't seem adequate, he filled her in on what he'd been thinking. "You know how it goes with making weight, Glory? It probably wouldn't be the worst thing in the world if they left you isolated in a hermetically sealed isolation unit. Different things that drive you nuts, like the scent of French fries and cheeseburgers, because you can't have any what with making weight, would waft no farther than the hermetically sealed door. Inside the sealed unit you wouldn't have to deal with that. You wouldn't have to stay up nights clutching your gut, wishing you could hold a vat of grease aloft and drink it. But the thing is, they don't put you in a hermetically sealed unit. They put you in the middle of the lunchroom, third period."

"Dan, aren't you mentally stronger for having to fight off the scent of fries and burgers?"

"Not that I've noticed."

With each passing second, he made a further adjustment to the way Gloria Serpentino looked. So that the initial disappointment—she wasn't one who'd be in the Magical Fifty but for her *attitude*—had already passed to acceptance, which by now had transmogrified into pleasure. He couldn't remember having seen her before. She had long brown hair that was thick without being ample or unruly (though he loved unruly and ample), clean but not shiny. While she wasn't thin from what he could see across the table, she was closer to being thin than anything else. The Serpentino face was plain, but came alive when she talked, and more—here's what Biggie loved—came alive when she listened. To Biggie—so he formulated in the first minute of sitting across the lunchroom table—Gloria Serpentino was the kind of girl whom if you called pretty nobody would think to dispute you, though if you didn't, nobody would go out of their way to furnish the description. It was a little like Wing, who was really smart when you got to know him. Everyone agreed, too, when you pointed it out, but if you didn't go around calling him smart, nobody thought to bring it up. She wore jeans and a leather top with fringe extending from the arms, as if she were cast as a cowgirl in the school play. To Biggie—so he formulated in the second minute he sat across from her—she was a walking advertisement for a product he'd seen before but couldn't quite name.

By the third minute they weren't sitting across the table from each other but walking out of the lunchroom into the hallway. They stopped at their lockers to pick up their coats. In the fourth minute they met by the back door near the parking lot, which they soon cut across heading for Vine, their destination The Sergeant, the head shop where Gloria worked three afternoons a week. To her questions and observations, Biggie supplied questions and observations of his own, neutral stuff, crap like, "It's great that we have an open campus," and, "Yeah, my cousin goes to a place where they need a hall pass just to go to the bathroom," and, "All my cousins go to high schools in New Jersey. I don't know the policies there," that, Biggie figured, unless you listened to the minutest suggestions of each syllable and magnified them to the tenth power, probably wouldn't betray that you'd only spent a thousand hours thinking about her over the last month. When you did apply that level of scrutiny, though, it was pretty clear you had. Nobody would miss it.

The first few minutes with Gloria Serpentino passed like the blink of an eye, until you were standing with her in front of the head shop, looking down at her face as she looked up into yours, unclear how you'd arrived there, wondering if you were expected to kiss her, though this was broad daylight in the middle of downtown, and not a single word exchanged in your conversation face-to-face would strike anybody overhearing as personal, unless they took in, as Biggie did, the minutest suggestion of each syllable, then magnified it to the tenth power. "I'll meet you tomorrow, third lunch period, same time, same place," Glory said.

"Could we meet at our lockers instead? I meant that about the fries and cheeseburgers."

"And the craving for a vat of grease?" Gloria asked.

"No."

Gloria half smiled. Her eyes widened—the whole works rising, her brows, her huge irises, the pupils—as if she hadn't considered the possibility Biggie might mean what he said. "I see. Okay, Dan. We'll meet by the lockers."

"Thanks."

"And, Dan, we'll meet there every day."

Having the real face to envision, so that it wasn't always the combination of every pretty girl he'd seen around school mixed with every beautiful woman he'd seen on television plus the college girls he'd see walking around the Sunset Market, all with the bodies of *Playboy* models, the animated version of Gloria that came alive when she talked or listened changed everything.

It made Biggie feel he moved through less of a dream world and more of a real world, which was surprising when he thought about it, because, except for the fog, it had never occurred to him he'd been walking through a dream world. Other people out there you could certainly say stuff like that about; Jerry Bray, for example, with his fake hustle and the sense you always had when he walked toward you that he was about to clap you on the back and ask for your vote for President. Bray was a guy you could believe pretty much walked through a dream world. But Biggie was down-to-earth, meat and potatoes, what he saw in front of him all there was to it, that's what he'd thought; but now, after twenty minutes with Glory, face-to-face, he knew the lens had always been out of focus. Not that he regretted it. It wasn't the sort of thing that you could regret for an instant. The out-of-focus kind of guy he'd been, walking the hallways alive but where everyone else was a blur, thinking about people, he could now see, not as people but as the concepts they elicited in his imagination, Christ, had done nothing less than deliver him to Gloria Serpentino. Well, it paid off triple.

He talked it over with her two nights later. This, after two days of walking her every third lunch hour from the back door of the school down Vine, up Central, to The Sergeant on Crawford, a ritual he already considered he could probably live without, but barely; two nights of hours-long phone calls, forty-eight hours of finding a Gloria Serpentino context for everything he did and, if he couldn't find one, looking harder and scrutinizing until one emerged. "It's amazing, truly amazing," Biggie said into the phone. He was leaning back on his bed with his shirt off, watching his stomach which, it seemed to him, had shriveled practically beyond the ridges and muscle until the skin looked about to snap. The soundtrack for *Hair* was playing on the hi-fi.

"I know," Gloria said.

That was the thing with Gloria. Sometimes you could get away with telling her something amazing and she didn't call upon you to explain, she already agreed. In fact, sometimes, like now, she didn't even need to know *what* was amazing. "It's like all I've ever seen are shapes, figures in the mist, approximations. I mean that I'd look and get the basic idea, and then let the basic idea determine my attitude rather than the thing I was really looking at. It was a strange way to be."

"Were you that way around girls?"

Well, it was hard to imagine what else there was to think about. "Sure. I'd see the girl, for example, say a pretty girl, but there'd be no individual context, just a pretty girl category in my brain which furnished everything I already needed to know about her. Without that—who knows?—I may have even made an effort to get to know her."

"I don't believe that." That was another thing about Glory. She had a way of not believing a good two-thirds of what Biggie told her. But instead of making it seem like she was calling him out as a bald-faced liar, her disbelief made him take a closer look at himself.

"What?"

"That you didn't see human beings, just categories. That you never really got to know people, just assessed their type and relied on that general assessment to forge your attitudes."

"Well, I don't suppose in every case."

Gloria tried to be helpful. "Maybe you were only that way around girls or people you were trying to impress."

They were pretty much one and the same, Biggie didn't tell Gloria. "You're probably right. But do you see my point, Gloria? I missed the little things, details, nuances. Sure, I knew the sun gave off warmth and light, that the Earth and fuck-all revolved around it once a year, the general info kind of crap, but not the way the sun played off the puddles on our front porch after the rain. It's like I didn't *need* to know stuff like that."

"And now you do?"

Biggie wondered. Now that he thought about it, he wasn't even sure he wanted to be a guy who always walked around noticing things like the way the sun played off the puddles on the front porch after the rain.

It seemed like it could take a lot of time. What if you just wanted to go from point A to point B? "More than before."

"But it seems so pretentious to notice things like that all the time," Gloria said, "like you exist on a higher plane of consciousness than everybody else. There are people at school who are like that. Stan Weinberg. Liz Catrady."

Stan Weinberg and Liz Catrady were the biggest druggies at HPHS. They probably *were* on a higher level of consciousness than everybody else. While Biggie himself had never taken drugs, it had always been because he thought it might screw up his training, or that once he started he might never stop ("You remember Bluestone?" "The wrestler?" "Yeah, freaked out.") or, when he thought of it that way, because he didn't want people going around *saying* Biggie had freaked out, whether he had *actually* freaked out or not. He wasn't even sure *what* "freaked out" meant, other than that Wetzel was saying it all the time about one guy or another who'd once shown promise. But Biggie had never thought of not taking drugs because it would make him seem pretentious. "Do you think I'm pretentious?"

"No," she said immediately.

"Why not?" Lately it seemed to Biggie that all he had were pretensions, like being the greatest wrestler in the history of the world. Then there was his very persona of Killer Kowalski, who wasn't just a rough customer but had to be the meanest wrestler who ever lived. Nothing less would satisfy Biggie. That's when he wasn't praising himself for being so down-to-earth.

"Because you lift weights two hours a day and run ten miles a day and practice another ninety minutes at school and walk around breathing wrestling every fucking second."

How did she know that? In fact—not that the "every second" part was literally true—Biggie had been pretty afraid to let her know that, when you got down to it, despite all that stuff about his psyche and inner feelings he was always letting her in on, he *was* pretty much all about wrestling. *A dumb fuck, running, lifting, wrestling bastard.* Not that the inner feelings and probe-the-psyche stuff was a lie—when he did lie to her, which wasn't often, more likely exaggerations such as, "I never see human beings, just categories," she had a way of being all over him in ten seconds flat—but that it shined a light on things he'd never bothered to take a close look at, and sometimes didn't quite recognize what he saw. It seemed to Biggie now that while wrestling was all he was about in a nutshell—there wouldn't *be* a nutshell without wrestling—it wasn't the entire shell. "And I'm undefeated and unscored upon," Biggie said, regretting it immediately, not only because he feared that saying it—as opposed to thinking it a dozen times a day—might be the kiss of death, but that it sounded sort of pretentious when said aloud, like Biggie was at best idly boasting, at worst spewing a pack of self-serving lies.

"They don't really see the sun in the rain puddles every second. They just want you to think they do. While you, Dan Bluestone, really are undefeated."

"And unscored upon."

"Do you ever think about falling in love?"

Biggie stayed up at night thinking about Gloria, the specific vision of the oval face he stared at every afternoon after walking her to The Sergeant, not the general concept with its stereotypical assumptions reduced and shriveled to human size. But the words that came to mind, the product of half-hour-long rummages through his frame of refer-ence—the qualities beginning to define her in his imagination—had not much to do with the actual vision of the specific face that materialized before him in the dark. It was unclear to Biggie, too, if the qualities made Gloria pretty, or if her being so pretty made her these things.

Having Gloria's face to anchor his dreams, everything became clearer. And murkier, also. For example, Biggie thought it was a pretty rotten deal that he had two parents who practically devoted every second of their lives to making him feel great, as well as one sister who laughed at everything he said and pretty much found him to be asinine, though he knew she loved him anyway, if for no other reason than on general principle; for about eighteen years he had all these people working overtime in a single-minded quest to boost his spirits, and then Gloria Serpentino comes around and in forty-eight hours not only makes him feel half a foot taller than all these good efforts combined, but also pretty much shows him that on top of everything else, he'd been moping half lost through a murky dream world, untethered and wrong since the day he'd been hatched. In comparison, everything they'd done for him was the work of amateurs, well-intentioned but incompetent. When he looked at it that way, it made him feel unappreciative of Mom and Dad and Giselle, and everybody else he'd ever met in the murk who'd done nothing but be nice to him. He would feel even worse if he weren't feeling ten feet tall from Gloria.

"Here's what I think," Biggie said. "You may not want to know this about me, Gloria—" Biggie had already gotten into the habit of prefacing certain remarks to Gloria, as if warning her of dastardly realities to follow.

"Yes, *caveat emptor*. Thanks for reminding me, Dan."

"The reason I haven't fallen in love is that I've been afraid wrestling might get lost in the shuffle." Was that true? Biggie found himself saying things to her that, while intended to bare his soul, sparked more smoke than heat. Where did he get this stuff? Here, for example. Sure, he didn't want to get distracted and lose focus or anything the way guys did—guys like Wing, perpetually rhapsodizing over Sara Sherman (who wasn't even the one who'd pussy-whipped him)—guys like Wing who weren't earmarked for the State Championship anyway, pussy-whipped or not—but the main reason he didn't go around falling in love with every girl that smiled at him was that there hadn't been too many girls smiling at him, not too many full-blown high school girls anyway. Just

Mat Gals and girls who smiled at everybody—or who were probably smiling at some guy standing behind him. Still, if the stuff he said wasn't 100% true—there were probably dozens of other reasons, too, he didn't go around falling in love all the time, beginning with his being an all-around selfish bastard—it was certainly 100% true that he didn't want to see wrestling get lost in the shuffle.

"What girl who loves you would want to make you lose focus on wrestling, your dream, Dan? I don't get what you're saying. It doesn't make sense."

"You're right, Gloria. It's paranoia pure and simple."

"You're shy, Dan; I'll bet that's why you haven't fallen in love. But I didn't ask you why. I asked if you ever thought about falling in love. So: Do you ever think about falling in love?"

"I don't know." What startled Biggie more than anything else he'd said to Gloria—out of the mouths of babes, as Gloria told him once about some savvy insight her little sister Vicky shot out with—is that this was about the truest thing he'd told her yet.

"I think about it all the time," Gloria said, for *once*—to Biggie's relief—not taking him to task for his answers but providing one of her own. Which wasn't really true, Biggie thought, correcting the notion simultaneously upon perceiving it—another Bluestone Specialty he'd filled her in on—because she answered plenty of questions.

"I like that about you," Biggie said.

"What else do you like about me?" Gloria asked the next night. Biggie was on the bed in the same position, though *Tea for the Tillerman* played on his hi-fi, rather than the *Hair* soundtrack. By now he was only three pounds over. Saturday afternoon they'd wrestle Niles North, their last dual meet before Districts, and the extra slice of wheat bread he'd had with dinner—atop the grapefruit, salad, half-bottle of Fresca—made the acids surge in his stomach and his thighs inflate to double-size; he prickled sharply, under siege from within, when he wasn't feeling like he was pushing a wheelbarrow with one brick too many, the whole pile ever on the verge of toppling.

"Everything," Biggie said. "And you me?"

"Not everything."

"Wha?" Biggie exhaled, not surprised exactly, though not what he wanted to hear.

"Because I don't know everything about you. But Dan, I will."

It sounded to Biggie more like a threat than a promise. He liked that about Gloria.

They also talked about matters beyond the revelations of their inner psyches and nascent affections. Gradually, in fact, their topics had a literal agenda. Here, it seemed odd to Biggie, since they'd read each other's hearts as clearly as they dared, they didn't read each other's words and inflections clearly at all. "What do you mean by that?" Biggie might suddenly blurt when Gloria criticized a teacher he liked.

"That's your view but you're missing my point," Gloria might say back.

"That's your opinion."

"That's *your* opinion."

And for a moment Biggie would fear his life had spun back to square one, and then Biggie would laugh—or Gloria would—as if they'd staged the entire misunderstanding for their mutual amusement.

It seemed to Biggie, lying back on his bed, under siege from within, they understood each other even when they misfired. Especially then, when he thought about it.

With Districts approaching right after Niles North, *misfiring* wasn't a luxury Biggie could afford. Not now. But if he misfired, he'd catch the bullet and straighten its course.

Districts. All his life, when he'd dreamed about wrestling in Districts senior year, then Sectionals after taking Districts, then State after taking Sectionals, he'd pictured how nervous he would be. He knew the butter-flies would eat him alive. Even as an eighth grader, contemplating how it would be, one loss, one loose move away from not winning State, which would be intolerable, rendering his whole life until then a failure or a lie.

It wasn't just Biggie who suffered from District Madness during the week before their last dual, Niles North. Even Wing Terrill—who was no more likely to make it through Districts into Sectionals than Sara Sherman was to confess a decade-long fixation on Wing's ass—who hadn't spent, Biggie would bet, ten seconds of his middle school years throbbing with anxiety over how nervous he'd be when the time finally came senior year—Jesus, Wing probably never expected to wrestle var-sity— even *Wing* was glum and sullen during practice all week, grim and determined, a new Wing, whose transformation Biggie would have found startling if the guy wasn't lousy as ever on the mat when actually wrestling. The intensity on his face altered, but not his intensity on the mat; that was Wing, sobered with Districts right around the corner.

"When's the draw coming out? When's the draw coming out?" Wing kept asking Biggie, as if *Bluestone* administered the District draw. Same case could be made for Luigi Cravi. Even Jerry Bray stopped hopping around the wrestling room like a maniac, the fake hustle thinned out and sobered by the gravity of the looming occasion. Guys like Mandel and Hatch and Pelligrini would lean back against the wall during their breaks between drills, fixing their thousand-yard stares on points unknown. They were afraid of Districts, the way most soldiers—this Biggie read in History class—were afraid of combat. And the ones who weren't afraid—this was also on the books, a matter of record—were nuts.

Biggie was nuts. No two ways about it, driven insane by Districts coming up so soon. He was nuts all week going to his classes, walking down the hallway, no longer standing against the corridor wall passing time; he'd walk from one class to another and, if he had his way, wouldn't stay for the class but pace through the building like a watchman with a compulsion disorder. He was nuts during practice—nothing new there—nuts walking home, nuts pushing the pace on his nocturnal run, nuts not while talking to Gloria Serpentino every night but afterward, lying in bed replaying the conversations, supplying amendments and addendums to what he'd said, reports he'd submit during tomorrow's conversation as he walked her from the back door of Highland Park High School to the head shop on Vine. By now it seemed—ever since Mary Wellington died, really—he was operating on pure adrenaline. He couldn't sleep; he'd try, but sleep seemed a waste of time. Practice was (Biggie figured) not a waste of time, but practice wasn't Districts, either. Running and lifting and hoisting himself dizzy on the chinup bar wasn't a waste of time, but wasn't Districts either, where it would all pay off. Talking to Gloria Serpentino—here's what Biggie thought while thrashing around in bed the Friday night before Niles North after talking to her, something he'd reluctantly admit only here or if a car pulled over as he ran the streets and the driver, in the guise of innocently asking for directions, pointed a gun to the wrestler's face and demanded to know point-blank if talking to Gloria Serpentino, too, was a waste of time on the absolute scale of everything not actively Districts being a waste of time—*yes*, though it tore out Biggie's heart to concede it, that was the madness. And for the first time since he knew he was falling for her, not the abstract combination of faces generating further abstract concepts but the actual Gloria Serpentino, Biggie Bluestone, thrashing around in bed, feared he was letting her down.

—◇—

Niles North, Friday, February 5

The seniors addressed the squad. Their hands enjoined in the huddle, offering both prayer and rumination before the final dual meet of their high school careers. "We're a team," Jerry Bray said. "That's what I'll always remember about us. We're a true team."

Mandel took his turn. "We never gave up. Not one of us ever gave up."

"We're the Highland Park Little Giants," Luigi Cravi added.

Everybody nodded; Luigi's observation bespoke sagacious implications it might take years to tease out.

"There's a lot of love in this locker room," Wing contributed. "It's no coincidence. As Jerry said, we're a team."

"That's right. That's right, Wing."

"We leave our hearts on the mat," Blake promised. "That's what we do."

"We don't save it for the prom."

"Our blood and our sweat, too. Our tears."

As co-captain, Biggie spoke last since Bray went first. He looked around the circle into the grim eyes. "We'll put on a representative performance."

Suddenly leaping into the air, Bray shouted, "Go! Go! Go! Go! We're Little Giants!"

It seemed to Biggie now he should say something about Mary Wellington, suggesting they dedicate the meet to her, but amidst the high spirits and jubilation—the team was set to burst through the wall to take on Niles North—he couldn't see working in the somber dedication.

They all joined Bray's chant. As if they were charging onto Soldier's Field against the Packers, the Little Giants hustled through the high school locker room door into the gym, onto the mats to the inevitable smattering of applause. Nonetheless they proceeded with a furious flurry of calisthenics led by Bray in the middle.

"'We'll put on a representative performance,'" Wing said to Biggie as they leaned into the mats for the final stretching before introductions. "What's that supposed to mean?"

"Representative of *what*?" Cravi asked.

"The same shitty way we've wrestled all season," Wing guessed.

"Typical Bluestone," Cravi added.

For all the grim, battle-hardened determination they'd shown all week and in the inspirational circle, it surprised Biggie that they *did* put on a representative performance against Niles North. All season the team had been flat and erratic. So it went today in the final meet before Districts. Teagarden at 98, the first out on the mat, starting the show, setting the pace, was even flatter than usual, as if in screaming, "Go! Go! Go!" then bursting through the locker room doors as if taking the beachhead at Anzio, the steam evaporated. Same with Pelligrini at 105. Biggie wished the team *would* settle into a representative performance, a carbon copy of every other match they'd wrestled all year.

For once, his wish was granted. The precisely same old same old unfurled before Bluestone's eyes. Guys who usually won, won; the others lost. The ones who liked to hold on and stall it out performed to exact formula, as did the others who shot a bevy of takedowns and whipped in their half nelsons the instant they hit the mat, counters be damned.

Representative.

If they wanted to see the representative Biggie, they'd better look fast. He never had a match like this in his life. It was as if the representative dimension infused the wrestler with a long view, and he watched himself now through a double-long range telescope, crossing the mat, a distinct figure in slow motion. If you thought Bluestone was going sentimental, seduced by the madness, this his last match ever on the Highland Park mat before the Highland Park fans and the wrestling cheerleaders minus Mary Wellington, dressing in the goddam Highland Park locker room, the last time, piecing together that it amounted to the best time of his life, ever since sophomore year when he first wrestled varsity and could thus believe when he walked through the Highland Park halls pretty girls saw something other than a dreaming kid scratching his butt, a sheet of toilet paper stuck to his heel, you wouldn't know it if you watched him through the double-long range telescope. Biggie *wanted* it to be in slow motion, wanted to savor, but the guy tied him up, Biggie shoved him away as if shooing a fly, shot and caught the guy's heel as he moved backward—a move you usually made when the guy came *toward* you with his momentum, but this was Biggie Bluestone, representative, who'd read the book back to front—knocked out the other leg, normal single, automatically found the angle the split second they hit the mat—he could almost hear the guy whisper to himself in slow motion, from the other end of the telescope, "Here it comes, goddam, shit, fuck, crap, Bluestone's got me here"—rolled him for the quick pin. Thirty-seven seconds.

After his shower and toweling off and dressing, Biggie sat in front of his locker trying to feel sentimental. Last home meet. Bray, Wing, Cravi, Mandel, and Hatch also hung around, sitting in front of their lockers on the benches, staring at the floor.

Last home meet. Shit. It's over. Biggie tried to get himself worked up.

It reminded him too much of the last game of the football season. The team was awful—two wins all year—but the top guys—the quarterback Rory Pruskin; the halfback, none other than Jerry Bray—sobbed like abandoned toddlers as they got out of their uniforms for the last time. Biggie tried to get upset then, too—last home game. Christ. Shit. There go the fucking dreams—and kept trying as he'd solemnly nodded good-bye and walked through the doors of Plank Field for the last time, and was still trying when—according to Wing, who stuck around longer, consoling Pruskin and Bray through the emotional crisis—the wrestler was heard from two blocks away, laughing his head off.

"Next week Districts," he said to the circle of solemn seniors. While this was an incontrovertible statement of fact, Biggie felt guilty for pointing it out. It was like telling the guy he'd just pinned in thirty-seven seconds, "See you again in the State finals." Most of these guys were going to lose in Districts, first round. You didn't have to rub it in. Only Bray and probably Mandel and maybe Luigi would qualify for Sectionals; something Biggie himself had never done. Now here he was, taunting them for their imperfections.

"Districts," Bray said, raising his fist in the air, shaking it at his co-captain,

"Districts." Wing raised his fist.

One by one they went around the solemn circle shaking their fists defiantly. "Districts! Districts!"

There wasn't much else to say. Districts next week. Nothing was over yet.

"You guys are my *family*." Luigi looked at Wing and Biggie as they rose from the bench and extended his fist. Wing placed his fist atop Luigi's. Then Biggie placed his fist atop Wing's in the totem pole, overwhelmed to find it welcome.

By then Bray caught on and conjoined his fist with the others, atop Biggie's, followed by Mandel's fist atop Bray's and Hatch's atop Mandel's fist.

The moment was still nice, certainly worth getting worked up over, but with Bray's co-captaining-by-the-number commitment it became less of a sentimental memory and considerably more like an official team function, like being issued a jock strap.

Afterward Luigi and Wing went to Virginia's. Bray and Mandel and Hatch included themselves for the first time all year.

"I'll meet you later," Biggie told the group.

"Last home meet and he won't come along!" Luigi shrieked. That was Luigi for you. Family.

"Sentimental guy that Bluestone," Pete Hoffman grinned. Last week he'd been admitted to Yale. You'd think he'd be satisfied without launching the sarcasm bomb.

"Biggie has to call Gloria Serpentino," Mandel said, as if reading the bus schedule to a senior citizen's tour group.

Dad was in the living room reading the paper, stretched out in his favorite chair, a green Saarinen that was a wedding gift from Biggie's grandmother.

Biggie often wondered if his dad read every last article, or if for him reading the paper was like listening to music was for Biggie sometimes as he drove the Dart up Sheridan Road, his mind wandering, usually drifting toward winning the State Championship. But at least you could talk to Dad while he read the paper, you could carry on complete conversations as he went from story to story, Dad letting you carry the load but sometimes offering salient observations if salient observations were called for. And if you quizzed him on the stories he was reading—to test if he was really paying attention—his dad would provide a pretty thorough analysis of damn near every story in the paper, including the stuff he'd read contemporaneously with offering the salient observations. Whereas Biggie pretty much appreciated it if everyone would shut up so he could concentrate.

"Last home meet?" his dad said as Biggie walked past.

"And not a day too soon," Biggie said.

Dad had a way of looking at Biggie, tilting his head slightly, minutely raising his brows, as if the adjustment of his head position might help him to better process what his son said. "Is the State Tournament what it's all about, Biggie?"

His dad could go days without talking to you beyond the daily bulletins, then pick the moment when you're charging downstairs to call Gloria Serpentino for initiating an in-depth discussion.

"Same story. It comes down to how you do in the State Tournament. If—when—I take State the offers will fly in. That's what they say, anyway. And they're seldom wrong," Biggie added.

Dad nodded. "You're determined to wrestle in college, then?"

"Wha? Sure."

"Coach Gosley wrote to you?"

Dad knew very well Coach Gosley wrote to him, if you count a scrawled, "Give me a call. Come down for a visit," beneath a form letter as writing. That letter had come last week, along with ones from Western Michigan and Minnesota, all form letters, in addition to the form letters he'd previously received from Illinois and Indiana. Yet another form letter, delivered to Coach Wetzel at the high school, though addressed to Dan Bluestone, came in from Northern Illinois, where Gloria was going, a development Bluestone was alternately ashamed and relieved that he hadn't yet filled her in on.

In addition to tilting his head slightly and raising his brows when you were being cryptic, Dad had this way—Biggie was beginning to see it more as strategy than mannerism—of restating things you already told him, asking a second time out of genuine interest, as if that might spur you on to tell him things you hadn't revealed, even to yourself, because you didn't want to go around repeating stuff you'd already told him or had otherwise committed a stance about. "If you call it *writing*. I showed you the letter."

"I could call Coach Gosley if you wish." Dad looked openly at Biggie, as if the option were worth considering.

That's another thing Biggie figured he really needed. Maybe Mom would pick up the receiver and add her two cents' worth. ("In addition to being a fine wrestler, Mr. Gosley, you'll be interested to hear that Biggie's a good boy."). He was touched that his father wanted to help, but that's just not the way you landed wrestling scholarships at Big Ten schools. It kind of annoyed Biggie that this was something he needed to point out.

The odd thing was Dad probably *could* call up Gosley, and Gosley would talk to him, what with being a hotshot professor at Northwestern, as famous around campus as Gosley. *Technically*, it was just as likely Gosley had a kid who wanted to major in sociology at Northwestern, and that very instant Gosley was offering to call Sanford Bluestone on his son's behalf. It might tip the scales, all things being equal, if Coach Gosley knew his old man was a top guy on campus, too, though Biggie still had a hard time imagining they gave those kinds of considerations much weight. You didn't get to be a top ten wrestling program by going out of your way to recruit a bunch of professors' kids.

Christ, they'd probably hold that against him.

"Thanks for offering, Dad, but I wish you wouldn't. You know. Not now anyway. Plus, with winning State, these things take care of themselves. It would be better if I worked it that way."

Dad appeared to think it over. "You'll let me know?"

"Is that you Biggie?" Mom asked now from the hallway as she walked into the living room. She was dressed in the robe she always wore before getting dressed up to go out for the evening. Dad pretty much wore a suit at all times. In Biggie's observation he was *always* ready to go out, or be called to the lectern. Sometimes Mom didn't remind Dad in advance that they had plans, she just walked into the living room and told him she was ready. "Are we going somewhere?" he'd hear Dad ask from downstairs. The problem with always being ready to go out, though, if Dad was any indication, was that you tended to spend half your life waiting around the living room for Mom to be ready. Or you started getting ready at the same time as Mom, though you could have waited an hour to get ready and you'd still end up waiting. Biggie wondered if this was something

Dad knew about Mom before they got married, or was it just part of the "for better or worse" deal.

"I'm Giselle. Biggie's downstairs."

"Don't be sarcastic with your mother," Dad said, as if he just might call Gosley if Biggie didn't change his caustic ways.

"It's an honest joke."

"Great match, Biggie." Mom kissed Bluestone on the forehead to congratulate him. His parents had been up there in the stands with Cravi's parents, the moms nattering away, both dads wishing they were somewhere else but being good sports about it, happy to indulge in the family activity. "You were really wonderful."

"As always," Dad added from the Saarinen. "My son the wrestler."

"Biggie, how are you?" Mom asked.

That was another thing about his parents that was enough to give you a complex. Every time he turned around, they wanted to know how he was. "Terrific."

"Can you talk for a moment, please?" Mom sat on the couch next to Dad's green Saarinen.

He sat down in the black easy chair across the living room and waited. He crossed his legs and folded his arms, then unfolded his arms and leaned forward, forearms on knees. As inconvenient as these discussions were, Biggie liked them and would like them a lot more if they didn't usually result in his going to Camp Herzl for four weeks, or having to be about a thousand times more fastidious about taking out the garbage.

"We haven't talked much lately," Mom began. "With everything that's been going on with Giselle—"

"I haven't felt ignored, if that's what you're wondering."

"You knew Mary Wellington, too," Dad said.

"It's okay. I mean it's not okay that she's dead, of course, but I'm really okay, under the circumstances."

Dad nodded. "Is there anything you'd like to talk about?"

"No." Biggie shrugged. "Thanks for asking, though. I mean that."

Dad closed his hands together and smiled. "Well, okay."

That was Dad, happy to cut to the chase, then get back to the paper.

The thing was, Biggie suspected this wasn't really what he was doing. Not that they weren't interested—Biggie was certain there was nothing that interested them more than how he or Giselle was doing—it meant a thousand times more to them than how they were doing themselves—but the way it went with these discussions, his parents always began talking about one thing before they got around to their real interest. They'd ask him about school, bring out nuances and subtleties, before, just when Biggie thought he was home free, cutting to Herzl or his lackadaisical approach to the garbage. Even when Biggie *knew* it was coming, he managed not to see it coming. While he knew they were playing him like a puppet, it always worked. The stuff they told him to do flat out without setting him up with the diversionary tactics he had this way of categorizing as advisory, not required.

"Have you talked to Giselle?"

"Did she say I said something?" When you grew up with Giselle as your sister, a lot of distorted accusations had this way of being thrown in your face. "I didn't do anything."

"We know you didn't do anything."

"We thought perhaps you had the chance to talk to Giselle," Dad said.

"I guess."

"And have you talked to her?" Mom asked.

"Is this some kind of psychological ploy?" That would be yet another proclivity about his mom, the school social worker. The wrestler often had the impression she was trying out her psychological theories and stratagems on him before setting them loose on the general enrollment of Evanston High School.

Whenever he asked her that question, which was weekly, his mom had this way of laughing reassuringly, as if Biggie was the most perceptive kid on the planet. They didn't ask for much. Sometimes Biggie felt guilty his parents didn't have a kid like Pete Hoffman, who really was a smart guy. He figured you could torture his mom for hours and she'd never admit, even to herself, that she'd want any other son than the one she had (Biggie), but you had to think that if a genuinely smart, perceptive kid like Hoffman were her son, Mom would walk around in a perpetual state of satisfaction and mirth.

Dad wouldn't exactly mind, either. In fact, when Biggie was younger, before his dad sort of accepted that Biggie was more inclined toward the mat than mathematical conundrums, there were times he'd thought that if you tortured Dad—not right away, but maybe after the third day—he'd break down and *admit* he'd rather have a son like Hoffman, if not Professor Pete Hoffman himself.

"Anyway," Biggie was saying, "how am I supposed to talk to Giselle? She's always off in her room or away with Lauren Gelfin or doing whatever she does when she's not in her room or off with Lauren. Listening to records, I guess. The only time I see her is in the morning when we drive to school. Have you ever tried talking to Giselle in the morning?"

Mom smiled and nodded. Bluestone might have felt like he was in Mom's office, subject to her prompting, were she not in her bathrobe and hairnet.

"He has a point," Dad conceded.

"Not that I'm so great to talk to in the morning."

"He has a point there, too."

"It would be nice if you talked to her," Mom said.

"What exactly am I supposed to talk to her about? If I ever catch her in, that is."

Now Mom frowned. He took this for another psychological ploy.

"Giselle's always looked up to you," Dad said.

"Sure."

Dad looked at Mom now to continue. He'd done his best with the block of granite.

"She's been having a terrible time," Mom said. "Did you know she's been cutting her classes? She screams at her friends. Biggie, your sister's spending hours at a time crying in her room. Have you noticed that?"

"That I've noticed."

"Mr. Anderson called yesterday." Mr. Anderson was the school counselor, a colleague of sorts of Mom's. Freshman year he'd often had this image of Mom and Mr. Anderson huddled together, conspiring against him, but Anderson really was a pretty nice guy the two times Biggie actually met him, which was last year when a group of juniors got together to discuss college plans, after which Anderson announced he'd be writing them each a letter of recommendation based upon his impressions, a biographical sketch he'd like them to submit, and their record.

"I hope you mean my *wrestling* record," Biggie remembered interjecting.

Mr. Anderson had looked at Biggie and smiled slightly, awaiting elaboration.

The one guy within the town limits of Highland Park who didn't know he was a wrestling big shot was the guy who'd be writing his letter of recommendation.

"What did old Anderson have to say?"

"*Mr.* Anderson," Dad reprimanded.

"He said you always look like you're a thousand miles away, but then you say something that shows you've been there all along," Mom said proudly.

That was probably the nicest thing anybody from that high school had ever said about him, any adult anyway, besides Coach Wetzel, who was always saying nice things about him to the Highland Park *Life*. Still, from the way Mom beamed at the recollection, you'd think it was the highest praise imaginable. He wondered how excited she'd get if she had a son who was not only right there all along, but looked it.

"That's what everyone likes to say," Biggie said. "That I'm a thousand miles away. If I go to college at Lehigh or someplace like that"—Lehigh was a big wrestling college in Pennsylvania—"they'd be right."

"My son the comedian," Dad said.

Mom frowned again. "Biggie, people are saying terrible things about Giselle at school."

"To Giselle?"

Dad nodded. "She's your sister, Biggie. You don't have to say anything, but an awful thing has happened. It would be nice if you, as her brother, talked to her. She'd appreciate it. I'd appreciate it, too. So would your mother."

Before they added that Mr. Anderson would appreciate it, Biggie said he'd talk to Giselle. "Don't blame me if she screams." He stood up.

When he was through talking to his parents Bluestone felt like he was expected to salute before heading downstairs with his marching orders.

Biggie regretted the last crack about Giselle screaming at him. If she was really in such bad shape that *Biggie* had to bail her out, nothing else had worked. After all, his dad was a hotshot sociologist, and Mom worked with troubled kids every day. He didn't even mean it, either, about the screaming. Plenty of times he'd talked to Giselle and she didn't yell at him. As often as not, if you counted as talking such exchanges as, "Pass the potatoes, Giselle." "Did you say please?" "Please." "Okay, Biggie, if you promise not to finish them." "Why not? Because *you* want to finish them?" Christ, probably Giselle thought *he* yelled at *her* all the time.

Biggie called up Gloria Serpentino to file his daily report. "*Another victory on the books. Biggie Bluestone winning by pin,*" Biggie said, as if he were a radio announcer. "Thirty-seven seconds to be precise."

Gloria didn't say anything.

"That's right," Biggie said.

"Dan Bluestone, my hero."

Biggie didn't bristle at the crack, but wondered if such comments could ever get on his nerves. "Yes, your hero. As well I should be."

"How long's the match supposed to go?"

"Six minutes, by the rulebook."

"Does it bother these guys," Gloria said, "when you pin them in thirty-seven seconds?"

"Well sure." Here's another thing Biggie had never told anybody before, if mostly because it was hard to imagine anybody else would want to know. "Back in sophomore year when I first started wrestling varsity, I had to get past feeling sorry for guys when I pinned them, with their girlfriends and everybody watching." While this was true—Biggie distinctly recalled feeling sensitively about guys he'd pinned sophomore year—he'd only pinned two guys all that year. It occurred to Biggie now he might have racked up more pins if he hadn't felt quite so sympathetically about their humiliation. Whatever intimations of guilt he'd felt, he'd gotten over it by junior year, luckily, when he really started to pin people. Now, when he couldn't get a guy to last a minute against him, the thought seldom crossed his mind that he was feeding these guys a dose of public shame. He even had the impression they didn't mind all that much, like it was just part of the game, no better or no worse than any other way to lose—"Can't win 'em all."—that kind of shit you told yourself when you were licking your wounds. Looking at it that way, Biggie felt like a throwback to an earlier era, when guys would sooner die than be pinned. And if they did get pinned—Biggie recalled reading this somewhere—they didn't get a moment's sleep until a string of championships cleansed the stain from memory. Christ, he remembered getting upset—back in middle school—when he'd *read* about guys getting pinned. Thirty-seven seconds? Intolerable.

"I don't know about these guys. Really. Maybe I thought they were like me, back when I felt sorry for them. If a guy pinned you so fast, it was like he could take you in his hand and crush you anytime he wanted. With people watching. He could probably kill you if he wanted to. You'd be at the guy's mercy, even though the guy's your same weight and roughly your age. Humiliating. Maybe there are guys out there who could do that to me, but it's nothing I'd want to know about. And it's not like you have anybody else to blame. Out there on the mat it's dog-eat-dog."

"No beta dog, you."

"I don't know." Beta dog? "I think I'm different from half these guys—maybe all of them but guys like Berkenmeier, Dixon Boyd of North Chicago. Bob Stuth of Deerfield, too—I can sense these guys caving in when I find the angle and slip in the half. Like they know the game's up and so they quit, resigned to their fate. Or they don't want to be hurt so they accept the inevitable. It's a pretty disgusting statement about human nature, when you think about it."

Gloria didn't say anything right away. Biggie could picture her on the other end of the line squinting as she pondered Biggie's latest sweeping utterance. Suddenly, though, the silence was unsettling, so to salvage the insight Biggie added, "Nothing against these guys, Glory. It's just that sometimes I think I'm from an earlier era."

"Yes," Gloria said finally. "You're like one of those Greek philosophers, I guess, doubling as a soldier and a statesman."

"That would be doubling as a soldier, *tripling* as a statesman." Bluestone was suddenly amused with himself. He got that way a lot, which was a pretty good quality, though not one you necessarily admired in others. If you hated somebody, you'd probably hate them doubly if they considered themselves a laugh riot on top of everything else. He decided, since he could never tell when Gloria was ridiculing him, rather than tease out the implications of every syllable, he'd simplify his life by taking her literally. Biggie Bluestone, Philosopher, Soldier, Statesman. A throwback, he suspected that was the era they should throw him back to.

"You're right as always," Gloria reflected.

"Of course, if I *were* around back then, I'm sure I'd find plenty to whine about. Jesus, Gloria, if I were around back then I'd probably be telling everybody I belonged to future times."

"Like 1971?"

"That would be when." Biggie said, "I guess that brings us full circle."

"Dan, can I ask you a question?"

Biggie snickered into the receiver, not so much at Gloria as at himself. Here he was having a serious conversation on the phone, discussing matters he'd never articulated before—possibly matters *nobody* articulated before, though you had to figure if so, it was for good reason—and mostly what he found himself wondering about was whether Gloria was in her room now, talking to him with her clothes off. You didn't want to think she was sitting back in curlers with goobers coming out of her nose. Biggie figured when he was older, his wrestling days over—assuming he wasn't coaching somewhere, or, realistically, a famous guy like an actor or a politician—maybe even a sociologist like Dad—he'd do well to land one of those jobs where you spoke on the phone all the time. That way if he ever got bored and there was a woman on the other end of the line, he could picture the woman with her clothes off. The problem was, half the women out there you wouldn't want to see with their clothes off. With his luck, when he dialed up and some woman answered on the other end, it would always be one of those who sounded like you really wouldn't want to see her naked, who sounded like she was leaning back in curlers with goobers coming out. Now, though, Biggie promised himself if he ever got into that situation, no matter what the woman sounded like on the other end, he'd always picture Gloria Serpentino. She'd be his saving grace. "Can you ask me a question? I don't see what's stopping you."

"I only ask because I know you lift weights and run and think about wrestling every second of the day."

"I think about other things sometimes."

"I know you think about me," Gloria said.

Biggie envisioned Gloria's long hair swaying on the other end as she sits forward naked on her bed. Through the sheaf of her long brown hair he could see the aureoles of her breasts. Bluestone snickered: if he was really different from other guys, it was probably because—at his heart and core—he was more of a pervert than the regular run.

"What are you laughing at, Dan?"

"Did I miss the question you were going to ask?" Biggie wondered.

"Okay, Dan. I know you're all about wrestling and everything—I don't want you to think I don't realize that or don't approve—I like that about you, Dan, that you're dedicated and purposeful—I understand that you're a really strong guy, but why are you so good?"

It's because of my family support, Biggie thought, which made him think suddenly of Giselle, whom he should probably be tracking down right now to sit down and set her straight, if he were half the guy Gloria thought. "What?"

"Why are you such a good wrestler, Dan?"

"Do you mean what drives my motor? Stuff like that?" He almost said *shit* but caught himself. He didn't want to send Gloria the signal that the stuff she wanted to know about was shit. It was stuff. Still, he hoped she didn't want to know about motivation, crap like that. Not that it wasn't important, but sometimes Biggie had the impression people thought stuff about him mainly relating to why he runs the roads and lifts weights and prances across the mat like a maniac. Or if they didn't think *that* about him—it was hard enough to imagine himself ever crossing anybody's mind, except Mom and Dad's and maybe Giselle's every other blue moon, and now Gloria, if he got carried away; you didn't find Berkenmeier thinking about him up in Mundelein—he'd read articles about athletes where they were spread out on the slab and dissected, their least impulse analyzed by some guy who barely knew them and probably had no more insight into human behavior than Jerry Bray, pathologizing them into a quivering mass of inferiority complexes and obsessive compulsions, as if that could explain the first thing.

"No, that's not what I mean," Gloria said.

"I'm twice as strong as anybody, is what it comes down to. In high school that's enough. Next year in college, though, well, that's a different story." Saying this immediately depressed Biggie. Despite the truth of the information, it reminded him about the letter from Northern Illinois he'd not yet mentioned to Gloria, as if, if he'd told her and she insisted he go there—a scholarship was a scholarship—he'd drop all his lifelong plans and fall into line just because she'd batted her eyes, a pretty girl, and asked him. Sheesh. By not telling her, he felt like he was executing a small betrayal, not like he was turning her in to the Red Chinese but as if he were kissing her and dreaming of another woman. Small like that. When Bluestone finally told Gloria—he knew he'd have to—he wondered if he'd cover his butt and pretend he'd gotten the letter that afternoon, his lie yet another betrayal. When he thought about it, the betrayals were piling up at a pretty fast clip considering he'd never kissed her and, when he did try to tease out the meaning of each syllable when she mocked him, wasn't even all that certain she liked him.

"Other guys are strong, Dan. Other guys lift weights and run the roads and practice feverishly; you know that's so. It's more than physical. You must tell yourself things. Dan Bluestone's not the only jock in the state of Illinois. Dan, when you're on the mat what makes you better?"

Biggie tried telling her. "This will sound strange. I wrestle with complete abandon, Gloria. Full intensity, full tilt, that's what I give out there every second. I'm fearless. That's what's different about this year. I mean, a lot of guys leave something in the reserve tank. That way if they lose, they can hold on to their sanity. They can say, 'I lost, sure, got pinned fast,

but I didn't quite have it out there. Another day I'd have handled the ox.'
Or they don't like thinking their next breath might be their last breath.
They don't like their legs turning to rubber, their hearts bursting like a
tire, their lungs shattering to shards. I'm not like that, not this year. If
they take it full tilt one minute, they'll die the next. But I know if I don't
pin the guy in thirty-seven seconds I'll be twice as tough after a minute,
ten times as tough after five—they know it, too. That's why they cave in,
now that I think about it. They know at their core I'll take it to the end
of the road, and they won't. Or can't. But Gloria?"

"Yes, Dan."

"You have to be twice as strong as the other guy to think that way, and
they have to know you're twice as strong." Which is why Killer Kowalski
dressed in pink tights and feathered sequins and hopped around the ring
like a madman, that's what Biggie thought, even if pro wrestling wasn't
any more real than a painting was real, or a foreign film, or the image of
a naked girl on the other end of the line, her aureoles emerging through
her sheaf of thick, swaying brown hair.

"Dan, did you ever take English class from Miss Dall?"

"Sure. Last year."

"I don't know if I should say this."

"That's okay. I remember Mom typed up a paper I wrote for Miss
Dall. When I got the paper back right beneath the B- the old bag scrib-
bled, 'Well typed.' That was the praise. Mom felt great about it, anyway.
Plus, you can say anything you want. It's not like *I'm* wearing a muzzle."
Which made Biggie think again about the letter from Northern Illinois
and probably about a thousand other things he wasn't telling her.

"Why do you call her an old bag?" Gloria asked.

"What am I supposed to call her, the 'old thoroughbred'? 'Old #64'?"

"Why can't you call her 'Miss Dall' and leave it at that?"

"There'd be no law against it," Biggie admitted.

"And she's not an old bag."

"Nor is she old #64. See my point?"

"What point?"

"No point," Biggie admitted.

Pointless bastard.

"Miss Dall read us this poem about this boy, Icarus. It's from a Greek myth. Icarus and his father, Daedalus, were being held captive. Daedalus was an inventor, so he made wings out of feathers and glue so that they could fly away. Daedalus warned Icarus not to fly too close to the sun or the glue of his wings would melt. But once he started flying, Icarus became so exuberant that he forgot about his father's warning and soared so high that the sun did melt the glue, his wings fell apart, and he fell into the sea and drowned. This poet thought Icarus was a hero. I still have the poem:

> *Never regret thy fall,*
> *O Icarus of the fearless flight,*
> *For the greatest tragedy of them all*
> *Is never to feel the burning light.*

Why I spend so much time talking to you, why I liked you from the start, Dan, is that you're not scared to fly too close to the sun."

For a second Biggie didn't say anything, then: "I thought it was because I'm a handsome devil."

Now Gloria didn't say anything. For a moment Bluestone pictured her sighing as she gripped the phone. He waited a few more seconds.

Not a handsome devil.

"Thank you," was all Biggie could think to say.

And why I like you is because you noticed, he thought later, and wondered if it were true. She saw things about him he'd never thought about himself. Did it matter if what she saw was true?

He did a long set of pushups, pondering, then walked up to Giselle's room to see if she was around, pondering; he knew if he *wasn't* afraid it was because he was an idiot, or else there was no angle he could play in *admitting* he was afraid, even if to himself only. Pretending he wasn't to others, not that anybody asked—when you played that angle, a thousand cookies crumbled all at once, then a thousand more before you knew what hit you—or because he'd decided—when? he wondered—*if* he lost, he could deal with all that later, *after* he lost—no scholarship and fuck-all to be certain, and nobody looking at him anymore like a legend or myth made flesh walking down the school halls. If they did notice him at all, they'd see him as the conceited bastard whose wings melted—even Mom and Dad might see him as diminished, though they wouldn't admit it to themselves, and Giselle would have a bit less to bray about, a bit less cachet with *her* friends—he liked it that she got a kick out of being his sister—and Gloria? Would Gloria still see Biggie as the guy whose heart feared nothing and soared?

How long had he talked to Gloria? Two hours passed like twenty minutes when he talked to her. Twenty minutes passed like two hours.

If he ever kissed her or licked her breasts or lay under her in the darkness, their clothes off, it would be a bonus, be extra, be gravy and icing and sizzle. That's what Biggie decided lying in his bed. It was his goal, that was true, but it would be in addition, surplus. Bluestone wondered if, when he took State, he'd feel as good as he did in this moment. He would—Christ, he'd feel as he'd never felt before—but this moment must be something like it would be, an intimation of that sensation; though when you thought about it, it wouldn't exactly put a damper on everything if she thought he was a handsome devil, too.

In the middle of the night Biggie woke up, looked around until he could make out the shapes in the dark—his desk, his dresser, his record player—gave a thought to rolling out of bed as long as he was up and tackling the chinup bar before taking a run. A bonus run. For a second,

Bluestone closed his eyes to concentrate, as if cleansing his soul of all thoughts, or to fall back asleep. Biggie pictured Berkenmeier across from him, circling the mat, daring Biggie to shoot so that he could counter. He pictured moving in deep on Berkenmeier's leg, the guy—he could see Berkenmeier's muscles almost rivaling Biggie's own, his blond military crewcut—Berkenmeier was bigger, quicker too—pushing Biggie away, off balance. They hit the mat at an angle.

Biggie thought, "Fuck I'm scared, scared shitless."

Nice that Gloria didn't think so.

The Journals, Saturday, February 6

After his 500 pushups and fifty pullups, Biggie topped off his five-mile run with an extended sprint from Forest. It was another warm day for early February, probably fifty degrees. This being Chicago, you couldn't trust it, though, and everyone Bluestone saw was bundled up as if crossing the Siberian tundra.

If his shoulder throbbed as it usually did when he ran in the mornings ever since the accident, if his knee was killing him, if his groin felt like he'd wrench it in two with his next step, according to the laws of general principle, this was all shit you can't notice, or that's all you'd ever notice. Biggie fumbled with his keys at the door, showered, tackled a grapefruit sprinkled with saccharine and half a Fresca, won a long stare-down with an Oreo, then walked down the hall to Giselle's room to set her straight.

Nobody there.

His parents weren't around either—they were at a luncheon at the Palmer House downtown, as Mom reminded him with a note on the counter, including the directive to take the garbage out by the time they return. Biggie wished they were here, so he could tell them that if he were going to talk to Giselle—if he *had* to, per their order—if Giselle herself *wanted* him to—the least she could goddam be was *around*.

He looked back into the living room, pictured Berkenmeier slightly off balance, one foot jutting out of alignment, driving in and lifting the leg before Berkenmeier could respond, kicking out the other leg, hitting the mat at an angle, the image so real Biggie was disappointed to find that he wasn't driving for a pin in the State Championship at Assembly Hall downstate in Champaign, in front of 15,000, but was standing in his living room, walking toward his sister's bedroom to see if she's there but not answering.

Halfway down the hall Biggie heard the mailman, then turned an abrupt 180 and charged out to the porch in his gym shorts and t-shirt. He approached the mail as always with an acute jolt of expectation. If most days the mail brought nothing, no Eastern Illinois, no Wisconsin-Parkside, certainly no Northwestern, after an instant's disappointment he'd double his expectations for tomorrow's delivery.

Dad was good for about a dozen letters and sociology journals a day; Mom was always writing involved correspondences with everybody she's ever known. Even *if* Biggie got a letter, it could be hours before it emerged from the pile. On the bottom of the pile today was an envelope on Northwestern stationary, the name *Roy Gosley* above the insignia.

Biggie stared at the envelope a moment, holding it aloft, as if contemplating a delicate artifact. He fought the impulse to rip open the envelope. He remembered once ripping open a letter from his uncle, in his haste tearing his $50 bar mitzvah check in two. While his uncle was happy to replace it, the incident didn't quite confirm to one and all that Biggie'd turned the subtle corner into manhood. Biggie walked into his dad's study, found the silver letter opener—about a thousand years old, his parents' wedding gift from a distant cousin that Bluestone had spent half his boyhood dreaming was the original sword of Zorro—took a deep breath, gently scraped the silver opener beneath the seal, then pulled back the flap without tearing the works in two.

Dan:

We've been following your impressive progress closely and congratulate you on your outstanding senior season. We hope you're still keeping the Northwestern Wildcats in mind for your college plans!

Best of luck in the state tournament.

Roy Gosley

Beneath the type, Coach Gosley scribbled, "*It was nice seeing you earlier this year. Don't hesitate to call.*" Enclosed with the letter Biggie fished out a wrestling brochure and another brochure, *Northwestern: A Big Ten Experience*, extolling the singular virtues of the place.

Biggie read the letter again, then twice more.

You spend half your life waiting for a letter, one day it comes, you take the deep breath, refrain from tearing it open—treating the fucker like an artifact—delicately negotiate its flap, then it turns out the thing was written by a *Xerox* machine. How was he supposed to take the last sentence, anyway? "Best of luck at the State Tournament." Just a "Hi Biggie, we'll take a look when the tests come back."

He walked back to the living room, then placed it with the rest of the mail atop the coffee table. Bluestone took a final look at the letter, shook his head, then walked down the hallway into Giselle's room.

When she didn't respond to his knock he opened the door.

Back in middle school, if he walked into Giselle's room without permission and she'd find out about it, she'd erupt until Mom and Dad rushed in like you'd committed a felony—which it would be, Biggie conceded now, assuming she wasn't your sister and it wasn't your house and Giselle herself couldn't be found poking around in *your* room all the time, and you'd walked out of the room with an armful of items. Then Dad, after waiting for Giselle to settle down, would deliver a stern lecture—even if Giselle overreacted, it was hard to argue you'd gotten lost and after desperately wandering found yourself there, thumbing through her records—with Mom shaking her head, you'd let her down once again. ("And one more misstep, Buster, you'll find yourself in juvenile detention.") Well, Biggie couldn't recall any such times, not at the moment. In the last year or so, the rules had changed. If you wanted to borrow a pencil or an album without asking, she didn't make a federal case out of it, unless she caught you reading her diary.

Her *diary*? Did Giselle keep a diary anymore? *Dear Diary, this is Giselle.* When she was a little girl, she kept her diary under lock and key when not pressed to her heart. Had she outgrown that? Biggie wondered, wandering around her messy room.

Back then, Giselle had this way of assuming that if you were a human being, you'd sacrifice your first-born to get your hands on her diary. He remembered years ago passing Giselle's room *en route* to Mom and Dad's and seeing his sister lying on her bed contemplating the pages of the small booklet before deliberately, then furiously, applying pen to paper, but with such a peaceful look on her face that it wouldn't cross his mind that she was about to accuse him of anything.

What had happened to that little girl? Sometimes when he thought about Giselle, what he still saw was the little girl with the peaceful expression. He stood in the middle of her room and wondered if he was being fair. Nobody thought of Biggie now the way they thought of him back then. (He'd been an earnest kid with a thousand questions he needed answered *now*. On the other hand, he wasn't big on being imposed upon himself, quick to turn sullen. (Biggie saw that *that* much of his character had emerged unscathed.)) If he wasn't always the strongest kid in his class—dating back to the morning in the sixth grade he'd fallen out of bed into a pushup stance, that was the official memory, but before then also—people would have swatted him away as they would a gnat.

Jesus, if he didn't have a sister who, when they weren't busy thwarting each other's every move, laughed at everything he said back then, he'd be curled into the fetal position right now, gnawing on his arm.

Suddenly the wrestler was overwhelmed by this image of his little sister reading her diary, not crying in her room, not leaving the house for hours at a stretch whenever she could, excited about joining the Brownie Scouts, later founding the Mat Gals, before people at school said things, at peace with her world. He couldn't pretend, either, that this was average crap that she was going through and shrug it off philosophically, like wondering if your pimples disgusted everybody within a hundred-mile radius.

Biggie quietly left Giselle's room and walked down the hall toward the front door to look outside. Maybe in a past life he'd been a spy? He'd gone through a stage as a small child when he'd ask his dad every ten minutes if they'd had any relatives who were spies. A famous one, a guy Biggie could identify with and model his behavior? None that Dad knew of, it turned out. That was the problem with being Jewish—your ancestors were never spies and cowboys but dressmakers and rabbis. Biggie coughed and walked loudly back to Giselle's room, wishing he had a table to knock over or a can to kick. He'd whistle if it didn't make him feel so ridiculous. Christ, he wasn't *spying*, he was being a big brother. Without knocking over the lamp and the pile of books he opened the chest of drawers by her bed.

What was he supposed to do about it if people were saying things to her, as Mom said? Throw them against the wall? If there was some guy she was in love with, for example, what was he supposed to do, track the guy down? If so, should he warn the guy away or encourage him? The problem with having a sister was, if she was in a mess, you wanted to go around cleaning up the mess, just for general purposes. It wasn't the same thing as hearing about other people's messes. You had to make a big deal about it. That was the system. Because you couldn't just *know*, you didn't want to know. When you thought about it, it also came down to being a lazy bastard, too. So you didn't spend a lot of time investigating her thoughts and feelings.

Still, Biggie knelt by Giselle's night table, thumbing through the pile of notebooks he found in the drawers, where he knew they'd be. There was other stuff in the drawers, too, but with the other stuff, he made a point of not looking.

In the notebooks, mostly, there were passages about crap she did with her friends, speculations about whether guys would say "Hi" to them or acting like they didn't care if the guy did, or passages about whether or not guys—girls, too—were acting like they were on drugs. Endless speculations about whether somebody liked somebody. Jesus. In one section Giselle mentioned something about having a crush on Jim Durkee, who was a guy two years ahead of *Biggie*. It seemed pretty unlikely—Durkee being such an older guy as well as something of a hick—but he had to figure Giselle wasn't entirely dreaming this stuff up. This particular passage was from two years ago when Giselle was a freshman. Biggie didn't read on for fear she'd actually *gone out* with Durkee or whatever you did when you were fourteen; not only didn't he want to hear about it, but *if* he heard about it he'd probably have to track Durkee down at Western Illinois or Silo Tech or wherever the hick Durkee was going to school these days and call him to account. That was the system, so Biggie moved on to the next notebook.

Reading these notebooks made Biggie happy he didn't go around writing in journals and keeping diaries. Just his luck, if he kept a journal into which he poured every thought, he'd probably die or disappear; then people would read the notebooks, religiously poring over them for clues as to what made him tick. "Gee, that Biggie was sure a dull bastard," they'd say, despite themselves. That's probably why he didn't keep one in the first place, in addition to being a lazy bastard.

On the theory that he didn't have all day before somebody came home to find him on his knees in his sister's room reading Giselle's intimate private reflections—though how secret could they be if they were not under lock and key but piled haphazardly in a drawer anybody could see if they happened to be in her room rifling through her drawers? Biggie rushed to the last notebook, underneath the others at the bottom of the drawer. Here most of the recent entries were short.

Went to the hospital tonight with Lauren. Mary's mom and dad were there. Her sister, Myra, came later. Went to their house afterward for dinner, then went back to the hospital. When it got late the Wellingtons asked us to stay at their house.

And:

Mary had surgery today to relieve the pressure on her brain. They still don't know if she'll live. People at the hospital are nice. I sat in the waiting room with Lauren and Suzy and Jeanette. Everybody talked about Mary then tried not to talk about Mary, then I got really mad nobody was talking about her, then I got mad at myself for getting mad. Lauren yelled at me to shut up.

I'm so scared.

Then there weren't any entries, nothing about when Mary died—for which Biggie was thankful. Nothing about what people said afterward, of the funeral—which Biggie recalled now, an image of himself stalking the place from the midst of his fog wanting to dedicate the State Championship to Mary, with everybody looking at him tolerantly but with (now he senses) the minutest sense of trepidation, as if they were about to be browbeaten by the village idiot. What followed were several blank pages, as if Giselle, sensing the record was incomplete, reserved space to go back and fill in later. After half a dozen empty pages, Biggie found this:

Mary, I always think about when we met. I always think that you would talk to me about my problems, even when we were fighting with each other.

I always think that you'd defend me when Suzy accused me of flirting with Jack Greenblat. I think of the times we cut school and drove into Chicago with Suzy and Missy and talked to these guys at Oak Street Beach. I think about tryouts for wrestling cheerleaders and how mad I was that you made it and I didn't, mostly because I'd have to run Mat Gals without you. I think about Mr. Bender's geometry class when we'd pass notes and laugh so hard Mr. Bender would yell at us, which made us laugh more until he wanted to send us to detention. I remember everything we talked about, every word, about your mom and dad and sister and parents and my parents and brother and everyone we knew, what we thought about everything, and what we liked so much, what we hated. I remember every Friday night and Saturday night, sitting at the table at your house or mine with Lauren and Suzy and Missy and having eating contests.

The entry ended there. Other entries were the same but ending in the middle of a memory, in the middle of a sentence. Sometimes Giselle would mention a single day, picked at random, it seemed, and list seven or eight things they'd done with each other. *Said hi to Jack. Tried to borrow Mom's car to take to Skip Nordick's party. Studied for Geometry. Told Mr. Warnerheim we were born in Albania. Drove by Stuart Blazer's house and shined the lights at his room and honked the horn until his dad ran outside. Got high with Mark and Kirk and Lauren. Called Jamie Hilger a bitch, which she is. Talked on the phone for three hours.*

Often she'd write about driving back to Oak Street Beach way down Lake Shore Drive in Chicago to see if those guys were still there, or to look at the waves. *Mary loved the lake*, Giselle wrote.

He shut the notebook and sat on Giselle's bed and stared at the floor catching his breath. *He* loved the lake. It was a small thing, ordinary, something you probably didn't think to mention too often. You assumed a person loved the lake; it was un-Chicagoan not to. Yet that Mary loved the lake suddenly made him feel a loss that was nearly incalculable. Sitting on Giselle's bed, his stomach churned; oh, he was angry at his insensitivity for never bothering to know that about Mary, for never saying, "Sure, I like the lake too." The commonplace made him feel closer to her in ways he hadn't—and wouldn't have—anticipated, and he found himself wishing she'd loved reading about Xerxes instead, or Persian history. If she were ordinary, she could be anybody; that was the goddam fuck-all. You *wanted* her not to be just anybody, to be unique, special, vital in ways nobody had seen before, but she was just an ordinary girl, at least in the eyes of Giselle, a girl who liked the lake and would help you with anything and got a kick out of passing notes in class and ruminated endlessly on the nuances of saying "Hi" to guys and was wary of being grounded. You could buy a similar unit at the supermarket. You could wander a thousand miles on foot, Biggie figured, then look up, open your eyes and there it would be: identical units, no better, no worse. But not a single one of these units would be Mary Wellington.

The wrestler wanted to stop: Why am I doing this?

On the last page he could bear looking at, Biggie saw this:

Why did you jump on the car trunk?
Why did I drive on and turn?
Why did you fall?
What did you think
When you stood and threw up?
Did you think I tried
To kill you? Mary,
Do you think that still
Wherever you are?

There were plenty of other entries, too, some saying, "I'm sorry," over and over for pages; others "I love you," over and over again for pages. "I thought we'd go to college together," plenty of stuff like that. Biggie glanced at these until he couldn't look anymore.

Well, he'd found what he was looking for; he hoped it was worth it. Biggie rearranged the notebooks to approximate as closely as possible the way he'd found them, smoothed out Giselle's bed, looked another time around the room, its soft warm pastels and teddy bears and piles of books and magazines and pictures of dogs and horses and rock stars—one of James Taylor, another of Janis Joplin—then went downstairs to call Gloria.

Though not right away. He lay on his bed staring at the ceiling, then fell asleep.

Dreamed of Mary Wellington touching his face.

Rescue, February 8-10

If Giselle suspected you of ransacking her journals and reading to your heart's content, you wouldn't need to spend the rest of the year wondering. Nor would she keep the issue between the two of you. Three minutes after she'd let you know, she'd let everybody else know what a slimy, slinking, spying bastard you were. Even when she was wrong, word got out fast.

Biggie took it as a good sign on Monday morning when, driving his sister to school, Giselle, riding shotgun, didn't scream.

"Are you going to be home later?"

"When?"

"After school? For dinner?"

"When are *you* ever there for dinner?"

"I would be if I could *eat* dinner."

Giselle looked at her brother and rolled her eyes.

That night, after he'd methodically devoured half a bowl of rice, a grapefruit, a thin slice of roast, a slice of cocktail rye, a large salad with diet dressing—a feast for a Monday—Giselle was in her room. He'd *heard* her in her room as he ate, minutely chewing each bite to make it last, but that didn't necessarily mean she'd answer when he knocked, or was there to begin with.

Still, after he knocked, Giselle asked Biggie to come in. She was sitting on the floor by her bed pouring over a history textbook. It always surprised him to see Giselle study, like a face suddenly appearing in a picture you've seen a thousand times. She *liked* school until Mary Wellington died, in a way he never had except for sports and looking at girls. "Hi."

Biggie instinctively looked at the drawers he'd rifled through the night before. Luckily, Giselle was sitting in front of them. "I just wanted to say hello. See how you were doing."

The thing was, while Giselle was capable of being meaner to Biggie than anybody he knew, she was also nicer to him than anybody he knew, except his parents, who didn't count really. When he thought about it, she was nice to him a lot more than she was mean. He was nice to her, too, quite a lot. Still, he'd never before knocked on her door just to say hello.

"I'm doing fine, as you can see."

"Yes, you are."

"Did Mom and Dad put you up to this?" Giselle had this way of shaking her hair as a nervous mannerism, the way other people might crick their necks.

"You know Mom and Dad," Biggie said. "Sending big brother to the rescue."

The one thing he could count on, if he wanted to get along with Giselle, was making fun of Mom and Dad. He wondered if, when they were old and gray, in an old folks' home probably, he'd still have that ace up his sleeve. "Remember when Dad . . ." Now that he thought of it, Giselle could pretty much count on that, too.

"They said people have been saying things. At school."

Giselle looked at him blankly.

Before Mary Wellington, he didn't think he'd ever talked to Giselle for ten seconds without her giggling like a maniac—even when she sneered at him, it was punctuated with maniacal laughter.

This blank stare was going on half-a-minute already.

"Any truth to that?"

"People are jerks, Biggie, you know that."

"That's what I was going to tell you, Giselle. I had it all prepared. Giselle, I was going to say, people are jerks."

She laughed.

"Or else they're assholes and bastards!" Biggie added.

That got a snicker.

"I knew a guy," Biggie announced, on a roll, "he was all three. He'd take turns."

The stuff he was saying *was* really funny, at least when he said it to Giselle. It wasn't his fault if they were the only ones who could figure that out.

"If you think he was bad," Biggie said, flying now, "you should see his sister."

Even Biggie laughed. That didn't happen too often. Half the fun with Giselle was making her laugh until she was reduced to whimpering while you held a straight face, demonstrating, as she grunted and cackled uncontrollably, that she was a functional moron. This was one of those things you never thought about for two seconds, which turned out to be important.

When the laugh-fest stopped, Giselle opened up.

Biggie thought she might have opened up even more, except he had this way of contradicting her perceptions; he warned himself against this tactic as he contradicted her, taking the other side as devil's advocate, but his warnings only served to further encourage himself. "They don't mean it that way," Biggie said to practically everything Giselle told him.

What she said was this: People—mostly girls she'd known since elementary school, with whom she'd fallen in and out of friendships a dozen times; others she only recognized, nameless—looked at her a certain way. Or she would go into the girl's bathroom at school and would tell by the grimaces on their faces as she walked in that they'd just been talking about her.

"Maybe they were constipated," Biggie said.

Giselle glared at him, then sighed. "Don't believe me. I don't care if you do."

"I believe you."

"Then try showing some compassion." She was still glaring at Biggie, chalking him off as a traitor.

"It's terrible they're saying this stuff. I just wonder if they're really saying it."

"No. I'm dreaming it up, Biggie, because it feels so good."

She was right, that was the thing about Giselle. A lot of times in the heat of the moment she'd fire off accusations that sounded extreme, but for all their melodrama there was more than a grain of truth. This had been demonstrated by events time and again. She'd say things that *sounded* off the wall, but you usually found out a few months later that she was right.

"What about what Lauren Gelfin said?" Lauren Gelfin, who was the only friend of Giselle's who hadn't abandoned her, was quick to tell Giselle what everybody said: that during the accident Giselle was drunk and high, that she was angry at Mary for saying "Hi" to Skip Peterson, or jealous of Mary—Giselle mentioned half a dozen rumors that Lauren repeated, ranging from Mary making wrestling cheerleaders to Mary being model thin, the object of Skip Peterson's affections—*returning* those affections, Biggie noted—and in a sudden rage—premeditated, according to sinister reports—she'd driven in circles trying to kill them both.

"Christ," Biggie said.

"And if that's what some people are *saying*, it's what everybody else is thinking."

"Not necessarily," Biggie was about to say.

"Then I went to see Richie Havens last week." Last Saturday night Giselle had gone to a concert by Richie Havens, who played at McGaw Hall down in Evanston, where they sometimes held concerts when they weren't having wrestling meets and basketball games. She needed to take a break from her life, Giselle said, so she drove down with Lauren. When she went into the concession tent, among the thousands in attendance crushing in, she saw Tracy Warner, a girl from school. Giselle didn't think Tracy saw her, but as Tracy was walking away with her beer, Giselle heard her saying to the guy she was with, as he was sipping his beer, "Did you see that girl? Giselle Bluestone. She killed another girl from our school."

"And that's what people are saying," Giselle said.

"You didn't kill her. It was an accident. Christ."

"I try to get away and that's what I hear. I can't get away," Giselle said. "I don't know what to do."

"*Tracy Warner* said that?"

"Biggie, it's not just Tracy Warner. *Everybody's* saying it, except for Mr. and Mrs. Wellington. They know I didn't kill her."

"I'm going to talk to Tracy Warner."

"Biggie, I miss Mary so much." Suddenly Giselle convulsed. One moment she was talking plainly, listlessly, setting Biggie straight, the next, without any transition he could see, crying in convulsive waves. Huge tears fell down her face as she shook and rolled in the fury.

"It's not something you're going to get over like snapping your fingers," Biggie said softly. "People are jerks, like you said. They're insensitive," he said a while later. "They don't mean what they say."

"They don't?" Through her tears Giselle looked up at her brother, doubtfully. While Biggie was always good for a word to the wise, shot from the hip, she had a way of believing him, or so Giselle's look suggested, as if both knew he possessed privileged knowledge, which, for reasons of temperament, he dispensed but grudgingly.

"They really don't."

Tuesday morning, as he drove the Dart into the HPHS parking lot, Biggie had the kind of idea he didn't *know* was an idea until he was already implementing it. Giselle was riding shotgun, staring straight ahead. Beth Weiner, the neighbor who usually drove in with them, had called in sick. "Good old HPHS," the wrestler said as he turned off the engine. "Kind of makes you want to wax nostalgic, just saying it. This is the school I wrestle for, Giselle. The old blue and white."

"Shut up, Biggie."

"Let's go."

Usually Giselle peeled off as soon as he stopped the car. Back in the halcyon days, she was halfway across the parking lot whooping it up with her friends by the time Biggie collected his books in the back seat and locked the doors.

"What are you doing?" Giselle said as Bluestone hustled to walk beside her.

"Nothing."

Biggie continued to do nothing as they walked into the school, then cut off to the North Wing and Giselle's locker. "Is there something you wanted to say?" Giselle demanded as she picked out her books for her morning classes.

"No."

When they got to her homeroom, Giselle hesitated by the door. "Are you going to follow me in to homeroom, Biggie?"

"Do you want me to?"

"No!"

After second hour, when he got out of Spanish, he stopped by room 117S. Giselle walked out, staring at the floor.

"Surprise!"

He walked her over to the East Wing like a detective escorting a convict, then cut to the gym.

All these people, Bluestone thought as he left Giselle in the East Wing. Christ. Some of them grew up with her, these people who'd been her friends, whom she'd gone to slumber parties with and practiced curling each other's hair and swapped confidences and whose tears she'd dried when they were down—Giselle was known among her friends—her former friends, Biggie thought—as a crisis *specialist*—calling her a killer, if only as a point of clarification to somebody else, probably not even believing it, certainly not giving a thought to how it would sound to Giselle, when word got back. It hurt these same girls that Mary Wellington was dead. Biggie understood that. Hurt them more than it hurt him. Perhaps when they lashed out at Giselle, they were expressing profound sadness and fear—"Nothing personal, Giselle"—knowing it could have been any of them, any second, except they were destroying somebody else in the process. Even if it wasn't his sister—if it was a stranger, say, not just a girl, either; but Biggie caught wind of what was going on—he liked to think he'd do the same thing—he knew he wouldn't, of course, knew it wouldn't cross his mind. But at this moment, walking down the halls of the same high school he walked every day, people he saw every day clearing a path as if the scowl on his face might erupt into a volley of blows if they crossed him, he thought he would walk the world if it would spare a single soul what Giselle was going through. Bluestone had this sudden image of himself escorting the helpless and the frightened from state to state. Nothing would stop him, either. Still, if he knew he wouldn't walk the world, Giselle was his sister.

After fifth hour, after he'd walked Gloria from the cafeteria to The Sergeant and walked back, Biggie stopped by 217N. "You don't have to do this," Giselle said when she saw her brother. By now she wasn't surprised.

Biggie slapped his palm to his forehead.

Still, Giselle didn't instruct him not to.

After sixth hour Giselle said, "You're not going to do this every day, are you, Biggie? I mean, you have classes to go to, right?"

"Right."

"Because I get your point," Giselle said. "Everybody gets your point." Giselle motioned down the empty hallway, most everybody having left the HPHS campus before sixth hour. Biggie himself had wrestling practice to attend to and couldn't stand in the halls forever.

"I don't care. You see?"

"Will you please let me decide?"

"We'll see what it takes." The wrestler shrugged, "Are you sure you don't want me to?"

"Biggie," Giselle said reproachfully, and then surprised him. "I don't know."

Still, as he walked Giselle to the school's front door and gave her the keys to the Dart—a first in human history—Bluestone hoping Wing Terrill would drive him home after practice in the Fiat—he thought again what everybody—not everybody, but the girls, all of Giselle's reports were about *girls* saying things, not that Biggie imagined guys knew better—guys probably didn't have the *imagination* for it—saying what they did, not to Giselle, not to her face, of course—if so, you could trust Giselle to let *you* have it in the face—but in ways they knew would get back. They wanted to hurt her, when you got down to it.

It made him wish he wrestled for a different school.

He walked her on Tuesday and Wednesday. Thursday as well. Shit, he was burning off calories for Districts and every bit helped. By then Giselle wasn't bothering to protest. Bluestone didn't have the impression she was happy he was there, but she didn't try to evade him or look everywhere but next to her as they walked, as if his presence was coincidental. By Wednesday they had a lingering discussion outside 264S about Mom and Dad's collective idiocy, to be resumed when Biggie appeared after her next class to oppress her again.

If anybody noticed, they didn't say anything to Bluestone. He didn't run around mentioning it right and left. Even Gloria was spared.

By Wednesday, Biggie wondered if he was doing this for himself. Of course, who else? For Giselle, too, but it's not like you're a selfish bastard all your life, then suddenly you're not a selfish bastard.

Day Before Districts, Thursday, February 11

"It's like I'm already through Districts into Sectionals, without a care in the world." Biggie shook his head dismally as he walked Gloria to the Sergeant during lunch hour.

"Sectionals come after Districts?"

It was amazing that some people—people who mattered to the wrestler—could be so ignorant. His mom didn't know if Sectionals was after Districts, or the other way around, or if there was such a thing as Sectionals. Giselle—an Official Mat Gal—used Districts and Sectionals as synonyms.

In that he'd never gotten through Districts to *qualify* for Sectionals, Bluestone couldn't truly blame them for not having Sectionals within their frame of reference. "Districts come first. Two guys in each weight class qualify for Sectionals. Then, at Sectionals, two guys qualify for the State Tournament in Champaign-Urbana."

"That's where the State Tournament is?" Gloria asked.

Bluestone wouldn't get impatient. "Right."

"But first you have to get through Districts and Sectionals."

"Right."

"Is it certain you'll get through Districts and Sectionals?"

"It's not *certain*." Biggie stopped as Gloria walked ahead. He wondered if he said that it was certain, he'd be instantly struck dead. You weren't supposed to walk around sounding too confident because that automatically guaranteed disaster. This wasn't merely one of the rules of sport but one of the laws of general principle, from what Biggie could surmise. You could count on being struck dead the second you owned up to such sentiment. "I could always get struck dead or catch a vicious parasite the night before—which is tonight," Biggie said. "But even if I caught a parasite, I'd still make it through Districts. That's certain, Gloria."

Now Gloria stopped and walked back to Biggie. Her auburn hair fanned out in a gust of wind. "Why did you stop, Dan?"

"I was just seeing if I'd be instantly struck dead for my arrogance."

Gloria's eyes looked glassy as she closed in on Biggie.

"Isn't that supposed to happen when you get too big for your britches? You tempt the Gods to make a statement."

"And were you struck dead?"

Biggie glanced at his body for a quick inventory, jangling his arms and shoulders. "No."

Gloria kissed him.

God almighty she kissed him just like that. In the middle of the sidewalk on Vine Street. In full view of the cars driving by and pedestrian traffic and customers looking through the picture windows of retail shops.

Within an eighth of a second Biggie began kissing her back, extending his tongue to become entwined with Gloria's. She tilted her head slightly. Biggie went with the tilt, then tilted in the other direction, raised his arms—still jangling—to pull Gloria into him as her arms raised to meet his embrace. All this was within the next eighth of a second.

Gloria rose within his arms, her breasts rising into his chest.

For another twenty seconds, tongues entwined—now Gloria's lips sucked Bluestone's—they held the pose.

"Christ," Biggie said when Gloria detached herself.

She stood now an inch away, smiling a zillion watts, then moved in for another kiss, a tap on his lips, an exclamation point.

"Christ," Gloria said, stepping back, before turning to walk down Vine.

Biggie hooked his arm under hers across her back, pulling Gloria into him as they walked.

They walked along like drunken sailors. Biggie wondered if the grin stretching his face from jaw to jaw would ever subside—he'd wear this grin the rest of his life, but would it always stretch jaw-to-jaw or diminish slightly—after he got used to the idea, after he took it all in—into an average-to-above-average smile?

Could he ever get used to this?

One day before Districts, and he didn't even feel like he was starving to death. Or, unknown to him, until this moment he'd been starving to death his entire life.

Gloria Serpentino.

"Do you believe in God?" Gloria asked.

"No."

Now Gloria stopped, not to kiss him again but to search his eyes, and Biggie steeled himself not to break into laughter.

"I guess I can see why somebody wouldn't," Gloria said. "There's Vietnam and poverty and injustice and civil rights. And then if you look at what happened to Mary Wellington."

Biggie had the impression Gloria was baiting him by mentioning Mary Wellington, as if by mentioning her, the dam would break, and he was supposed to respond by telling her the thousand things he hadn't told her, beginning with the fog he'd been in after he'd heard and went so long without calling her, and probably including the letter from the Northern Illinois wrestling coach he still hadn't gotten around to mentioning yet. Probably tossing in that this was the first time he'd kissed a girl, in case she was wondering about that, too.

"I can see, with all the external evidence, why somebody wouldn't believe in God," Glory said. "That's all."

No sooner do you kiss a girl than she starts quizzing you to see how you check out on the big issues. Biggie didn't *mind* the big issues, but if you answered *wrong*, there was the matter of never getting kissed again. Still, you couldn't really take a stance just to weasel your way in. You had to figure you'd slip up down the line, if you did weasel your way in, once you were really head-over-heels, and that would only make it a thousand times worse when she threw you to the wolves for being a conniving, scheming, lying bastard. Biggie said, "You're right about the external evidence. But that's not why I don't believe. I just never have."

"I believe in God," Gloria said.

"Well, that's fine."

"There goes our marriage and kids." Gloria kissed him again. While Biggie enjoyed it, he couldn't help wondering if she was kissing him off in style or letting him know she didn't hold his godless views against him.

"Just when I was about to propose," Biggie said after they had disengaged, "you find out I'm a heathen."

"It's good you were about to propose, because I don't go out with guys unless they propose first."

"You'd marry a heathen?"

"I'll take that for a proposal," Gloria said.

They stood before the head shop. Biggie moved in for another kiss, Gloria grinned and turned before contact, then turned back and looked into his eyes.

Before entering The Sergeant, she turned back again. Biggie stood silently watching her.

"Dan, until this second I didn't think you'd ever touch me."

The wrestler said, "You were wrong."

You'd figure wrestling practice would be different once you'd kissed a girl in broad daylight, carved out opposing metaphysical stances, then obliquely proposed to her, but it was the same Thursday practice as always.

Afterward he added an extra rubber jacket and headed downstairs for five miles around the oval. Biggie was circling around before it struck him that when he'd been working up a sweat with Wing and Luigi, Wetzel too, tossing them like rag dolls, the Thursday intensity a function of his life, Gloria Serpentino didn't cross his mind once.

Amazing.

There was nothing to worry about until the finals Saturday night against Bob Stuth. This was an un-District-like sentiment, practically guaranteeing that he'd be struck dead on the spot, but not even Stuth would give him a problem or be worth worrying about if he hadn't beaten Biggie last year at Districts, a black cloud that wouldn't evaporate until Saturday, assuming Stuth made the finals. Stuth was a nice guy by all accounts; to know Stuth was to *want* him to win, but wouldn't it be like Stuth to lose before the finals? For ten laps now Biggie concentrated on Stuth possibly losing before District finals, but lost interest in the middle of the third lap. There was no way Stuth was going to lose before District finals. Just like, even though the first rule of wrestling was that the guy you didn't think could beat you, beat you every time, there was no way these other guys at Districts would beat Biggie—even if he thought there was no way, thus guaranteeing defeat, according to the principles of wrestling. The laws of wrestling weren't physical laws, like gravity, but general guidelines, advisory, confirmed by the weight of a million exceptions.

Biggie thought that for a lap around the oval.

It was hard to picture Gloria going nuts—the way she'd be when he won the State Tournament—but Biggie pictured her beneath him staring into his face, going nuts, then immediately dropped the image, as if by virtue of thinking it, the image might never come true. In his experience, that of a veteran since puberty at visualizing hundreds of girls beneath him going nuts, that was the law with girls, no exceptions. After half a lap the image evaporated.

For eight laps, stepping up the pace, the sweat now spreading in his arm pits and trunk and groin, swamping Bluestone's face and hair beneath the knit cap as he churned around the oval—flying freely now—he saw Berkenmeier across the circle coming toward him.

Berkenmeier on the mat, shooting the crawfish series.

Berkenmeier setting him up for an arm drag.

Berkenmeier on top, slipping in the crossbody ride.

Berkenmeier tying him up in a tangle of muscle and leverage.

All of this will happen if Biggie bides his time, waiting for an angle. He remembered what he'd told Gloria about himself: He was a fearless bastard.

Killer Kowalski wouldn't wait. Biggie's fearless now.

From the whistle he attacks.

After his shower, Bluestone hit 172 on the scale; the weight plus the five-pound allowance.

Still, the wrestler thought he'd crack that night, doubled over by hunger pains searing his belly—a nice touch for his senior season, firing up a steak the night before Districts so that he didn't make weight, goodbye fucking Northwestern. Despite the admonition, Bluestone thought he might, nonetheless. He tried dreaming of Henrici's, the huge steak he'd devour to celebrate taking State, the flashbulbs popping as the famous owner comes up to their table to shake his hand.

"This is killing me." Bluestone instructed his mom, "Guard the kitchen."

He could overpower her and fire up a chuck steak if it came to that, but asking his mom *helped*. It sort of made firing up a chuck steak seem like a real option.

"Mom, remind me that all my life I've worked toward winning Districts my senior year."

Mom folded her arms. She didn't smile. She probably didn't like the idea of guarding the kitchen all night, though she would do it, Biggie knew. Even if she couldn't tell if he was kidding or not, Mom was so attuned to everything Bluestone said that she anticipated disaster.

"You've worked all your life toward winning Districts."

"Sectionals, too. And *State*," Biggie said.

Mom nodded. Practically the only thing she knew about wrestling was that she hated it because Biggie starved himself.

"Am I kidding about breaking into the kitchen and firing up the chuck steak and ruining everything?"

"Of course not."

"That's right," Bluestone said, and went back downstairs.

By 10:00, the night before Districts, senior year, lying in bed with his eyes closed, begging sleep on, Biggie thought, "Jesus, this is what it's like when there's *nothing* to worry about."

"You kissed a girl today," Biggie thought. "That should tide you over. Congratulations."

It tided him over for nearly a minute.

The moment he was about to call *her*, 10:05, turning on the light, Gloria Serpentino called to apologize.

"For what?" That's all he needed, on top of starving to death, ready to keel over if he's not struck dead for arrogance: He *kisses* a girl, finally, *sheesh*, and she calls with regrets she'd ever touched him. A special Bluestone pre-District law.

"For asking you about God," Gloria said. "That was bad manners."

"You were curious," Biggie allowed.

"Are you okay?"

"Why?"

"Every time we talk on a Thursday night you sound like you're starving to death. I don't see what the point is of all these boys starving themselves so they wrestle at a lower weight, when they could just wrestle each other at a higher weight without starving themselves."

"It's complicated. The idea is to wrestle at as low a weight as you can while still maintaining maximum strength or close. That way you can have a big edge over guys who aren't cutting weight."

"But everybody cuts weight."

"Not everybody," Biggie said, thinking about Wing. Christ, Wing Terrill. Wing's career would likely end tomorrow in the first round at Districts. It was enough to summon compassion, though calling 8-10 senior year a "career" stretched the point, Biggie thought. An experience, perhaps. Wing "experienced" wrestling. Still, the wrestler was suddenly overcome by a desire that the season be over; two weeks from Saturday his fate would be revealed: State Champ, the scholarship to Northwestern; eating again, too. Christ, eating again. "Half. Everybody cuts a little, but about half to the extreme. Those guys are highly motivated, sure. But some guys are so involved with cutting weight they think *that's* the point, and they forget all about winning the actual *match*."

"That's no good," Gloria commented.

"But understandable," Biggie pontificated. "Look, do you think I should try to enjoy these next couple of weeks, or obsessively wish they were over so I can already know what happened, and eat again like a maniac, too. Maybe, when I'm State Champ, we can have a pizza?"

"Do you have a choice?"

"That's a vote for enjoying it since I can't very well flip ahead the two damn weeks?"

"That's my vote, Dan."

"Christ, then that's what I'll do."

"You say Christ a lot."

"Do I?"

"That's why I asked if you believe in God."

"Sorry." He wondered if that's how he'd always be around girls he liked, walking around offending them right and left. Saying Christ, for example, when for all he knew they were big believers. Biggie bet if she weren't a big believer he'd probably *never* say Christ. The whole process was unconscious, too, that was the scary part. If he went out with a girl who liked old westerns, he'd probably walk around saying things to her like, "Old westerns are crap," sentiments he'd never voiced before and didn't really believe, all without thinking, just so he could get a rise out of her or screw things up.

"Don't you pray before a match?"

"Nope."

"Does anybody?"

"Wrestlers are always looking for an edge." If there was one thing Bluestone hated, it was guys who prayed before matches. "It's kind of phony, though. You know Jerry Bray? Jerry Bray—he's the Poster Boy for School Spirit—always prays before matches. Not to win, of course—that would be selfish—but that he'll do his best. Of course, that way he'll win. Christ," Biggie added. "Sorry."

"I'm happy you don't pray before matches."

"Why?"

"Because you don't believe, and I'm happy you wouldn't do something you don't believe in just to get an edge."

"Hmm. Gloria, if you don't believe, you won't get the edge anyway. It won't work. You'd just feel like an idiot." Not that feeling like an idiot's liable to *stop* me, Biggie thought. Half the stuff he did and *believed* he managed to screw up and feel like an idiot anyway. But a pure idiot, not two-faced. A single-faced idiot. Though, when you thought about it, there was plenty of stuff he didn't believe that he did all the time to get an edge: Take half of what he said to Gloria. Just not about wrestling.

"Are you happy we kissed today, Dan?"

With his luck, Mom was listening in on the other extension to see if he was off the line, just so she could make a call this instant. "Incredibly."

"Hmm."

"Are you?"

"I wondered if you thought I was contagious. First you didn't want to see me. Then you didn't want to touch me."

"I think of very little else than touching you." If you didn't count shooting in for deep doubles on Berkenmeier. Also, various sociological studies somebody should do. And tearing into the kitchen to fire up a chuck steak. Bluestone was confident he wasn't being two-faced, though; most of that stuff was subservient.

"Are we dating?" Gloria asked.

"Are we?"

"Do you want to?"

"That's why I proposed."

"Good," Gloria said, "because I don't kiss guys I don't date."

"We're wrestling Districts this weekend at Glenbrook South."

"So I believe you've mentioned, Dan. Then come Sectionals, if you qualify. And it's certain that you will."

"Will you come watch?"

Gloria didn't say anything. Biggie thought of the way she'd surprised him that afternoon, moving toward him, her chest rising into his, the surprise of her tongue in his mouth. "Dan?"

"What?"

"I don't want to. If you really want me to, I will. But I don't want to."

Biggie didn't say anything.

"Don't be hurt. I *want* to see you wrestle, I think. But everybody I talk to, when I bring up your name that's what they talk about. Biggie Bluestone the wrestler. Best in the state. The superstar, the hero. The guy who pins everybody in ten seconds, the guy the colleges are after. Wow! You're going out with him! Dan, that's the part of you everyone knows. I can only share that. I like the part I see and hear that nobody knows, the one who talks to me and listens to me and says all the perfect things. The one who kisses me in the middle of town, not because he's a hero and star, but because I kissed him first and he's thought about little else. I like *Dan*."

Sometimes people say things—things about you—which are so at odds with the way you see the situation, you'd have to peel yourself off the floor if you weren't starving to death and had the energy. "You're kidding. People say that about me?"

"*You're* kidding."

"No, I mean I know I win the matches and everything and get written up in the papers." That was true. There was even an article in the Highland Park *Life* that afternoon, sizing up the team's prospects for Districts. Wetzel called Biggie "likely the best wrestler in school history." Which was likely true, Biggie thought, touched that Wetzel thought to mention it. The article said the match with Bob Stuth, in the finals Saturday night, stacked up as the highlight of the District meet. "The *local* papers, anyway. But it's not like people are running up to me all the time and making it into a big deal. Nobody mentions it outside the guys on the team. If anybody else knows, you'd never know it. Or it's like they're just not impressed. People say that stuff? Whew!" Bluestone blew drunkenly into the receiver.

"Darcy Philpot,"—a pretty girl Biggie could vaguely visualize, whom he'd recently learned was one of Gloria's friends—"wonders if I ever actually *talk* to you. She says nobody's been known to have a conversation with Biggie Bluestone."

"He's a conceited bastard, this Bluestone."

"This dates back to elementary school, Dan. They also mention Giselle when I bring you up, though lately *they* bring you up. They mention Mary Wellington, too, when they bring up Giselle." Now Gloria hesitated again. "How is Giselle?"

"It's rough with Mary Wellington."

Gloria waited a moment for the wrestler to continue. "Don't be mad at me, Dan. I'd want the wrestling part all to myself. That wouldn't be fair to you. To Biggie. I'm happy we're dating."

"Maybe you'll go to Sectionals," Biggie said.

"Dan . . ."

"If *Dan's* your guy, does that mean *Biggie's* free to see Darcy Philpot?"

"Not on your life," Gloria said.

That's the way the conversation ended. It was odd; *Gloria* was odd, though, when you thought about it. It was hard to figure a normal girl would go for him, even considering he was a heroic supernova, on everybody's lips, cut from granite, given that he'd never had a conversation with anybody, according to Darcy Philpot.

If all she ever wanted was to date *Dan*, he decided he'd be happy. He hoped he'd want *more*, the full loaf, and that she'd want more, too, even if there wasn't more, really, but he'd be a happy bastard.

Pep Rally, Friday, February 12

Third period was cancelled. Instead, those students who could be lassoed, occupied the gym for the annual mandatory Day-of-Districts wrestling pep rally. The gym held over 2,000; from what Biggie Bluestone could see, standing in the middle of the basketball court, every seat was taken.

"With this kind of turnout we might have won a few," Luigi Cravi said.

"Maybe if we'd won a few there might be this kind of turnout," Wing Terrill said.

The squad was lined up in the middle of the gym, perpendicular to the half court line, waiting to be introduced. As the students filed in, the award-winning school pep band played abridged versions of "Light My Fire," "Spinning Wheel," and a medley from The Temptations. The pom squad, regulars at basketball games but never sighted within a dozen-mile radius of a wrestling meet—or the pom girls with a wrestler—did a couple of routines until the girl balanced on the top of the pyramid slipped off and fell onto the back of an unsuspecting girl who, hunched forward with poms on knees, squealed horrifically as they toppled to the floor. Both girls immediately leaped to their feet, clapping along, full of pep, shaking their poms at the assembling student crowd.

"Not an award-winning pom squad," Wing Terrill said.

"Least they're not standing in the middle of the floor like dipshits," Luigi noted.

After the poms, the wrestling cheerleaders led the crowd in a moderate cheer. "Give me an H! Give me an I!" Early that morning, they'd planted cardboard signs on the lawns of each of the varsity wrestlers, spelling out their names in large blue and white letters—a touch that, though this was the third year running that he'd found a cardboard sign on his lawn the morning of Districts, managed to surprise Biggie at their thoughtfulness.

When the wrestling cheerleaders finished their paces, Coach Wetzel, dressed in a blue serge suit, took the mic in the middle of the gym floor and waved at the students assembled. "We've had a productive season, a memorable season," Wetzel began, then droned on, giving pretty much the same speech he'd given last year and the year before. Biggie wondered if Wetzel really didn't detect the similarities and prepared the speech from scratch each year, only to fall into the identical rhythms. Still, how many different speeches could you line up about the wrestling season? If you needed to be upbeat, you couldn't say, "This season was a disaster and our tournament prospects worse. We're going nowhere. Plus, the guys are assholes. *Thanks for your support.*" Still, when you got past the fact that the speech was cribbed from the *Wrestling Coach's Manual*—or else, realistically, from fragments Wetzel recalled from his own scholastic days—Biggie always got fired up when he heard the speech. It wasn't that Wetzel was all fire and brimstone, like the football coach who made you want to run through the wall to beat the stuck-up cruds from Evanston High—even if your Mom worked for Evanston High, and the guys you'd met from Evanston were a lot less stuck-up than the cruds from Highland Park High—but what got Biggie fired up is that Wetzel *meant* what he said. He may have gotten the line from the *Wrestling Coach's Manual*, and everybody may restlessly wait out the speech until they could leave, but he *meant* with every fiber of his being that Jerry Bray, for example, represented the best damn spirit of HPHS.

While this was the third year he'd stood with the varsity in the middle of the gym for the pep rally on District Day, and there was something fishy about the mandatory razzmatazz—2,000 here now, but lucky to draw fifty for the meets, quite a few of those parents—District Day was Biggie's favorite day of the year. As a sophomore, he'd looked forward more to being introduced at the pep rally than he did to *wrestling* in Districts. And since last year had been so humiliating when he'd lost to Stuth, the high point of the entire enterprise was when Wetzel called his name and he stepped forward and waved to the crowd. Even a smattering of applause, but coming from 2,000 and not the usual fifty, hot-wired your spinal column, and since attendance was mandatory, you also had to figure a good dozen of the Magical Fifty were present, politely joining in the clamor.

Was Gloria there? Biggie wondered as Wetzel droned on. You'd think the girl you were "dating" would show up at your last pep rally, even—when push came to shove—politely join in the smattering. Gail Abernathy, Wing's girlfriend, showed up, even though Wing was the kind of guy (and indifferent wrestler) who might not show up himself. Even Bray was "dating." Congenial, smiling Bray had a *girlfriend*. Biggie watched Bray's girlfriend sitting in the front row, beaming, going nuts at each applause line. Wendy Penn was practically the captain of the crowd. You didn't find Wendy Penn making noises about "sharing" Bray. She *wanted* to share Bray.

"One of our best," Wetzel was saying. "We look for Jerry to go far in the Tournament. I can think of no one to better represent the blue and white."

Coach dished out the platitudes. Wetzel hadn't talked to Bluestone since Wetzel let him back on the team, not beyond the usual "Go get 'em, Biggie." Wetzel's specialty. Not even when they wrestled in practice. That's the sort of thing that happened after you threw somebody against the wall. They let you back on the team because they understood the fog, in addition to your being undefeated, but that didn't mean they weren't constantly on guard, expecting you to slip back into the fog any minute. He appreciated that he'd put Wetzel in an awkward position; in fact, Biggie wouldn't be surprised if Wetzel stayed up nights praying that Biggie himself became a coach one day, and a guy like Biggie came along and tossed him against the wall, though with all kinds of mitigating circumstances, just so Biggie could look back and understand and feel like jumping off the roof.

Was Wetzel an interesting guy when you got to know him? The rumination made the wrestler wonder. Did his wife find him *interesting,* or just a guy who said the same words over and over all the time, even if he usually meant them? Christ—not that he would get worked up about it, either way—did Wetzel's wife even *like* Wetzel? Did *he* like Wetzel? Did Wetzel find *himself* likeable? When he thought about it, it wasn't merely because he'd tossed the coach against the wall; he'd never talked to him before then beyond "When's weigh-in?" or "Does Waukegan look tough as ever this year?"—the kind of non-conversational place-holding shit you'd expect from a sophomore wrestling varsity, trying to be pleasant, wary of stepping on toes. Biggie wondered if Wetzel had expected more this season. The coach praised him to the skies every week in the Highland Park *Life.* Face-to-face, he *nodded* at Wetzel. Wetzel nodded back. At least Biggie managed not to turn away when they crossed paths. Had Wetzel hopes that they'd be a team, Coach and Star, like the Lone Ranger and Tonto, Auerbach and Russell, Nixon and Kissinger? All he got was a collision with the wall and the same perfunctory nods Bluestone had been dishing out since first wrestling varsity.

Biggie watched Wetzel introduce the team one by one, soberly voicing sincere platitudes. When Coach Wetzel finished introducing Scott Hatch, the 155, Biggie straightened up.

"The next guy," Wetzel said into the mic, "what can I say?" Wetzel looked at Biggie, paused, then waved to Biggie. Biggie Bluestone waved back. "There's a cliché you hear from coaches, that somebody comes along once in a career. I'm uncertain many coaches get somebody like the next kid once in a career. He's had the finest regular season in Illinois high school history. Undefeated, unscored upon. You all know who he is, the incomparable Biggie Bluestone!"

"When he's not tossing you against the wall," Cravi whispered to Wing.

Wetzel seemed to take a deep breath.

Biggie stepped forward. Wetzel walked over and squeezed his arm and said softly, "Good luck, Biggie."

Biggie looked up into the stands and waved with his free arm as if gazing down from a float. He looked for Gloria, and then Giselle, sitting with the Mat Gals, finding neither. Instead, his eyes fell on Pete Hoffman, seated with the JVs. When their eyes met, the Professor smirked, then shouted, "Big-*gie*! Big-*gie*!" Sitting next to Professor Pete, Rick Marx, JV 145, shouted out, "Big-*gie*! Big-*gie*!" Then Cindy Shelton, from the wrestling cheerleaders, caught on and joined in, "Big-*gie*! Big-*gie*!" leaping to her feet as if on cue. That only made him think of Mary Wellington, and for a moment Biggie thought that before the chant got out of hand, he should seize the mic and announce, as co-captain, that they were dedicating Districts to Mary Wellington. Soon the chant spread beyond the wrestlers and cheerleaders, slowly at first, out of the mockery Professor Hoffman intended (rehearsing for Yale) but generating a life of its own, overtaking the gym, "Big-*gie*! Big-*gie*!"

Wing beside him shouted "Big-*gie*! Big-*gie*!" and Wetzel himself, letting go of Biggie's arm, and those of the Magical Fifty in attendance joined in, Sara Sherman for all he knew, the chant reverberating through the suburban high school gym as Biggie Bluestone stood before them.

PART THREE: THE TOURNAMENT

Opening Night, Districts, Friday, February 12

In the preliminary round, Wing drew John Rucker from Deerfield, an All-Chicagoland fullback, as muscular as Biggie Bluestone but the *wrestling* temperature set lower. Still, Rucker was 15-5 to Wing's 8-10 and could pin Wing in twenty seconds if he knew Wing was a guy you could pin in twenty seconds.

With the regular season books closed, Wing Terrill went nuts, wrestling the match of his life.

Wetzel was in the chair for Blake's match across the gym. Norm Billings, the JV coach and assistant, was tending to Scott Hatch; Biggie, as co-captain, loped down from high in the stands where he'd been watching, his own first-round match an hour away, to assume the coach's chair at the edge of the mat.

It turned out that when you put Biggie Bluestone in a coach's chair, you couldn't shut him up. "Wing, get in there! Wing, set him up! Wing, he only circles *away*! Watch the single, Wing! Full intensity, keep pressing! Shoot! Now! Now!"

At the end of the period, Rucker muscled Wing to the mat and scuttled around for the takedown. Wing stood up and tore away within seconds. 2-1 Rucker.

Slowly, Terrill nodded toward Bluestone and shook his fist.

Ten seconds into the second period, Wing stood up from the bottom position and tore away. 2-2.

"Rucks, set up the single, Rucksy, you got the hug, Rucksy, he's stalling! He's stalling!"

The Deerfield coach's chair had been empty through the first period. But now Bob Stuth sat across the mat staring at Biggie Bluestone with his crooked fucking grin.

Christ, Stuth.

"*You've* got the hug and trip," Biggie shouted at Wing, wanting to take it back. Wing wouldn't *know* the hug and trip. "Ref," Biggie shouted, "Deerfield's stalling!" Sometimes, if a guy was stalling, you could influence the referee to call stalling by yelling, "Stalling!"

Stuth shouted, "Highland Park's stalling, Ref!"

It kind of made you want to beat the piss out of Stuth now.

With the score 2-2 in the third, Wing rode Rucker viciously until Rucker escaped—Wing driving with the kelly but wrestling too loose. Forty seconds left. Three times Wing drove deep on the double—Wing hadn't driven deep on the double since middle school—as Rucker fought him off and backed away.

Rucker squirmed off the mat again.

"Call the stalling, Ref! Call it!"

"Let 'em wrestle, Ref!" fucking Stuth screamed across the mat.

Nobody else was watching the match. In the preliminary round of Districts, one of thirty-two districts in Illinois, with four mats going simultaneously and maybe two dozen of the 3,000 settling in at the Glenbrook South gym having any idea—Wing's parents, Gail Abernathy (even Luigi Cravi was elsewhere, fifty yards across the gym, running in place, his eyes closed)—even those few weren't taking it in, Biggie was imagining, wouldn't remember by next week—but Wing Terrill, for whom qualifying for Sectionals had never crossed his mind, threw out the record book to wrestle the match of his life.

"Suck it up!"

"Suck it up!" Stuth shouted.

With twenty seconds left, the ref warned Rucker for stalling.

With fifteen seconds left, Wing shot the double again, and Rucker pulled him off the mat.

"Stalling, Ref. Come on, call it!"

The ref brought the whistle to his mouth as if to give the point, then pulled it out.

Five seconds to go: Wing moved in for the same hug and trip Biggie had practiced on him a thousand times, but that Wing himself had never tried before. Rucker under-hooked then tackled as Wing lifted. They fell to the mat, Rucker landing on top. For a moment Biggie had the sensation of watching in slow motion, imagining Wing rolling on top to *win* the match of his life.

He fell to his knees and screamed and waved his fist.

At the buzzer, Wing tossed Rucker to his back.

But the ref gave Rucker the takedown and predicament. 7-2.

"That was beautiful."

Wing was doubled over, forehead tilting toward his lap, ferociously breathing fierce, gusting inhalations, settling into steady wheezing.

Ten minutes after the match, they sat in the front row of the bleachers, Biggie watching Luigi Cravi manhandle a roly-poly behemoth from New Trier, Wing still trying to breathe.

Wing looked at Bluestone as if telling him to cut the sarcastic shit, then sat up and exhaled. "Beautiful?" *Wheeze.* "That was fucked."

Biggie didn't want to get into a big argument now about whether it was beautiful or fucked, or whether one precluded the other, or whether, in fact, it was neither. "I thought it was beautiful," he said, and left it at that.

A few minutes later, Wing's arms and trunk continued to twitch, but he could sit up without immediately pressing his forehead back to his knees and talk without gulping. "Six years of fucking wrestling. Six years of practice and having you beat me up every day, and Wetzel, shit, then Cravi working me over, and pulling on those fucking tights every Friday so guys like Rucker can beat the crap out of me in front of my parents and Gail. *Over.*" *Wheeeze.*

"In front of Sara Sherman and the rest of the Fifty, too. Don't forget them."

Wing looked at Biggie again to cut the sarcastic shit. *Wing* could be sarcastic every second, but when Biggie said something to lighten the atmosphere, it was inappropriate bullshit.

"Why'd I do it?" Wing rasped.

"Maybe so you could ask that question." Wing grimaced at him, so Biggie added, "*That* was fucked. You had him before the buzzer," because that's what you wanted to say after somebody lost the last match of their life and it was over, whether it was fucked or not.

An hour later, half of the 3,000 spectators rushed toward the mat where Biggie Bluestone took on Roy Petry of Niles West, 11-4 on the season.

"Big-*gie*! Big-*gie*! Big-*gie*!" Wing and Pete Hoffman shouted, the wrestling cheerleaders taking on the chant, the chanters multiplying until the gym shook.

Petry looked across the mat helplessly.

One minute and twenty seconds later, Biggie found the angle for the pin.

As quickly as the crowd assembled it disassembled.

Impressionistically.

By the end of the first round, everybody had lost but Biggie, Mandel, Bray, and Luigi.

"Fucking Districts," Wing muttered in the locker room.

———◦———

Second Day, Districts, Saturday, February 13

Mandel lost in the morning semis, then lost again to finish fourth in Districts. Bray won 5-2 over a kid from Dundee, qualifying for the finals Saturday night, then Sectionals next week. Biggie pinned a guy from Glenbrook North in a minute twelve, qualifying for the finals and Sectionals. Luigi won 7-6, qualifying.

Nine Little Giants down, three to go.

An hour after Luigi's semi, the HP wrestling team huddled over two large tables pushed together for lunch at Hackney's, a burger palace on Skokie Road in Glenview. Bluestone devoured a triple cheeseburger. The baskets of rings and fries were refilled like water glasses. He didn't want to go *nuts*. He wanted to be ready for Stuth in the finals that night. Stuth had won 8-0 in the semis.

"Fucking Rucker," Wing said.

"That's wrestling," Biggie consoled.

You think about Stuth non-stop for a year. When the time is at hand, all you can think about is whether to order another triple cheeseburger. In wrestling, you win even when you lose. You can eat triple cheeseburgers and fistfuls of fries three times a day from here on out.

You probably wouldn't *want* that. You'd probably prefer the memory of winning State to weighing 400 pounds. But you had to remind yourself.

"Fucking Rucker," Wing said.

"You had him," Biggie consoled.

Wing finally gets worked up about losing, wrestles like it's a competition; as justice plays out, it's the last match of his life.

Rucker won again that morning in the semis. The thing with *winning* was you could bet Rucker wasn't seated at some restaurant in Glenview overcome by injustice and the cruel fates, muttering, "Fucking Terrill."

Stuth probably hadn't given *their* match last year ten seconds of thought.

Like a demented war veteran, Wing couldn't let it go. "Rucker. Shee-it."

Wing's wound was *doubly* raw because Rucker won that morning. That's the kind of shit that drove Biggie nuts: If Rucker had lost that morning 15-1, Wing wouldn't be muttering, "Fucking Rucker." But he'd won, doubling the wound, and Wing figured with any luck, with any justice, with a little more English on the throw, *he'd* be in Sectionals next week himself, but it was just Wing's luck to draw the short straw.

This kind of shit drove Biggie nuts because wrestling didn't work that way. Sophomore year, for example, he'd lost 3-2 in District semis to a guy who lost 3-2 to a guy who went downstate, and that it should have been *him* sustained Biggie halfway through junior year. But while he knew you couldn't compare scores then evaluate judiciously, even last year, calculating that he beat a kid 4-3 who beat a kid 8-5 who beat a guy 12-7, the wrestler had nonetheless spent an hour determining with precision that he would have beaten the State Champ by twenty-seven points. Then, calculating a different series (and another hour down the drain) that he would have *lost* by thirty-one. *Sheesh.*

Just because Wing wrestled Rucker closer than the guy he beat that morning, you couldn't discount every other match Wing ever had where Wing was pretty much a half-ass fuck-up.

"You told me to wrestle every second full intensity, to leave my heart on the mat," Wing was reminiscing.

"When did I tell you that?"

"That's how you wrestle. By your example that's what you told me every day in practice."

There was a lot of truth to what Wing said; usually people assumed he won all the time because he was twice as strong as anybody else. It's not like you could go around correcting them on the matter, either, without sounding idiotic. ("It's not muscle, it's *heart*." "The heart's a muscle, too, Biggie.")

"Just to see what it was like," Wing said. "To see what it was to wrestle that way. So I take it up a gear like you tell me every day, Biggie. I leave my fucking heart on the mat. But you didn't tell me if I took it up a gear, fucking *Rucker* would take it up a gear. You didn't mention that." Wing looked at him as if Biggie had withheld the information out of cruelty.

"Just like Rucker to upset the apple cart."

"He's in the finals," Wing said solemnly, as if he'd heard Rucker was going out with Sara Sherman.

Did the general principle hold? As he grabbed another fistful of fries, Bluestone wondered if you went out with a girl that some other guy went out with, who went out with a girl that some other guy went out with, who went out with Sara Sherman, that it should have been *you* going out with Sara Sherman, given an ounce of luck or justice. When all along, while you're babbling to yourself about the vicious fates, pacing back and forth like a demented war veteran, Sara Sherman would rather implode sitting at home watching TV, occasionally glancing toward the notches on her bedroom mirror for every college nobody she's humbled.

"I may wrestle in college," Mandel announced to the table.

That's the kind of thing that happened at Districts; another thing that drove Biggie nuts. When you became a senior, after you lost, as you stuffed yourself with an endless succession of triple cheeseburgers, making weight suddenly became a distant dismal memory; what you were left with instead was unfinished business that was eating you alive like a tapeworm. Even if you were a guy like Mandel, lucky to place in

Districts, you find yourself making announcements to the table about how you were going to knock 'em dead in college.

It was sort of a ritual, like senior skip day, that you practically looked forward to from freshman year.

Even Mandel knew he wouldn't be wrestling in college.

"You could do it," Bray said enthusiastically.

"I may wrestle in college," Wing announced.

Wing, who could barely wrestle in high school.

"Anything for another shot at Rucker," Luigi nodded.

"Fucking Rucker."

Districts.

Saturday night, district finals. The Glenbrook South JVs cleared the four mats, then pulled a massive mat, *GS* emblazoned in the center, to the middle of the huge gym floor.

An hour earlier, Bob Stuth sat beside Biggie Bluestone, the two sprawled in the front row of an empty Glenbrook South gym. Biggie contemplating: *District finals*, trying to get fired up without falling into a trap. With somebody like Stuth, tall and lean but not too muscular, who you knew could wrestle like hell, sometimes you found yourself concentrating on what a great wrestler Stuth must be, a technological wizard, a master of defense and leverage, the perfecter of every move, to be so good with such a skinny, crappy body.

You could really overemphasize his greatness part of the equation, all because Stuth didn't look that tough.

Even though Killer Kowalski never talked to anybody as a matter of policy—so they'd think he'd be liable to stomp on their throat or tear their ear off—Biggie discovered that Stuth was such a nice guy you couldn't *not* talk to him when he sat down beside you. The persona worked best with guys you hadn't *already* spent a couple of hours talking to since sophomore year, before you'd dreamed up the persona. Otherwise, they tended to see through it.

Stuth began chatting away; Biggie chatting back about letters from colleges and Berkenmeier and Dixon Boyd, who was wrestling at 167 after all, a complication it was clear to both that neither had begun to contemplate, and even Rucker vs. Terrill last night, saying "Bob" every other sentence to let Stuth know he didn't hold anything against Stuth just because he was from hated Deerfield and last year had ruined his entire year.

"You're looking impressive, Dan."

"*You're* looking impressive, Bob."

"What's that chant? Big-*gie*! Big-*gie*!?"

"Mockery."

"Well, Dan, good luck after tonight."

"Good luck after tonight, Bob."

All the while Biggie knew—being such a suspicious bastard—that Stuth was setting him up; Stuth was such an all-around great guy that even as he knew Stuth was setting him up, he was still thinking that if he couldn't win, at least a great guy like Stuth took Districts. The title was in good hands, either way.

Stuth was such a nice guy that Biggie didn't mind talking to him, as depressing as it was.

"Who's recruiting you?"

Biggie thought of flattening Stuth with a catalogue of big-time places—Iowa State, Oklahoma State—to blow his mind. But you wanted to level with Stuth. "Nothing definite. After the tournament, maybe. I've *heard* from a lot of places."

"Tell me about it."

"Sheesh."

"Michigan wants me to walk on," Stuth said. "Penn and Cornell send me letters every week, but they think I'm going to Michigan. Otherwise,

I get the same form letters everybody does: Northern Illinois, Southern Illinois."

"Eastern Illinois."

"Western Illinois."

"Then it's down to Western Illinois or Harvard, Bob?"

"It's an excruciating decision, Dan."

"Penn? Cornell? Bob, what did you score on your SATs? 10,000?"

"20,000. What did you score?"

"I scored 20,001," Biggie said. "Ask my mom if you don't believe me."

"That's excellent," Stuth said.

Biggie nodded. "Have you talked to Roy Gosley?"

"Big Ten scholarships are for big time guys, Dan. Berkenmeier signed with Wisconsin. Northwestern's for guys who never give up points in their matches. Guys like the Icon don't talk to guys like me."

"Right."

"At Northwestern, you'll get to wrestle Berkenmeier the next four years."

As nice a guy as Stuth was, he wasn't such a great guy that Biggie wanted Gosley to sign up Stuth for Northwestern instead of him.

"Leave Berkenmeier for me this year," Stuth said.

Biggie had seen plenty of guys who would have been a lot better off losing in the District final, ending up on the wrong end of the Sectional bracket the next week. When you didn't have to win and might be better off taking it on the chin, come the Sectional brackets, it was hard to convince yourself that winning Districts was the difference between life and death.

You wanted to call yourself District Champ, though, and—so he didn't have to think about *wrestling* Stuth—he wondered if that was something he'd walk around doing, letting it slip in the way Pete Hoffman had been letting it slip into every conversation that he was going to

Yale. Biggie wondered if that's the sort of stunt he'd still be pulling ten years from now if nothing else worked out, a total bust, pushing thirty, reminding himself he'd been District Champ, as if that by itself might inspire him to pull himself up by the bootstraps and right the boat.

Whatever you'd say about yourself wasn't half as important as what anybody figured out for themselves once they got to know you—at least that's what you told everybody to show you were well-rounded. If you went around telling people, "Incidentally, I was District Champ back in high school. Pass the margarine, please," you'd probably add as fast as you could, "Of course, it doesn't mean anything to me. Pshaw." Except for other guys who went around waiting to slip in *they'd* been District Champs. Biggie could also see that happening: Sitting in a room with a bunch of burly guys, slurping beers, belching, reliving the old days nobody outside the room cared to hear about. Even then the truth was that there were probably a lot of guys who'd been District Champ, who met regularly—across the business table or in the courtroom—and the topic had never come up. If it did, a momentary curiosity might be aroused, but no major production, no immediate imperative to order a keg and flip on a ballgame. But you'd only be *pretending* to yourself it didn't matter—so the wrestler told himself as he watched the early finals from the bleachers—that you were so much different now, that that was all a lot of crap—"District Champ? Pshaw"—that you'd outgrown, the kind of idle posturing you could afford to do if you *took* Districts. The kind of luxury Bob Stuth already had, defending District Champ. Once you had the luxury you didn't have to go around telling people. It was enough to hold the piece of information in stock.

It was probably like being the richest guy in town. Between thinking about all the *shtarkers* who were a thousand times richer and driving yourself miserable hatching new schemes, you didn't think to let it slip too often. But if you weren't, you probably thought it would be kind of nice, in addition to having the assets, to be able to say you were the richest guy in town.

Even then, there'd be a million people around who'd be quick to tell you that none of that shit was all that important, anyway.

Stuth looked at Biggie across the mat the way everyone had since the Quadrangular back toward the beginning of the season: beholding the Loch Ness Monster. Stuth nodded. Biggie didn't nod back, feeling like an asshole—it was *Stuth*, after all—but enough was enough.

At the whistle Biggie was surprised to find Stuth was quicker than he, so when he set up for an inside angle Stuth circled away, slapping at Biggie's knees with his long arms after Biggie shot and *backed off*. He hadn't backed off since last year when he'd wrestled Stuth. That's how the first period went, Biggie working in, Stuth outquicking him, circling away, slapping at his knees.

"He's going to be tired now, Bobby," the Deerfield coach, Russ Perkins, shouted from the corner. "He's going to be tired!" Because Bluestone's matches seldom lasted into the second period, everybody figured he'd get tired.

The chant proved contagious. "He's tired, Bobby!" "He's tired, Bob-by," arising to dim the chants of, "Big-*gie*! Big-*gie*! Big-*gie*!"

"He's tired, Bobby!"

"Big-*gie*! Big-*gie*!"

"He's tired, Bobby!"

"Big-*gie*! Big-*gie*!"

Biggie stepped back, taking it in.

Christ, he *was* tired.

There was a *reason* he'd lost to Stuth last year beyond the fact that he'd wrestled like a dipshit.

Too much had happened, Mary Wellington, the stuff with Giselle, even Gloria, to say nothing of the usual bubbamagumba he specialized in, all crushing Biggie now. Balanced on the head of a pin, he couldn't sustain the gale force. For a moment he was outside the mat watching himself wrestle and saw nothing you can get too excited about; wrestling in slow motion, a study in lethargy. Bottomed out as if he'd already given everything he had, the barrel emptied out two weeks too soon. Biggie was disappointed in himself that he had let this happen, disappointed he wasn't doing anything about it. Noted the lethargy. Noted the chants rising in mockery. Noted Stuth rising beneath him in confidence as he stands and Biggie kicks out his leg and slams him back to the mat, though barely holding on. Noted the barely holding on. Noted Stuth standing up again, peeling Biggie's hands again but out of bounds, barely.

The tunnel he'd been in before the match he'd never gotten out of, Biggie thought, watching the two distant figures shift in and out of focus.

Or he'd never gotten in the fucking tunnel to begin with.

Now Biggie stood up again. Back in the tape, he let go his right arm and under-hooked the opposite leg and lifted with his force. For a moment he held Stuth off-balance in the air before kicking out the leg, hitting the mat with an angle, driving in the half upon contact. Stuth couldn't brace himself. A sickened look overcame his face.

Bluestone pinned Stuth as if he could pin him forever.

Three minutes and four seconds.

District Champ on the books. The wrestler walked into the stands with his placard and medal. Beaming, flashing the tokens.

Pete Hoffman was explaining, "The pin, though spectacular, was anticlimactic. The excitement was when there was approximately a competitive match. Could it be? Was it our imagination? Do our eyes deceive us? Are we dreaming? For three minutes the impossible had happened, transforming our sense of reality. Our assumptions were under siege, our world turned topsy turvy." Biggie had heard variations of this same dissertation before. When Hoffman wasn't telling you that he was going to Yale, he was always expounding on the ways the world was about to turn topsy turvy. After a while you saw his point.

"But it was all illusion. Three minutes of intrigue before the inevitable thud," Professor Pete said.

"Speaking of reality," Mandel said.

"He's practicing for Yale," Wing explained.

"Pete's going to Yale?" Biggie said.

Hoffman and Terrill were watching Cravi stall out the third period of the heavyweight final. 2-1.

"Luigi Cravi, District Champ," Wing said.

"Has a ring to it," Biggie said.

Sectionals Week, February 15-18

Rather than the usual maze of crawling ants, all Sectionals week, the wrestling room was organized into two distinct pockets, one including Jerry Bray, Bluestone, and Cravi, who had each qualified for Sectionals. The second, larger group consisted of Dan Blake, Pete Hoffman, Wing Terrill, Scott Hatch, Coach Wetzel.

Biggie was the one who needed to shed twelve pounds for Sectionals, so he found himself standing in the middle for drill after drill as the other wrestlers took him on in furious thirty-second flurries, then switched off. Nor did action stop after Biggie pinned them. Wetzel blew the whistle. The next guy charged in. Within several minutes Biggie couldn't tell one from the other. Twice in fifteen minutes did the drill last the full thirty seconds, both times against Cravi.

After drills were over and everybody left, he descended to the oval, floating lap after lap.

School? Floating from one class to the next, Biggie had the sensation that wherever he went, he was in the middle, that everybody watched every move he made, and when he walked down the hall—even as he walked Giselle to her classes—people he'd never noticed before smiled at the wrestler in quick bursts, as if everybody wanted to get to know him really well in thirty-second intervals.

The wrestler promised himself that Sectionals week would be the best week of his life, since there were no guarantees about *next* week. He'd seen plenty of others languish after their moment had passed—even Becker last year, after getting pinned downstate—discovered as imposters. "It's what it must be like to lose out for Homecoming Queen," Biggie told Gloria. The next week they were viewed as diminished figures, studies in ruin.

Still, he was touched that word was out that he was royalty, certified by taking Districts.

"You should ask Sara Sherman out, now that you're beatified," Wing suggested helpfully.

"Sara Sherman doesn't go out with guys unless they're beatified," Luigi added.

The three were standing in the hallway before fifth hour. Students passed in waves. While Wing spent a good part of *every* week standing beside Biggie in the hallway, this week his friend had covered him like caramel around an apple, as if Terrill could absorb some of the lopsided, spirited smiles directed toward Bluestone and Cravi.

In class, teachers went out of their way to lap extra attention. Or else went out of their way not to. When he bobbled the answer, the teachers set him straight reluctantly, hesitating momentarily. Perhaps they were wrong about the Treaty of Versailles. Perhaps Biggie Bluestone was right. He'd float to Civics and receive similar treatment, thinking every second not of the thousand smiles or the bounties granted those who qualified for Sectionals, but Berkenmeier.

Christ, Berkenmeier.

"He's the one," Biggie told Gloria. He'd debated not even *mentioning* Berkenmeier to her, but then felt like he was holding back because, after Wing made a big deal out of this being the opportune moment to ask Sara Sherman out, now that he was beatified by Districts, he hadn't shot back with the information that he already had a girl. "Thanks for the advice, Wing. I'll check with Gloria first about asking out Sara Sherman." While Wing was being glib and metaphorical—which he always was when he wasn't telling you off—he'd been obliged to protest. If you went out with somebody for years—like Wing with Gail Abernathy—you could make a big deal over Sara Sherman's ass and everybody thought you were being hilarious: Good ol' Wing. When you'd only gone out with somebody for days, you had ethical obligations. You didn't want to tempt the fates by going out of your way to be an asshole. Similarly, he couldn't hold back on Berkenmeier; fearing his reticence might play out in a loss at Sectionals.

That's one thing that drove Biggie nuts about himself. Here he made a big deal to Gloria about not believing in God, fearlessly beating his chest in the face of the fates, challenging the sun, yet he monitored his every move for fear those fates would strike back double at Sectionals and he'd end up a study in ruin. It made him feel hypocritical, the way not immediately pointing out that he *already* had a girlfriend made him feel hypocritical. "Berkenmeier was always a million miles ahead of me. Made it to State sophomore year when I'm barely varsity. Third in State last year when I lose in Districts. Took Junior Olympics last summer, pinning four State Champs. Christ, Gloria, I don't know what's going on."

Gloria looked up at him quizzically. Mostly he wanted to kiss her now. Since the first kiss last week he'd kissed her every day outside The Sergeant before floating back down Vine to the school. Still, parameters were set. He could put his arm around her or hold her hand anywhere, but unless they were standing outside The Sergeant, he didn't feel authorized to kiss her. Gloria had a wide mouth, too, and full lips that required a monumental act of will not to descend upon. If you weren't given the go-ahead but descended upon those lips anyway, you were liable not only to be rebuffed, but also to lose your privileges outside The Sergeant. That these rules were unwritten only cemented the importance of following them scrupulously.

"What do you mean?"

"Well, it's confusing." One thing he'd discovered about talking to Gloria—*further* evidence of his hypocrisy—is that if he peppered his monologues with proclamations of confusion, Gloria was far more likely to take him seriously. Otherwise—when he mentioned wrestling, for example—Gloria had a tendency to act like she was waiting him out before changing the subject.

"Welcome to the 20th century, Dan. It's all confusing. *You're* confusing."

"All year I think about Bob Stuth. I'm up at night visualizing angles and leverages and the crawfish series, then last Saturday I'm in there against him and it's as if I'm a thousand miles away, watching myself on tape. See? When I'm *in* there against him it's not worth getting excited about. Like the entire year before then didn't matter because when the time came, I wasn't in the mood."

Gloria thought it over. "*When Dan pins you it's as if he can pin you forever,*" she said in a radio announcer's voice, reading from an article in the Highland Park *Life* that had come out that afternoon.

"It was nice of Stuth to say it, *if* he was quoted correctly. A lot of times when they quote a kid after a match that the kid lost, the kid sounds like he should have won, so when you read it, you feel like throwing the paper against the wall at the injustice of this poor kid not winning."

"If they can't win on the mat, they'll do it in the papers?"

"Well, it's *wrestling*, after all. It's not like there's much coverage. They'd do it in the papers if anybody asked," Biggie clarified.

Still, it was nice of Stuth to say that. Even if it *was* sour grapes, Stuth was such a great guy it sounded like graciousness. Biggie figured if *he* lost, like to Boyd or Berky next week, even if he was praising the hell out of the other guy, it would come out sounding like sour grapes.

He couldn't wait for the Wednesday Waukegan *Sun,* which promised a preview of Sectionals, to turn up at the Highland Park Library (they wouldn't get it until *Friday*), so on Wednesday after practice Bluestone drove the Dart into Lake Forest and stopped off at Canfield's RX. One copy remained on the stand beneath the magazine rack. Biggie paid his dime. He didn't tear open the paper to the sports section, instead folding it civilly under his arm, then tossing the paper atop his books on the passenger seat. As he drove back to Highland Park in a faint drizzle, he considered whether he should even read the *Sun* once he got home. Though he didn't consider himself superstitious and was quick to point out to Gloria that he didn't believe in God, he often managed a sense of impending disaster. Bluestone figured he inherited it from Dad, another Depression lesson passed down. By going out of his way to buy the *Sun* just in order to read the Sectionals preview on the chance he might be mentioned, was he tempting the fates to deliver a blow? "*Yes,*" the wrestler feared.

The prudent approach would be to not even *read* about Sectionals, much less going one inch out of his way to buy a copy of the Waukegan *Sun* just to see his name in print, thus becoming an overinflated bag of crap awaiting the inevitable pinprick.

He'd cast his fate already just by driving into Lake Forest. All season long he'd managed not to overinflate into a bag of crap, if only because at HPHS, whether you were undefeated and unscored upon registered no impact on the seismic scale; nothing like whether you had landed a supporting role in the spring musical. But now, Sectionals in sight, the oaf starts pounding his chest like a self-absorbed lunatic! So Biggie was tempted to reach over and toss the *Sun* out the window onto the wet road, except that would probably be a thousand times *more* tempting to the fates. If there was one thing worse than being a self-absorbed lunatic, it was being a self-absorbed lunatic and pretending you weren't. Still, while you didn't want to go around bringing it to everybody's attention, there was the matter of general principle. If there was a special Sectional Preview Issue in which you were liable to be mentioned, you'd have to be even more of a self-absorbed lunatic *not* to buy a copy.

The story took half the front page of the *Sun* sports section:

The 167-pound weight class stacks up as the strongest in many years. Three Lake County wrestlers are worthy of winning State: Rick Berkenmeier of Mundelein, who was third at State last year and last summer won the National Junior Olympics in spectacular fashion; Dixon Boyd of North Chicago, up from 155 where last year he took second at State; and Dan Bluestone of Highland Park, who has quietly put together what's perhaps the finest season in state annals. Berkenmeier's already signed with Wisconsin for next year, and Boyd, the all-state halfback, has inked a letter-of-intent to play football for Purdue.

"Bluestone's believed to be the first ever to get through the regular season without being scored upon," said Mundelein coach Zach Reese. "But Highland Park hasn't had the competition. He hasn't wrestled anybody like Berkenmeier or Boyd. He's a tough kid, but Rick and Dixon are in a different universe than what he's used to. The Suburban League was soft this year." The winner of the projected Bluestone-Boyd semi-final will likely take on Berkenmeier in Saturday's eagerly awaited final. "One of the three's not going to qualify for State," Reese said. "That's how tough this Sectional is."

Wednesday night Biggie lay on his bed, the phone against his ear, staring at the roof. The soft Suburban League? It was enough to make him want to beat Berkenmeier to defend the honor of the Suburban League, Biggie told Gloria.

"*Is* the Suburban League soft?" Gloria asked when Biggie read the paragraphs.

That was the same question his mom had asked earlier, when he'd shown her the article.

"In comparison to Biggie," his dad winked.

They were at the dinner table, Biggie picking at a thin slice of roast beef, pretending it was the last vestige of a thick slice he'd already devoured, and half a head of lettuce touched with diet vinegar dressing. This was probably the hundredth kind of diet dressing he'd tried this season, and he'd been wondering if he wouldn't have been better off taking his lettuce with no dressing at all, rendering the roughage flavorless, slightly sour; all the goddam diet dressing did was remind him he was starving. He'd even said that to Mom—except for the goddam part—when she asked him how he liked the diet vinegar. "All it's good for is reminding me I'm making weight," he'd said sullenly.

"I *like* it," Mom said.

You could take the most flavorless, sour liquid, label it Diet Deluxe, and his mom would like it. She also liked grapefruit. "*You* should be the one making weight." Biggie asked, "Do you ever wonder how the two of us could be in the same family?"

"Every day." Mom smiled at Biggie.

Biggie blushed.

"The question was rhetorical," said Dad helpfully.

"So was the answer," Mom smiled at Biggie.

That was hypocrisy, too. What Giselle liked to say—"Biggie can dish it out but he can't take it"—Biggie knew to be true. The observation made him feel bad for Giselle, being the runt to a larger sibling who was relentless at dishing it out. Still, *everybody* was better at dishing it out, even Mom, who hardly ever dished it out—Biggie couldn't recall Mom teasing him *once*—nor was she teasing him now, he'd bet, as he looked at her across the table, still smiling at the wrestler with her rhetorical answer.

You didn't find Killer Kowalski taking it too well. "Good at taking it on the chin" wasn't one of the qualities Biggie mentioned in the report to the seventh-grade class back when. Killer dished it out exclusively.

"Compared to *me*, it's soft," Biggie cracked over the phone to Gloria.

"Modesty becomes you, my prince."

"I *am* being modest."

"That's what scares me," Gloria said.

"Giselle?" Biggie asked Thursday morning as he walked her to her first period class. By now Giselle didn't bother anymore to protest her brother's glowering presence. If anybody else took notice of it—as Biggie'd imagined they had two weeks ago, when he'd begun walking Giselle to her classes—by now the spectacle was routine. ("By *coincidence* they have the same schedule," everyone figured.) "Has anybody been saying anything to you lately, good or bad?"

"You're always on my shoulder, Biggie. Who's going to say anything, good or bad? When would they get the chance?"

"Stuff might get back to you, though."

"Nothing's gotten back to me lately, thanks."

"Good."

But she didn't tell him to stop, which was depressing in its own way. *Next* year he'd be off to Northwestern. By now, twenty colleges had written, yesterday another post card from Roy Gosley, congratulating him on taking Districts "so impressively." He wanted to tell Giselle that if anybody said anything *next* year, she should let word out that he was only twenty minutes away in Evanston on a wrestling scholarship, but he felt like he was abandoning her by even mentioning it.

"If anything gets back to me, I'll know who to tell," Giselle said.

"*Whom* to tell," Biggie corrected. "Giselle, has anybody ever said anything to you about me?"

They'd had this conversation often—usually Mat Gals telling Giselle that Biggie was so cute and mus-cu-lar in his wrestling togs—though not since Mary Wellington died. "About you? Sometimes."

"I don't mean about wrestling, particularly. Does anybody ever tell you, say, 'Your brother, Giselle, he's too big for his britches.'"

Giselle paused in the hallway. Two weeks ago, she practically ran to her classrooms. "No, of course not. Nobody's ever had anything bad to say about you, Biggie, ever." Bluestone knew she was kidding. "How would they know? Nobody's ever *talked* to you. That's why everybody thinks you're such a nice guy. I'm the only one who knows otherwise."

"Well, keep it to yourself."

"I expect Gloria Serpentino knows, too, what an idiot you are."

"That's what she likes best about me."

Giselle looked at him quizzically, as if surprised to realize her brother was adept not only at dishing it out, but also at dishing it right back to himself. Quizzically, also, as if the phenomenon of her brother and a girl from the known universe finally made sense.

"Plus, you're a wrestling hero," Giselle added, helpfully.

A classroom hero, too. Pretending.

Aside from Jane Bennett, none of the girls from the Magical Fifty were in his classes, but they'd fall in love with him if they were. It was pretty clear—Biggie, the hero, pretending—that they were nonetheless falling in love with him outside the classroom, assuming they subscribed to the Waukegan *Sun* or had tracked down past issues.

His teachers regarded Biggie deferentially, warily, the wrestler's forbidding presence enforcing a level of scrutiny beyond their confidence zones. These teachers not only subscribed to the Waukegan *Sun*, but also read the sports pages and considered its proclamations sacrosanct. If they considered the Suburban League schedule soft, they kept it to themselves. ("We know Dan Bluestone personally," they're composing in Letters to the Editor. "Not only is he a fine gentleman, as well as personally irresistible to ladies of every stripe due to his heroic nature, but the Suburban League schedule is first rate, too.")

Pretending.

It's all an act, that's what stunned Biggie as he sat in English class fifth period, basking in his heroism and the bashful stares of adulation from classmates and teachers alike that they were managing to keep to themselves. At this moment Mr. Allison was talking about *For Whom the Bell Tolls.*

"Hemingway had a code. 'Grace under pressure equals courage.' Does anybody have an idea what that means?" Mr. Allison peered around the room. Half the class raised their hands as the other half feverishly scrutinized their desktops. "Dan Bluestone. Grace under pressure equals courage?"

"Wha?" Biggie said, looking up from his desk. Mr. Allison looked at him indulgently. This class was the closest he had to a favorite, though he hadn't answered a question—or asked one—all term. He'd been called upon and said things in response but hadn't really answered a question Bluestone-style.

"What do you think it means?" Mr. Allison said.

"Means to me, or means to Hemingway?"

"Please."

"It means if you're under pressure, and you act with grace, then that's what courage is."

Mr. Allison refrained from rolling his eyes. "That's what it *says*. But what does it mean? Can you tell us, Dan?"

"Wha?"

"If you behave decently in times of stress, then you're a brave and admirable human being," Deborah Fleck broke in.

Fleck, Christ.

Deborah Fleck pretty much answered all of Mr. Allison's questions. Sometimes nobody else would be able to answer them, until Mr. Allison finally got around to calling on Deborah Fleck, but more often she'd go ahead and answer Mr. Allison's questions anyway, breaking in when Mr. Allison called on somebody else. While the habit annoyed the hell out of everybody, at the moment Biggie resolved to ask Deborah Fleck to marry him if he ever had a conversation with her. That's why—Biggie imagined—the class hadn't tarred and feathered Deborah Fleck by now and run her out of town on the rails. While you wanted to kill her when she kept jumping in to answer all the questions, she got you off the hook often enough that half the time you wanted to marry her, too.

"That's what I meant," Biggie said. Everybody laughed.

After she answered the question Mr. Allison had directed toward you, you could always say, "That's what I meant," and get a big round of laughter. That was another reason nobody had killed Deborah Fleck yet. Biggie had used the line twice before that term and it never got old. Even Deborah Fleck could be counted on to smile transparently, as if setting you up to deliver the punch line was the reason she jumped in to answer the question.

"It's not falling apart when all you want to do is fall apart," Biggie said.

"Very good, Dan," Mr. Allison said. "But why do you need a *code*?"

"Why do I need a code, or why does Hemingway need one?"

"Please."

"Well, maybe, I suppose, so when you're under pressure you don't have to go back to square one and figure it all out. It's probably tough enough deciding what grace is, without the bullets flying at you or whatever. You have a blueprint to follow, a code, so you'll know how to act. If you *already* know what grace is, you can concentrate on the bullets flying at you."

"Or whatever," Deborah Fleck said.

"The particulars, I mean," Biggie said. "The incidentals."

"Very good, Dan."

Fleck smiled approvingly.

"But Mr. Allison," Biggie continued, "isn't it courage to forge your way without a code? To invite the complications in?"

"What's your view?" Mr. Allison asked.

Bluestone wondered. "What if you thought X was grace, but it turns out Y was grace, X just suited your nature; does that mean you didn't act courageously, though you thought you were? I mean, what happens when the deck keeps reshuffling? When the complications are overwhelming?"

Mr. Allison paused. "The code may be a metaphor for our desire to make concrete those abstractions that sometimes erupt under the pressure of a particular circumstance—with the bullets flying, or whatever,"—here Mr. Allison nodded thoughtfully at Biggie—"leaving us with nothing at all. Nada, nada, nada, as Hemingway says."

"That can be the loneliest place there is," Deborah Fleck offered, wrinkling her nose, another habit of hers that drove Biggie nuts, as if she hadn't so much thought of the observation as smelled it.

"But Hemingway didn't intend it as a metaphor," Mr. Allison continued, "any more than Robert Jordan was a metaphor, or Lady Ashley in *The Sun Also Rises*."

"Or Jake Barnes's wound," Deborah Fleck offered.

"Dan, that's why literature may live more profoundly in us than the people we talk to every day, or the trees swaying in the breeze you watch through the window during class, or the way the grass smells after it's fresh cut. The people we read about, when we identify with them, are flesh and blood, but they also provoke in us concepts we sort out until the day we die."

"Some things *are* black and white even if the deck keeps reshuffling." Biggie loved this. He knew in ten minutes—the result of reshuffling the deck, Bluestone-style, contemplating the dualities—he'd look back and feel ridiculous; for *now* it was the best time he could remember having in a classroom. "Who is this masked man?" the wrestler imagined his class-mates wondering, moved at his golden soliloquies. Pretending. "You can take what's real and place it in a different situation, different parameters, Mr. Allison, and render it hypothetical." *Render*? Where was he getting this stuff? "But that doesn't mean it wasn't real, just because the deck was reshuffled. It doesn't mean you really acted courageously, retrospectively speaking, when you really didn't and looked the other way."

Why not just announce he didn't *know* he was suspended from foot-ball junior year, in case anyone else thought it was courage or even knew he was suspended in the first place?

Mr. Allison moved toward the window and gazed outside, appearing to consider the dissertation. "Dan, you ask interesting questions, if on a rather high level of abstraction."

"What's the relevance to the code?" Deborah Fleck demanded.

Biggie decided he wouldn't marry Deborah Fleck, then wondered why it was that whenever he tried to say something meaningful, he ended up sounding like Professor Irwin Corey.

That's when it hit him, thinking about Fleck and her Fleck routine, and that every time he opened his mouth in class to make a point, Professor Irwin Corey seized his wits.

It was all a circus act, all *shtick*, all a routine, a code, a mask so other people couldn't see you; so you didn't have to see them and collapse under the sheer massive weight of your helplessness. Helplessness? He felt he was drifting off balance, and stared at Mr. Allison as if for support.

Helplessness! So you didn't have to glimpse yourself either and stare into the abyss. You didn't have to wonder about the relevance and fuck-all. Nobody had a clue. Mr. Allison? Spent half his day hoping Deborah Fleck would shut her trap.

They were out of their depth without the mask. With no code to light their way home, they were lost at sea. Even Berkenmeier? Berky probably *believed* the shit in the *Sun*, that's how clueless he was (and wouldn't it be something to talk it over with Berkenmeier, sitting in the stands after the match, chewing the fat about how none of this crap mattered—Biggie, perhaps, gesturing toward the mats spread out across the gym floor two tiers below, Berky nodding in agreement—and how it also mattered so much it was unbearable, you couldn't overlook that either—it was the other reason for the code—because without it what did you have? Who were you? Code my ass, Biggie would say. Yes, code my ass, Berkenmeier would say, and lucky for us). Though you probably didn't want to go around shooting off your mouth too much about the circus aspect, because what was that but a different kind of mask?

And Wing Terrill? With Wing Terrill you knew it was an act. He never pretended otherwise; that was clear, once you figured it out in the first place. Had Wing figured it out? For a moment Biggie had this vision: All these people walking around naked in a conspiracy of silence, most silent even to themselves. Because once you broke the silence, the breaking would never end. Even for his dad—"Dad, is it all an act, really?"—he'd bet it was all a shtick, an act, a code. A mask. So why not Killer Kowalski? Why not Professor Irwin Corey? Why not Biggie Bluestone?

Why not Biggie Fucking Bluestone?

"Let's ask Dan. Tell us, please, Dan. Tell Deborah. What's the relevance to the code?"

Fucking Fleck. The relevance is, read the goddam Waukegan *Sun*, Biggie wanted to say. Also, the wrestler was inclined to stand up in his seat and yell, "The jig is up!"

"Perhaps what Dan is suggesting," Mr. Allison quickly read his silence, "is that the code is not an end, but a beginning."

"That's what I meant."

Mr. Allison said, "May I speak with you after class, Dan?"

With a lot of teachers you'd rather they didn't ask to speak to you after class; such colloquies had this way of ending up with the teacher furiously filling out a detention slip. At best a warning with stern intimations about your next breach in deportment. Mr. Allison, though, was just as liable to tell you about a magazine article he thought you'd be interested in, or something he'd read in a book that reflected off something you'd said in class a month back. Half the time, with Mr. Allison, you couldn't remember what it was you said in the first place. You had the impression, too, he didn't *expect* you to remember. As if nothing *surprised* him where kids were concerned.

Never surprised, never disappointed? Was that Mr. Allison's jig?

Biggie still didn't feel all that great about Mr. Allison's asking to see him immediately after he'd issued a wisecrack. But with Mr. Allison, he'd probably just tell you to use fresher material. As Biggie walked circumspectly to the desk, he noticed Deborah Fleck milling around. Fleck again, being Fleck. She often did her Fleck routine after class, as if she wanted to give you a chance to run up to her and tell her how brilliant she'd been or ask her to marry you for taking you off the hook. He nodded at Deborah, who wrinkled her nose at the wrestler, and immediately apologized. "I'm sorry, Mr. Allison, about that crack."

"I wanted to wish you luck this weekend," Mr. Allison said, "in Regionals."

"You mean *Sectionals*." Biggie felt like an asshole. It was just the sort of correction Deborah Fleck would make.

Mr. Allison stuck out his hand. "I mean Sectionals, Dan."

"If it *were* Regionals," Biggie said. "I could still use the luck."

Luck aside, Biggie still felt he was onto something monumental as he walked out of class trying to reel it all in: none of it mattering because it all mattered so much it broke your heart to contemplate—or the opposite side of the coin; you convinced yourself it mattered because you couldn't allow that it didn't matter at all, so you slipped on the mask, maybe never taking it off.

From that moment on he promised himself he'd feel unburdened, though he knew the moment couldn't last any more than this week could last without turning into the weekend where Boyd and Berkenmeier waited. Still, for the moment, he understood something that loomed just beyond the pinprick of recognition; for as long as he could remember he'd tried to reel it in. For example, it was no accident he'd fastened onto Killer Kowalski, years ago. Even then he sensed what he now saw everywhere. He thought again that it was liberating; while it was the kind of knowledge that answered everything, it also answered nothing at all.

He watched the faces walking down the hall, staring into their eyes. They still smiled at him in quick bursts. He knew the names of one out of a dozen, tops. One way or another, they'd be his co-conspirators in the game of silence; he had to love them for that; though one by one he figured they'd drive him up the wall. He didn't even *like* half of them. And those were the ones whose names he knew. He didn't even listen to Gloria or Giselle; how could he take on more?

And then Bluestone saw Myra Wellington, walking out of the shade into the slanting sunlight of the hallway where Biggie stood watching the circus. He wasn't sure he'd seen her since the wake. In that moment, though, it hurt that she was so beautiful; Myra Wellington was probably the one person in the school, other than Gloria, who would understand him—not entirely, of course, not the wrestling Bluestone, not the working-out Bluestone, or the Irwin Corey given to flights of rumination, not the Bluestone who daydreamed half the day about Gloria when he wasn't daydreaming about every other girl in his orbit. She'd probably known his kind since the first day of middle school: Grade A American beef, if dimmer than most.

She wore a long black dress and a brown sweater, her black hair tied back—*is* that her? Biggie wondered—and he stood against the wall and steeled himself to look into her eyes, as if he were cementing his legs deep into the mat, willing himself to stay balanced. Christ. For an instant her eyes met Biggie's, and then she passed, leaving the wrestler with a thousand things he wanted to say to her and knew he never could, unless he was somebody else. Knowing, too, she had a thousand things to say to him, were she somebody else—and wouldn't it be worth giving her the chance to unburden, were she so inclined? Not that he'd ever touch her face; there'd never be anything like *that* between them. There was a code here he didn't quite understand—because it would help, it really would, and not just help him.

Biggie promised himself if he saw Myra Wellington again—well, maybe he'd make a point of it—he would pretend he was somebody else. He would wear that mask. Hadn't that been what he was doing all along? He'd convince himself it didn't matter, if necessary. He'd take Myra Wellington by the shoulders or hold her hand and—fuck what? Biggie wondered—he'd try.

Because he was Biggie Fucking Bluestone, and when Bluestone pinned you, it was as if he could pin you forever.

Opening Night, Sectionals, Friday, February 19

After Wing Terrill promised to drive Luigi Cravi into Waukegan Friday night for the first round of Sectionals, he asked Biggie to come along.

"You might want to go later. *I'll* drive Luigi. We weigh in at 4:00. The first matches are at 7:00," Biggie said.

Wing assumed a wounded frown, a Wing Terrill specialty. When Wing didn't get the point, he had this way of letting you know he got the point as far back as last year. Wing also assumed you knew he really didn't get the point until now. There were a thousand interlocking assumptions at work. "I know the matches are at 7:00. So?"

"So? So you'll get us to Waukegan at four then hang out until seven?"

"Just like a wrestler."

"Maybe Wetzel can arrange for you to step on the scales so you can weigh in," Biggie said. "Bring along a jock strap just in case."

"Always do," Wing said.

Wetzel would be driving up with Bray and the assistant coaches. Biggie's parents were driving up later with Luigi's parents, arriving at seven. The cheerleaders were coming up later, along with about a dozen Mat Gals. That was it for HP.

The Fiat was too small to cart both Biggie and Luigi, so Biggie ended up driving all three in the Dart. From Highwood he cut over to Sheridan Road, then north on Sheridan the twenty miles into Waukegan.

"I love Sheridan Road because it's so scenic," Wing said.

Sheridan Road *was* scenic, at least through Lake Forest.

"It takes you anywhere in Chicagoland," Luigi said.

"All you have to do is exit when you get to anywhere." Wing.

"In twice the time as the highway." Luigi.

"The idea is to get there when we weigh in, not an hour before so we can sit around starving to death." Bluestone still hadn't adjusted to the fact that Cravi could plop on the scale after eating chuck steaks all day and imagined by now that he never would. There were a thousand aspects to the wrestling experience heavyweights like Cravi never got to sample, such as living on grapefruit and oatmeal and Fresca, tapering down to water, and breaking into a thousand jumping jacks in a rubber suit every spare moment that you weren't thinking about driving over to the sauna at Ft. Sheridan.

It was the sort of fact you could never adjust to.

"Here we go again."

"Only Biggie knows what it's like to be a wrestler."

"That's right. The only thing anybody else knows about wrestling is the *wrestling*."

"Bluestone's not even being funny." Luigi.

"He thinks he is, doesn't he?" Wing.

"Fucking Bluestone." Luigi.

"Happy I brought it up." For the first round FB drew Nick Frankes of Belvidere, a senior, 17-9 on the season. He'd never heard of Frankes, but when he tried to visualize the kid, what emerged was a tall, skinny, acne-scarred guy with a tendency to cradle, who liked to hook the leg and lean into the crossbody ride. A leg rider, which was almost as disreputable to wrestling purists as being a heavyweight, though Biggie reminded himself that he didn't *care* what the other guy was like. Did Killer Kowalski care? Still, Frankes had made it to Sectionals, which was more than he could say about himself until now, and Biggie couldn't quite fight the sensation that he was walking into an ambush.

The Waukegan High parking lot was full when they pulled in at five of four, crammed with school buses and cars and wrestlers in letter jackets briskly walking toward the Waukegan locker room.

"We forgot our letter jackets. Because we're so cool," Luigi said.

Cravi was right. There *were* Highland Park letter jackets, but nobody wore them except a few football players who didn't know better, and a bunch of kids from sports like swimming or cross country who had no other way of letting you know they were athletes, so they took the deep breath and shelled out for the letter jackets. Otherwise, if you wore the HP letter jacket, you signaled to everybody that you were socially immature, or else supported the war and were probably hot to enlist the day after graduation. Jesus—this Biggie always liked about the place—they didn't even have a *prom* for lack of interest.

The flip side? Some teams, less sophisticated in their priorities, required school buses to travel to Sectionals, while at HP you fought it out with Luigi over who would drive, while Wetzel drove up with Jerry Bray and the assistant coaches, parents and cheerleaders to follow later.

The Glenbrook South buses unloaded as they walked across the lot to the Waukegan locker room. Fifty yards ahead, Coach Wetzel walked with the assistant coaches and Jerry Bray. The Poster Boy was wearing his HP letter jacket; it was rumored that Bray slept in his HP letter jacket.

Some of the girls piling out of the Glenbrook South buses wore braces and weighed ninety pounds, a good two years away from being full-blown high school girls; dozens upon dozens of others, emptying from the buses before Bluestone's own eyes, made the wrestler imagine that at Glenbrook South there was a Magical 500.

"We're the blue and white!" Cravi shouted at the Glenbrook South buses.

"It hurts to say this. At Glenbrook South, Sara Sherman would be average." Wing.

"That's because she's not *pretty* enough." Cravi.

"I was just thinking about that," Biggie said. It was one more thing about going to HP that made you think you were born wrong.

"They may have a Sara Sherman, but Sara Sherman wouldn't be her." Luigi.

"Wouldn't be *she*," Biggie corrected.

"Good to have you along."

"Considering I drove."

"Is Gloria Serpentino coming to watch her hero tonight?"

Bluestone looked at Wing to stave off the inevitable speculation on how Gloria would rate at Glenbrook South; because if the look didn't work, he was fully prepared to follow up with speculations about how

Gail Abernathy would fare, which you could bet wasn't any better than Sara Sherman; then shrugged at Cravi. "It's a free country."

"I'd like to talk to her before she dumps you," Wing said.

"You two can sit together and discuss how great I am," Bluestone told Wing.

"*Does* Bluestone have a girlfriend?"

"He *says*," Wing said.

"What's the point if she won't even show up to watch you in Sectionals?"

Bluestone gave a thought to strangling Cravi right there in the parking lot, in front of the Glenbrook South buses, except with Cravi you had to take the question at face value. He possibly didn't know what the point was. "She doesn't like wrestling. She doesn't see the point of cutting weight."

"Who does?" Wing said.

"Tell her Sectionals are *important*." Cravi was really getting worked up, as if a principle was at stake that Fucking Bluestone didn't *get*.

"That'll work." Wing.

"I hadn't thought of that." Biggie.

"Then you can solve world hunger," Wing said. "But first things first."

"We're the blue and white!" Luigi shouted again at the Glenbrook South buses, still unloading, as they walked toward their fate.

They weighed in by teams, rather than by weight class, but still Biggie looked around for Berkenmeier and Boyd, couldn't see them, then made a point of not looking around for a tall, skinny, leg rider who would be Nick Frankes.

After weigh-in, Biggie followed Wetzel in the Dart to an old-fashioned diner in downtown Waukegan. The diner was in what looked like a long, old-fashioned trailer, where they sat at a large, round table in the rear. The table also struck Bluestone as old-fashioned. Humphrey Bogart was liable to break in any second, firing. He ordered a double cheeseburger and coleslaw. No fries because he'd need to weigh in again tomorrow morning.

"I'm proud of you boys," Wetzel said to HP's three District Champs. Cravi, Bray, Bluestone. Wetzel raised his water glass.

Jerry Bray raised his water glass. "To Coach Wetzel." Biggie feared Bray would wax nostalgic, but the Poster Boy left it at that, as if no words could summon depths adequate to expressing what an honor it was to wrestle for Wetzel and the blue and white of Highland Park.

"To Coach Wetzel," Luigi said quietly.

"To the blue and white," Biggie said.

Bray pushed aside the basket of rolls and extended his fist to the middle of the table. Luigi placed his fist atop Bray's. Biggie placed his atop Luigi's fist.

Two hours later, four mats worked simultaneously in the Waukegan gym.

That Biggie sat atop the third tier, in the last row, stood as a practical concession. If the wrestler could have peered in through a hole in the roof, that's where he'd go, looking through the opening at Wing and Luigi two tiers below and his parents across the floor sitting midway up with Luigi's parents, Bray's parents seated behind them, and the 2,500 screamers crammed into every inch of the first two tiers and most of the third.

Fucking Sectionals.

He didn't think he could breathe. He tried to think of nothing, then tried to think of pain—how crucial it was to push the wall, to force fucking Frankes, if he lasted, which he wouldn't, into a spot Frankes had never been, until Frankes thought if he kept this up he'd keel over—and then Biggie closed his eyes and thought about a day in winter when he'd run five miles at the crack of midnight, then topped it off with thirty pullups, a bonus set. What was Frankes doing then? Beating off! It could have been any of two dozen days, but he chose the one after he'd almost been run over by Gloria Serpentino and cracked his shoulder, then after practically cursing at the beautiful girl he saw through the window—did he think she was beautiful then, or is that the kind of thing you pieced together later, your chest swelling?—running on his way, as if the faster he ran the farther he could get from the beautiful girl in the car and the pain in his shoulder. It was the luckiest day of his life. But what he thought about was picking himself up and continuing the run. He thought about bench-pressing 360 pounds, and when he let down the weights and staggered around dizzy for two or three minutes, lying back down on the bench, then pressing the weight again. What was Frankes doing then? Blowing his nose, then turning back into the pillow.

Two sections below, Wing and Luigi leaped into the air and waved their fists as Jerry Bray peeled away to win 6-5 over a kid from North Chicago on a last-second escape. Biggie found himself on his feet screaming to save his life, then returned to his last row bleacher seat drenched with sweat and chilled. He took a deep breath and found his lungs could barely locate oxygen. Then the wrestler found that an axe was hitting his gut; he doubled over in his bleacher seat, then bounced up and tore down the three tiers into the locker room and an empty stall. The stink from a hundred guys unloading rose to meet Biggie as he plopped down on the filthy seat. Still, he was weakened, and glancing later at his bleached face in the wide, communal mirror, noticed a jaundiced tint, as if he'd contracted malaria at the old-fashioned diner. The lighting itself made him dizzy.

Getting his breath back, Biggie collected himself. What had happened? He stared at himself in the mirror, a pillar of strength again in front of the stalls as groups of wrestlers moved around him in steady streams.

Realistically, Frankes had only one card to play: the "surge of adrenaline." With the blood flowing again in his arms and shoulders, the fog clearing, the malarial gloss lifted, Biggie assured himself that that was Frankes's only angle. Like the ninety-pound ladies you read about who lifted semi-trailers in a surge of adrenaline to free their trapped toddlers. Right now, Frankes was talking himself into a monumental surge of adrenaline: Frankes was the only line of defense against Bluestone the Barbarian, who'd rape and pillage his village unless fucking Frankes responded instantly with a monumental surge of adrenaline. Christ, Frankes was *counting* on that surge, Biggie would bet. Except—here's the actuality poor Frankes would soon stare and blink at—it only worked if your toddler *was* trapped beneath a semi. You could *pretend* your toddler was trapped, pretend in your dreams, pretend triple-speed like you've never pretended before, but when you opened your eyes, you didn't have a toddler, nor were you a ninety-pound woman; you were just facing a ferocious madman, certifiable, across the mat who was ten times as good. That was the Frankes predicament in a nutshell. Plus—here was the fucking thing—on Frankes's best day, if Frankes had a surge of adrenaline, Biggie Bluestone would respond with a double surge.

Later, Biggie sprinted to mat #3 when his match was called, strapped on his leg band, leapt into the air. He was fresh, loose. Nick Frankes of Belvidere lumbered over, a tall kid, frail. Not that he'd fall into that trap. Frail-looking guys could be snakes. Thin arms become steel wires.

Still, there was a reason Frankes was 17-9, not 24-2, not 26-1. At the whistle he stepped forward and backed off as Biggie came toward him, a little like Bob Stuth build-wise, move-wise, without Stuth's moxie, that's what Biggie figured within ten seconds. Biggie surged toward a cross single leg drop to the opposite leg, but it was a fake, a move invented on the spot, at the last second swiping Frankes's right ankle. For a moment Frankes bounced on his left foot, soon kicked away. Frankes grunted, summoning a monumental surge of adrenaline, presto, as Biggie leaped forward—not too high, warning himself, so Frankes couldn't work the mountain path and slip under him for an escape of his own and possible tilt—this was sloppy, Biggie knew—and underhooked both shoulders crushing Frankes into the mat. Twenty-seven seconds.

To his right, Stuth was beating a kid from Libertyville, 6-2. This was the second year running Stuth had made it to the Sectional semi-finals. Stuth would face Berkenmeier tomorrow morning, a match Biggie'd love to see, but his hands would be full. Kitty-corner, across the gym, Berkenmeier was pinning a kid from Arlington Heights after throwing him onto his back with the suddenness and grace of a lumberjack felling a tree. The huge coils of his arms glistened in the lights as he worked the pin with methodical, unhurried precision. On the mat adjacent to Berkenmeier, Dixon Boyd, Mr. Universe, toyed with another muscular Black guy from Rockford East. Though the match was lopsided, it was worthy of a quarterfinal downstate. Junior Smith, whom Biggie had never heard of, was 22-2 according to the brackets, quicker than anybody Biggie had ever himself wrestled since Boyd sophomore year. With his massive shoulders and triceps, he looked like he could bench press the moon. As Biggie watched, Boyd let Junior Smith up, took him down again, let him up, took him down now to his back, let him up after Junior Smith furiously wiggled to his stomach, beginning the same pattern again with startling suddenness, until Boyd became bored with the gratuitous exhibition of flurries and tosses, up 24-9, point made—to Biggie?—then worked the pin with an arm bar hook and trip, a combination Biggie couldn't remember seeing in a photograph in *Advanced Wrestling for the High School Athlete*. It was impossible to imagine tomorrow morning. "Fuck," Wing said, sitting beside Biggie in the second row.

Biggie draped a towel around his neck, squeezed his headgear. "Boyd's better than last year."

"I could do that if I gave it the college try," Hoffman said.

"He's a man," Coach Wetzel said beside Bluestone and Wing. "He's a man."

"He's a man," Wing agreed.

When somebody was really tough, the ultimate tribute was that the guy was "a man." That's one thing that got Biggie about wrestling; the sentiment always diminished the accomplishment, implying that the guy you'd beaten was an adolescent, if not in reality a girl. Biggie heard that kind of talk about himself all season, too. "Bluestone's a man this year." Like he'd just had a bar mitzvah or opened a bank account. All it meant, though, was that you looked really tough on the mat, whereas a lot of guys who really were men probably wouldn't look that tough on the mat. His dad, for example, wasn't somebody you'd necessarily call a *man* if you saw him in wrestling togs.

Truthfully, Biggie much preferred "stud." That's what they said sometimes. "Bluestone's a stud this year." "Yeah, he's a stud."

Biggie preferred that.

Still, when Biggie phoned in his progress report to Gloria later that night, "Dixon Boyd's a man," is what came out.

"You said this was a high school competition."

"That's how it's advertised. They ship in some men for show, though. For legitimacy."

"I see."

"*I'm* a man," Biggie pointed out.

"Prove it."

"Wha?"

"Come over right now and prove it."

It was always a mistake not to take her seriously. "Gloria, I got Dixon Boyd tomorrow at ten. He's a man. I have to weigh in at eight."

"Which gives us plenty of time, Dan."

"Okay, I'm on my way over."

"Good."

"Fine."

"Are you here yet, Dan?"

"You see, Gloria," Biggie said, "I don't have to prove my manhood. I don't need to run into the woods and beat my chest, or shout my name through the streets, 'Big-*gie*! Big-*gie*!' That's for Dixon Boyd. For the great Biggie Bluestone, it's enough to talk on the phone to Gloria Serpentino."

"And beat off to the image of her lovely face as you listen to her lovely voice?"

"And beat off to the image of her lovely face."

"Dan, I hope you win tomorrow."

"I wish you'd be there."

"I wish you were *here*," Gloria said.

He pictured her lying back on her bed, her long brown hair swaying over the receiver, her lips pursed. He could see her tongue. He hadn't kissed her since this morning standing in front of The Sergeant. "I wish, too."

"Call me tomorrow," Gloria said.

Biggie wondered if he played every card he had, pushed every button, threw a fit, told her he loved her—did he?—Christ, he wondered—pleaded from his knees, tore off one mask and flipped on another, signed over his first-born and future earthly riches—threw in Wing's future earthly riches for good measure—if he could get Gloria Serpentino to watch him wrestle.

Second Day of Sectionals, Saturday, February 20

At six, Biggie tumbled out of bed into his sweats and rubber suit and wool cap and ran three miles to stay loose, then fixed a cup of oatmeal, half a grapefruit, warmed up the Dart, picked up Wing and Luigi, then cut over to Sheridan Road for the scenic Saturday morning drive to Waukegan. For the moment, refusing to think of Dixon Boyd, Biggie had the sensation of keeping time at bay. The radio was tuned to BBM-FM, set so loud the speakers crackled. James Taylor was singing "*You've got a friend*," Biggie and Luigi and Wing screaming along. As always when he listened to the radio, Biggie thought of Gloria Serpentino. But now he also thought of Wing, along for the ride, and Luigi in the back seat, who'd won last night, screaming along, and his parents, who'd drive with Giselle to Waukegan later that morning with Luigi's parents, and the carloads of Mat Gals and cheerleaders driving up to Waukegan later that morning to scream their hearts out—and mean it, too; not screaming Biggie-style, clarifying in his imagination an obscure point—and another dozen teammates driving up later, and here Biggie and Wing and Luigi letting go, windows open, the late February morning air blasting through, screaming "*You've got a friend!*"

It was easy to believe it was true. Wing and Luigi anyway. Gloria certainly. They weren't necessarily whom he would have *chosen* as friends. It wasn't how he'd envisioned friendship as a kid—what had he thought back then? Guys who'd be on his wavelength, with whom he'd talk over everything, who'd work out with him and watch his back and never have a bad thing to say about him—guys who saw Biggie as being better than he saw himself, that's what he would have wanted—and go out of their way to call him up; and a girl who'd sit in the stands watching him wrestle, hands fixed in prayer—though, like Biggie, she wouldn't believe—crestfallen, tears streaming down her face if he lost, with everybody watching her because they knew she was Biggie Bluestone's girl.

That kind of shit—though it still sounded good, Biggie had to admit. What he got instead were two wisecracking idiots who didn't even *like* him, judging from anything they ever said, who hung out by virtue of the their weight classification proximity, random teammates, that's how arbitrary their affections—*sheesh*, the best they'd ever say about him was to call him an asshole, but *affectionately*—plus a girl who wouldn't cross the street to watch him wrestle—and yet, this was the thing, screaming out "*You've got a friend*," bundled up *en route* to Waukegan and the Sectional semis and Dixon Boyd, in a half-freezing, half-overheating car with Wing and Luigi, he felt the corny song in his very heart and breath.

He wasn't going to stand in line for an hour at Customer Service and exchange these guys, no, and Gloria was his girl, same deal, Wetzel his coach—the wrestler was going nuts now, certifiable—Giselle his sister, the Mat Gals his gals, braces and knee socks and attention spans notwithstanding.

Basking in sudden largesse *en route* to the Sectional semis.

"*I can't get no satisfaction,*" Mick Jagger sang next. "*I can't get no satisfaction!*"

"*I can't get no satisfaction!*" the three friends screamed along *en route* to Waukegan.

Who can? Biggie wondered, though this song raised another issue worth mentioning. "If he spoke grammatically, would he get more satisfaction? What do you think? Or maybe if he stopped *whining*!" Biggie shouted over the song and the rackety heater.

"Fuck you!" Cravi shouted from the back seat.

All was well in the Bluestone world, two hours pre-Boyd.

Jerry Bray lost 8-2. Biggie watched from the tunnel, pacing back and forth across the warm-up mats.

Afterward, Bray collapsed into the front row of the bleachers, then buried his face in his hands; Coach Wetzel sank beside him and placed an arm over Bray's heaving shoulders, consoling the best damn representative to ever wear the blue and white.

Not ordinary or pedestrian. Not run-of-the-mill. Biggie thought of the night in mid-winter when he'd taken off on his nocturnal run and been hit by a car, saw the beautiful girl through the window (well, he was lucky, that was the point), continued his run. He thought of bench pressing 360 pounds, staggering, benching 360 again in another minute. Two reps in sixty seconds, the Bluestone world record. He thought of his shoulder killing him, swallowing the pain because what else could he do? He thought of endless bike rides, the tires deflated for extra resistance, Biggie keeping pace, pedaling furiously; he thought of dreaming every moment of his life, he thought of the pain that would chop his lungs like an axe until Biggie was breathing through a crushed thimble. That moment would be welcome, the *sine qua non*, as Professor Pete would say, as Deborah Fleck would say, as Biggie Bluestone thinks now, the moment he'd step on the throttle with everything he had, every breath and ounce of gristle and splinter. Dixon Boyd, welcome in.

He thought of Dixon Boyd moving in on his leg like he was gliding through water. Biggie kicking away, scuttling around, a front headlock-knee tap, Boyd falling to the mat with the thud of a meteor crashing to earth.

Well, Boyd didn't know from Dan Bluestone, the best regular season ever. 29-0, 25 pins. Quote unquote.

Second in state, my ass.

Killer Kowalski takes the mat: Barely glances at Dixon Boyd, Mr. Universe. Fastens his ankle wrap. Shakes his arms and shoulders, bouncing on the mat, stares straight ahead into the stands seeing both less and more through the tunnel, bearing in as he'd never born in before into the eyes of Roy Gosley, fifth row, straight ahead, furiously scribbling notes as his eyes meet Biggie's and—this Biggie could swear, though the tunnel distorted everything he saw as being more vivid than the quotidian world beyond it—Roy Gosley winked.

Unscored upon lasted eight seconds. Boyd went in on Biggie's left leg, lifting it in the air, kicking out the far heel, breaking Biggie down before it registered, sealing the wrist two-on-one; then Biggie lifting off his base, broken down flat again, lifting off again—tried to stand up, slammed down, tried to Granby roll, tried to whizzer, tried to steel himself and burst through. Beyond the mat, he could hear people screaming—in the middle of getting the piss beaten out of him detected Hoffman calling his name, "Big-*gie*! Big-*gie*!" and Mandel's voice chanting along—but screaming at numerous removes, as if the chanting was such a distant memory Biggie couldn't be certain he was hearing it now. Shook his head. He heard Wetzel screaming for him to peel Dixon Boyd's hands. Excellent advice.

Three times Biggie stood and tried to peel Dixon Boyd's hands. Three times Dixon Boyd slammed him to the mat, finally working in the half. When Biggie spent the last minute of the period fighting off the immense pressure of the turn, it was like holding a train at bay.

You spend every second working out (this Biggie thought of telling Gloria), some guy's still twice as strong and fast as you. Biggie wondered if the principle held, a universal law like gravity or the wind spitting in your face. You spend all your time studying, some guy's still twice as slick with the math calibrations. You study at the feet of Akiba, spending every spare moment picking up stray snippets, you can bet some guy who wouldn't know an aphorism from a horseshoe still barks out twice the wisdom. Those were the immutable laws. And while every Bluestone has his Dixon Boyd, every Boyd has his Berkenmeier. You've got a friend. Well. He'd be just Biggie now. Not even Biggie. Plain old Dan. ("People used to call him Biggie. Had a girl named Gloria.") 2-0 after the first.

Biggie won the flip—couldn't get over it—and chose top, then hung on for dear life, Boyd a stallion trying to buck its loose-strapped saddle—Biggie not even a rider—with switches, standups, whizzers, hip hoists, stuff Biggie couldn't name, holding onto Boyd as if cleaving to a mast—not a saddle now, the metaphor itself overwhelmed by the sheer fury—in a hurricane—waiting for the pain, please, now reeling Boyd to the mat, now tripping the ankle the instant he broke free—separation between them but Biggie flying back to cleave to the mast. Still, the hurricane wins, Boyd pulling away Bluestone's hands one minute in. 3-0. Biggie flying forward, tying him up, squeezing, pushing him off, moving in, his center of gravity low (Boyd won't shoot in beneath him), never allowing the separation (Boyd would kill him), blocking everything full force, a moment of hip toss, a moment of whizzer, he couldn't shoot on Boyd, couldn't counter—this was Dixon Boyd, after all, not the soft Suburban League schedule—Boyd was too quick, coming at Biggie triple-speed. Fastening a headlock, Boyd tosses him down like a rag doll, out of bounds at the buzzer. 3-0.

Now Biggie's down, breathes deeply again, again looks into Boyd's expressionless eyes.

Stands up, Boyd holds him aloft in the air like a pillow, slams him down; Biggie scuttles, Boyd catches him, pulling him into the circle with most of his force—this Biggie guesses, would say if you asked—Biggie pulling away full force, Boyd hooking his legs, squeezing out the clock. One minute to go.

And then it happens. The axe to his legs, breathing through a thimble. Welcome in.

Biggie switches and rolls in overdrive, scrambles to his feet before he knows he's on his feet, 3-1, in on the headlock, looks to the opposite knee—all before it registers; to think on the mat, to evaluate and calculate and weigh one against the other, is to have Dixon Boyd on your legs, lifting, tossing you to your belly before it hits you—you're done—the mat slamming your belly before the realization—that's where thinking gets you, where pacing yourself lands you, contemplating your options like choosing which apple to pick from the tree—well, not with Dixon Boyd you don't—don't reach for the knee, pick the far ankle—why? *That's why*, he thinks—a fraction of an inch from the edge of the mat—and Biggie knows in one minute he'll be dead, a carcass hauled off with ropes, that's his fate, he can't push this far, nausea bursting through his chest, blood in his eyeballs until he's dizzy, then dead; is it worth it? Boyd's face across the circle, up 4-3, thirty seconds to go, fending Biggie off now, welcome pain, not a stallion but a mudder, a sloppy track now, moving furiously through the mud, Biggie in for a double, gone, in for a hip toss, blocked, in for a single, gone, in for a throw, Boyd still twice as strong but they're both dead now, furiously surging left, Boyd surging right to counter, timing it now by feel, turning his surge right with Dixon Boyd's momentum, tumbling on top. Well. 5-4.

Wetzel and Cravi charged onto the mat to lift him aloft. Wing charged in from the stands, Hoffman and Bray and Mandel following like squadrons of frantic ducks. In their clutches, Biggie stared at Dixon Boyd, who was staring blankly at his coach, who stared back at the wrestler, who stared back at the coach, who now stared at Biggie in the clutches of the mob, passed out, coming to.

His breath returned after half an hour. Biggie was in the shower then. His head cleared after twenty minutes as Biggie stood in front of the locker staring at the floor.

Luigi was pinned in 52 seconds. This Biggie learned over lunch at the old-fashioned diner. If he must have known it before, now he took it in as he ate a triple burger.

"You beat Dixon Boyd. You beat Dixon Boyd."

"You beat Dixon Boyd."

"Best match I've ever seen," Wetzel was saying, "at the high school level."

That was Wetzel. As if he'd barnstormed the country, watching matches at different levels, Biggie thought, his head still clearing.

Can you get sunstroke when you're not in the sun?

"Or any level," Wetzel said.

Biggie walked into the bathroom and looked at himself in the mirror. He looked exhausted but the same, no black eyes, no tears in his scalp, his nose didn't quiver. What did he expect, Killer Kowalski blinking back? Or a marching band?

Berkenmeier beat Stuth 17-4. Biggie must have heard that before, too, though now it registered. Six hours until Berkenmeier, he told the mirror.

"And now all I have to do is beat Berkenmeier," he said when he returned to the table, then drained a glass of water, then yelled for the waiter and ordered another burger.

"Berkenmeier couldn't even pin *Stuth*," Wing said.

"Toyed with him, though," Luigi said.

"Who doesn't?"

He beat Dixon Boyd in Sectionals. Biggie wondered if the reason he'd thought so much about Berkenmeier was so that he wouldn't have to think about Dixon Boyd. Second in the state last year, better than ever, runs into a buzz saw, that was Biggie's take. 29-0, 25 pins, none of it mattered until Dixon Boyd. "Ten times as good, and then *I* become ten times as good." He thought of running to the pay phone in the rear of the diner, cramming in a fistful of coins, letting Gloria know the neat symmetry of the equation he'd become, momentarily. "Last second takedown," he'd tell her. "I love you," he'd say. Would he mean it? Jeez. Though shouldn't he go out with her first, a real date, the works, as opposed to the ritualized make-out session—one kiss, no more—standing in front of The Sergeant? What was the works? Don't tell me those kisses weren't real, nobody's fingers were crossed, Biggie thought. Knowing Gloria, she wouldn't go out with him for the works. But that was a different

Biggie, pre-Boyd. He wasn't sure he bought it—it was nuts—but in this moment, sitting in the old-fashioned Waukegan diner with Luigi and Bray and half a dozen teammates along for the ride—Wetzel, too—Biggie knew he was fated, hand-picked, everything he'd done—not much, true, but he'd *wanted*, he'd tried, you couldn't say he hadn't worked, heretofore to be viewed in the context—("Yeah, I remember the kid, a strange boy, always lifting weights, running the roads, not a brainy kid, they say he grew up to beat Boyd in the Sectional semis, last-second takedown")—a monster, they'd say (but in a good way, in the best way ever). All crap he'd sort out with Gloria, post-Boyd, yes, but—here was the thing—post-Bluestone, too, post-the-exact-guy-she-knew, and couldn't she tell?

Biggie wanted to *entomb* the moment so he could feel it, savor it, succor it, know it tomorrow—he'd beaten Dixon Boyd, Mr. Universe, last-second takedown—*that* Bluestone, they'd say—with no Berkenmeier gunning over his shoulder, not yet, still six hours away—because it wasn't sealed, really, when you thought about it. Everything he felt in this moment, Berkenmeier could take away double, that's what he'd have to face. Biggie looked up from his extra burger. Everybody was looking at him. Had he said something? "Not yet, please" out loud, startling the HP crew. ("You see, Gloria, that's how the world is, post-Boyd. Post-Boyd, pre-Berkenmeier, anyway.") Everybody stares at the monster. ("Gloria, who can blame them? You think they're not curious?") They covet what he has, Biggie imagines, besotted with his post-Boydian grandeur.

"Because it wasn't thirty down one to go, it was one down one to go, Gloria. It was—this is what kills me, because you want to hold on, you want to savor, to entomb, but the train leaves the station, the train doesn't go in reverse, it doesn't wait, and you have to be a tiger out there, not a human being, if you see my point, Gloria." Well, it was just one to go, that's all that mattered, not the one down. The one down was done. Still, though disappointed he couldn't savor now or entomb the moment, what was the alternative? *Not* beating Boyd. Which could have happened if he hadn't gone with the train and leaped into the abyss; he could have lost 3-1, not bad, licking his wounds right now, wondering the rest of his life—if that's really the way it was, and you never got over this stuff—but the moment was symbolic, Biggie thought, of his life ahead, and he'd let go, gone with the surge, remade himself—now here he was, anyway, in this restaurant, Boyd down, done, Berkenmeier to go.

"Berkenmeier's next," Coach Wetzel was saying, "He's a monster."

That's another thing about Wetzel. When he wasn't snubbing you because you'd tossed him against the wall in a fog, he was telling you that Berkenmeier was next up in the bracket, as if you didn't know who Berkenmeier *was*, or weren't paying attention.

"Berkenmeier? I was hoping to draw Huckman!"

Wing spit his water back into his glass. Mandel coughed, his Coke gone down the wrong pipe. Bray almost choked on his fries.

Huckman was the Libertyville guy Stuth beat yesterday. *Yesterday* Bray would have pointed out to Biggie that Huckman lost to Stuth, first round. ("I don't get it, Biggie. Better check the brackets.") Post-Boyd, pre-Berky, everyone not only got the joke, *Bray* even found it hilarious.

Even Wetzel smiled slightly, which didn't happen too often.

"Biggie's a monster," Bray said.

That sealed the post-Boyd apotheosis. If there was one step above being a man, a stud, it was being a monster.

Biggie suppressed a dastardly howl for fear the table would short circuit.

"Biggie'll handle him," Wetzel said softly.

Not *how* he'd handle him, Biggie noted, taking another breath, looking around the table; because the train leaves the station, Biggie thought, whether a particular Biggie Bluestone wanted it to or not.

"Biggie's a buzzsaw, Biggie'll take him," Luigi generously agreed.

"Bluestone's a stud."

"That's better than being a buzzsaw," Mandel commented.

"Who can take whom, the buzzsaw or the monster?" Hoffman posed.

"Yeooow!" Bluestone howled at the table, because what else could you do, pre-Berkenmeier?

"Yeooow!" he yelled again.

"Yeooow!"

Still, he found himself fastened to the idea, teasing his imagination like a song he couldn't get rid of and looked to hear every time he turned on the radio, though there were better songs he'd pass over, flipping the stations; this could last for weeks, until one day he heard the song and it was suddenly just a song he'd heard a thousand times before, no mystery there, no secret or revelation anymore, no read-out of his heart.

After lunch, Biggie drove back south to Highland Park, dumped off Luigi, dumped off Wing, and drove home, where he had the kind of conversation with Mom—Dad was off in the den, working—that always convinced Biggie the bassinettes had been mixed up back in the maternity ward. "Great match," Mom said, the same way she'd say "Great match" when he beat a fish from Niles East. "Does this mean you *made* the State Tournament?"

"I haven't *made* the State Tournament, Mom. I need to win tonight, either in the finals or—if I lose in the finals—against the guy who comes up through the wrestlebacks, probably Bob Stuth."

"Stuth again. Didn't you beat Bob Stuth last week?" Biggie was surprised she remembered.

"Yeah, but this is this week. The scores don't carry over. We start with a blank slate."

"That doesn't seem fair."

"Mom, it has *nothing* to do with being fair."

"Don't be touchy, Biggie. I know it's stressful for you."

"It's *not* stressful for me," Biggie said. "Anyway, I either have to beat Berkenmeier—that's the guy on the refrigerator—in the final, or probably Stuth."

"Oh Biggie, good luck," Mom hugged him before he could turn around and escape downstairs.

Mom didn't discern any distinction between pre- and post-Boyd—that was clear.

He hated being rude to his mom—touchy, too—as a general matter, but did she have to push his buttons hours before Sectional finals? You didn't really want to start doubting yourself now, cursing yourself for being a rude bastard to your mom, who'd done nothing but sing your praises since you were hatched; frantically pacing your room because, if virtue was rewarded, realistically, you didn't have a prayer.

You didn't find Berky lamenting that, all things considered, he wasn't a *nice* enough guy to take Sectionals. ("Bluestone might have taken Sectionals," they'd say, "but no *mensch*, he. Didn't deserve it. Character deficiency.")

Biggie bet Ma Berkenmeier wasn't accusing Berky of cracking under the stress. It probably wouldn't come up, even if Berky really *were* cracking. They were probably too busy practicing the crossface half nelson.

Biggie hustled back upstairs. "Sorry I was so touchy, Mom. You know. The stress."

"You're the best son in the world," Mom said, which Biggie didn't mind hearing right now, on the off-chance virtue really was rewarded. "Can Luigi still qualify for the State Tournament?"

"He'll need to wrestle back," Biggie said, standing in the kitchen politely to provide further clarification, though Mom merely smiled.

She *liked* the idea, Luigi's wrestling back.

He made his way downstairs, miraculously slept an hour, ran a mile, no more, rumbled back to the Dart and headed north on Sheridan, picking up Wing and Luigi.

Biggie, standing in the middle of the circle, waits for Berkenmeier to approach, thinks Berky's half an inch taller. Human scale. You pictured him a *foot* taller. The chant—"Big-*gie*! Big-*gie*!"—is already accumulating from a low rumble. Berkenmeier, crewcut blond hair, lazy smile, rangy as the side of a wall, the All-American wall, a refrigerator, looks at him slightly askance—no surprises here—and pumps Biggie Bluestone's hand.

How long have I dreamed about you, Berky? Fantasizing spins and whizzers and deep doubles? Berky running, Berky working out every day with the Olympian, learning the real insider dope. Little Berky getting the piss beaten out of him by Ma and Pa Berkenmeier. Berky drilled by his brothers—big stars themselves—since he was a tyke. Then third in the state last year, won Jr. Olympics last summer, rated #1 in the country, now the immovable object, the irresistible force. Dreaming Killer Kowalski. Yet the moment comes and all you get is an intimation of contempt on the edge of the face, looking slightly askance. No games, no con, no psyche-out. As if Berky was beyond the games, the shtick, the con. Well, it held.

Smiles into Berkenmeier's face as he squeezes his hand. "Good luck."

"Heard good things about you, Blue . . ."

"Stone," Biggie says, no offense, "and it's mutual."

"Looking forward to this," says Berkenmeier.

"The match of the century."

So the match was routine. You can have your hype, your 2,500 screamers, your Waukegan *Sun*. Nothing. There's still the majestic and the routine. Routine. Not by Biggie's standards—unscored upon until the match of his life against Dixon Boyd. Or Berkenmeier's, 32-0, 28 pins, defeated Boyd himself at the Christmas tournament. Same town, same gym. But the sort of routine thing you get when two guys square off. One moment one has the edge, the other the next.

A superb technician, strong as an ox (strong as *Biggie*, he had to admit), full of advanced takedowns—sweeping in the double leg, picking the cross ankle, the inside trap, Berky knew it all, that was clear to Biggie from the get-go. But Biggie could keep him in his sights. Berkenmeier working the twelve-hour shift, blunt, brutal, a clunker pressing forward, a machine (but a clunker—that surprised Biggie); you could keep your hand out of the grinder. All you had to be—here's the catch, thinks Biggie—was everything Berkenmeier was.

And push and push past pain's door, to want pain's door, to want to burst through, so that when everyone shouts "Suck it up," it's already too late, after the fact. Berkenmeier coming after you, a clunker, the arsenal basic, the technique relentless—what did Berky see? A buzzsaw, Mr. Universe, meeting the pressure and then some—but Biggie meeting him force-to-force, blocking, gripping his wrists, feinting to one knee (Catch that, Berky), scrambling away, fighting the duck under, the reverse lifts, the front headlocks, throwing in the kitchen sink. Feeling Berky get his leg with twenty seconds to go, Biggie peeled back, stretched furiously, his life depending on it, slapped Berky's tricep, gripped, pulled in, he was pulling pain's door off its hinge, scuttled around at the buzzer. Takedown.

Berkenmeier won the toss and chose up. In the back of his awareness there was plenty of screaming, but—here was the thing—you couldn't pay attention to the peripheral shit—couldn't be *aware* of it, even if you were—couldn't think twice, either, about how much you *wanted* it, wanted to win, for Gloria, or for all the hours and dreams you put into it, or that you were dedicating your season to Mary Wellington—every thought put you at one remove, so you weren't paying attention when Berkenmeier moved in with the leg sweep and you bounced on your belly, still collecting yourself for the surge of adrenaline—which proves mythical after all. A dozen wristlocks Biggie peeled off, the hammerlock, the twisting knee lock, the chicken wing, a head scissors once which Biggie fought off, tumbling out of bounds with Berkenmeier's knees squeezing his ears. Berkenmeier wrenching the wrestler's shoulder, as if he knows Biggie's shoulder's dead. But Berkenmeier pulls at his legs, stands—Biggie's legs are in a vise now, until they blank numb, Berky twisting, but not turning his trunk or his upper arms as he crawls across the circle. Stalemate. Then Berkenmeier breaks him down again, pries in the half, the three-quarter, through sheer force, Berky's own surge of adrenaline, Biggie leans forward—huge risk here—Berkenmeier *follows* him forward, slapping Biggie's head to the mat—before it registers—but riding too high as Biggie's hand slides across his back—Biggie squeezes out and slips around for the reversal. 4-0.

Riding is pain. Not reacting but enforcing, smothering, covering Berkenmeier like a tarpaulin over a rushing brook. Berky was discouraged now, Biggie could tell. He didn't know quite what to do anymore—everything he tried worked *almost*, then Biggie slithered around—Biggie slinking in, slipping out—he lost heart, Biggie thought, the effort still there full tilt, but not the imagination, Berkenmeier back to basics, a strongboy like Biggie reduced to strength but purely, a volcano ever on the verge of eruption, a furious bull but suddenly tamed, resigned, Biggie knowing what to expect—the volcano, the bull—until Berkenmeier started reacting to *him*, not forcing, too far behind with half a minute to go, divining desperate counters for reversals and near falls—prying an arm behind Biggie's back—Berky got that far—to swing him over for the reversal and predicament—not *that* far, though. The match of the century ended in a standoff in the middle of the circle, Berkenmeier forcing, Biggie forcing back. 4-0. Bluestone, Sectional Champ.

Afterward Biggie charges into the stands. "*Now* I'm going downstate," he says to his mom.

"Nice work, Biggie," Mr. Cravi says.

"Nice work, son," says his dad.

"Luigi's next," he says to Mr. Cravi.

Biggie stands in the tunnel. Everybody congratulates him. Other wrestlers, then more wrestlers. Every coach in northern Illinois shakes his hand. People he recognizes, people he doesn't quite. "You beat Dixon Boyd, you beat Berkenmeier," one after another tells him, sometimes posing the declaratives as a question, as if they might be mistaken and corrected. "Thanks," Biggie says to each, not quite answering. "You're a man. You're a monster." "Thanks," Biggie says, squeezing their hands.

Because Biggie beat Berkenmeier, Stuth was out of the wrestlebacks. Afterward Stuth hugs Biggie as he stands in the tunnel.

"Maybe he really is a nice guy," Biggie says to Wing as Stuth walks away.

"You beat Boyd, you beat Berkenmeier," Wetzel told Biggie, standing in the tunnel.

"This reminds me of the reception line at my bar mitzvah."

Wetzel laughs.

He looks into the stands. The Mat Gals are crowded around Giselle, jabbering her ear off, hugging her, pressing his sister as if on the verge of hoisting *Giselle* on their shoulders.

"You're Dan Bluestone, Highland Park," a Glenbrook South cheerleader tells Biggie later. She has long blonde hair, electric blue eyes, a curious, amazed smile.

He's dressed now, walking into the stands to watch the wrestlebacks.

One by one the wrestling cheerleaders seek Biggie out. "Biggie, oh Biggie, you were great. Can I give you a hug?"

Biggie doesn't see why not.

Every five minutes Wing wanders off; every five minutes Wing returns. "You're a monster," Hoffman tells him. "This is big. This is really big."

An hour later from the top tier, Biggie watches Berkenmeier beat Dixon Boyd 6-3 in the wrestleback final. Style is everything. That's what amazes Biggie, beguiles him, would confound him if pressed to the point of contemplation. He shuts down Berkenmeier the machine, 4-0. Routine. Scrapes by Boyd in the luckiest match of his life—though he'd beat him again if he had to, as he won't have to now, thanks to Berky—next week in the State final. He was Biggie Bluestone after all, besotted in grandeur, busting down pain's door. Yet here Berkenmeier controls Boyd throughout, the score much closer than the match, the result never in doubt—unless you know it's Dixon Boyd (though the Boyd of this morning, not the Boyd now), the style favoring the methodical over the spontaneous, Berky strong enough to thwart the flurries—so if you didn't know any better ("Well, who can say?" Biggie thinks) you'd think Berkenmeier was everything advertised, everything Biggie always feared he was.

"That makes you the best in the country," Roy Gosley said, sitting beside Biggie, interrupting his reverie. Where did Gosley come from? How long was he here?

Probably Gosley wanted to embrace him.

The Northwestern coach patted Biggie's shoulder and laughed, squeezed the pressure point in Biggie's screaming shoulder, jovial, avuncular, winking into Biggie's face but letting him know who's boss, who's Mr. Wrestling, that's what Biggie thinks. "Boyd, then Berkenmeier," Gosley said. "I'll see you next week in Champaign. I'll *call* you this week. We could sure use you next year."

As Biggie watched Gosley walk away, Gosley turned around. "What's that they call you, Dan? That chant?"

"Wha? Oh, Biggie. Biggie Bluestone. Back in middle school I was pretty big. It stuck, I guess."

"Biggie," Coach Gosley repeated. "Biggie Bluestone."

"That's right."

"Two guys in a row you don't pin," Wing says.

Biggie looks at him.

"I'm beginning to think *I* could beat *you*."

The kid who beat Bray 8-2 in the semi lost to Crockett in the final 7-4, eliminating Jerry Bray, co-captain. The guy who pinned Cravi won the final. Luigi won the first round wrestleback in overtime, then led for half the consolation final, spent the second half slammed to his back by the 300-pound Waukegan heavyweight, 10-3 the final score, Luigi out.

Driving back, Biggie flipped from station to station, looking for the song to define the untethered euphoria; each song was promising, though he'd move on halfway through, the songs suddenly too sad to bear, clobbering Biggie, as if each love affair was doomed to fail because love itself was so much larger than the two who wanted it, they didn't *know* they wanted it until too late, that's how it seemed to Biggie steering the Dart south on Sheridan Road with Wing dozing off in the passenger seat—Biggie's changing the stations driving him to such intense distraction Wing blanked out, pushed beyond tolerance—and Luigi in the back seat, staring out the window, cold tears glazing Luigi's face, or warm tears filtered through the cold socket as Luigi bit his tongue, murmuring "Shit" over and over—"Shit, shit, shit"—as if—this Biggie liked thinking—the songs themselves broke Luigi Cravi's heart.

"He crept up on tiptoes out of nowhere. Suddenly he was sitting beside me," Biggie was telling his dad late Saturday night about Roy Gosley. Immediately after getting home, he'd placed his *Outstanding Wrestler—Waukegan Sectional* trophy on the hallway bureau, descended downstairs and collapsed on his bed. Thought of calling Gloria to report, decided he shouldn't, then almost did. An hour later he was up, bundled up in sweats, running five miles to take off his edge, then found Dad still up in the living room reading the paper.

"Did Coach Gosley say anything or just sit?"

"Nothing *flat out*. Not the official pitch, if that's what you mean," Biggie said.

"He said that they could use me next year."

His dad looked pretty tired—it was after 1 a.m., Biggie bet—as he smiled at Biggie.

"So I guess you're right," Biggie concluded. "He just *sat*."

"Do you still want to go to Northwestern?"

"Sure. You know that. Ever since the seventh grade, when you'd drive me to the meets."

Biggie thought his dad was going to offer again to give Gosley a call. Biggie pictured it: "My son—whom you've been *halfass* recruiting all year—and no, your methods don't impress me—wants to go to Northwestern, Gosley. I asked him and he said 'Sure.' That's for the record. Off the record, ever heard of Sanford Bluestone?"

Maybe his dad *should* give Gosley a call.

But his dad didn't float the notion now. Biggie figured he understood that, if he really made that call, Biggie'd die of embarrassment. Unlike his mom, who didn't seem to mind much if Biggie died of embarrassment. Instead, Dad nodded wearily at the trophy on the bureau. "You've earned that."

"Well, thanks."

"You've worked for it, Biggie. I know you've put so much into it. Your lifting weights, your running, your isometrics. I remember when you were fourteen and would do the Canadian Air Force exercises. Remember when you'd carry me on your shoulders for a workout? We still have those pictures somewhere. Biggie, you'd spend so much time by yourself back when you were a kid, reading about sports, doing pushups," Dad reminisced. "This must be very gratifying for you."

"It's better than a punch in the nose," Biggie allowed. There could be a thin line between being amusing and being a wiseacre; sometimes Biggie would consider he was still on one side of the line, whereas his dad would think he'd crossed, so he added, "I appreciate the sentiment."

Every year or so Dad issued an "It's not the result but the effort" lecture, usually following Biggie's season-ending calamities, so Biggie could tell everybody, "Sure I lost, but it's the journey that counts." He usually appreciated the gesture, too, but it was nice to hear a "You earned it" lecture for once, as a variation on the theme.

"I'll probably sleep with the trophy tonight," Biggie added.

His dad laughed.

Unlike his mom, who had never laughed at a single thing Biggie said, his dad sometimes found him amusing, or at least could appreciate that Biggie was trying. Whereas his mom was liable to say, "Don't sleep with the trophy, Biggie. That's silly. You'll break it."

"You have a gift. I realized that tonight. I knew you were good, but not like that. I don't know where you got this gift." Dad shook his head in bewilderment then ceremoniously—*his* sense of humor—extended his hand to Biggie. "My son, the wrestler."

Corny as it was—when Dad wasn't busy working he had a tendency to wax sentimental—one of a thousand things he'd inherited from his dad, now that he thought of it—that's when he wasn't feeling like he had been dropped from outer space, or (Giselle's pet theory) the milkman—it was sort of nice that Dad thought he had a gift. Of course—this got to Biggie now—he'd always *assumed* Dad thought he had a gift. What was Dad doing all these years if he wasn't thinking that Biggie had a gift?

Mom was the one, though, who was always spouting off about how talented and bright Biggie was, how he could do anything with enough sweat and brain power. Dad was objective. *He* didn't see a monster just because it was progeny.

When Mom was feeding Biggie that line of crap, it was probably all he could do not to step in and contradict her. "But there's no *gift*. The kid's just a worker."

"Gosley also said he'd call this week," Biggie announced, then went downstairs.

Half an hour later he could hear his dad still moving around in the living room and thought of going back upstairs to thank him for coming along tonight, or saying he had a gift, or—Christ, he felt like he had to say something—offering those times to call old Gosley for him, even if the last thing he needed was Dad calling Gosley.

The phone rang. Biggie charged from his bed to the door in time to hear Dad upstairs talking into the receiver, asking where Giselle was, telling her he'd pick her up now. He didn't speak harshly. That was hard to do around Giselle sometimes. You found yourself speaking harshly to her even when you asked her to pass the potatoes.

Biggie went upstairs to wait for Dad to return with Giselle. Occasionally he looked over at the bureau where he'd placed the Outstanding Wrestler trophy. He was dead tired, as his dad must have felt by now. He couldn't remember thinking of his parents as being tired before. Whatever it was—driving to Waukegan to watch him, or his dad staying up past 1 a.m. for Giselle to come home, congratulating Biggie when he comes through the door in his sweats, telling him he has a gift, not mentioning *once* that's not why he was up, as if it might spoil Biggie's moment, then making a point of not yelling at Giselle when she called—they had double the energy for. Triple.

All while Biggie was dead tired but couldn't sleep—that's how great he felt, because there weren't too many days in your life when you beat Berkenmeier and Boyd in Sectionals—as if the adrenaline that had driven him doubled back through his veins. Wanting more.

Biggie pictured Berkenmeier up in Mundelein taping *Bluestone's* picture to the freezer door to remind himself what the best in the country looks like.

———— ❦ ————

The Boyfriend, Sunday, February 21

"Undefeated Dan Bluestone of Highland Park pulled off a major upset in beating Mundelein's Rick Berkenmeier 4-0 in the 167-pound final," Gloria read over the phone. Sunday morning. Biggie lay on the floor after his five-mile run, followed by forty pullups and forty chinups, then 300 pushups. *"Earlier in the day Bluestone beat Dixon Boyd of North Chicago, last year's state runner-up at 155, 5-4 on a last second takedown."*

"Interesting," Biggie said from the floor.

"They didn't say those were the first runs scored against you all year."

Runs? That was Gloria.

Before his morning run, Biggie had already scoured both the *Tribune* and the *Sun-Times*, from which Gloria read now.

"And that's just the *Sun-Times*," Gloria said. Now she read from the *Tribune*, which didn't specifically mention the Berkenmeier and Boyd matches, but ended their brief coverage by revealing, *"Dan Bluestone of Highland Park, the winner at 167, was awarded the trophy for Outstanding Wrestler,"* though the way Gloria read it, you'd think he'd won the trophy for Obnoxious Wrestler.

"I'm admiring the trophy as we speak." This wasn't *technically* true. The trophy was still on the bureau in the upstairs foyer, so Mom and Dad and Giselle could take turns admiring it. "I slept with it next to my pillow."

"Hmm."

"Dreaming of you, needless to say," Biggie hastened to add.

"Dreaming of me. Dan, can I ask you a question?"

"Sure, Gloria, ask."

"You don't sound like you want me to."

"That's because when somebody asks if they can ask, it's my experience that they pretty much want to tell you what a jerk you are. They either make a statement, I've noticed, or ask a question that is *really* a statement, something like, 'Why do you wear your underwear on the outside?' But *go ahead*," Biggie said.

"I see," Gloria said. "Thanks for the permission."

"You can ask a question if it's *polite*."

"Dan, why do you wear your underwear on the outside?"

"I was hoping nobody noticed."

"You're not an asshole, Dan, so you don't have to act like one."

But he was being an asshole, that's what drove Biggie nuts, because he didn't want to be. In fact, it practically took a monumental act of will yesterday to prevent him from calling Gloria *during* the Berkenmeier match to file updates.

"Funny that I hear about my boyfriend's triumphs by reading the newspaper," Gloria said. "It makes me wonder if you *are* my boyfriend."

"I'm sorry, Gloria, for being an asshole." He didn't add, "Plus I'm sorry you *forced* me to be an asshole," for fear it sounded too idiotic, even coming from him. Or that if he'd not been one—if he'd followed every impulse and called her last night the moment he got home to provide the blow-by-blow—a nice guy at heart, a pushover, a sap showing he *cared*—she wouldn't be calling him this morning—this Biggie was certain—reading from the papers, asking why he didn't call.

"*Are* you my boyfriend?"

"You don't know?"

"Aren't we being mature," Gloria said.

Biggie paused. "Is it up to me? Does it have to be all of the above? Can I be your boyfriend but you not my girlfriend?"

"So you can date those Glenbrook South girls?"

Biggie wondered if just because you won Sectionals—were voted Outstanding Wrestler by the coaches—if Glenbrook South girls would suddenly start showing up in Highland Park, searching door-to-door. One day you can barely get Highland Park girls to say hello to you, the next day Gloria's asking you if every hotshot girl on the north shore is after you, and—talk about being an asshole—the possibility strikes you as legitimate.

"It has to be all of the above," Gloria said.

"Yes, naturally."

"Well, naturally I accept," Gloria said. "Thanks for asking."

"Does that mean we go to the prom?"

"They couldn't drag us to the prom, Dan, even if there was one."

"Because we're too sophisticated?"

"That's right."

"I have a question for you, Gloria, uh—"

"Say it, Dan."

"Am I still an asshole?"

The question wasn't idle. Because the reason he *didn't* call Gloria last night to file the report, in addition to lighting a fire under her, to getting her off the dime, to hurting her—well, he *was* an asshole—into asking *him* where they stood, well, to fucking motivate her because he was a dipshit—because *he* could have just asked her, after all—was because if he'd called last night he would have had to tell her about Roy Gosley sitting beside him in the stands, and if he told her about Gosley he'd also have to tell her that Northern Illinois was after him, once and for all—you sort of had to disclose one if you disclosed the other, particularly if you were boyfriend and girlfriend *officially*, or else you really were an asshole. In fact, you were an asshole for *not* telling too. Either way you lost, and Biggie wondered if this would be a final statement about having a girlfriend.

Sheesh. No wonder nobody ever understood what he was talking about. People gave him far too *much* credit, when you got down to it.

"You're very handsome, too."

"I'm *handsome*?"

"And I'm beautiful, Dan. Correct?"

"Correct," Biggie said.

"Thank you, Dan. I believe you're getting the hang of this."

"It's true. You are."

"Will you call me tonight, Dan?"

You spend two months talking to a girl almost every day on the phone, you never run out of things to say—Christ, you're just scratching the surface, Biggie thought now, staring at the receiver, contemplating yet another run (because he needed the routine, the routine's how he got here, beat Boyd and Berky—and what's Berky thinking *now*?), he needs the conversations with Gloria, too, relies on them, and she understands everything you say, understands your point even when you don't have a fucking point (though she convinces you that you do and you see, Christ, she's right, I really am amazing), then the day comes when you run out of things to say that you haven't already told her two dozen times, except for the things you didn't tell her so you wouldn't have to tell her *other* things, being the kind of slinky bastard you are, and *that's* the precise moment you close the deal, sign the papers, formalize the agreement, become boyfriend and girlfriend. Jeez Louise. He wondered if that's how it was for Mom and Dad, too—though, when he thought about it, it was hard to imagine Mom and Dad being boyfriend and girlfriend at all.

———————

State Tournament Week, Monday, February 22

Monday night Coach Tepper of Indiana called, asking if Biggie had *formalized* his future college plans.

"Not yet. Still looking." Tepper probably didn't want to hear he'd been thinking about wrestling for Northwestern since he was a toddler. "I've been thinking about Northwestern, though," he added, to be fair about it. "Nothing formalized, though."

Except for Gloria Serpentino.

"They're a fine program," Tepper said. "But if you haven't decided, keep an open mind. We're an excellent program."

"Yes." *Indiana* an excellent program? He could probably wrestle for Indiana *now*. You didn't want to say, "Excellent in what sense, Coach Tepper? Compared to Lake Forest College?" Indiana was the Big Ten, but barely, wrestling-wise.

"I recommend that boys go to the school where they would find the best fit, not only academically and athletically, but in terms of promoting their growth as men and productive citizens. Our wrestlers fare very well after graduation, Dan. Very well. That's something you'll want to consider."

Biggie saw Tepper's point. If he signed with a dipshit outpost like Northwestern, he'd be lucky to catch on as a shipping-receiving clerk at General Binding. "I will."

"I've seen it often," Coach Tepper said, "that when boys go local, when they've grown up wanting to wrestle or play football or basketball at Tech, Dan, they end up wishing they'd gone away to school. College is a time to venture from the backyard, to leave home and spread your wings. Northwestern's a wonderful institution, too, but they're local, Dan. At Indiana University you'll be close enough that your parents can drive to our meets, yet far enough away from home to enjoy the full benefit of the college experience."

And spreading my wings, Biggie thought, envisioning Icarus in bright red Indiana togs.

"Keep us in mind, Dan. We'd be an excellent fit."

"I'll keep Indiana in mind. Thank you."

"I'll call next week so we can plan your visit, Dan. Plan on meeting our wrestlers, touring our campus, and seeing for yourself firsthand what a quality experience Indiana University offers. I look forward to meeting you."

"Meeting me again. We've met before, after the Northwestern meet in December. I'm the guy who introduced himself."

Salt Tepper began a dissertation now on how impressed he'd been that Biggie had taken the initiative—it showed exactly the kind of guts and class they were looking for at Indiana University—recovering so nicely that Biggie had the idea Tepper really did remember. There was no reason he *shouldn't* remember, except that probably a dozen guys a week were showing all kinds of guts and class by introducing themselves. He hadn't sounded like he'd ever met Biggie. Still, what was Tepper supposed to say? "Dan, I especially remember your crossed eyes. Plus your fly was down"? What got to happen, though, is that he had Salt Tepper off balance. A month ago, he'd have been stuck for a response. Now he was jawing with a Big Ten coach, springing verbal conundrums like it was Terrill or Cravi. He felt so relaxed, in fact, he had to bite back the impulse to ask Tepper about blow jobs at old Indiana U.

Coach Tepper wished him luck downstate.

If having the edge talking to a Big Ten coach was a novelty, the novelty began to wear off ten minutes later when the phone rang and it was the Illinois coach, Monte Safredo, asking if Biggie had yet firmed up his college plans. "Nothing firmed up."

"I know it's late in the game, but we offer tremendous opportunities at the University of Illinois."

Biggie felt obliged to mention he'd been thinking about Northwestern. "Plus, I just got off the phone with Coach Tepper."

"Both great schools," Coach Safredo said. "At Illinois, though, in addition to providing one of the finest educations in America, we offer the advantage of being an *in-state* school, yet far enough away from Chicago that you can experience the best of both worlds. Close enough to home, Dan, yet far enough away."

"Interesting."

Safredo worked that angle. "We're a large state university with all the educational and social opportunities, son, yet a close-knit group, a *family* offering the comforts of home. How does that sound to you, son?"

"It sounds fine."

"Have you thought about a major?"

"English or sociology, I guess."

Illinois was tops in those areas.

"We wrestle at Assembly Hall, the best facility in the country," Coach Safredo said. "I look forward to seeing you and meeting your parents this weekend."

That's just what he needed, Safredo asking his dad what he did for a living. ("Oh, I'm a Professor at Northwestern, Coach Safredo. I'm a big shot there, too, just like Roy Gosley.")

"Fine," Biggie said.

When Safredo hung up, the phone rang again. Before tackling his homework—another series of simple-minded sentences requiring translation to equally simple-minded Spanish—Biggie waited for Mom to yell down, "Biggie, it's for you. *Michigan* on the line. When you're off, take out the garbage!" A great thing about college was that, from what he'd heard, nobody yelled at you all the time to take out the garbage.

The call was for his dad.

Biggie felt like yelling upstairs to keep the line clear for Coach Gosley trying to get through but went upstairs and knocked on Giselle's door instead.

Giselle was sitting on the floor staring at a large map of the world. She didn't look up when he entered. "Biggie, if you could go anywhere, where would it be?"

"Northwestern," Biggie said, "but I'm keeping an open mind. The important thing is to find the right fit. Indiana and Illinois just called."

"I mean to visit." Giselle wrinkled her face in that way that told you she was upbraiding herself—probably for trying to carry on a conversation with Biggie. Within the last year, Giselle had acquired the expression. It wasn't the sort of expression you were born with but picked up and perfected.

"*Sheesh*, I'll be lucky to make it past Champaign next week."

"You'll win. I can't imagine you losing this year. You beat Berkenmeier. He was rated #1 in America." Giselle looked up. Her eyes weren't red, though that didn't mean she wouldn't burst into tears any second. She still had that tendency.

"Now that I've beaten Boyd and Berkenmeier, they're showing an interest."

He remembered when he was in this room rifling through Giselle's diaries, trying to pin down her secrets. He was happy he had. Without that, he wouldn't have bothered walking Giselle to class, which was a pain in the butt for all concerned, probably made no difference, and Giselle didn't appreciate; but it made him feel like he was doing something. That was the point of reference all along—Biggie had to admit—but it was better than doing nothing, unless doing nothing turned out to be better; but you could never bank on that.

Still, it didn't hurt Giselle any that her brother was the best thing HP had ever seen: Bluestone, Star. "It's been interesting at school. People I don't know have been coming up to me to say hi."

"Hi," Biggie said.

"It's like they think *I* made State."

"Rather than your supernova brother."

Giselle wrinkled her face again, this time not because her brother was such a dipshit, but the school at large was, if not humankind in general.

"Any Mat Gals going to Champaign?" he asked.

Giselle went over a list of who *might* go. This was pretty flattering, that all these girls were taking off from school—or considering it—to drive three hours to watch him wrestle in Assembly Hall, but when they got there, most wouldn't suddenly start paying attention. Mostly it was a chance to party with 10,000 other kids who had descended upon Champaign. That's probably why some cheerleaders were so devastated when guys from their team lost at Sectionals. In addition to the Mat Gals, the wrestling cheerleaders, who the rest of the year were the JVs, were driving down. They'd sit by the mats and scream their hearts out during Biggie's matches.

Biggie didn't want to emphasize the JV cheerleaders. Mary Wellington would have been one, and he didn't want to set Giselle off. Contrarily, it *might* be worthwhile, he thought, standing over Giselle, to give her a chance to talk about it, so Biggie went ahead: "The wrestling cheerleaders are coming down, too, of course. You know, Cindy Shelton, Rona Lefler, Kerry Lipschutz, Julie Beamer . . ."

Giselle looked up and smiled at Biggie as if to say, you lucky dog.

There was even talk of getting a busload of students from the school to come down; there was always talk like that. In the end, even when more than one guy qualified, all you ever got were six or seven regular students signing up, not enough to qualify for a bus, so a bunch of guys—all from the team—ended up borrowing somebody's parents' station wagon, or else driving down with the coaches. Still, Biggie liked the idea of a list circulating around school. "Sign here for the bus to Champaign to watch Biggie Bluestone wrestle at State."

Giselle wrinkled her face again. It occurred to Biggie that it might be an allergy rather than commentary on the stupidity of the world at large.

"Is Gloria coming?"

"Gloria Serpentino?"

"When I mention her you always act like you don't know who I'm talking about. I can see why you'd act like that around *Mom*," Giselle said.

"Sheesh," Biggie said.

"If you don't know who I'm talking about, then you've been kissing somebody you don't know every day in front of The Sergeant. It's all over school." Giselle turned from her map again. She had this way—despite Biggie being her big brother and hero—of smiling at him like he was her nephew. "This Geography project is due tomorrow. Talk to me *now*, okay? Tell me about Gloria."

The odd thing was, once it started tumbling out, it turned out that he had a lot more to say about Gloria than he thought he had, and it made Biggie wish there were people he could talk to once in a while about shit like this, other than Gloria herself. For one thing, it turned out it *bothered* him that she'd never show up for his wrestling matches—he told Giselle Gloria's excuse, too, about "the wrestling Biggie being the other Biggie, everybody's Biggie. She wants the Dan Biggie for herself," a sentiment Giselle found as unconvincing as Biggie now realized he found it, but pretty touching, too. "That's part of me, too, the wrestling part," Biggie told Giselle.

"Is there another part?"

For another thing, it turned out—Biggie discovered—that it bothered him a lot more than he let on, even though they were "boyfriend and girlfriend," officially, by dint of oral contract, they hadn't, technically speaking, been on a date. "It's like I have the warranty for the new TV, but not the TV itself."

"Have you ever asked her out?"

"Good question." Now that he thought of it, after the two times he'd asked her out—which sort of sealed their fate as a couple, though she'd turned him down—there had been a lot of jostling about ("I wish you were here now." "No, I wish *you* were *here*.") that kind of indicated that he'd been pretty content just to talk to her on the phone.

"Ask her to a movie or dinner," Giselle suggested. "Have you done more than kiss her?"

This was rather more than his sister was entitled to know. In fact, he couldn't see asking Giselle if *she'd* done more than kiss one of the maggots she'd gone out with—or even *kiss* them, for that matter—because, one, he didn't want to know, and two, he'd want to beat the piss out of the guy if he knew. "No. Keep that to yourself, please."

"You sound like you think Gloria's going to fall in love with you because you're such a great wrestler."

"No, that's why everybody *else* falls for me. Gloria falls for me because of Dan."

Giselle lowered her chin to her palm. Biggie had the impression she didn't remember Dan.

"Here's what you do, Biggie. I say this as a girl. Walk downstairs to the telephone. Do you have her number memorized? If not, look it up and *then* memorize it immediately, if there's space in your brain next to the wrestling records. Dial the number, ask to speak to Gloria. Identify yourself. After the preliminaries, ask her to come to Champaign this weekend for State. Don't sound like you won't mind if she came along, tell her you'd like it. Then, Biggie, tell her you'd really like it. And then Biggie?"

"What?"

"Tell her she can stay with the Mat Gals."

That's all he needed, Gloria in the lion's den with the Mat Gals.

"Do it now," Giselle said.

"Yes ma'am." Biggie saluted his sister.

"And one more thing."

"Ma'am?"

"After she agrees to come down to Champaign, get off the phone."

He didn't do it *now*, though. *En route* to the phone downstairs, Biggie found himself stepping into the living room to tell Mom and Dad about the calls from Tepper and Safredo.

"Illinois and Indiana?" Mom said.

"They're coming out of the woodwork now," Dad said.

"They haven't actually *offered* anything, but they make a lot of noises about visits and the pleasures of making my acquaintance. In wrestling they don't like to offer you a scholarship unless you're going to accept that same second. They don't have that many to offer, so if they're waiting on your response and you turn them down, they might lose out on another guy."

"An interesting procedure," Dad said.

"I think that's how it works." That was true. The wrestler was operating on general principles. It wasn't as if there were a recruiting manual explaining all the ropes and innuendoes, and not too many guys from HP had won wrestling scholarships.

"This must be a wonderful time for you, Biggie."

Which reminded him of the telephone and Gloria Serpentino. "You bet, Mom."

Still, they didn't want him to go yet, so he shot the breeze more with his parents. Going downstate was a bit like being elected President of the United States probably, that was the thing. Your parents telling you how proud they were of you, and you practically getting on your knees and thanking *them*. ("Mom, Dad, you *let* me lift weights. You never made a big deal about it that I wasn't studying." "That's because you were studying, too," Dad saying. "You didn't neglect your studies." "That's because you gave me good habits," Biggie saying. Mom even getting up and hugging him, a tear in her eye.) And all along you still had to govern if you were elected President, because it probably didn't matter so much if they revered you and you turned out to be a lousy president, like Andrew Johnson or Warren G. Harding. That would be quite a different conversation. ("It's your fault." "No, it's *your* fault.") Just like you still had to win State, once you got to Champaign.

Anyway, Biggie thought that it was nice to say the stuff. Christ, now he felt like circling back to Giselle's room and telling her he owed it all to *her*, except—this was Giselle, too—she'd probably yell at him for not calling Gloria yet. (Though there was no reason *she* couldn't call *him*, and tell him, now he was on the subject—what? Biggie wondered—and then he'd tell her everything about her he was nuts about, being so cute and smart and understanding his point against prohibitive odds (kissing him, too, in front of The Sergeant every day, to the salacious voyeurism of HP). Well, she owed it all to Biggie, and he owed it all to her.)

Once he finally got downstairs and broke away it was too late to call Gloria—not that she wouldn't be up, but her mom and sister wouldn't be, since they were probably annoyed as it was with Gloria tying up the phone constantly. It worked the same way at the Serpentinos' in Highwood as at the Bluestones' in Highland Park. It was also too late, realistically, for Gosley to call and offer that scholarship. They didn't make those calls at 11:30 p.m. on the off-chance you'd be lying awake, waiting for the call. Not something that was going to happen at the Serpentinos', either.

Biggie turned the stereo to a low hum—*Share the Land*, his new favorite album by The Guess Who—and fell asleep thinking about Gloria in Champaign watching him wrestle, her long hair falling to her shoulders, her lips open in surprise and wonderment, everybody watching her, checking her reaction when he pins the guy or even—this wasn't going to happen, no sir—when he loses, the tears falling from her eyes like tiny care packages, fists clenched prayerfully, mouthing his name, and then she makes love to him later, the State Championship Trophy on the headboard above the hotel bed, licking every inch of his body, calling his name, "Big-*gie*, Big-*gie*" louder now, louder, then louder still.

———◦———

State Tournament Week, Tuesday, February 23

At 11:30, he met Gloria at the front door of the school, outside the principal's office and the main hallway.

Biggie was in the same nostalgic mood as last night. If the image of the naked Gloria gave way, the sentiment didn't. First, Gloria took his hand the second she saw him. Before they were boyfriend and girlfriend, as of two days ago, she'd wait until they safely cleared the school grounds. Second, he found himself telling Gloria, "You know, this is pretty cool, don't you think? Not to get too abstract on you, Gloria. I mean the whole business of having a girlfriend. From my perspective, of course, it's nice to have some girl—you—waiting at the door at 11:30, then off we walk hand-in-hand into the sunset toward The Sergeant. I mean, it's something I look forward to, even when I'm not thinking about it. *Especially* then," Biggie added.

"You don't think about it?"

"Naturally, I think about it always. Even when I'm having the worst day. This is hypothetical, because I haven't really had a worst day since yesterday, when we became girlfriend and boyfriend—"

"Sunday," Gloria corrected, squeezing his hand reproachfully.

"Even then, I don't think it would be as bad or calamitous or horrific or whatever—it's like the shit wouldn't hit the fan, but just miss—knowing I have, well, a pretty girl waiting for me come 11:30 sharp."

"*A* pretty girl?"

"Gloria Serpentino waiting for me."

Gloria spun around and kissed him, right on the corner of 4th and Elk, four blocks from the prescribed spot in front of The Sergeant.

"It's nice to know I brighten your day," Gloria explained.

"And I yours?"

She kissed him again.

They were walking again up Elk when Biggie further violated the proscription and placed his arm around her back, pulling Gloria into him as they walked, leaning on one another for support. It reminded Bluestone of one of those World War I movies where Tyrone Power or somebody helped a wounded guy hobble from the foxhole to the first aid tent behind the lines.

Gloria's brown hair was lighter in the sun. Biggie looked through it, down to the sidewalk, and up toward the railroad tracks as they passed the St. John's Station into town. Biggie had the sensation—nothing new, lately—that the entire town and fuck-all, if not half the north shore, scrutinized his every move. *Our* every move, he corrected himself. "I want you to come to Champaign this weekend. Don't worry about transportation or a place to stay, that'll be taken care of. You can stay with Giselle and the Mat Gals."

"I'll get to meet the whole family." Whether that was good or bad he suspected that Gloria didn't know herself.

Biggie squeezed her. "It's the State Tournament. I know the wrestling part of the deal isn't your part, but Gloria, it's *my* part. It's not like there are dozens of parts to me and wrestling's just one of the happy gang. It *is* the happy gang. Look, I might not even get to see you too much down there. It's a madhouse."

"You're really talking me into it."

By now they were in front of The Sergeant. Biggie wondered, now that they were boyfriend and girlfriend, if she'd allow him a *second* kiss as they stood before The Sergeant's picture window, bundled up in coats on a sunny Chicago afternoon in late February, her co-workers watching, no doubt, through the picture window. "*Please.*"

"I'll call you later," Gloria said, then lightly pushed him away. At The Sergeant's door she spun around. "You're very polite, Dan. It surprises my friends to hear that."

"Thank you for noticing," Biggie said.

He thought Gloria was about to offer another observation, but instead she said, "You're welcome."

State Tournament Week, Wednesday, February 24

Luigi, Wing, Hoffman, and Scott Hatch came by to work with Biggie during practice, along with Jerry Bray. Bray, though too light to be useful, couldn't bear the thought of a wrestling practice without him. They traded off working Biggie for drills, but—from what Biggie could tell—all were out of the wrestling mode. Even the Poster Boy resorted to standing against the wall cheerfully clapping his hands, "Big-*gie*! Big-*gie*!

Big-*gie.*" Luigi screamed at Bray to shut up; which didn't stop Luigi from chanting, "State Champ! State Champ! State Champ!" the second Bray shut up. He was pleased they bothered to show up at all, and pinned them repeatedly in short order, even Luigi, who over the course of two days had fully made the conversion back to football and now mostly tried not to get injured as Biggie tossed him around like a tackling dummy. When he told Wetzel he was going down to hit the track and work up a sweat in the basement dungeon, nobody complained.

Biggie made weight by Wednesday after practice. All-time personal best, 1971.

For dinner, the wrestler had an extra slab of roast beef to commemorate the all-time record, an extra half-grapefruit, extra half-head of lettuce in his salad, then was debating whether to chance a half-scoop of ice cream when Roy Gosley called.

Just like he promised.

"Dan, your two matches at Sectionals—against Boyd and Berkenmeier—were the finest back-to-back matches I've ever seen for a high school wrestler, and that's going back forty years. Berkenmeier was rated #1 in the country. You made him look like"—here Roy Gosley chuckled—"a high school kid."

Biggie didn't know what to say. He'd had the drop on Salt Tepper, but this was Mr. Wrestling, and you couldn't very well tell Gosley they *weren't* the finest back-to-back matches he'd seen in forty years, or that he hadn't really been at it forty years. He didn't want to stand in the wind, either, saying, "Shucks, sir, every dog has his day. Probably Berky'll pin me next week at State" to the great Roy Gosley, just to show he wasn't a brash wiseass. "He's tough. He's *real* tough."

Gosley began giving Biggie the Northwestern routine, nothing he hadn't heard before—he'd heard it *yesterday* from Tepper and Sofredo. But with Northwestern the stuff was *true*, it was like going to the Ivy League, yet it was big-time wrestling, his dad probably the most famous guy on the faculty, and—Christ, this occurred to Biggie—he'd seen the beautiful co-eds in the stands, not like Champaign and Bloomington where the *assumption* was reasonable, but at Northwestern he'd seen *firsthand*. Evanston was closer to DeKalb, too, where Gloria would be at Northern; there was that first and foremost. "I've gone to wrestling meets at Northwestern since I was a kid," Biggie said. "I've always wanted to wrestle for the purple and white." ("The purple and white." Talking to Coach Gosley, you felt like suiting up and tearing onto the mat right now in your purple and white.)

"Hold your horses," Gosley chuckled. "You'll redshirt freshman year—while Drake Watson's a senior—then wrestle varsity four years straight."

"Yes, sir."

"Four years is an eternity in wrestling, Dan."

Biggie thought, this *conversation* is an eternity.

"We'll talk about it this weekend. Dan, tell me straight out. Do you want to be a Northwestern Wildcat?"

"Yes sir!"

Bluestone sensed the Icon Incarnate was mildly disappointed that Biggie didn't snarl.

"That was Coach Gosley," Biggie told Mom and Dad in the living room. "Northwestern. How's their Sociology Department, Dad?"

Mom crossed the room and kissed Biggie. Dad stood beside her and shook his hand. Though they were so corny about it, they'd probably been waiting for years to drool all over him; any excuse would do.

Ten minutes later, in the middle of a set of clapping pushups, Biggie thrusting himself in the air, clapping his chest between repetitions, the wrestler got another surprise.

A knock on the glass door of the downstairs entrance.

Sweating from his set, his veins firing, face set in a glower, shirt off. The look didn't encourage solicitors selling magazine subscriptions.

It was Gloria.

Gloria.

He opened the door like a maniac before she'd turn and walk away, or the image would prove an apparition.

"You looked like you wanted to kill me."

"I thought you were selling magazine subscriptions."

She was wearing a light brown cloth coat, as if she'd stolen away—this Biggie liked thinking—before she could talk herself out of it. More likely, her mom saw her in the coat and warned her, "Don't visit the Bluestone boy. He's bad news."

"Here I am," Gloria said. "I hope you're not mad."

"Here *I* am."

"Well dressed, Dan."

"I don't dress for school until morning," Biggie said, staring at her.

"I mean it." Gloria ran her hand over his bare chest. His legs quivered as if she'd traced his name with an ice cube.

"Christ."

"Oh, Sweetie, you say Christ a lot for a guy who doesn't swear too much. And who's Jewish to boot." Gloria kissed his shoulder.

Christ.

Could she really be this beautiful? Gloria Serpentino? The sound itself made his legs *quiver* again. Biggie wondered if there was some deficiency in him because he wondered if Gloria was as beautiful as he thought she was. There had to be a point where you stopped wondering about superficial crap like that, a point where you only cared if she was beautiful to *you*, as they always said in songs. Even *that* was superficial. The guys out there who had fully shed their superficiality probably didn't even care if their girls were beautiful to *them*, that's how deep they were. Did Dad walk around asking himself these questions? It was odd, when he thought about it. Nobody ever called you superficial if you found sunsets and mountain streams and opera beautiful, but if you found a *woman*—who was about a thousand times as important in Biggie's book—beautiful and valued that for its own sake, at face value, everybody always yelled that you were superficial; so you ended up yelling back, "I mean *inside* her skin. She's beautiful *inside*," just to get them off your back. But when you got down to it, most guys were probably superficial bastards like Biggie, who had nothing against inner beauty so long as nobody rubbed their noses in it—you could wind up going to operas if you didn't watch yourself, or driving out to catch the sunset over the lake—and thought there was a hell of a lot to be said for outer beauty, too.

Gloria Serpentino was beautiful in the half-light of the Bluestone basement. If the extent of her beauty surprised Biggie, he was seeing her for the first time, really, now. Her face was plain and asymmetrical but filled with mystery and light, her eyes playful and mischievous but turning suddenly an intensity of somber, probing consideration. They encouraged each other, standing in the rec room. Long brown hair, thick and gorgeous—nobody would dispute that—more thin than not, lithe, average height, raw, down-to-earth like nobody he'd ever seen. Christ, it didn't do her justice. *Average* height? There was nothing average about her, let alone her height, that's what Biggie thought, taking her in. Those were the parts. The sum of her parts times a thousand equaled her whole, but could you tell a girl that? They probably liked to think the parts were fine, too. But the whole was the game, what counted, what kept you searching over mountains and oceans, and driving out to sunsets, acting like a maniac always on the verge. Imminent. This nobody knew. These were Gloria's parts, which Biggie was in the process of negotiating firsthand once she removed her fingers from his chest, his legs still quivering—it could be *never* and he'd die happy—a guy who'd kissed Gloria Serpentino, stood in his basement as she ran her hand across his chest, was officially boyfriend and girlfriend with; he'd been in the mix, yes, nobody could say otherwise—now she kissed his lips, running her tongue along his lips before he opened his mouth and met her tongue with his own. Christ.

Biggie dropped to his knees. By now her blouse and bra were off; he couldn't see her breasts in the half-light as they crashed into his chest and he lifted and carried her into his room, lowered her lightly to his bed, and Gloria said his name. Gloria stripped her pants off before Biggie hit the bed. "Dan, close the door," she pointed. Now he could hear the TV upstairs. Mom yelling to Dad about a dentist's appointment. Walking through the darkness he felt his way to the hi-fi, turned it on: Carole King's *Tapestry*. The room was totally dark, so he opened the shade above the hi-fi, where a slant of artificial light cut across the floor. "I can't see you with the door closed. I want to see you."

"It's not *about* seeing with your eyes, Dan. That counts, but it's seeing with your skin, seeing with your hands. Here," Gloria took Biggie's hand and directed it over her breasts. He lightly traced her aureoles. He closed his eyes as his hands combed over her pubic hair, his quivering fingers feeling the way inside, her surprising wetness as he straddled her then took off his clothes and lay beside her, two naked bodies over the covers, then under the covers, their limbs and trunks entangled, breasts pushing into chest, seeing with their skins. "You see with your heart and soul and dreams, too, Dan. I really think that, so don't laugh. That's why people make so many mistakes in love. They see with their eyes only. Or they see with their dreams and hopes but not their eyes."

"Love is a crapshoot is what you're saying."

"Dan, you've said it all. But if you see with your dreams and your heart and your soul, you'll never have anything to regret."

He didn't want to think where she learned this stuff.

They weren't to make love. That was the rule, firmly established.

Biggie kissed her again, swimming and fluttering in her mouth and breath. This lasted minutes that seemed like seconds that seemed like hours—that's how time hit the wrestler now. He'd never been more patient in his life. "Well, what would happen if we ended up making love tonight?"

"We'd love it. But I'd never talk to you again, Buster."

"Because you'd see me with your eyes, I guess."

She squeezed Buster tighter.

He could lick every inch of her body. He could lick her wetness, now no longer surprising but alive with predictability. He could lick her shoulders and thighs and the bottoms of her feet. He could suck her metatarsal. When she moaned he could lick her neck, her leg always hooking Biggie's, too. When it unhooked she immediately re-hooked it, "That's too close," she murmured once, as his penis brushed her, Gloria's voice box vibrating against his tongue and breath.

"You're gorgeous," Biggie said. "You're the most gorgeous. I'll say that for you."

"Probably half the girls in Highland Park have been down here like this." Gloria's head lay against his chest, her hands clasping Biggie's.

"Every night in my dreams."

"You have a nice setup down here, Dan. I practically *share* a room with Vicky, my sister."

"I know she's your sister."

Gloria blew in his ear.

"Move in here."

Gloria playfully moved her hand through his hair. "I might, if you keep this up."

"I mean it." He did. Now.

"How does it feel to be inside that body?" Gloria squeezed his arms. "I mean these muscles are pretty amazing, Dan, you have to know that. You don't have a shred of fat, either, just like a slab of rock face. Fuck-all, Dan, if you think I'm beautiful; *you're* like a force of nature. How does it feel to walk around inside a sculpture?"

"It's a blast."

"Sometimes when I talk to you, I feel—I used to feel this way, any-way—like you've built yourself into this rock so nobody can see inside."

"Works well on the mat, too."

"I think I'm being unfair," Gloria said.

"You know me."

"Maybe that's how I expected you to be."

Gloria lifted her head and began petting his chest, until he ran his hand along her cheek and held it, hooking his eyes as they talked. "I was driving around tonight, Dan. I hadn't really done that since we met. A lot of nights I just stay home, waiting to talk to you. It's as if I spent every hour worrying about my parents' divorce, and suddenly I hardly give it a thought and I'm all wrapped up in Dan Bluestone."

"*Now* you really are," Biggie said, entangling her arm.

"So here I am, wrapped up in Dan Bluestone."

"Thanks for stopping by on your drive."

"But my mother's still miserable, Dan, and my parents are still getting divorced, and Vicky still doesn't know what hit her. Here's Gloria, though, happy as a lark. She's got the guy she wanted."

"That's good or bad?"

"Oh it's good, Dan." Gloria kissed him hurriedly. "But I wanted you to know that I may not be everything you think. I may just be hiding away."

"I guess I don't want to see you as some kind of answer, either."

Gloria laughed. She rocked in his arms and laughed. For a moment their legs unhooked—quickly re-hooked, Biggie noticed—and Biggie caught her rhythm, laughing until his bed rocked like a dinghy, laughter intensifying with each tremor, until he feared his bed might collapse to the floor. Not that he cared, now, rocking Gloria, Gloria laughing in his arms, catching her breath, rubbing his nose with her own. "No, Dan 'Wrestling Is Everything I Am' Bluestone. I don't think anyone would ever think that you're looking at me as the answer."

"I'm beginning to see you as the question!" Biggie said.

This inspired another round of laughter. "Stop it, Dan!" Gloria said.

It *wasn't* fair, though. Even as he rocked her on his bed, he thought it wasn't *fair* to say he didn't look to her as the answer. The hell he didn't. Fuck if she wasn't. She filled in the blanks, crossed the T's, turned out the lights, turned them back on with a brightness reflecting everything everywhere he looked. Every fucking thing. She turned his feelings inside out. Hers was the voice he wanted to hear when he swept the floor or ran along Sheridan Road through the night. She whispered the secrets he'd always wanted to hear.

But wrestling was different. He thought of the kid he'd been, going to sleep at night dreaming of winning State Championships, an odd kid with a palpable yearning to be, well, just who he was now, a human being equal to the one dream, anyway. Bluestone said as much—though it was odd, too, vaguely preposterous, to find himself holding Gloria Serpentino in his arms, sticking up for his sport and the kid he'd been.

"I only mean there's an imbalance. I don't want to get too caught up, okay, in this." Gloria looked around the room. "In us. Not anymore than I already am. That's why I didn't want to make love. It's powerful, Dan. Anyway, you're going to Northwestern or Michigan and I'm going to Northern Illinois in DeKalb. End of story."

"Northern recruited me," Biggie told her suddenly.

Add impetuous to vaguely preposterous.

He didn't *want* to say it, not yet. You spend a month not telling her about recruiting because you'd have to tell her *her* school was after you, too, feeling like a slimy guilty bastard every second, then it suddenly pops out like a tooth.

Biggie steeled himself for the eruption.

"I know," Gloria said softly.

"You *know*?"

"You're the greatest wrestler in history, Dan. Of course you could go to Northern if you wanted. Give me some credit."

"I should have mentioned it earlier."

"I want you to go where you want to go, that's what I want. You need the Big Ten. I'll be in DeKalb."

Later she told Biggie, "When my friends wonder what you're like, I tell them you're the *nicest* guy. You really touch me. I mean that, Dan. It's such a surprise. Of course, my friends all think you're cute and handsome and fuck-all."

"*I'm* cute and handsome?"

"They think that all you do is work out and run and build up your muscles, that you never talk to anybody. They think you're a monster or something."

"That's *good*," Biggie said.

"They *envy* me," Gloria said.

Later, Gloria stared into his eyes. "I'm sorry I'm such a mess."

"You're not a mess."

"I'm sorry to rain on your parade. You deserve better."

"You're not raining on my parade."

"Oh, I'm bringing you down to Earth, Dan."

"I'm flying untethered."

"G'won," Gloria laughed.

Biggie said, "I make things more complicated, too, than they have to be. Who doesn't? Christ, you should see half the guys I know, talk about complicated. These guys think seven times seven equals two, and two times two is 49. But I'm the world's specialist. *I'm* the mess. I'm raining on your parade, Gloria, not the other way around. I'm bringing *you* down to Earth."

"I'm flying untethered," Gloria said.

Later.

"I just want to see you with my eyes *and* heart and soul and dreams."

"I don't see why not," Biggie said.

They stood in the dark kitchen sharing a glass of water, staring into each other's eyes, saying nothing.

It was almost midnight.

"I better go. Wouldn't want you tired for the weekend, Dan."

Biggie nodded.

Gloria kissed him again.

Mom walked into the kitchen in her robe, her hair as startled as her eyes, recoiling as if she'd spotted Queen Elizabeth embracing her son next to the refrigerator.

He kept his arm around Gloria as she smiled at him and turned to face his mom.

"I thought I heard some noises in the kitchen." Mom smiled at Gloria.

Mom would smile if she saw Genghis Khan.

"This is Gloria."

Anybody else would go back to their room, but Mom had to start a *conversation* with Gloria. She teased out that Gloria was going to Northern next year, that she lived in Highwood, her dad was a mechanic, Vicky was her sister. Before Mom fished out whether Biggie had made love to Gloria—Gloria would have told her, too, that was the thing with Mom, told her about the special prohibition on fucking, everything but was okay, until Gloria felt like she was seeing Biggie not only with the heart and soul and dreams, but the eyes, too. Refrained from telling Gloria, "I didn't think Biggie would ever have a girl over." Bluestone managed to steer Gloria out of the kitchen and halfway toward the front door, Gloria pulling back toward the kitchen. "*Dan,*" she protested.

"Will you be in Champaign this weekend?" Mom managed to work in, following them into the hallway before he got Gloria through the door.

"I'll be there," Biggie said.

Gloria smiled at Biggie and spun toward Mom in the hallway. "Mrs. Bluestone, I wouldn't miss it for the world."

When Bluestone came back from walking Gloria to the Buick parked on Sheridan, he knew his mom would be waiting in the kitchen—Jesus, she'd bring in Dad and Giselle to work him over, too—armed with 8,000 questions.

The kitchen light was on, a note on the counter.

Biggie, she's cute.

Downstate, Thursday, February 25

"Big Dan Bluestone's a buzzsaw, a machine, a monster, a stud, a comer," Wing was saying in a radio announcer's voice.

"You're right, Wing. They don't call Big Dan Bluestone *Biggie* because he wrestles small. The man's a man," Luigi commented.

"Thank you, Luigi. The man's a force of nature. Incidentally, fans listening at home, no hot potato can resist his charms. Yes, he'll be heard from come the finals Saturday night."

"Tell these guys to shut up. Please."

That's the way it had been all the way down from Chicago Thursday afternoon. If it were anybody else driving, they could blast the radio. But it was Wetzel driving. Wetzel kept it tuned to WBBM, the all-news station.

"They'll need to reckon with Big Dan Bluestone. King of the brackets at 167. This is Wing Terrill, news radio sssseventy-eight."

The hissing was the signature of the main guy who read the news on WBBM.

"Wing, you're a douche bag. This is Luigi Cravi, news radio ssssssseventy-eight."

Wetzel drove, along with Luigi in the front seat, Wing and Biggie in the back of the official HP station wagon. "Wing Terrill and Luigi Cravi are along for moral support," was how Wetzel made the authorization case to the principal.

"And now a word from our sponsor," Luigi said. "There's something about an Aqua Velva man."

"Something truly perverted," Wing added.

His parents were driving down after work with Cravi's parents. They'd found a couple of hotel rooms in Monticello, twenty miles outside of Champaign, where every room was booked. Luigi's folks didn't care for wrestling any more than his folks; they were there to watch Biggie, and to watch Luigi lending moral support. Biggie wondered if he ever had a kid if he'd find himself driving all the way down from Chicago to Champaign to watch the kid lend moral support. It wouldn't surprise him either way. Mrs. Cravi called last night to see if they could hook up with a ride. "We wouldn't miss it for anything," she'd told Mom.

Enough of the Mat Gals signed on to secure a school bus; they'd come down with the JV cheerleaders and several guys from the team—Mandel, Bray, Blake, Hatch, Hoffman. Giselle would go along on the bus, as would Gloria. The bus wouldn't leave until tomorrow morning at 5:00, early enough to get there for the first session, though it was hard for Biggie to imagine Giselle showing up that early. One of the advantages of qualifying for the State Tournament, it turned out, was that you didn't have to catch the bus at 5 a.m., but could drive along in the official station wagon the day before.

"Thanks for the encouragement." Biggie looked over the brackets for the thousandth time.

"Shut up, you two," Wetzel piped in.

Count on Wetzel to come through.

Wing looked wounded, staring out the window.

"What'd you weigh before we left?" Wetzel asked Biggie for the fourth time, "174?"

Wetzel's luck. A State Champ in the works, but the stud freaks out and doesn't make weight.

"173." One over the given allowance. He was sure he'd dropped another pound already from the sheer effort of trying not to listen to Wing and Luigi.

After they pulled into the Holiday Inn Urbana, Biggie and Wetzel in one room, Wing and Luigi, with Hoffman and Bray and Blake and Mandel and whomever else they could pull into the other—Biggie pictured those newspaper photos of fraternity boys piling into phone booths or Volkswagens, that's how it would be one room over while he tried to sleep—not that anybody else had it better; it's not as if Berkenmeier would be hiring a chopper to fly back up to Mundelein between matches—Wetzel spent half an hour prepping Bluestone, the first legitimate coaching he'd gotten in three years from the ex-Rutgers football star. "Downstate it's not always the best wrestler, Biggie, it's who can adjust to the distractions. There'll be 15,000 at Assembly Hall tomorrow."

Not 15, like at HP.

"There are parties all night at the hotel. There's endless commotion and noise pouring through the walls as you lie in your strange bed. Do you have a favorite routine? A pattern of superstitions before a match, Biggie? Not downstate you won't."

He'd been dreaming of wrestling downstate since he was in short pants, and Wetzel assumed he'd get distracted by the partying down the hall. "I understand," Biggie said. "It's not the better wrestler, it's the better *focused* wrestler."

"It's the better focused wrestler, that's correct."

"But it doesn't *hurt* to be the better wrestler," Wing noted.

The problem with running in a strange city is that you couldn't really break into a sprint and get the nerves firing too much, couldn't get a rhythm going or sustain a fantasy, because you had to pay attention to where you were.

Groups of guys in sweatsuits were running all over Urbana. It still struck Biggie that a lot of schools sent half-a-dozen guys downstate. Not that it threw him to see the hordes of wrestlers bobbing through the streets in their sweatsuits. A lot of those schools were from downstate, which weren't as tough as the suburban sectionals—still, plenty of downstate guys took State, something nobody from HP had ever done—but for Biggie, who hated running in packs—it was tough to get the veins firing when you had to advance a conversation—also, there was the matter of having to *beat* the other guy when you ran—you didn't exactly want Jerry Bray finishing stronger, even when you were out for a casual run with the pack mainly to loosen up—so they were worth watching even if as a rule their Sectionals were easier. There were also plenty of lone guys like Biggie running, plenty more packs of two to six. He kept his eyes open for Granite City sweatshirts. The guy he drew tomorrow morning, first round, was from Granite City, Daryl Workman, a junior, 21-8 on the season.

While Biggie kept his eyes open, he went over keeping his arms in close to his trunk and exploding with the hip throws and back tosses. He visualized a series of penetration steps, reminded himself to lift with his legs—this was the State Tournament, after all. Against a lot of guys, he could get by with just using his upper body. Against Daryl Workman, realistically, but he didn't want to look sloppy. If nobody he'd wrestle was nearly as good as Berkenmeier or Boyd, you couldn't overlook anybody; that was the deal downstate. You had to be a little terrified and Biggie did his best to take that view to heart. Although both the *Trib* and the *Sun-Times* listed Biggie in their State Previews as the favorite at 167, Daryl Workman possibly never heard of him. They had their own frame of reference in southern Illinois, their own icons. They didn't consult the *Sun-Times* State Preview. These guys in the brackets probably hadn't given *Berkenmeier* a thought all year. They had different styles of wrestling, too, Biggie emphasized to himself as he ran slowly. And you knew if a school sent half a dozen guys downstate—Granite City did every year—that their guys, the Daryl Workmans, knew what they were doing on the mat. Not just a few moves and muscle, the Bluestone formula. Biggie ran, trying to get worked up and terrified, then turned around after a couple of miles and ran back.

Wetzel was watching an Andy Griffith rerun with Luigi and Wing on Channel 9. "You're back," Wetzel registered, then turned back to the set.

The three looked pretty engrossed.

After drinking a glass of water, he cut over to Luigi and Wing's room next door—the door was open—and fell to the floor for a set of pushups.

Downstate.

His parents called when they checked in at the Inn in Monticello, twenty miles away, with Mom going on for ten minutes about how much they wished Biggie luck tomorrow, how proud of him they were, all the crap they were telling him these days every time he left the house. "I need to get some rest, Mom," Biggie broke in. "Enjoy Monticello."

The instant he hung up, Gloria called. "Enjoying yourself, Dan? Are you by yourself?"

"It's a blast," Biggie said. "I just had dinner—that's salad and a grapefruit—in the Holiday Inn coffee shop. Wetzel's still down there talking to half a dozen other coaches—the place is a convention. Wing and Luigi are prowling the Holiday Inn hallways looking for cheerleaders. They can't get any cheerleaders from HP to talk to them, but they expect to score down here. It's not a matter of their *personalities*, it's the location."

"Are there a lot of cheerleaders at the Holiday Inn?"

"Not enough for Terrill and Cravi, but it's teeming." Every room in the joint was crawling with wrestlers or cheerleaders or coaches. Or else guys like Wing and Luigi, along for *moral support*. "Maybe I'll get a cheerleader myself. Wing promised to bring one back in the spirit of moral support."

"Put your hands on your dick," Gloria said.

Biggie obliged.

"Think of me," Gloria said.

"Have a good trip tomorrow with the Mat Gals. Maybe you could stay here tomorrow night?"

"Wetzel would love that," Gloria said.

Not only was Gloria willing to watch him wrestle, but she knew the coach's name.

You couldn't just sit in your room doing nothing but waiting for the time to pass and thinking terrifying thoughts about Daryl Workman, 21-8.

Biggie pulled on his coat and walked outside into the cold February night and began walking. A full lap around the Holiday Inn. The high school world had already descended upon Urbana. Yelping girls were running up and down the hallways, yelping guys chasing them. Yelping guys ran down the hallways, yelping girls chasing them. Any moment he expected to see Terrill or Cravi yelping down the hallway after a yelping girl.

Right now there were probably guys along for moral support all around Urbana thanking their lucky stars they didn't have to wrestle tomorrow. *Downstate.* Probably, if you'd gone to a lot of parties, you felt like you were missing something. He always felt like he was missing something when he wasn't invited to parties he'd heard about, when he heard about them, as if some pretty girl was liable to seize the chance to hustle over and reveal that she worshipped the hallowed ground he walked on. At the parties he'd gone to—all official functions—no girl had ever run up to him, even when he was off sitting by himself in the kind of brooding contemplation that pretty girls were known to find sexy. It crossed his mind, too—Biggie not encouraging the notion but not fighting against the flow either, giving his mind free reign—that here *he* was, the focal point, the star, the greatest season in Illinois history—not that he'd scratched the surface of his abilities or aspirations—and all these other kids were the ones yelping through the halls like young seals, half of them probably *coupling* later, the hope of which could send you through the halls yelping—*coupling*. Christ, he felt like yelping himself while he circled the Holiday Inn trying to do something as his thoughts ran, other than sit in his room trying to read—impossible—or watch TV—impossible.

Forty-eight hours and his fate would be revealed.

It was probably a little like your wedding, Biggie figured. You wanted to savor the moment, but you had a thousand things to pay attention to and everybody looked like they were having a million times more fun than you, about a hundred people congratulating you every time you turned around, then running off to look for more fun, but it was your wedding, after all, and damn if you weren't having the time of your life.

That's what he decided as he paced around the Holiday Inn. This was the time of his life, like it or not.

Trumpets, Friday, February 26

After Biggie slept ten hours, he woke up to find Wetzel in the other bed snoring like a freighter. The wrestler threw some water on his face and took a run to slap his drowsiness awake. Back from the run, he found Wetzel gone; probably looking for Biggie, as if the wrestler had freaked out from all the distractions and bolted for South America. The wrestler showered, then came out of the bathroom to find Wing and Luigi sitting on Wetzel's bed, Wetzel straightening his tie in the mirror.

"We had a cheerleader for you, but you were out like a lamp." Wing.

"I had her instead. Knew you wouldn't mind." Luigi.

"That was a girl?" Wing.

Wetzel stared in the mirror, straightening his collar. "You boys are sounding like a couple of juveniles."

"But happy juveniles," Wing said.

On the drive to Assembly Hall, nobody said anything, and he was so grateful he wanted to thank them. It had never been a good idea to talk to Biggie before a match, and it would have been a worse idea now. They pulled into the lot at 7:04. Weigh-in was open from 7-8. Wetzel had lined up their credentials by phone the night before, so they walked through the side door and secured their passes. A dozen scales were lined up in this huge weigh-in room—what it was ordinarily Biggie had no idea (possibly a banquet hall, except that it was beside the locker room)—where a couple of hundred wrestlers milled around with their coaches. Biggie idly looked around for Berkenmeier. Couldn't see him. After half an hour of climbing the walls, Bluestone weighed in, one under. Wetzel patted him on the back and cheered. Then Biggie walked through the locker room, out the door, onto the arena floor.

Here it was. Eight mats spread across the floor. Wrestlers rolling around already. The first matches were scheduled to start at nine. It would be eleven before Biggie wrestled, but he wanted to sink into the mats—though suddenly he thought of Gloria riding down on the bus with the Mat Gals and cheerleaders, barely past Collinsville by now—and walked out to the middle of a mat where he lay down and rolled back onto his shoulders. He closed his eyes, arched into a bridge, spun around—slowly—into a front bridge. After several minutes, he stood by himself in the middle of the mat while practicing feints, hip heists, and penetration drills where he leaned in so deep he flopped to his belly against the soft mat. Downstate. He practiced numerous deep back arches—effectively tossing the air through the air—and landings, forward and backward somersaults, as teeming wrestlers in pairs practiced sit outs and rolls.

When he passed the practice mat on the way back into the locker room, he shot half a dozen singles against the wall, his palms barely brushing the wall padding as he shot back to his feet. Biggie Bluestone never felt quicker in his life.

There was nothing to do but wrestle the damn match. Daryl Workman of Granite City, fuck you. It hardly seemed possible, too. Biggie gazed up into the stands, imagined all of the 15,000 seats filled, then walked back through the locker room, where so many wrestlers and coaches and officials said hello to him in the mindless, offhand, sincere, curious manner of an initiate identifying fellow initiates—that's what it was, a functional organization, a convention—it was pointless not to say hello back, or to swear in their faces, "Christ, can't you see I have a match in two hours?" Then the wrestler walked out the same door he came in, to the parking lot where Wetzel waited for him with Wing and Luigi.

They went out for breakfast. Nobody said a word to Biggie; he said nothing back.

After that it was a madhouse, a circus, a zoo. Biggie took in even less.

Chaotic moments descended upon the earth and rose like helium balloons before the air they landed in could be breathed. Then onward to the next balloon. That's how it seemed.

Out of a crowd of 15,000 he could pick out Mom and Dad, easy. He could pick out Giselle, give him half-a-minute. Gloria, he knew, was in the middle of section 228A. He didn't have a clue where that was, other than on the second tier, but knew within seconds he'd zero in and spot her from the floor, such was their chemistry and instinct. That's what he would have thought.

Biggie pacing the locker room. He paced the hallways outside. The fuck of it was, Wetzel was right. You really hated to give Wetzel credit, but he nailed the target. This was to every other match he'd ever had what LaSalle Street was to the game of Monopoly. You could focus like a maniac—he was a maniac himself, he was Killer Kowalski—and there were *still* 15,000 people out there. Fuckers all.

Though it turned out, this Biggie discovered long before he lined up across the circle from Daryl Workman of Granite City, 21-8, Sectional runner-up, there weren't too many of the same people looking at *you*, not with eight mats, wrestlers scuttling back and forth across the floor like rodents as their names are called with their match numbers, their mats identified—this all stuff Wetzel took care of—and then the moment was at hand, you were lined up across from Daryl Workman, and fuck if it's not a lot like every other match, State Tournament or no State Tournament, 15,000 or the sole companionship of your dreams, so kiss my ass, that's what Biggie thought.

At the whistle he moved in on Workman, a tall, thin guy, gawky, a leg rider, Biggie guessed. Workman moved in, grabbing Biggie's headgear—because you only had to take one look at Biggie Bluestone, identify the undefeated record from the published brackets, to see what he was about, muscle and explosion—Workman with nothing to lose, no chance, free as the breeze, nothing at stake but his dignity—trying to tie Biggie up, squeezing, to draw him in close so Biggie couldn't set up anything from the full range, protecting against the straight away angle. Biggie's in low on the hips as Workman reaches in, explodes in a lift, steps across with his right leg to hook Workman above the right knee, drives clear through him as they hit the mat, Biggie driving his elbow past the ear on contact with the mat, easing in the half before he senses it's there (Wing was right, he was a force of nature), though Workman's already on his back, already pinned in thirty-two seconds.

Time slowed up again. Wetzel shook his hand vigorously as Biggie wondered where everybody was. Then Wetzel placed his arm on Biggie's back. Now he noticed the JV cheerleaders, Rona Lefler, Cindy Shelton, Kerry Lipschutz, Julie Beamer—they'd arrived mat-side just as he worked the turn for the pin—hugging each other, then staring at him bemused, as if wishing he'd delayed the stick for their arrival. Then Biggie saw his parents in the second tier, sitting with Giselle and the Mat Gals and Gloria. Wing and Luigi, too. A hundred feet across the floor, Berkenmeier was up 12-0 in the second period. Biggie charged up to the second tier, worked in a few words with his parents ("Why do there have to be so many mats?" his mom asked. "I'll raise the issue with the Tournament Director." "My son the wiseass," Dad said proudly to Mr. Cravi), worked in a few with Giselle, chatted up the Mat Gals—they'd come all this way, after all ("Could you see from up here?" he asked everybody. "How was the drive?")—though it seemed Wing and Luigi were up to the task by themselves, working the Mat Gals, none of whom he could recall the two showing the least interest in before—nobody but Bray and Hoffman and Mandel *watching* the matches. Probably they hadn't watched *his* match. After a round of peppy congratulations, his parents went back to their conversation with Luigi's parents.

She was there all along, at the edge of the third row, second tier, wearing a black sweater and jeans, looking straight ahead, smiling to herself as Biggie played the Camp Director, greeting each, knowing she was there, that he'd get to her last—he enjoyed this, building the tension, taking an extra word with a Mat Gal here, an extra comment there to Mr. Cravi, working the crowd—a new Biggie if there ever was, which was the point—casually then, at last, walking down the row to Gloria, to whom he says, "Miss, how was the view?"

Gloria rose with her outstretched arms, staring into his eyes outlandishly like they were standing in front of The Sergeant in the privacy of Elk Street as if—this occurred to Biggie, also—playing her role, the two of them part of this show, Camp Director and Girl. Hand-in-hand they walk up the concrete steps into the hallway circling the second tier.

"I can't believe you're here."

"That was fabulous, Dan."

"G'won."

"You g'won."

They were standing against the wall at the end of the hallway, Biggie with his arm around Gloria.

"You're just saying that. I know. But it was pretty amazing. Nobody's paying attention, it's a zoo, a circus. I mean, do the cages keep the animals out, or the people out? You have to wonder. But still the sound descends upon you like you're suspended in the middle of a seashell. You wrestle in complete privacy, Gloria—it's a lot different than HP—though, theoretically, 15,000 people still watch every move, to say nothing of everybody else—for instance, my mom's sister and every relative up and down the Jersey coast—who wants to know how I did, she's probably on the phone calling Jersey right now—'One down, three to go, Sis'—well, here's what I want to say: I stayed focused, that's the thing, I was in the cave, the fog. I didn't notice any of that, not even the noise till afterward."

"Take a breath, Biggie."

He did, was for a moment overcome by a wave of dizziness, as if he'd hyperventilated posing with one arm on Gloria's shoulder, the other hand against the wall, the dizziness followed by a wave of nausea that nearly snapped him in two. When the waves passed and he braced himself for another, they were gone.

Gloria kissed him, not melodramatically as she had in front of the Highland Park section of the second tier, the Camp Director's good ol' gal playing the role she knew Biggie wanted, but with a tenderness as alarming as it was reassuring. "A lot of kids say they want to be State Champ, I'll bet, but the next week they dream about being fire chief. You should have seen me back when I was a kid. I *still* change my mind every week. Sometimes I want to be Biggie Bluestone's wife, sometimes I want to be an astronaut," Gloria was saying, staring into his eyes.

"Will you write to me from space?"

"Dan, I love your parents and sister."

"They love you."

"How do you know that?"

"Why wouldn't they?"

"Your mom was telling me even when you were a little boy, you'd do your pushups. While other kids were asking if they could stay up to play with their tinker toys, you'd go out to take a run around the block."

"She *told* you this," Biggie said.

"It was so cute."

That's all he needed, Mom regaling the Mat Gals and cheerleaders—Wing and Luigi, too—and half the second tier with stories of little Biggie's inspirational determination. "I thought I could trust Mom to use her judgment," Biggie said dismally. "Plus a measure of common decency."

"She's your mother. She's *proud* of you. This is her moment, too."

"Next she'll be saying that when I had that accident in my pants in the third grade, she thought nothing would come of me."

"Giselle's great, too. I really think we could be friends. I don't say that about too many people."

Giselle, at least, he could trust not to humiliate him with sentimental retellings of her brother's most embarrassing moments. "Other guys have to worry about their matches, I have to worry about what my *mom's* going to say. How about my dad? Did he stick up for me? Did he deny anything?"

"I don't think your dad was listening." Gloria squeezed his hand.

"That's why they're still married." Still, he wouldn't have minded if his dad had rallied to his defense; realistically, there wasn't much he could do when Mom went off like that. Knowing Dad, he'd only wind up correcting Mom: "You're wrong, Minnie. He didn't run around the block. He ran around the block *twice*."

"How was Giselle? Was she interacting with the other girls?"

Gloria turned and looked strangely at Biggie. "Don't worry, Dan. Your sister's a popular girl. She's a great interactor. Giselle interacts very well. She's the opposite of you. She *talks* to people."

"Keep Luigi away from her, too."

"I promise."

"Well, we better get back before Mom recites my bar mitzvah speech."

"Sorry I missed that one."

"I'm sure it's not too late."

But they didn't go anywhere. They stood against the wall watching everybody walk by. People glanced at Biggie in his HP sweats, "167" stitched across the back, then glanced at Gloria, holding their look a few seconds longer until they passed. Biggie hated guys like he was being—holding up a pretty girl for public display, so everybody could see how great he was—but as much as he hated the way he was being, he loved standing against the second-tier wall of Assembly Hall with Gloria Serpentino. "I can't believe you're here."

"I know. Me too."

"Will you sleep with me at the Holiday Inn tonight? We can send Wetzel to stay with the Mat Gals. That's a fair exchange." That's where

Gloria would be, with the Mat Gals at a Vacation Best outside Urbana. "Wetzel would like that, too, I imagine."

"I wish I could."

"That's what I mean. I wish you could."

As they walked back, Coach Safredo, the Illinois coach, emerged in the second-tier hallway and cut a beeline toward Biggie. "Nice match, Dan. Business as usual, I see. How do you like our facility?"

"Great facility."

Safredo extended his hand. Biggie shook it with a quick pump.

Over the next two days, he'd shake Safredo's hand approximately thirty-seven times.

After he posited Gloria back with the Mat Gals in the second tier, half of them already disappeared—his next match wasn't until tonight, against a kid from East St. Louis Lincoln who won 7-2 in the first round against a kid from Peoria Woodruff—he went out for lunch with Wetzel. Terrill and Cravi came along for moral support. He thought of asking his parents along—they probably expected to take him out for lunch—but he knew they'd ask the remaining Mat Gals and cheerleaders and Gloria, along with Mr. and Mrs. Cravi. They'd pick up the bill, too. A circus he didn't need, with the kid from East St. Louis Lincoln already in his sights. Biggie explained to Gloria, "I need to focus. With you I'm addled, scatterbrained, a feather fluttering in the gale force."

"That's fine. I'll tag along with Giselle, or ask your Mom for your bar mitzvah speech."

Sometimes he couldn't tell if Gloria toyed with him because she loved him or just liked busting his balls.

Business was as usual at the Holiday Inn. Every table teeming with wrestlers and coaches playing musical chairs.

"A lot of wrestlers under one roof," Wing said.

"You'd think they were offering a grapefruit special."

Biggie ordered a steak sandwich, medium, along with a side salad. He'd have to run after his match tonight to work off the steak, but he'd run anyway to dull the edge and tire himself out. Sheer adrenaline burned a pound or two.

Safredo walked through the restaurant, working every table. He shook Biggie's hand again and winked at him. As the Illinois coach, Safredo was the Meet Director. He *had* to pull this kind of gladhanding shit. But Biggie could tell Safredo loved every second of it, though there weren't more than three seniors in the whole tournament, at most, who'd sign with Illinois. The other State Champs would either wrestle someplace else, or, as was mostly the case, weren't good enough for Illinois. Still, in twenty minutes Safredo shook the hands of fifty kids, none of whom he was recruiting—except Biggie—and more than a dozen coaches, none of whom would likely ever have a kid who'd wrestle for Illinois.

"I asked around," Wetzel reported. Anthony Burroughs—the East St. Louis Lincoln kid he'd wrestle tonight—got in unbelievably quick on the single, was pretty basic, though, on the bottom, and possessed a vicious crossbody ride he'd turn for back points. "A great rider, that's the word."

"Thanks." Not that Biggie didn't *want* to know—he'd spend the afternoon envisioning himself breaking the crossbody or sitting out and throwing hip heists so Burroughs couldn't hook his leg in the first place—but the reports were often based on one or two matches. Probably Wetzel talked to a guy who'd seen Burroughs wrestle the Peoria guy this morning and remembered him working the crossbody for back points. You were liable to go nuts guarding against the crossbody, when the kid wasn't that big on it in the first place, just happened to see an opening. Anyway, there was plenty of stuff guys worked against other guys that they never tried against Biggie, having their hands full with the turk or the double or half a dozen throws. Still, it was nice of Wetzel to ask around.

Then Roy Gosley walked in.

"Do I hear trumpets?" Wing said.

Gosley didn't work every table like the winking Camp Director, back-slapping, shaking every hand, kissing babies, Christ, setting up contacts, establishing footholds with every coach in Illinois on the chance that five years down the line, Stump of Collinsville might coach a supernova he'd direct Gosley's way. Unless you knew better, you'd think Gosley wasn't any more of an interactor than Biggie. Gosley caught sight of Biggie, charged over, shook his hand, "We'll talk tomorrow, Dan," then nodded at Wetzel and walked out of the Holiday Inn Restaurant.

"Is God double-parked?" Wing.

"Maybe he forgot his wallet." Luigi.

Gosley inspired awe. It wasn't just that he *was* Mr. Wrestling, imperial, austere, on TV every time the NCAAs or Olympics came around. You were fucking privileged to talk to the guy. Even Wetzel was impressed to hell with himself that Gosley nodded at him, coach to coach. Wetzel beamed at Biggie as if it suddenly hit him that he coached a guy who could *wrestle*. You practically *could* hear trumpets.

"Was that Roy Gosley, Mr. Wrestling? Didn't I see him on Johnny Carson?" Luigi.

"I'll be a monkey's uncle! I believe it was!" Wing.

"I'm Luigi Cravi!" Luigi yelled at the door. "Pleased to meet you, Pope Gosley!"

"Behave yourself, you two," Wetzel said.

After lunch Biggie took another walk around the Holiday Inn, then lay down on his bed and watched the ceiling. Four hours until the quarterfinals. Wing and Luigi, stint of moral support discharged after lunch, wandered the halls. He wondered what Gloria was doing now.

While he loved his mom and dad and wouldn't trade them in for any other parents—each set came with a set of problems, he'd bet; you'd lose either way—he'd be lucky if Gloria ever talked to him again when they were through working her over. Well, it was out of his hands.

Anthony Burroughs was 29-2, according to the brackets. The kid he beat was 24-4. Biggie liked the numbers, derived a security from the quantification, though records were meaningless since they'd wrestled different guys. Not a single common opponent. Nobody Anthony Burroughs had wrestled had wrestled anybody Biggie had wrestled. Different parts of the state, they may as well be different planets. Still, you had to figure a guy who was 29-2, even from a different planet, who beat a guy 7-2 who was 24-4, could wrestle.

Nothing the fuck to worry about, that's what he told himself. He only had to find an angle. "Really, all I do is swing into the guy's momentum," he told Gloria once. "Momentum surges, I call them." That was his game. The Bluestone Formula. Finding a way to swing into the guy's momentum then exploding full throttle. Say they were locked in the middle of the mat. Burroughs may be swinging one way, countering against the force of Biggie's swinging the other, so Biggie suddenly turns with everything he has and swings the same way Anthony Burroughs is going, stepping outside his foot as he does. Foot position was essential, though Biggie had gotten the toss on guys when his footwork was awful, by sheer force of muscle and explosion. He couldn't count on that forever. Biggie thought it over, lying on the hotel bed. Swing one way so the guy swings the *other*, then switch and swing with the momentum, stepping outside. That's all there was to it, though on the mat it took a thousand forms, on feet or knees, vertical, lateral, outside position, as simple as Biggie imagined it, as complicated as he made it.

Imagining it now.

Biggie napped two hours. Dreamed of tosses. Of Gloria watching him in the thick lethargy of dozing off just before sleep, just her face, standing over his bed, looking down trying to tell him something.

It was nice of her to come to Champaign. He could focus on that. She didn't have any interest in wrestling. None of these people—none of the Mat Gals or JV cheerleaders or guys on the team—were her friends. Probably she'd never talked to any of them before. She didn't know his family, either, yet here she was thrown in with them for two days, which could drive even Biggie nuts, and he was *in* the family. It was an ordeal, true. And then Biggie makes a big show of playing the boyfriend, the melodramatic hug and kiss for the benefit of the second tier, then carrying her away for a private conversation just so he could show everybody where the matter stood. At the least, she probably thought she'd get to *talk* to him once in a while, maybe hold his hand and feed him a lot of drivel about being a hero and star, sharpening her edge but meaning it at the same time too, during a spare moment when he wasn't focusing on wrestling.

On the other hand, she was his girlfriend.

They'd agreed on that, though they'd never gone anywhere but The Sergeant during third lunch hour. This was the State Tournament, only the biggest event in the history of Biggie Bluestone's life. You wouldn't think he was being all that unreasonable in wanting her here to see.

This was the thing. If the wrestler was an abstraction to Gloria Serpentino, now he was concrete.

For dinner a large salad and muffin, plain, in the Holiday Inn coffee shop, with Wetzel. Wing and Luigi materialized, taking a break from walking the hallways.

When it came to meals, he knew he could count on their moral support.

Though he was Killer Kowalski in the cave and spoke to nobody.

Anthony Burroughs of East St. Louis Lincoln. An amazingly muscular Black kid, squat, about 5-5. That was Biggie's assessment, seeing Burroughs for the first time, strapping on his leg band.

Is that how people saw *him*? Amazingly muscular? Preposterously, stupendously? You couldn't really ask.

Behind the scorer's table on the main floor he noticed the JV cheerleaders, staring at Bluestone as if awaiting their cue to burst into formation.

For the quarterfinals, the eight mats from the morning session were reduced to four. You'd think it was a lot more, as the session moved crisply. So what does Biggie do? He thinks of Mary Wellington. She should have been here tonight, with the JV cheerleaders, staring at Biggie for the signal. He didn't want to make more of it than it really was. There were a lot of things Mary Wellington should have been doing now; cheering for Biggie Bluestone on the floor of Assembly Hall wouldn't rank too high on the list compared to meeting a guy she loved and having children someday and laughing with her sister Myra and a thousand other things. In fact, Biggie never had the impression Mary understood wrestling, whereas some of the JV cheerleaders—Cindy Shelton, for example—knew a surprising lot about the sport. Cheering at Assembly Hall would be on Cindy Shelton's list, he'd bet. But it registered now. He'd promised himself a thousand times he'd dedicate the State Championship to Mary Wellington. He'd never gone so far as to do so *out loud*, though, and to do so now—when guys were scrambling for any source to psych themselves up into a rabid frenzy and bring on that adrenaline surge—even if only whispering to himself, struck the wrestler as singularly cheap. Biggie Bluestone was sorry she was dead from a thousand perspectives, half of them involving Giselle; he'd *not* win the State Championship, lose this very quarterfinal match if that was the deal to bring her back without saying he would, but Mary Wellington was not going to come back. Still, the wrestler almost swore it to himself. Almost said, "This one's for Mary." Then for a moment he thought of dedicating the championship to *Myra* Wellington, in Mary's honor, but Myra Wellington did not want the championship, realistically; it was probably far down on her list, though Biggie had no doubt she'd put it at the top if that was the deal to bring Mary back. Someday he liked to think he'd talk to Myra Wellington and tell her all this, the works, thinking of dedicating the championship, the rationale against it, that he'd stood on the edge of the mat before the State quarters and thought of her. While that wasn't likely, he *liked* thinking so, imagining it.

Thinking about the Wellington sisters took twelve seconds.

Biggie closed his eyes, launched into a set of jumping jacks, almost ran over the referee hustling to the circle.

"This is the State quarterfinals, Biggie," Wetzel yelled from the coach's chair. "I don't have to tell you that."

Anthony Burroughs had never wrestled anybody he wasn't twice as strong as, and Biggie wasn't too certain that wasn't still true. He tried everything—sharp head shirks, duck unders (like ducking under a volcano), head snaps; he worked the legs when thwarted, reached for ankle picks, tried inside taps. Nothing. The underhook was out of the question with a guy like this. Christ, Burroughs underhooked *him*. Biggie felt the resistance to his surge, exploded into the momentum stepping over Burroughs's far foot, the patented Bluestone toss as Burroughs exploded into the momentum stepping over Biggie's far foot, patented Burroughs for all Biggie knew, so to any of the 15,000 watching it looked like nothing happened, two guys hugging in the middle of the circle.

Biggie couldn't get elbow control, he couldn't get inside control, couldn't get shit. Still, the game was the toss, the game was to trick the momentum. Explode into the surge. This could take a thousand forms.

They were pushing into each other when Biggie stepped outside his left foot with his own right, stepped backward with his own left, all in a fraction of a second, with Anthony Burroughs flying on top of Biggie and swinging on over, a classic lateral drop, though landing *after* the buzzer. It didn't count, though Wetzel roared to his feet screaming the drop beat the buzzer. 0-0.

Still, the lateral drop made all the difference. Burroughs sat out and Biggie sucked him back, tried to stand up—here's what Biggie was waiting for, he knew the chance was there with Burroughs's short, massive legs and he was the guy to do it, the stud, the monster; nobody had cradled Anthony Burroughs before, he was sure of *that*, it took Biggie Bluestone. Caught him in mid-stand up, bringing his knee up toward his head as Biggie drove his left arm over Burroughs's shoulder and around his chest, his right arm around the other way—over Burroughs's broad back and his knee—walked him forward hunched in his arms with all the force he had until Burroughs was on his side ready to turn, trying to somersault away instinctively, working in the direction of the cradle—not hearing the crowd now, driving Burroughs—drives his left knee into Burroughs's side now until the squat kid has turned—this is the match already, he's got a near fall here, three points—though he needs to be careful, too, not to pin himself—using his left leg as a post, stacking Anthony Burroughs, man mountain, on his shoulders twenty seconds into the second period.

"Business as usual," Biggie said to the guy from the Chicago *Tribune,* who intercepted him as he walked off the mat, immediately regretting the comment. "The kid was strong, but his legs were short, so I knew if I tried it, I could swing him with the far side cradle. Of course, if I missed it, he'd whizzer and take me to my back."

"You knew that the first time you saw him?" The sportswriter chewed on his pen as he looked at Biggie.

Biggie shrugged. "It's not like anything else worked. But that's the key to wrestling downstate. You have to take a guy who's really good and show him something he's never seen before." This Biggie regretted saying even more than the "business as usual." "Or something he's *seen* before, but not done nearly as well," he amended, which made him sound even worse.

The guy asked him about his record. 33-0 now, 27 pins. Only one guy scored on him all year—Biggie mentioned that, too; not intending to, but it was as if the reporter had slipped him a dose of truth serum—that's what Biggie told Gloria—mainly by asking him a question while wearing a *Tribune* badge.

"Jesus," Biggie told Gloria, "I practically gave him my bar mitzvah speech."

"I had to be lucky to land the cradle," Biggie continued with the reporter. He couldn't leave it at that. "But I wouldn't have been lucky if I hadn't thrown it in the first place."

Max Miller, according to the badge. He was a beefy, middle-aged guy dressed like a harmonica salesman. "I've been reading your stuff for years," Biggie said, which was true, but made him sound like he was sucking up, on top of being an insufferable jackass.

That wouldn't stop Killer Kowalski. He was surprised he didn't *tell him* about Killer Kowalski.

Max Miller nodded, staring over his pad at Biggie. "College plans?"

"Sure, I have college plans." Biggie wanted to leave it at that. "Wherever I go there'll be a water cooler in the hallway."

"I'm sure that can be arranged," Max Miller said. "I hear everybody's after you."

So he told Max Miller about driving to Northwestern since he was a kid. But Illinois and Indiana were also in the mix, he added.

"You'd make a great spy." Gloria was lying on the hotel bed in the Holiday Inn, three hours after the match.

"I reveal nothing unless asked, that's my policy."

"I'll remember that," Gloria said, "the next time I want to plumb the deepest secrets of Dan Bluestone."

"I imagine by now my mom has told you those," Biggie said.

Here was the thing. When the *Trib* guy was talking to him, Biggie looked up into the stands and saw Gloria—his parents, too—Christ, throw in the Mat Gals—not to mention Wing and Luigi and Bray and Mandel and Hoffman—not bad for Giselle to see, either—watching Max Miller of the *Tribune* interview him. "'Look, Ma, no hands,' that's what it was," Biggie told Gloria. "'Quiet please, big shot at work.' That's what loosened the skids."

"You are a big shot," Gloria said, kissing his chest. "I don't think I really understood that until today. This is a really big deal."

"Well, it's not because I haven't told you every other conversation."

After the interview, Biggie charged into the stands, worked the second tier like he was Safredo, miraculously refrained from unhooking Gloria's bra and waving it in public view, then charged back down—Christ, he shook Safredo's hand coming and going—into the weight room, peeled off a set of benches and presses, not too much weight, just working his muscles, a gentle sweat, surging on adrenaline, hopped on the scales—one over—then ripped off four miles on the indoor track in his rubber suit, three dozen other wrestlers in their rubber suits in pursuit—including Berky, he envisioned, plotting his revenge. He couldn't bear to weigh himself. One *under*. Showered.

Twenty-four hours I'll know.

Wetzel was waiting in the Coach's foyer, milling with his colleagues, "Taking notes on which round's coming up," Biggie told Gloria. Wetzel drove him back to the Holiday Inn, cutting over to the restaurant where the coaches congregated, and Biggie went to the room where he collapsed on his bed counting the seconds.

Twenty-four hours.

He couldn't hear any sounds from next door, Wing and Luigi already afoot, already elsewhere tonight, though he heard the slightly muffled noises of yelling and music and the rumbling of footsteps shuffling distantly and the voices of girls. Luckily he was the one guy who didn't care he was missing out, he told the ceiling, closing his eyes.

Ten minutes later—600 seconds by his count—there was a knock on the door.

Gloria.

"I shouldn't have come. I know you're focusing here in your cave." Biggie looked at her. "Exercising your legendary will and discipline," Gloria added.

"Mom mentioned that, too, I see."

Biggie took Gloria's hand, pulling her across the room to the bed. He put his arm under her neck and she placed her hand on his head, ruffling his hair as they lay on the covers.

"I won't stay long, I promise. I know you need your rest or whatever. Cindy Shelton drove us over with Robin Weinberg and Maggie Pescola of the Mat Gals. They went to a Glenbrook South party with Wing and Luigi on the other side of the motel."

"Why is it I'm the one in the semis and everybody else gets to have the fun?"

"It's the price of deification," Gloria whispered in his ear.

"But I am having fun," Biggie said.

"Bet your life you are, Buster."

"When you showed up the other night I had the best time in the history of the world."

Gloria looked at him and frowned. "The world? That's all? Just the world?"

"Plus other galaxies."

"Bet your life, Buster."

It was nice, lying with Gloria, bantering mindlessly about everything and nothing. But Biggie couldn't shed the theme. He wanted to tell her. "Twenty-four hours and I'll know. It's pretty amazing to contemplate. I mean, when you consider how long this has been in the works." He wanted to mention that in a way this was really nothing, from a wrestling perspective. Next year at Northwestern he'd see guys ten times anybody he'd face here, and that went for Berkenmeier in the finals tomorrow night, though first there were the semis in the morning. "I saw Gosley when I was in the weight room. The Northwestern coach."

"You've told me who Gosley is. I know who he is."

"He said he looked forward to talking to me tomorrow. Christ, that's twice he's said he's looking forward to talking to me tomorrow. If he'd talk to me now, he'd save time tomorrow."

Gosley also told him that he thought Biggie's cradle was "brilliant," a Gosley phrase. He would have mentioned that to Gloria, but it was hard to make it sound like Gosley was calling the *cradle* brilliant, and not Biggie. You didn't often think of cradles as being brilliant. Or lateral drops or pancakes, for that matter. A silly discernment, Biggie knew; if it were Max Miller of the *Trib* he'd offer the interesting information freely enough. "Gloria, the thing is, I never really thought this would happen. They make a big deal these days about the idiotic kid with the dream. Anyway, *Mom* makes a big deal about it—"

"I've heard *you* mention it a few times."

"Well, Mom had to get the idea from someplace. I doubt she imagines I ever had a thought in my head back then. You know what they say, 'It's not that the horse sings well and hits all the right notes and shit . . .' But the thing is, while I always *assumed* it would happen—Christ, I kind of assume I'll be President of the United States someday, if you catch my drift—I'm not sure I ever thought it would, not in recent years. Never really *thought* I'd be lying here in the Holiday Inn the night before the State semifinals, and then the finals, with a girl in my arms."

"Make that a beautiful girl in your arms," Gloria said.

"There were always guys my age who were better than me, that's the thing. It's like I was a Little Leaguer hitting .500, which sounds good, but there were always other guys hitting .600, so you couldn't exactly say that I was earmarked. I worked, I lifted weights, I ran, Gloria, I was twice as strong as anybody, but I was a cut below the top guys. It seemed like they always had the big-time coaching or the older brothers who were stars, while I consulted the photographs in *Advanced Wrestling*. I never really knew what I was doing on the mat other than hustling. Emotionally, too, I was out of it. Like I expected everything to change magically if I kept pushing, everything to fall into place, but all along I knew I was standing out there in the wind with my fly down, toilet paper stuck to my heel. Muscled, sure, but clueless. Even at the beginning of this season I made a lot of noise, at least in the family. Maybe to Wing and Luigi.

"But then it began to come true. A few things happened, I guess. There was the psycho stuff, which I won't go into, not now, but it changed the way I attacked on the mat, and then I figured something out, what I'd been doing all along when things worked but finally it hit me—you work the other guy until you can explode in the direction of his momentum, that's the whole game, though you have to pay attention to incidentals like putting your foot—or your knee or whatever—outside his in the direction of the surge—then everything became clear, I guess. Also, there was the issue of pain. Nobody wants to go through too much pain out there, Gloria, but I learned I could, that I could knock on pain's door and break it down and emerge on the other side, and other guys couldn't. And then, well, Mary Wellington died. That happened. Something else clicked then, but I didn't understand it, really. Still don't. That's not the point. Gloria, you know when other people walk around saying, 'Why her? Why not me?' I think that's what happened to me. Not 'Why wasn't I the one out there who fell off the car and got killed?'—though I must have confronted that too—no, not 'Why not me to fall off the fucking car'—well, to fall prey to all the bad crap out there—though that was part of it—but the flip side, too, you see. 'Why not me?' for the good crap, too? 'Why not Biggie Fucking Bluestone?' Since I'm never more than one step away from the cow pie, 'Why not me?' for taking State with the college coaches and the big schools after me, for example, since all I've ever done is dream about it and work out five times a day and run more miles than you can count. Why the fuck not me? I mean, they have a lot of crap I don't, but I have a lot of stuff they don't have, either. Stuff they couldn't dream of. That's part of what happened too."

"They don't have me," Gloria said, squeezing his hand, looking through his eyes with such intensity he swore she could see the psycho stuff he mentioned and on through it, and the great concept of the momentum surge, and every pushup he ever did, Mary Wellington, too, and through Mary Wellington and on through Gloria herself to everything he meant. "You need your rest, sweetie. Good luck tomorrow."

It was 11:30.

⸻ ◆ ⸻

State Championship Day, Saturday, February 27

Biggie woke up at six, ran two miles to loosen up, pictured Killer Kowalski entering the ring, did 200 pushups outside the motel door, tiptoed back through—Wetzel was still sleeping—and showered. When he walked back into the room Wing and Luigi were sitting on Wetzel's bed.

At 7:15, in Assembly Hall, Biggie made weight.

"Christ!" he told Wing as they sat in the Holiday Inn coffee house after ordering the jumbo ham and cheese omelet, extra potatoes, muffin on the side. "You can't identify with what I'm going to say, but do you know how long I've looked forward to this day?"

Wing looked at Luigi and rolled his eyes.

"Here we go again." Luigi.

"This day when I don't have to worry about making weight anymore. Never again. Until next year, anyway."

"You've mentioned it daily." Wing.

"I've heard it, too." Luigi.

"Don't overstuff yourself," Wetzel said, as if this weren't Biggie's feverish routine all season.

"I don't believe that's possible." Wing.

"Is it a man, or is it a garbage can?" Luigi.

"Coming from Cravi, that's a compliment." Biggie.

"A lot of guys are too nervous to eat before the semis." Wetzel looked at Biggie with what the wrestler took as concern; it occurred to Biggie that Wetzel liked him, wanted him to do well for reasons other than that it made Wetzel himself look good. That he really means this shit and wants the wrestler to take it to heart, find it useful, apply it like he was taking apart an automobile motor. Though Wetzel also knew Biggie knew more in his little finger than he ever would, was more interested than Wetzel ever was. Half the time he'd assumed Wetzel was filling up the air, summoning words because the situation suggested words were called for, but knowing they were approximations, notes that a real coach would reject for the good information that made all the difference.

"There's a semi-final round this morning?" Biggie asked, before ordering a large cookie for the road.

"You don't want to puke out there."

"I don't want to puke out there," he agreed.

Back in the motel room, when Biggie collected his gear, the phone rang. He thought of not answering, then thought it was Gloria.

"Biggie, I was hoping to find you."

"I'm just leaving, Mom."

"Good good good good luck this morning."

"Thanks, Mom."

"Here's Dad."

"Hi, son."

"Dad."

"Good luck out there."

"Thanks. I'll see you at the arena."

Killer Kowalski was on his own, off to the wars.

In one form or another Biggie had the "Good luck, I mean, really good luck out there" conversation a dozen times.

Giselle ran up to him, what could he do? The JV cheerleaders the same. Gloria kissed him, smiled, kept her distance. Even Wing and Luigi, who knew better. He didn't want to be an asshole about it, the State semi-finals and fuck-all, they had every damn right to wish him luck—Biggie acknowledged as much, good natured as always—but you didn't find too many people wishing Killer Kowalski good luck, that's what he'd bet.

Even Safredo shook his hand to wish him luck. "Business as usual, Dan?"

"That's right," said Biggie Bluestone.

"Good article today."

There was a pile of sports sections on the bracket table. The fucking *Tribune.*

There was Biggie in the lead story.

Show them something they haven't seen before, or show them better.

The kid he drew in the semi was a huge, oafish, lanky kid from Lockport Central. An immense chest, long knotty arms, no muscular bulk. If Biggie was a monster, Blue Grabner was an octopus. He was 32-1 on the season. The next mat over, Berkenmeier drew an unbeaten kid from Rock Island who'd beaten Anthony Burroughs in their Sectional final.

At the whistle, Biggie stepped toward the kid, waiting for Grabner to meet his pressure, though Grabner backed away, Biggie diving for his ankle as he headed backward. Biggie circled back toward the center, feinting toward the legs—he figured he could shoot on the guy but wanted to get in a toss early—then pushed forward into the massive chest, harder now so the kid would push back and he would catch the surge or back up so he could kick in with the turk. Instead, Blue Grabner loops under to Biggie's left—Biggie reacting to the left—and swings under with the high crotch toward his own back—Biggie in overdrive sure he'll catch the mistake right now for the early stick—and swings Biggie over, landing before Biggie swings over on top as the ref blows his whistle.

Biggie's already in the circle, hopping up and down in place.

"That's out of bounds, he was out of bounds, can't you see he was out of bounds," Wetzel's screaming at the ref, who's holding up three fingers for the near fall. "These are the State semis, ref. You can't do that! You can't rob a kid."

"One more, Coach, and your wrestler's disqualified."

The crowd's erupting. Even from the second tier he thinks—though Biggie blanked it out, focused—he hears his *dad* screaming, among 15,000 voices, "He's out of bounds. Don't count that, ref. He's out of bounds!" Even *Mr. Cravi's* screaming. "Pay attention, ref. They're out of bounds!"

"You coach and I'll call them," the ref says quietly to Wetzel. Wetzel's shirt is drenched through to the armpits, a vein bulges in his temple. *The Wetzel vein,* Hoffman called it, though you never saw Wetzel get too worked up; the coach was usually implacable in the corner.

Biggie thinks he hears Wing shout, "Who paid you off, ref!"

The ref looks at Wetzel and raises a finger. "That's one point green."

"I didn't say anything!" Wetzel screams.

"He didn't say anything!" half the crowd shouts, he'd hear later. Vaguely hears now.

Grabner glances at Biggie, who smiles awkwardly and walks over to pat Wetzel's arm. Neither will remember what he says. Wetzel sinks into his chair.

6-0.

Biggie tries to stand up and Grabner releases him, 6-1, moves toward the circle. They're on their feet. Keep the fucking elbows in this time, he reminds himself, shoves Grabner backwards, who backs up from the shove, rights himself, then stumbles over his scrambling feet.

Biggie watches from the circle as Grabner bounces on his butt five feet away. He pictures himself flying atop Grabner, applying the half, turning him, gripping the mat with his toes.

"Get him! Hustle!" Wetzel shouts. "Biggie, *please*. What's with you? *Get him.*"

Wetzel kicks his leg in the air.

Standing still in the middle, he watches Blue Grabner, who looks at him, stands up, moves back toward the circle.

Biggie surges ahead, lower now, thinks about an arm drag—Grabner's arms are away from his trunk—surges forward again as Grabner underhooks the high crotch and swings back to his shoulder. Biggie knows it's not a mistake, wouldn't fall for that again, reaches down to break the momentum, but it's too late, he's already on over, flying with the flow, almost free and then his bad shoulder jams the mat and he's not over but scuttling upside down. The Octopus squeezes his hands and stacks the monster, not a fluke this time, onto his ear. Biggie knows there's nowhere to turn which won't swing him onto his back, so the wrestler arches, snaps the grip in two, bridges onto his neck until it feels like the sucker will break, explodes over onto his belly, flying into a sit out and switch, though Grabner hangs on until the buzzer.

"Would you keep your arms in, *please* Biggie," Wetzel screams.

11-1 after one period. For a moment Biggie thinks of glancing into the second tier, shakes the thought. 11-1. This guy could do this all day, he thinks. No, he thinks.

After that, Biggie dominated. Hooked a whizzer from the bottom position, reached underneath and jammed the Octopus to the mat, pulling out the far arm, coming over on top for a tilt and predicament points. 11-5. Again jammed Grabner's head to the mat on the whistle, tore him down with the two-on-one, drove his head in Grabner's side with every ounce of fire he had, slipped the half deep in the cave, though he's dizzy, lightheaded, not seeing pain's door. Grabner swings him over but the kid's not that great, no Dixon Boyd, no Berkenmeier, Biggie catches another tilt. 11-7.

Four times in the third period he lifted the Octopus, returned him to the mat, broke him down, though Grabner sucked his arms and legs into a shell. Once Biggie pried an arm for a single arm bar but couldn't work the tilt.

What's it sound like when 15,000 people stand on their feet and scream, "Stalling, stalling! He's stalling, ref! He's stalling!"?

Finally the ref warned the Octopus, warned him again after Biggie went for the head trap as Grabner sucked in, called the point after Biggie pulled in his legs. 11-8.

But he wasn't going to turn the guy, that was the thing. He could lift and slam him all night, but the kid was going to stall and the ref wasn't going to call it again, not in the semis of State, that's what Biggie knew. He couldn't find the angle, there were no surges with the Octopus sucking in his arms and legs, bunching in, bouncing up, suddenly scuttling across the mat. So Biggie let him up, 12-8. Got the high crotch and turn—the Octopus spent now, wilting—for the takedown,

12-10, Grabner lost in pain, backing up, waiting it out, Biggie knew he had the surge, thought of letting him up driving in with another high crotch, but was breaking down himself suddenly, a rabbit tossed into a lake, wonders if this will kill him, wonders why the door won't let him through. And the ref says twenty seconds, twenty seconds boys, with a matter-of-factness that bordered on the violation of a confidence, that's what Biggie thought—there had to be more than twenty seconds, had to be an eternity. Had to be time to consider every fucking question he'd ever consider. So he began to let him up then rammed in the half nelson, too high, Biggie knew, Grabner held his ground, not surging, palms and feet pressing into the mat, butt pointed toward the huge scoreboard hanging from the Assembly Hall ceiling, that's what it looked like from the second tier, a rabbit, he'd hear later. Biggie fuming with the half, turning, ten seconds to go now, moving into it as he never moved into a half nelson before—what choice was there?—Grabner's shoulders sinking down now but he's too high, so Biggie moves in deeper, squeezes, Killer Kowalski on the rampage roaring for his life—he's got the near fall now, he's sure, 13-12 if he's counting right, though he wants the pin now, he wants it, driving to the mat as the kid swings through the other side at the buzzer.

Biggie returns to the middle of the mat. Jumps up and down in place, throws little punches in the air as if pummeling a ghost. His neck and chest convulse, his cheeks blank numb and spin, then rest in place. Well, he's spent his coin. And he likes it; that was the thing nobody understood. He likes it when his forearms throb and the bones in his face quiver and he blanks out and his legs wobble and his shoulder wails. And Grabner leans on his side, arms outstretched, poised—so it looked from the second tier—to negotiate the mat with the sidestroke.

The referee huddles with the side judges. Wetzel screaming. The Lockport Central coach screaming.

"That's three points near fall, green, two points reversal red if red got it in time. Did red get it in time?" Biggie hears the ref, whose name is Bannock, ask the side judge, who looks at him ponderously, seems to study Biggie Bluestone standing on the mat.

Thinks it over, staring Biggie in the eyes, nods his head.

"14-13 red." Bannock lifts Grabner's arm.

Wetzel's still screaming at Bannock. Biggie walks off to the warm-up mat, collapses to his knees, lifts up to see Gloria staring down at him from the second tier, her fists clenched, tears glazing clearly visible from sixty feet away, and wonders if it's real. Behind her, sitting past Gloria, sees Giselle and his parents. Now Gloria leaning over the railing two tiers above him poised to jump, that's what his heart says, fuck-all, the thirty yards between them incomprehensible, Gloria sobbing now as she watches her guy.

That much he accomplished, anyway.

Biggie walks outside in his wrestling togs, circles the arena until the noises inside are a faint echo, shivers in the late winter afternoon, breaks into a run. Feels his neck quiver, his shoulder die, his cheeks blank numb, his forearms spasm.

Twenty minutes later, back in the arena, he walks up to the second tier. That's when he hears it, some cornball outside the concession stand reading aloud from the morning's *Trib*: "Though it's an open question if Bluestone can be scored upon." The guy, wearing a porkpie hat below which long thin sideburns extended like tributaries, a coach from down-state, Biggie guesses—looks into the air as if the air's listening. "Not more than fourteen points!"

Then he turns to see Biggie walking toward him. He blinks half a dozen times beneath his porkpie hat. Sucks in his breath.

As Biggie walks past him toward the tunnel landing to the second tier, the man breathes an audible sigh of relief.

Ten seconds later Camp Director Safredo emerges from a cluster and shakes his hand. "Tough break, son."

On the second tier, Wing sees Biggie first and runs to him. "That was fucked. Who paid the ref off?"

"That was fucked," Luigi echoes.

"Sure," Biggie says.

"Fuck it, Biggie," Wing says. "Where were you anyway?"

"I took a walk."

"Gloria's looking for you, your folks are looking for you, *Wetzel*'s looking for you. They practically sent out an all-points bulletin. We figured you'd left for the Gulf of Mexico."

"That's an idea," Biggie considered. "What about Giselle?" he added. "How come she's not in the search party?"

"I believe Giselle went out to lunch with the JV cheerleaders," Wing said.

"Good to know I can count on my sister for solace and comfort."

"I don't honestly think Giselle's your sister," Luigi said.

The thing was, they hated it that he lost but nothing had changed, Biggie yet undiminished in their eyes. That's what happens when you beat the crap out of somebody every day in practice: They *know* how fucking good you are. They hated it for *Biggie* that he lost, he'd bet—he fucking hoped, anyway, *sheesh*—but also for themselves. "Yeah, Bluestone's my pal. He's the best ever in Illinois." They lost that. All crap maybe, reflected glory, the grandeur betraying their own poverty of spirit, but still he'd loved the idea of people saying it about him, of *that* meaning something to them, the right to look somebody in the face and idly boast they knew Biggie Bluestone back when. It was nice having that. Something *they* could live without, Biggie thought as he stood on the second tier with Wing and Luigi. A lot of the Mat Gals stared at him, smiling sympathetically. They knew he lost—they'd have to know, he figured—though likely it didn't mean all that much to them when he was winning, other than that he looked pleasingly mus-cu-lar—a monster, a stud—and for Giselle, who took this stuff seriously, the Mat Gals knew it meant something to Giselle, more than to Biggie himself at times. Giselle *needed*. Were she here and not off to lunch, you wouldn't have to guess how Giselle was taking it.

The world falls apart and clarity issues forth.

The Mat Gals, watching him now, sympathetically, not "Serves the fucker right for never talking to us," were sad. For him, he liked to think, with an immediacy filtered through the prism of several removes, as if they were joined at the hip, but as distant cousins. For Giselle, their leader again, now she was back on steady footing, the head Mat Gal, the President of the Mat Gal Society of Illinois for all Biggie knew.

But his parents and Gloria. "They're the ones, let me tell you," Biggie thinks. Out looking for him now, bearing the enormity, crushed to *pieces* on his behalf, reduced, halved, they'd die every death he ever died if they could, the very idea so unbearable the wrestler, Biggie Bluestone, just from this standpoint wishes nobody loved him.

A half hour later he's on the mat again, the consolation semi-final, wrestling the guy the Octopus beat in the quarters, 8-2. This kid from Rich East, Biggie doesn't think to check his season's record, or visualize takedowns, or enter the cave. Lucky he showed up. Walking around Assembly Hall looking for Gloria and his parents, who were looking for him, that's when he hears his name called over the PA. Mat #3, straps on his band, shakes the guy's hand, presses the guy, who backs off lazily, tired from the consolation quarters he'd wrestled one hour before. Biggie reaches for the ankle pick, lifts, knocks out the leg, drives with the half on contact. The guy wiggles a while as Biggie digs in, stretches out, weight distributed to his toes as if his feet might puncture the mat. Fifty-two seconds.

"Back in the saddle," Wetzel says. He looks at Biggie closely, grabs him by his good shoulder. "Are you okay?"

Biggie says, "Sure."

"Could have used that earlier," Wetzel says. "You didn't wrestle smart."

"You're telling me."

"You don't know everything."

"What?" Biggie says. "Did I say I know everything?"

"Don't freak out on me again, Biggie," Wetzel sighs. "Do you hear me?"

After Biggie showers and dresses, leaving the locker room, he sees Gosley walking in his direction. "Dan Bluestone."

Biggie smiles, glances down.

"You showed me something, Dan, I'll say that," Roy Gosley was already saying. This was outside the locker room. "You came back after a devastating defeat to beat a kid—kid can't wipe his ass, but anyway—in thirty seconds. That shows me something. A lot of guys in your shoes, the big favorites with the big press, forfeit the consolation matches like it's beneath their dignity."

My shoes, Biggie thinks. "And it was fifty-two seconds, sir."

"The Lockport kid got you with the fireman's twice."

I remember.

"The way you keep going forward, pushing, pushing to beat the devil, you're vulnerable, Bluestone. That works in high school. Any college guy will eat you alive. But we'll work on that." Gosley claps Biggie on the shoulder.

He smiles at Biggie. Biggie smiles back.

"Are you interested in being a Northwestern Wildcat?"

"Yes sir."

Roy Gosley, already looking over Biggie's shoulder, nods. Pumps Biggie's hand. "I'll talk to you later."

Gosley starts to walk away.

"*When?*" Biggie says, then says again, louder, until Mr. Wrestling turns around, "When?"

In the third-place match he pins the Rock Island kid in thirty-seven seconds, working the hip toss again, timing his surge. Half in the cave, half out. Third sounded better than fourth, but that wasn't it. There was a kid across the mat. That's what it came down to; there was another guy across from him, pitting himself against Bluestone on a mat. Where else would you want to be? Biggie's surprised to find that he's pleased with himself. Berkenmeier beat this kid 4-2 in the semis this morning. A lopsided 4-2, but still.

In the finals Berkenmeier beat the Octopus 12-1, dismantling every move. Berkenmeier didn't push forward at all costs, didn't hatch his throws from reverie and the photographs of *Advanced Wrestling*. When they hand out the medals after the match, Biggie shakes Berky's hand. Berkenmeier nods curtly, smiling lazily. "Nice work." "Nice work."

Christ, Berkenmeier still hasn't heard of him.

Biggie shakes the Octopus's hand. The kid from Rock Island's hand.

"Third in the state's great," his dad says. Now they're waiting in the Courtesy Room at Assembly Hall, where Gosley said he'd meet Biggie to talk. "Bring your parents if they're here," Gosley added.

He did and brought his girlfriend too.

"We're so proud of you," Mom said.

"You were proud of me when I learned how to tie my shoes."

"Don't be edgy," Dad said.

"I'm proud of you," Gloria said. "I've never been third in the state at anything."

"I still think you're the best wrestler," Mom said.

She thought this was the Chicago Symphony and the issue was a matter of taste and interpretation. "Mom, that's why they have the tournament."

"I know third isn't what you wanted, Biggie," Dad said. "I know you're disappointed."

"But it was incredible the way you came back," Gloria chipped in. Under the table she brushed his knee. He thought of that night she'd suddenly appeared. It seemed like a long time ago. "Gloria, I was younger then. Now I've learned, now I'm seasoned, now I've swallowed the bitter pill of defeat." *That's* what he should tell her. Melodramatic shit that suited him, or about the guy with the cartoon hat and corny flushed face who was so terrified when Biggie walked past him. "Oh my heart, Gloria!" Sheesh.

"First he was ahead, then everybody was screaming something, then you went ahead, then he went ahead," Gloria said. "Very exciting."

"It's the crowd participation," Biggie said.

"I mean it."

"Yeah."

"You beat Berkenmeier, the State Champ," Mom reminded him.

"I guess that makes me State Champ." Biggie looked down at his hot chocolate, filled with cream and sugar from the vending machine. It was his second cup. "It's not likely I'm going to kill myself," Biggie said, "in case you're wondering." He looked at the group, frowned.

"Because if you did, I'd kill *myself*." Gloria squeezed his knee.

Dad raised his eyebrows and winked at his son: Nice, but who is this girl?

Biggie wondered if it was such a great idea leaving Gloria with his parents all day.

Dad looked at his watch. Mom went to the restroom and returned. Now she looked like she was ready to attend the opera.

"You're sure Coach Gosley said he'd meet us here?" Mom asked again.

"With my parents."

After another forty-five minutes, still no Gosley.

"Maybe they'll form a search party," Biggie thought.

"Where is he?" Mom said.

Biggie stared down his fourth hot chocolate. "Where do you think?"

Such a Gentleman, Sunday, February 28

Late that morning Biggie drove back with Wetzel and Wing and Luigi. It was just as well he didn't drive back with his parents. School regulations, Wetzel said.

By now his parents were convinced that third in the state and snubbed by Roy Gosley was the preferred position, toward which Biggie would have done well to aspire in the first place. This in addition to telling him 12,000 times how proud of him they were, which reached the point of diminishing returns after the 11,000th, coming from them, who had a way of being proud of him when he managed to brush his teeth two days in a row.

He was their boy. There was a time when he pooped in his diaper. The bar was low.

"Call Gosley tomorrow," Mom instructed Dad after they'd driven down from Monticello for breakfast, before they drove back.

"Mom, Gosley still has our number. But they're looking at a lot of guys. Third in the state is fine, but they have a lot of guys to choose from, including State Champs."

"How many are 35-1 with 29 pins?" Dad said. "A lot of colleges would love a kid like that."

Biggie was amazed. Dad knew his record. "I'll preview the call for you, Dad: 'Thanks for calling, Professor. And if I have any advice for the Sociology Department, I'll call you.'"

"Tonight we're going to Henrici's," Dad said. Henrici's was the expensive steak joint on Skokie Road. Biggie pretty much got through the season dreaming about Henrici's. He'd envisioned going there as the reigning State Champ, with the owner showing up at the table, shaking his hand, the steaks on the house. Flashbulbs popping. To his surprise, he'd found himself revealing this to his dad as they packed the suitcases into the Chrysler.

"Same steaks when you're third in the state," Dad said.

"We'll ask Gloria along," Mom said.

Mom and Gloria had struck up quite a friendship through the course of yesterday's adventures. Their bonding theme: How do we nurse poor broken Biggie back to health and prosperity now that fate has revealed who he is? Gloria had even kissed him good night, last night, in full view of his parents, with such intensity they could have been standing in front of The Sergeant in full view of half of Highland Park. Mom and Dad had turned away, out of embarrassment or mercy?

He couldn't escape feeling that Gloria was taking his temperature.

It was an unusual first date, when you thought about it.

On the drive back, Wetzel transformed from yesterday's angriest man in America. Emerged from the depths of Biggie's betrayal. It made Biggie wonder if there really was a regulation about having to drive back the kid you drove down with. He wondered if it was like Wetzel to cite a fraudulent policy for an opportunity to apologize.

As soon as they hit Centralia, the contrite Wetzel was saying, "Third at State is damn good, not only the way you came back against Lockport,"—Wetzel made it sound not like a city so much as a mouthful of arsenic—"but your wrestleback and the third place match. Biggie, the Rock Island kid was undefeated until Berkenmeier. Almost *beat* Berkenmeier. You handle him in thirty seconds. All the coaches were raving about it."

What else are they going to talk to you about, Biggie thought. Freaking out?

"We've never had a kid at Highland Park who was third in the state," Wetzel said.

That's surprising, Biggie thought, considering the terrific coaching.

"I know you're disappointed and let down. I was disappointed and let down, too, yesterday. I let it show."

"Don't worry about it."

He wasn't sure he was supposed to *answer* Wetzel, so much as permit the coach free reign in his monologue. "With any other kid I've coached, third in state would be like Hanukkah in summer." Although Wetzel himself wasn't Jewish, the coach often sprinkled in a Jewish reference. That's why he's lasted so long at Highland Park, went one theory advanced by Wing. "To you, third in state is like they *cancelled* Hannukah. That's why you're so good. A perfectionist. You wanted more. And you gave it more than lip service."

Someday he hoped to give Gloria Serpentino more than lip service.

"Sometimes I wonder if somebody took your intensity for wrestling and applied it to everyday life, what would happen?"

Now Biggie looked in the back seat at Wing and Luigi, who were both conked out, thus permitting Wetzel free reign in the department of shirt-sleeve philosophy on the intricacies of Biggie Bluestone, wrestling, the world at large, and the relationships therein, without interruption and commentary. This was a new side of Wetzel, now that word was out and everybody knew what there was to know. Biggie kind of liked this side of Wetzel, when he thought about it. Which he wasn't exactly inclined to do at the moment.

Last night Biggie was asleep by eleven after his parents drove him back from the Courtesy Room at Assembly Hall, Gloria providing the lip service in full view. Then they drove her back to the Days Inn in Urbana. As for Wing and Luigi, from the looks of it, they may not have gotten back at all. This morning, at breakfast, a giddy Luigi mentioned meeting a girl. He had her phone number on a strip of paper tucked in his back pocket.

"When you dial her number, I suspect they'll answer, 'Northbrook Police.'" Biggie.

"Northbrook Zoo." Wing.

Good to see his pals were up late suffering on his behalf. Now Wing and Luigi dozed off in the back, their faces creased into satisfied smiles, reliving the highlights of their field trip to Champaign-Urbana.

"I really wonder that, I'm not just saying it," Wetzel said.

"You mean about ordinary, everyday life?"

"You'll let me know when you find out, won't you, Biggie?" Wetzel turned to look at Biggie as if he really wanted to know.

"You'll be the first," Biggie said.

His parents were already home when Wetzel dropped him off, Mom on the phone with her sister, Giselle in her room, door closed, Dad in the den churning out the lecture notes.

Business as usual.

He went downstairs, surprised to see they hadn't moved Gloria in.

Mom was talking about Biggie. "He was wonderful; you should have seen him, Ada. He won all his matches but one, and in that one he came from way behind. But listen to this: the young man he wrestled fell down in the match. Others would have jumped on the boy, but Biggie didn't. He didn't want an unfair advantage. You would have been so proud of him. It's all everybody was talking about. He's become such a gentleman."

That was the family line now, Biggie thought. Third in the state in skills, but tops in sportsmanship.

Killer Kowalski, Miss Congeniality.

For a moment as he looked around downstairs at his weights, and the same floor where he'd done millions of pushups, and the chinup bar, he felt a loss so overwhelming he wanted to run through the plate glass door. His heart raced out of control—Biggie envisioned the muscle racing out of the chest cavity, down Sheridan Road, past Sara Sherman's house and Wing's house, skirting over the lake, all the way into Indiana.

Still, when he moved over to the weights, he began to lose himself. Biggie thought he'd be too down in the dumps to work out—what was the point?—too late now—crossing the room seemed impossibly beyond his initiative. But by the time he was on the second set of curls several minutes later, 180 pounds on the bar, more than he'd lifted for curls since football season, he had a steady rhythm going; his pores opened up, his breathing became natural. He did his presses with 220, three sets, which he'd never done before, and his arms ached fiercely with each repetition until, by the final set, he was dizzy, concentrating solely on form and explosion. Then—which was ridiculous, really—he took 260 pounds and swung the weights over his head, behind his back, for a set of deep squats. As the weights swung overhead Biggie grew lightheaded, dizzy again, and thought for a moment he'd topple onto the rec room floor, but this was his all-time workout record; he righted himself quickly, squaring his body beneath the weights. Still, his knees quivered, and the tear in his shoulder screamed. Trying not to buckle, Biggie steadied himself for a moment then sank into a squat, rose, grunting, counting each repetition out loud until he had thirty, then another twenty. Although with each further repetition he wanted to end the set, he never wanted it to end.

About the author

Don Eron lives in Boulder, Colorado, and is the author of *And Go to Innisfree, Presner the Remarkable* and *Killer Kowalski Takes the Mat*. He is a graduate of the Iowa Writer's Workshop and has twice won creative fellowships from the Colorado Council on the Arts. An academic labor activist, his writing on academic freedom has been cited in petitions before the US Supreme Court, the Inter-American Commission on Human Rights of the Organization of American States, and the National Labor Relations Board. He is the publisher of Contingency Street Press LLC, a literary micro press.